MIDNIGHT DESCENDING

Books by Lisa M. Green

The Awakened Series

Dawn Rising
Darkness Awakening
Midnight Descending

Standalone Novels

The First

See the rest at *lisamgreen.com/books*

Newsletter

Sign up for updates and information on new
releases at *lisamgreen.com/newsletter*

Light can only be seen in Darkness…

MIDNIGHT DESCENDING

AWAKENED ~ BOOK THREE

LISA M. GREEN

TRIDENT PUBLISHING

ISBN: 9781952300066 (hardcover) / 9781952300073 (paperback) / 9781952300080 (ebook)

Library of Congress Control Number 2020925985

First edition published in the United States of America in February 2021

Trident Publishing
Atlanta, Georgia
tridentpub.com
contact@tridentpub.com

For my parents

*Thank you for ensuring that fairy tales did not die
alongside my childhood. I'll always be that little
girl asking for one last dance at the ball.*

ERESSEIA

THE KNOWN WORLD

Mare Dolor
(Sea of Sorrow)

Mare Dolor
(Sea of Sorrow)

Vanito

Eadon

Rasenforst

Ramolay

Perdita Bay

Enchantress's
Tower

Imperium

Menos

Bramosia

Mare Dolor
(Sea of Sorrow)

A glossary is located at the back of the book.

Awakened

In waking dreams I glide on thorny paths
Trampled upon by those who wish to harm.
The briars all but broken in their haste
To rid the world of what must come to pass.
The roses dying, dying in their bed;
A thankless death to purge the unseen past.
An unknown path I take through the darkness
To reach the grail I do not wish to seek.

Through sylvan screen, I know he's waiting there,
An unwilling specter in my dark thoughts.
Never seeking, always finding, poor soul.
He does not want this, a burdensome crown
Upon his weary head, crushing down hope
And freedom from what he knows he must do.
This fearful dance will set the world ablaze;
Embers ignite, dreams fading into dust.

But dreams are shadows of the waking world,
Weaving a web of whispered promises.
In the end, pricks may sting and thorns may bite;
The spell was cast, but death did not take me.
Fumbling, stumbling, crumbling mind.
In death I'll not be someone's rotting corpse.
In sleep I lie in dreams that do not die,
Awakened by one who knows my true name.

PART ONE

THE WAKING WORLD

But dreams are shadows of the waking world,
Weaving a web of whispered promises.

Chapter 1

AURIANNA

Follow the path that draws you.

She felt "drawn" to have a showdown.

Aurianna stomped along the tunnel under the bay. Stomping felt right. It felt purposeful.

The tunnel would take her to the stairs leading to the upper levels of the Imperium, home of the Kinetics.

Her home. Once upon a time. Before betrayal had taken everything away.

"Where are you going?" Pharis's words echoed against the stone walls surrounding them.

"Where do you think I'm going?"

"You can't possibly think confronting my father right now is a good idea?"

"Why not?" *Follow the path that draws you*, the Arcanes kept telling her.

He grabbed her arm, forcing her to face him. "Because it's madness! He'll have you arrested and probably me as well if we're honest about it." He took hold of her other arm and pulled her closer, peering into her face with raised eyebrows. His expression was hopeful, his tone pleading.

"He's not going to arrest you, Pharis." His nearness was making it hard for her to think. She tried to wrench herself free, but his hold was firm.

Pharis's nostrils flared as his gaze landed on her lips. He opened his mouth, obviously struggling to find the right words. Finally, he managed to whisper, "Maybe, maybe not. But he'll definitely arrest you if you show up alone. Safety in numbers and all that."

"I don't need your help."

"I'm not talking about help. I'm talking about—"

Aurianna took advantage of his distracted expression to yank her arms free.

"Hey, wait!"

She took off without him, resuming her stomping march without another word.

When she reached the stairs, Aurianna slowed. She peeked around every corner as she wound her way up to the main level. The only way to the Magnus's chambers was across the entrance foyer and up a different stairwell. Guards blocked that level from this side of the Imperium. She would have to find a way to reach the other side of the main hall without attracting their attention. Or that of other Kinetics. Or Voids.

Aurianna was beginning to see the flaw in her plan, but she wouldn't admit that to Pharis, who was practically on her heels. They were lucky no one had passed them on the stairs by now. She cracked the door and peeked out at the massive entrance to the building.

A sudden yearning overcame her, a desire to see for herself what damage had been done to the outside world. She had tried so hard not to think about the events of that night, but now she wanted—no, needed—to know the truth.

Theron and Sigi had taken turns scouting the area outside the Imperium. She had not understood their reports. The aftermath of the rooftop confrontation—the night that had changed their lives forever—was confusing, and she needed to see it for herself.

Tiptoeing wouldn't help, so Aurianna decided haste was key if she were to reach her new objective. She could hear Pharis whispering her name. She knew he would wonder where she was going now but would continue to follow.

She didn't really care. She was going outside to inspect the damage.

Amazingly, two guards were walking away from the exit, and no one else was in the main hall. Aurianna slipped up behind their retreating forms, hoping to reach the door before either of them doubled back.

But she wasn't counting on Pharis not following right behind her. A soft "psst" echoed in the cavernous space, and she looked back instinctively. He was standing in the middle of the room, yards away. He threw his hands up, raised his eyebrows, and mouthed *where are you going*?

Just then a shout rang through the hall. The guards had made their way to the far end of the room and were already walking back.

Damn it.

Aurianna saw Pharis's eyes grow wide as he realized their predicament. She cursed him silently. There was no choice but to run for the exit and hope they could avoid capture.

Their footfalls on the marble floor echoed loudly. She reached the giant door and threw one side open, barely pausing to glance back.

They dashed across the bridge. Aurianna took a left and didn't stop until she arrived at a massive rock wall, which was halfway to the stables. Here they could pause to catch their breaths. A full moon illuminated their surroundings and cast long shadows in the night.

She sat on the ground where the guards wouldn't see her, taking in a lungful of air as she threw a meaningful—annoyed—look at Pharis. He stared back as he stood hunched over, his hands on his knees and gasping a bit. Finally, he said, "What the bloody hell are you doing?"

"Me? I'm not the one who alerted the guards!"

"Where are you going? I thought you wanted to see my father."

"I do. But I also wanted to see what happened out here."

Pharis's face softened, but she felt a pang of resentment in her chest. She didn't need his pity.

He nodded slowly, backing away. "Okay, let's go. We'll have to keep an eye out for guards, though I doubt there will be very many since it's almost—"

The clanging of a bell cut short his words. Peering over the rocks, Aurianna could see the giant clock above the Imperium's entrance, far above the doors through which they had just made their escape. The hands on the clock face pointed straight up.

Her heart sank.

Pharis sighed, sinking to the ground. "Curfew."

"What do we do now?"

"How should I know? You're the one calling the shots, apparently."

"I'm sorry. I guess you're more used to getting your way . . . everyone around you bowing and scraping to do your bidding."

"I'm not . . ." Cocking his head, Pharis narrowed his eyes at her. "That's ridiculous, and you know it. What's really going on here, Aurianna? Why are you trying to pick a fight?"

"I'm not!" Aurianna stormed off. She still needed to see the town, to understand what had happened. But first, a detour to the stables.

As yet, no one had been to the stables to check on Oracle, her horse. And the black-maned creature had been on her mind a great deal, causing her no small amount of worry.

Sigi had already tried and failed to see her sister Hilda to make sure she was safe. No one else had any immediate family at the Imperium. Besides Hilda and her friend Sebastian, Aurianna's only concern was for Oracle.

Sneaking around the back of the building, Aurianna crossed down and around to the stall where Oracle was kept. The mare shook her head, neighing and whinnying. Aurianna's mood softened as she pressed her forehead against the animal's, inhaling her horsey scent and blowing her own breath into her friend's nostrils. Oracle immediately calmed.

"Good girl," she whispered, her voice hitching with unspoken emotion. She could feel Oracle's agitation pick back up with Pharis's approach. He didn't speak.

After several minutes of silent discourse with her horse, Aurianna knew they needed to go. Quietly promising to visit again soon, she led the way back out. The town would be her next stop.

When she arrived at the entrance to Bramosia, she could see nothing to match the situation Theron and Sigi had described. But as she crept further in, remnants of a disaster began to show themselves. There were no demolished buildings or flattened structures as she had feared, but piles of crumbled stone lay strewn across the ground, holes ripped into the sides of homes and vestiges of recent fires.

But…how?

The singularity had been contained. *No,* she told herself, *the sphere of Energy Javen created had been contained.* But it had been merely the catalyst. *She* was the singularity. Either way, Aurianna had taken that power and absorbed it within herself. Or so she had thought.

No one had died, as far as she was aware. Her conscience pricked to remind her of the truth. Someone had indeed died.

But she pushed back those thoughts—*No no no no...*

This just didn't make sense. Why was there any destruction at all? Aurianna had prevented the explosion that blast of Energy would have created.

She could sense Pharis behind her, but he didn't make a move to touch her. Maybe he was afraid she would yell at him again.

Maybe she would.

Aurianna wanted to be alone, to run off to the stables and gallop off with Oracle into the night. Her friends would be safer if she weren't around anyway.

But she couldn't just leave without saying goodbye. Sigi deserved that, at least.

Finally, Pharis spoke, his voice soft in the stillness of the night. "I don't think this was your doing."

Slowly facing him, Aurianna mimicked his gentle tone. "And who do you think did it? Your father?"

"I wouldn't put it past him."

"He isn't capable of... all this." She waved a hand at the damage surrounding them.

"Maybe not, but there's no way you could have done this. I was watching you the whole time."

I'm not leaving you!

Aurianna remembered his words that night on the roof—mere days that seemed a lifetime ago. As she had stood encased in a ball of blazing Energy and heat, his sapphire-blue eyes had been full of unshed tears, but his gaze had never left her golden-amber one.

She shook those thoughts from her head before they over-whelmed her. "Whatever. Right now, we have to get back."

"I'm not sure that's going to be possible."

"I didn't see any guards outside the building. We'll just have to be quiet and careful going back in." Aurianna glared at him as she spoke.

"I just..." Pharis sighed with resignation, gesturing to the path back to the Imperium with an outstretched hand. "Okay. Lead the way."

They made it back to the front entrance, not a guard in sight. Aurianna reached for the handle to pull the door open a crack, just enough to peek in.

But it wouldn't budge.

She pulled again. Nothing. Aurianna then tried throwing her weight against the door. It didn't move.

Spinning on Pharis, she crossed her arms over her chest. "What now?"

"That's what I was trying to tell you. With the curfew, the front doors were bound to be locked."

"How are we supposed to get back?"

He shrugged. "Teleport?" he suggested, an amused twinkle in his eyes.

"Not funny. Also, not helpful." She slumped beside the locked doors, rubbing her temples with her palms.

"Well, do you have any ideas? I don't think staying here is a good plan. Guards could come by at any time." Pharis stared at her, then at the door, then out into the night, obviously racking his brain to come up with a solution.

Also scanning the area for inspiration, Aurianna asked, "Are they all locked?"

He leaned against the door, his shoulders slumped in frustration.

"Yeah. All the doors will stay locked until sunrise." Pharis's eyes glazed over with a faraway focus. Then he seemed to come back to himself, taking her hand and pulling her behind him as he made his way around the left side of the Imperium.

With a yelp of surprise, Aurianna allowed herself to be dragged for a moment before regaining her composure. As she started to yank her arm out of his grasp, she realized they had stopped at the edge of the cliff. Perdita Bay stretched out in front of them and off to their right.

"Let me go."

He dropped her arm, a brief flash of hurt in his eyes. But he just raised his eyebrows.

Aurianna was getting exasperated with the man. "What?"

A mischievous look crossed Pharis's face. "Remember when we were searching the tunnels that time, the night your—Ethan found us?"

"Yes. What's your point?"

"Remember that door we found?"

She felt stupid for not thinking of it before. "Think we can open it from the outside?"

"Why would anyone see the need to lock it? It's worth a shot. Plus, the vegetation-covered rocky bit shields it if any guards think to look in this area. If I remember correctly, the only open part is the side of the ledge facing Perdita Bay." His excitement was growing. "I'm fairly sure I can find it. Based on the direction the bay was from the door, it has to be around this side of the cliff."

"How are we going to get down there?"

Pharis regarded her as if she had suggested something stupid, like taking a dip in the bay. "Have you forgotten how I got you to safety that night, after the Volanti attack?" He offered his hand with a grin and asked, "Do you trust me?"

She felt a smile stretch her lips even as her cheeks warmed. "Yes."

Without giving her a chance to reconsider, Pharis scooped her up, one arm under her knees and the other supporting her upper back. Aurianna barely had a moment to wrap her arm around his neck before he took a running start and leaped over the edge of the cliff.

She was hardly more prepared for the sensation than she had been the last time. A whoosh filled her ears, and her stomach dropped then jumped up into her throat. But this was a much shorter trip, and Pharis was already slowing.

"I can't just hover in midair," he whispered, his voice breathy in her ear. "So I need you to help me find it as quickly as possible."

Aurianna studied the face of the cliff as they slowly floated down. Far below, she thought she spied what could have been the shrubbery-enclosed "porch" to the secret door. She nudged Pharis and pointed.

When she looked up, his eyes were on her rather than the cliff. His gaze dropped to her lips as his own gave the slightest twitch.

She forgot where she was—who she was—as she leaned in, the chill in the night air failing to cool her suddenly heated skin. Her grip around his neck tightened as their hungry lips met and clung, tongues tasting, hands gripping.

Pharis—somehow, inexplicably—spun her around to face him, his hands beneath her thighs, encouraging her to wrap her legs around his waist.

She locked her ankles, tightening her muscles to pull herself closer. Noises echoed in the breeze, and she wasn't sure whether they were hers or his or some combination.

Her stomach jumped again.

Falling. Their descent was out of control.

Pharis broke off the kiss, and his mouth became occupied with curses instead. It didn't take long for him to regain his composure and his equilibrium, however, and he halted their freefall. He peered over his shoulder to get his bearings and took them in the direction she had first pointed.

Then she heard voices.

Who in the world would be using that door besides them?

Aurianna raised her eyebrows questioningly at Pharis.

He nodded. He had heard the voices as well.

When they had first encountered the door from the other side, the view was blocked on most sides by a wall of vegetation that practically enclosed the ledge. Even the top was covered by a roof of rigid interwoven greenery that extended far past the rocky overhang.

The whispered words were coming from the covered area outside the door they'd been seeking.

He managed to land them softly where the foliage was thick on the covered rock that overhung part of the enclosure. He knelt down and began to slither to the edge on his stomach.

She poked him in the side to get his attention, shaking her head violently when he looked back.

He pointed to his eye then down, indicating he wanted to observe whatever was happening on the ledge below. Pharis slowly inched forward and leaned his head down past the top bit of shrubbery.

Several voices started shouting at once.

His body went rigid, and he yanked his head back, cursing loudly as a stream of bullets rent the greenery where his head had just been. He clutched her arm, and they stood on shaky legs, inching back to lean against the cliff wall. Smoking holes could be seen near the edge of the foliage, right where Pharis had been only a moment before.

Aurianna began to shake.

Images flashed through her consciousness. She vividly remembered the horrifying moment when she thought she had lost Pharis to that same fate. It was as if she experienced again the moment when her entire world had focused on his face as the bullet was bearing down on him. His expression had been of absolute peace and only the slightest twinge of fear—a gleam of resignation in his eyes. He knew he faced his mortality and had been completely willing to do so.

Aurianna hadn't wanted to see. She had stopped time with the bullet mere inches from Pharis's still form. But the visual was seared into her memory forever.

And here they were again, life and death just beyond their control.

Control. How ridiculous that she could so easily forget the powers burning within her.

Lifting a hand, she aimed a spark of white-hot Energy mixed with Fire into the vegetation just in front of their feet. A sizzling sound, as well as the acrid smell of burning foliage, accompanied the formation of an opening. Aurianna could see several faces through the now-gaping hole.

A massive gun was also trained on them through the charred perforation.

Pharis already had his hands in the air in a gesture of surrender, their position clearly indefensible against such a weapon.

Aurianna briefly contemplated wrapping her arms around him and tipping them over the edge, hoping he could fly them to safety.

But the man holding the gun seemed like he could and would shoot them down. And falling to their death was also not part of the plan—not that they had much of a plan.

She raised her hands slowly, wary of the man behind the gun and his intentions. Would he shoot first and ask questions later? Were they about to die?

But a muffled order had him gesturing with the gun for them to climb down. Pharis moved to go first, but the man, never lowering his weapon, shook his head and nodded at her. Careful not to make any sudden movements, Aurianna sat on the roof and lowered herself slowly through the hole. Several people aided her.

Who the hell are *they?*

She studied the group. A half dozen people were crammed into the tiny area outside the door. A few had weapons trained on her. Two still faced the door, obviously wrestling with the lock.

Pharis jumped down, refusing to accept help.

A hush fell over the group, and Aurianna wondered if they recognized him. If they intended to hold him for ransom or use him as a bargaining chip, this would go from bad to worse rather quickly.

From the shadows at the back of the enclosure stepped a female with dark hair, light eyes, and a solemn expression. Aurianna sensed she was the leader.

Aurianna thought she looked familiar but couldn't think where she might have seen her.

Pharis's reaction to the woman was stronger. He gasped and stumbled backward.

Aurianna started to ask him who she was, but he was slowly retreating as the woman advanced, his steps taking him dangerously close to the ledge behind him. Aerokinetic or no, the element of surprise left the outcome in question, especially considering his current distracted state.

His eyes widened in confusion and pain, and he shook his head as if in denial.

Aurianna was about to shout a warning as his right foot stepped just shy of the edge. But the female suddenly reached out and took his arm, pulling him away from danger. Their faces inches apart, Pharis and the woman stared unblinkingly into one another's eyes. Pharis didn't even seem to register the other woman's hand gripping his arm.

Aurianna felt her hackles rise in a territorial instinct.

Finally, the woman spoke. "Another step, brother, and this will be the shortest reunion in history."

Chapter 2

SIGI

Just inside the arched stone entrance to the tower, Sigi sat alone, biting her fingernails as she waited for her friends' return. Theron had gone out on patrol earlier in the evening, and Aurianna had stormed off several hours ago. She hoped they were safe.

And my Regulus as well.

Was he still her Regulus? Sigi didn't know what anything was anymore. Being a Kinetic was a gift from the Essence, from the gods. Since she had left home as a child, her life had been in service to Eresseia, and by extension, the Magnus, and other Consils.

She had always been loyal to the Imperium. Her years of study as a Kinetic and her training and time in the City Guard were a testament to her and her fellow guardsmen's commitment to the Magnus and to the people who depended on them.

But who were those people exactly? Was she not sworn to protect the people of Bramosia—of all Eresseia, in fact? Who would stand for them when the leaders would not? She had never thought to question the parameters of her loyalty or service. She had never felt the need to doubt or discern who she could trust. Yet she was questioning her decisions of late and the side she had chosen.

The Regulus—Pharis—would make a far better Magnus than his father ever had. Sigi wasn't so devoted to the Magnus she couldn't see what he had become. But the treason she had committed left a bad taste in her mouth.

Perhaps their first step should have been to contact the Consils.

The role of the Consils was to advocate for the people of the region they represented, to be a voice for non-Kinetics across Eresseia. Laelia seemed to believe they couldn't be trusted either, but she refused to give any reasons why she felt that way.

Power was a corruptive force, Sigi knew. She had watched the Magnus over time and seen the little things that didn't quite add up. But she had never thought his abuse of power would reach this level.

She and her friends were hiding out in a tower that had been locked with a magical spell—a spell Aurianna herself had somehow managed to break. The spell had been intended to imprison Syrena—Aurianna's mother—to keep her away from Ethan—Aurianna's father, the man Syrena desperately loved.

Sigi shook her head. Nothing in their lives made any sense anymore.

A sound echoed down the tunnel before her, and Sigi's head shot up, her hand on her weapon, alert for trouble. A prickling sensation glided across her skin.

But the figure coming into view was only Theron. Rhouth, his furry fox companion, was faithfully scampering along behind him.

Sigi didn't want him to know how worried she'd been, so she merely arched a brow and inquired casually, "So, anything new out there tonight?"

"There's quite a bit of damage."

"We already knew that."

"More than we thought. I was able to scout out Bramosia more thoroughly."

"But how is that possible?"

"Well, I . . . walked up into the city and stayed out of sight until curfew, when the guards left to take their posts—"

"No, I mean, how could she have damaged the town? The rooftop barely even had any damage, apart from those stone barriers she erected. She contained it. We saw her." Sigi's forehead wrinkled in confusion then smoothed as she got an idea. "It must have been the Volanti attack the night before."

Theron casually leaned against the stone of the arched entrance, nodding as he crossed his arms. "It might have been them, to some extent. But they didn't get close to the Imperium, and that's what concerns me."

"I thought you said you were scouting out Bramosia."

"Yeah, but you can see the roof of the Imperium from the Consilium. I climbed up to the top to have a look at the city. And even from that distance, the extent of the damage to the Imperium roof was noticeable. Massive actually."

Rhouth had curled up at Theron's feet, twitching her tail lazily, her eyes focused on Sigi. She could have sworn the fox was staring her down.

"Massive? I don't get it. It wasn't like that when we left."

"I know, but there's a helluva lot." He shrugged. "It's scorched up pretty bad."

Burned?

Aurianna's Pyrokinetic abilities were beyond anything Sigi had ever witnessed. "But she contained it. We saw her."

He threw up his hands. "I'm just telling you what I saw. Whether she's responsible or not will be irrelevant."

Sigi nodded her understanding. "They'll blame her either way. The Magnus will come after us for this." Exhaling loudly, she wiped her clammy palms on the sides of her pants. "Any ideas about where we should go next?"

He shrugged. "Your guess is as good as mine. We could head out to my parents, but it wouldn't be long before they'd search for us there." Fear drew shadows across his tanned face. "And I'd prefer not to involve them in this mess."

"Yeah, I know what you mean." Sigi leaned back in her chair then threw her hands up in exasperation. "I don't know what to do about Hilda. I can't even get a message to her."

"I know, Sigi. We'll figure out something. I don't think he would hurt her—she's just a kid. But she's a smart kid. She'll be fine."

"I hope you're right."

"Sigi, I want to . . . that is . . . I mean, who knows what tomorrow will bring. And I wanted to tell you . . ." Theron stared at her for a moment, his face flushed and his mouth opening and closing. But he eventually gave up trying to articulate whatever it was he *wanted to tell her*. Shaking his head, he pushed himself off the wall and walked past her into the room without another word.

Sigi glanced over her shoulder, resisting the urge to call him back as she watched him plod with heavy footsteps up the stairs. Theron was clearly exhausted from his excursions. He had been gone for many hours.

They were stuck here, unable to communicate with loved ones in the outside world for fear of alerting others to their presence. The "others" were mostly her fellow members of the City Guard— men and women she had trained with, served with, shared meals with. And she had no idea who among them she could trust now or who among them were so loyal to the Magnus they couldn't see what he had become.

All this paled in comparison to the one thing which twisted in her gut every time she thought about it. Her little sister, Hilda, was still locked away inside the Imperium, not knowing what was going on and probably worrying about her as well. Sigi had asked Ethan to get a message to her—if he could do it without risking everyone's safety. She hoped it had been successful and Hilda knew her big sister was thinking of her. She appreciated Theron's assurances Hilda would not be harmed, but she wouldn't rest easy until she was sure her sister wasn't being punished for Sigi's role in what had happened three nights ago on the rooftop.

Not that she had done much, but she had taken a stand and made a choice. She had chosen her friends, and she had chosen her Regulus.

She needed to make sure her sister didn't pay a price for those choices. But unless Hilda happened to be outside the Imperium when they were on one of their scouting missions, Sigi had little chance of knowing.

Voices echoing within the tunnels had Sigi standing and drawing her weapon.

Aurianna and the Regulus had been gone for far too long. This was most likely them. But something seemed off. The footsteps and whispering seemed like more than two people, and both of them knew to be more careful than that. Sound traveled in the underground passageway.

The echoes also made it difficult to tell how far away they were. Sigi waited a moment then shouted, "Who's there?"

A brief pause, then the whispering resumed. Finally, she heard a familiar voice.

"It's us, Sigi. But we have company."

Aurianna sounded strained, so Sigi stayed alert, weapon in hand. "What's that supposed to mean?" She narrowed her eyes, squinting into the darkness.

"It's...We...nothing to be concerned about. Please don't shoot."

A moment later, Aurianna's face appeared around the corner, followed closely by the Regulus, his face so pale it seemed to glow in the near darkness. Right behind him was...

No. Not possible.

Sigi blinked to clear her sight, but there was no mistaking that face.

Mara Jacomus, the former Regulus, had been missing for almost a year and was presumed dead. Yet there she stood, a female version of her twin brother, who walked just ahead of her...

With a weapon trained on his back.

Sigi raised her gun slightly but was unsure what to do.

The Regulus spoke next. "Ms. Hellswarth, please lower your weapon." He spoke the words without any emotion, and Sigi wondered if he had been drugged.

Aurianna reached the entrance first, the frustration in her eyes seeping into her tone as she spoke. "Sigi, I assume you know who this is. Please put your weapon away." She placed her hand atop the barrel of Sigi's gun, pushing it down.

Sigi yanked it back up as her confusion took a back seat to her sense of duty. "But they've got a gun on the Regulus."

"I imagine there's no point in calling me that anymore." He sounded more relieved than concerned.

"Perhaps we should let them in to explain what's going on," Theron called from behind her. Glancing back, Sigi saw he was standing near the bottom of the winding stairwell, his hand hanging loosely at his side, but his weapon still firmly holstered.

"Why should we let them enter? We don't know who they are. What's the point of having someone guard the entrance if we let just anyone in?"

"Well, good thing I'm not just anyone." It was the—Mara who

21

spoke, her voice so familiar to Sigi. There was no denying this was truly the eldest child of Darius Jacomus—oldest by mere moments and therefore groomed to be the Regulus.

Sigi finally lowered her weapon. The people following their friends walked in like they owned the place, poking into the corners before finally lowering their weapons as well.

"How about we all put our weapons away for the moment?" Theron said, his voice calm and low.

Sigi had to hand it to the man: he knew how to defuse a tense situation, even one as strange as this.

Meanwhile, she noticed the Regulus—*what am I supposed to call him now?*—looked like he was about to pass out. So she ran over and pulled a chair over for him. Nodding his thanks, the man plopped down like he'd been running for days.

"Where are the others?" Aurianna asked.

Sigi sighed, rolling her eyes despite the current situation. "Where do you think?" She nodded her head up to Leon's room. Neither he nor Laelia had been outside that room in ages. She wondered vaguely if someone should check on them, but she'd be damned if she was going to do it.

"What about Syrena and Ethan?"

Sigi hesitated, wondering briefly if Aurianna wanted her parents here for this or if she preferred them to remain absent. "Same situation, I imagine." When her friend grimaced, Sigi almost laughed at the absurdity of their current state of affairs. "Sleeping, I'm sure." She had to bite her lips to contain her smile.

Poor Aurianna. She so desperately wished for a family, but I doubt she imagined it quite like this.

Then Sigi frowned. "Where did you go? Get locked out with the curfew?"

"Yeah."

Theron moved soundlessly to meet them in the open area of the tower, his hand still hovering near his holster. The hunter stood beside Aurianna, who was facing the group of men and women now standing in their temporary home—three females including Mara, and five males, all of them well armed. Theron cleared his throat. "Someone gonna start explaining, or what?"

Aurianna began, a tad defensively it seemed to Sigi. "We were locked out of the Imperium because of the curfew, but Pharis remembered this door we had found the night we met Ethan. We ..." She hesitated, chewing on her bottom lip. "These people were there already, trying to get into the Imperium. Pharis almost passed out from shock, and Mara's group managed to break the lock."

"They were trying to break in?" Sigi was incredulous. How could Aurianna have led these criminals right into their hideout?

But the girl shook her head. "No. I mean yes. But they were actually trying to find *us*. They heard what happened. Of course, by this point, I suppose everyone's heard about it." A pained expression took over Aurianna's face.

The Regulus picked up the thread. "Look, you obviously know this is Mara, my twin sister. You've seen her many times, so you can verify that fact. But the situation is complicated, Mr.... Uh..." He blinked rapidly and shook his head a bit as he addressed Theron. "I'm not really sure what to call you."

"Our given names are fine, Regulus. I'm Theron."

The woman who looked like Mara Jacomus smiled sardonically at the Regulus. "You don't even know their names? Really, Pharis, how very snobbish of you."

"It's not ... I'm not ... we've been ..." The Regulus sputtered, and Sigi felt herself blush in sympathy for the man. He sighed. "Things have been a bit crazy around here, as you can well imagine. But .. Sigi, right?" When she nodded, he continued. "Sigi is a highly

23

trained member of the City Guard. She's loyal to a fault, and I trust her with my life."

Sigi stiffened and said, "I *was* a City Guard, Regulus. But no more, it seems."

The Regulus shook his head. "If we are scrapping the formalities, just call me Pharis. Anyway, the title's no longer mine." He glanced over at his sister before turning back to Sigi. "And you *are* all those things. You are loyal to the people of this land, and to me. And that counts for a lot in my book."

While Pharis described Sigi, several of the strangers fidgeted, looking increasingly alarmed. One of the women raised her weapon again and aimed at Sigi. Theron leaped in front of her, his hand out in a pacifying gesture. "What's the problem, friend?"

The woman seemed uncertain but said, "He says that one's a guardswoman. So she works for the Magnus. Which means she can't be trusted. She has to leave."

"I just told you, I trust her!" Pharis stood up suddenly and almost knocked the woman with the gun off balance as he got in her face. "Put your weapon down. Now!"

"I don't take orders from you." The woman turned to Mara and raised a brow in question.

Pharis spun on his sister, his eyes wide. "Wait. You're their *leader*?"

Mara walked over and put a hand on her twin's shoulder. "You might want to sit back down for this. Deena, put your weapon away. If my brother trusts her, then so be it." She waved a hand around nonchalantly. "Pharis, do sit so I can explain everything to you."

He did with a snort.

"First of all, I'm not *the* leader, but I am *a* leader. I'm in charge of these bozos here." Mara jerked her thumb at the newcomers. "They took me in when I came to them. But I've—"

24

"What do you mean *when you came to them*?" The Regulus—*Pharis*, Sigi reminded herself—narrowed his eyes at his sister, his voice taking on a dangerous edge.

Mara sighed, running her hand through her hair in a gesture Sigi had seen her brother perform on more occasions than she could count. "Look, Pharis. You know I wasn't happy, not with the way things were at home. And especially not with the way our father was handling things. We agreed on that."

"We *agreed* he was a lousy father and a lousy leader. We *agreed* you would make a better Magnus when your time came. We *did not* agree you would up and disappear out of our lives!"

"True. But, brother, something had to be done."

"You just left, Mara! You left me to deal with everything! I thought you were dead. I had to take on a role I never wanted. And I grieved for you."

"I know, and I'm sor—"

"No! I lost Mom. I lost you. And then this"—he waved his arms in Aurianna's general direction—"insanity entered my life. And now I don't even know what's going on or whose side I'm supposed to be on."

Sigi felt an upwelling of compassion and a curious connection to this man who seemed to share her confusion. But it was a bit strange to hear her own thoughts coming from the mouth of the man she had looked to as a future leader—someone who should have no doubts about his place in the world. And yet, here they both were, cut adrift from their responsibilities and everything familiar.

Aurianna interrupted her thoughts. "Excuse me, but let's not forget it was, in fact, *you* who came to get *me*, bringing the 'insanity' with you. I didn't ask for any of this."

Mara spoke next. "Indeed. We've been watching these events play out, and I have a proposal for you."

"And what is that?"

"Come and speak to the resistance. Let them know where you stand and what your intentions are. Tell them you—all of you—are not with my father. Tell them you'll aid us in overthrowing the entire system he represents."

"Overthrow?" Pharis and Aurianna said in unison.

Mara nodded. "That is our ultimate goal. To bring the regions into a system of self-governance. Why should they be made to depend on Kinetics when they can handle things themselves?"

Sigi spoke before she thought, her voice low and full of conviction. "What you speak of is treason."

"Treason?" Mara replied. "Can you honestly deny the Magnus is a threat, then?"

Sigi glared at the woman. "I have served your father faithfully for several years now. I support the system even though I have lost respect for the man currently in charge of it. You were to inherit the position and power to make the necessary changes. Why not fix the problems from the inside, *Regulus*?" It was strange referring to the woman as Regulus once again, and Sigi could see from Mara's eyes that she was taken aback at the title being thrust upon her so suddenly. "Why not stay to find the solutions from within? Your brother planned to do just that, I gather."

Pharis nodded. "I did. And I agree . . . Sigi. The best way to make changes is from inside the system."

Mara addressed her brother. "And I would have agreed with that as well, had I not seen just how hated the Magnus is by the people he's supposed to be helping. A revolution *is* coming, whether we like it or not. The people won't listen to your cries of *but I'm different from my father*. They will simply tear you down along with him."

"How do you know all of this?" Pharis demanded.

"The Order of the Daoine walks among the people. We have

scouts who bring back news of what is said in the marketplaces, in the streets—in people's homes when they think no one is listening."

"The Order of the Daoine bombed the irrigation systems in Bramosia." Sigi glared at the woman, indignation flaring in her chest. "There is no excuse for that."

Aurianna said, "Theron and I saw the people after the fact. They were bringing the water up from Perdita Bay themselves. Without powers, without help. I think that was perhaps the point."

"Indeed," Mara said.

Sigi was livid and whirled on Aurianna. "You're defending a terrorist group?"

"No, I don't agree with their methods," Aurianna reassured her. "I'm just saying I think I know what their intent was. The ends don't justify the means, but perhaps we can help find a better way to accomplish the same thing."

Sigi narrowed her eyes and whirled on Mara, a sudden thought taking hold. "How are these non-Kinetics able to use weapons?"

Mara allowed a corner of her mouth to quirk up as she took a step back. "Does it bother you so much that the people are able to defend themselves?"

"The City Guard exists to protect the people. But we're not talking about average citizens. We're talking about a militant group. So how are they able to build and fire guns? It's a valid question."

Mara nodded slowly, conceding the point. "Aye, I guess it is. The guns we have don't work like yours. They don't need Kinetics to function. I don't know a lot about the manufacturing of the weapons, but they use some sort of explosive material to mimic elemental power and produce the force needed to propel the bullets. The same explosive material used to blow up the water system."

Aurianna perked up at the last part. "Explosive material—like on the train? Where did it come from?"

Mara shook her head. "No, that had nothing to do with us, I assure you." When Aurianna continued to glare at Pharis's twin in suspicion, the woman shrugged. "Like I said, that's not my department. I'm just here to make the world a better place."

Pharis appeared as if he might implode with his barely contained impatience and rage as he listened to their exchange. "But why make me think you were dead, Mara? Why put me through that?"

"It was necessary for everyone to think I was dead."

"Even me?" The tone in his voice was full of a deep sorrow that Sigi knew all too well. Grief over the death of a loved one was a precipice that could never be fully crossed. One always stood just at the edge, unable to either step back or fall into its depths. Over time, the grief lessened, but it was a feeling that stayed with you. Always.

"Especially you. If you believed it, then everyone else would too. And Father would call off the searches for me."

"But why?"

"I wanted to see what he and the Consils would do moving forward. They assumed the Daoine kidnapped me, but when no demands for a ransom came, they finally began to think I might be dead. And that's when their true natures kicked in."

"What do you mean?"

"You really have no idea, do you?"

"What?"

"While you lot have been running around chasing after Enchantresses and exploding trains, the Magnus and the Consils have been laying their own little schemes."

"You mean they're working together?"

"Together? No, not exactly. They *pretend* to be on the same side, but I'm sure they each have their own secrets and agendas."

"Like what?"

Mara's expression hardened. "Like...kidnapping the subject of a prophecy and using her as bait to draw out said Enchantress."

A sound from above made them glance up. Syrena—Aurianna's mother, and the "Enchantress" in question—stood on the staircase, one foot halfway to the next step. Ethan was just behind her, his mouth set in a grim line.

Ethan spoke first, his words harsh. "So, I was right. He hoped to use Aurianna's identity to somehow lure Syrena out of hiding, coax her to show her face again. She couldn't get out of the tower on her own, but she was deliberately staying hidden, keeping herself away from his prying eyes. And Darius wanted to get his hands on her... or even just a glimpse of her. Even after everything."

Mara nodded. "We think that's at least a part of it. The Order has known about your situation for some time. My father has caused a lot of pain for a lot of people."

The room went quiet.

"The Consils are no better." Laelia's bitter voice cut through the silence like a knife.

Sigi saw that Laelia and Leon had finally left the confines of their shared bedroom and had halted behind Aurianna's parents on the stairs. She wondered how much they'd heard of the strange conversation going on in the tower's great room. She suspected quite a bit since they weren't demanding introductions or explanations.

All four of the newcomers descended to join the group as the members of the resistance eyed one another.

Nodding again, Mara strode forward. "Aye. And that's why we're here. We want you to join us in stopping all of them."

Pharis sputtered, "I can't just join your resistance, Mara. They—"

"Not you, little brother. Her." Mara pointed at Aurianna. "Our leader wants her on our side."

"You mean you want her *powers* on your side."

"That too." Mara's tone had taken on a hard, unapologetic edge.

Sigi could tell Mara believed in this cause and supported the resistance wholeheartedly.

Aurianna shook her head. "First of all, we have enough of our own problems to deal with right now. There's damage out there that we didn't cause. I didn't cause. And we have a very pregnant girl who has been asleep for a few days. We need her to explain to us just what the hell is going on."

At Mara's look of confusion, Sigi pointed to the corner where Belinda lay, still unconscious. "Weeks ago, that girl was not pregnant. Now she seems almost full-term. We need answers. Not more questions. And we don't need your help."

"We're not offering. We're asking for *you* to help *us*."

CHAPTER 3

AURIANNA

A steady rhythm—a gentle rise and fall. Black hair mussed and contrasting with the white of the bed linens, smooth tanned skin which appeared darker to Aurianna in the dim light of the bedroom.

Pharis breathed in and out. Life moving forward with careless abandon.

If only it were that simple.

Aurianna watched a moment longer before ever so carefully easing out of bed. Rest alluded her this night as it had for the last couple. She left Pharis smiling slightly, an outward reaction to a dreamworld she wished she could share.

In another world, that smile might have kept her there, might have convinced her to crawl back beneath the blankets and *accidentally* wake him.

But this was not that world.

When she made the slightest sound while turning the handle of the door, Aurianna froze, hearing the rustle of the bed linens behind her. Praying to the Essence for Pharis to go back to sleep, she waited a few beats before trying again.

Outside the room, she picked up her pace, hoping not to cross paths with anyone on her way down. The circular hallways which wound around each level of the tower were empty as far as she could tell, so she glided down the stairs on silent feet.

Reaching the bottom level, she glanced around the great room briefly. Sigi was on watch, her back to Aurianna as she sat in a chair and fiddled with one of her weapons. Most of Mara's group were resting in shifts in empty rooms upstairs, but a couple eyed her from the corner of the main room.

Javen might have been working for them. The thought arose from her subconscious. He had been unhappy and angry at the Kinetics for so long, even seeming to show empathy for the Voids because he had almost been one of them. His Kinetic control had barely manifested, his power only just enough to keep him in training.

Javen's words on the rooftop had seemed to indicate he had his own reasons for what he did, but the Order of the Daoine was the only group, as far as she knew, to harbor ill feelings toward the Kinetics.

Aurianna chose to ignore the resistance members and walked over to her friend. Not wanting to sneak up on the woman with a weapon in her hand, Aurianna cleared her throat as quietly as she could. True to her guard training, Sigi didn't startle. She just peered up as Aurianna pulled over a chair to sit beside her.

"What time is it?" Aurianna asked, stifling a yawn.

"A little after midnight, I think. You've been asleep most of the day."

"I wasn't sleeping, not really." As Sigi's eyes widened, she hastened to add, "I just mean I'm having trouble sleeping."

Sigi's eyebrows were raised, her nostrils flaring as she fought to stifle a grin. "So...how are things?"

Aurianna sighed, stretching her legs out in front of her. "Just say it."

"Say what? I'm just asking how you're doing." Realizing she had spoken louder than she meant to, Sigi threw a glance at the strangers on the other side of the room and lowered her voice before continuing. "I might be fishing for a bit of gossip, but don't think that means I don't care about the rest."

"The rest of what?"

"You. Everything." Hesitating, she looked away and added, "Javen."

At his name, Aurianna squirmed, her back going rigid. "I don't want to talk about it."

"About *that*—" Sigi nodded to the upper levels, "or about the other stuff?"

"None of it."

"Why?"

"What do you mean, *why*? Because I can't, Sigi." Her shoulders hunched with the weight she was carrying. "I just can't."

Shrugging, Sigi bit her lip and put the weapon she'd been messing with on the ground at her feet. Leaning forward to rest her weight on her knees, she said, "The Imperium is strictly enforcing this curfew, as far as we can tell. From midnight until dawn, no one goes in and no one goes out."

"By *the Imperium* you mean the Magnus?"

"I...yes. The Magnus."

"I know this isn't easy for you, Sig. Your loyalty has always been to the Magnus and the City Guard." At her words, Sigi's eyes began to tear up, moisture glistening in the corners. "Sigi, what's wrong?"

The girl shook her head, touching a hand to her mouth as she pursed her lips. "Nothing." Sigi waved away Aurianna's concern. "It's just...you called me Sig. Javen used to call me that."

A burst of anger had Aurianna on her feet. "I said I don't want to—"

"This isn't just about you. We were his friends too, you know. And we knew him much, much longer than you did."

And just like that, the anger deflated into a calm stillness. Hanging her head, Aurianna closed her eyes and slumped back into the chair. "Yeah, I know. I know. But I shouldn't have trusted him. It was my job to fix things, and all I did was mess it up worse. I let him get inside my head because you guys were ignoring me—"

"We weren't ignoring you. Javen said—"

"I don't care what he said! I don't want to discuss him."

"Fine. Then let's talk about the damage out there. Theron said it's bad. You saw it, I presume?"

"I did, and I don't understand. I contained it, remember?" Panicked, Aurianna let out a whimper.

"Yes, you did. But I guess residual damage was bound to happen with something so volatile. Doesn't make it your fault, though."

A voice behind them caused the two girls to spin around in their seats. "And speaking of, how about we talk about what happened up there?" Theron walked around to sit in a chair beside Sigi, resting his elbows on his knees as he stared at Aurianna expectantly.

"I've explained as much as I know about the singularity and whatever I did. The Arcanes say the singularity is a moment in time when everything becomes infinite and can go in any direction." Aurianna tried not to think about Javen's words on the rooftop, but they still came unbidden.

I am giving you your destiny, Aurianna. Your reason for being here. Your singularity.

What is the singularity?

You are.

Shaking the horrifying thoughts from her head, she continued. "When we reached that point, it opened up the time loop. Before then, everything was in a closed loop, and no one could change anything. Except for me, apparently."

Sigi scrunched up her face. "So, when did this time loop first start?"

"They won't say. But now things can be changed, and the future is unknown."

"Well, that means your timeline in the future should be corrected and better now, right?"

"I don't know. I need to talk to Simon. And if you want a better answer than what I'm giving you, you'll have to ask the Arcanes yourself."

Theron frowned in thought. "I actually tried knocking on their door on my way upstairs yesterday, but no one answered."

Strange, Aurianna thought.

Theron continued, "But that's not what I mean. I'm talking about the other thing—how you moved outside of . . . I honestly don't know what you did. Not to mention whatever you did to the Regulus—"

"What she did to the Regulus is none of your business." Pharis had woken up and come downstairs without them noticing. Winking at Aurianna, he added, "Nor is what he did to her."

Theron looked as uncomfortable as Aurianna had ever seen him as he gaped up at Pharis and back down, not sure how to respond. "No, Regulus. We were just talking about what happened with the . . . ah . . . err . . ."

"The whole me-not-dying bit, you mean?"

"Yeah—and everything else."

They stared at Aurianna. Her cheeks felt hot as she realized everyone was waiting for an answer.

An answer she didn't have.

Only she did.

"I . . . Simon once mentioned a Kinetic power. He called it Chronokinetic. I guess it's pretty rare, but—"

"Chrono? As in time? You're saying you were messing with time?"

"We travel through time with the Aether Stones. Why is this so hard to believe?"

"Did you have an Aether Stone on you?"

"Well, no, but—"

His brows furrowed, Pharis was gazing at her intently, an expression of wonder on his face. "Just before I . . . right when the bullet hit me, I thought I saw you across the roof. But you had been behind me. That's the whole reason I . . ."

Don't say it. I know what you did. And you shouldn't have done it.

Sigi's voice was a whisper. "He saved your life, Aurianna. Regulus—Pharis, thank you."

His forehead was still wrinkled, his eyes still on Aurianna. "Well, I guess she didn't need saving, after all." Unspoken words danced in his eyes, but he only added, "Especially since *she* saved *us* from Ambrogetti's giant ball of Energy."

Aurianna was desperate to change the subject. "I've been thinking . . . there's a lot of damage out there, and whether I caused it or not, it won't matter. The Magnus or the Consils—or both—are going to come after me for it. I think it's better if I leave so you all aren't implicated."

"What?"

"There's no reason for everyone to go down with me. It's me they'll be after. We left . . . a dead Kinetic on the roof, and the town is in bad shape. They'll blame me, and I refuse to be responsible for getting anyone else killed or in trouble."

"Aurianna, no." Pharis stood and tried to grip her arm, but she shook him off.

"I've already decided, Pharis. I'm a danger to everyone. I shouldn't be here, putting you all at risk."

"Don't be—"

A soft noise in the opposite corner of the room, just beyond where the rebels were standing, caused everyone to jump.

"Where am I?" a frightened-looking Belinda asked.

CHAPTER 4

AURIANNA

Everyone gathered around the extremely pregnant girl, all gaping and speechless.

Belinda was noticeably larger than she had been when they'd brought her to the tower after the ordeal on the roof. Four days ago.

Somehow, of all the things they had seen and experienced recently, *this* was the most bizarre.

Aurianna stared along with the others, trying desperately to resolve the conflicting thoughts within her mind. Javen, the man she had thought was in love with her—the man who had taken her innocence under false pretenses—had clearly impregnated the girl.

But how?

Obviously, Aurianna knew *how*. But how could Belinda's stomach be growing at such an alarming rate? It was unnatural, and it unnerved Aurianna.

She knew the others felt the same.

They waited for the girl to finish the food Syrena had laid out for her. Upon waking, food and drink had been Belinda's first priority, apart from finding out where she was.

Until that moment, it hadn't occurred to Aurianna to wonder how Syrena had gotten food into the tower during her months of captivity, much less for her and her friends. They just seemed to have it available. But when Belinda requested food, Aurianna watched the woman—she could not think of her as *Mother*—conjure a platter of bread, cheese, and fruit out of thin air.

Ironically, the fact that it didn't faze Aurianna to witness such an impossible feat unnerved her even more. No Kinetic had that kind of ability. It was something . . . other.

And Aurianna suspected it might explain some of her own experiences.

Refusing to think on it any further for the moment, Aurianna cleared her throat as Belinda washed down the last piece of bread with a large glass of juice.

The girl nervously rubbed a hand across her swollen belly, sadness plain on her features. She scanned the assembled group, tears forming in her eyes as she shook her head in bewilderment. "I don't understand."

Theron stood in the back of the group, but he was the first to respond. "Well, neither do we. But I'm betting you have a much better idea of things than we do."

"No, I don't. Javen said . . ." Belinda's voice trailed off as she squeezed her eyes shut. Suddenly, she opened her eyes and focused on Aurianna. "I'm sorry. I just thought if I could make him like me . . ."

"Looks like you succeeded quite well on that front." Aurianna knew her tone was harsh, and she didn't care. The girl might have been young, but she had made mistakes they would all have to live with.

"No, he—I mean, yes, I tried to seduce him. But, in the end, he just used me. Told me I was fulfilling a greater purpose. I didn't realize what he meant until . . ." Belinda gazed down at her belly, placing her hand upon it once more. "But that was just a few weeks ago. I'm huge! How is this possible?"

And how did Javen manage to bypass the birth control in the water supply?

Seeing the naked terror on the younger girl's face, Aurianna began to regret her words. She leaned forward, trying to soften her tone. "There seem to be a lot of questions none of us can answer right now. The more we search for answers, the more questions we get. We're going to keep trying though." Placing a hand on her shoulder, Aurianna thought about the times she had wanted to strangle the girl who now sat alone and afraid before her. Now all her anger dwindled away. "In the meantime, I think you should stay here with my . . . with my parents." Aurianna ignored Belinda's wild-eyed look of puzzlement. "They'll keep you safe until we can find you those answers."

But the girl was shaking her head violently. "No! I want out of here. I want to find my family!"

"I'm afraid we can't let you do that." Leon's deep drawl cut through the girl's hysterical cries. "We can only guarantee your safety inside this tower. The Magnus is hunting us and, right now, you're not safe anywhere else."

Instead of continuing to argue, Belinda simply stared off into nothing, an air of sadness surrounding her.

Aurianna hurt for her. She knew what it felt like to yearn for family as well as to be caught up in things you didn't understand. She stood, a lingering ache across her back reminding her of the injury she had sustained during the Volanti attack several nights ago. The healers had tended to the wound and the pain, but memories of that night would remain with her forever.

Even more memorable was the flight Pharis had taken her on, exposing his massive Aerokinetic gifts to her. The experience had been both terrifying and magical.

That night she had begun to realize how much they had in common. How much she cared for him. And how much he cared for her.

But...Javen.

He was dead. And she had killed him.

Pharis was alive because she had made a choice. Sure, the others might eventually find a way to forgive her, but Leon...Leon would never be able to get over her killing his best friend, no matter the reason.

Wasn't she also the reason they had been in danger to begin with? Wasn't her very existence the cause of their pain and suffering? If it weren't for her being there, none of them would be hiding out in a tower, hoping the guards wouldn't find and imprison them.

No. They would all be dead—killed by the blast of Energy Javen had created by chaining those Voids together...

"What happened to those Voids?" Aurianna heard herself asking, her voice shaky with emotion. She stood up and faced the others, waiting on the answer she wasn't sure she wanted to hear.

Theron spoke up. "When I was scouting earlier, I could see the roof of the Imperium. It was a fair distance, mind you, but all I could see was the damage. No bodies to be seen."

"So, they...found him."

"I guess so."

She startled at a hand on her shoulder. Ethan.

"They're all right, child. The Voids, I mean. Well, perhaps *all right* is not quite correct. But they will live."

Aurianna felt a weight lift from her. She beamed back gratefully. "Thank you."

Ethan nodded before hugging Syrena to his side.

Her parents. She could hardly believe she had found them. Never mind they were only a few years older than she was now. Had Larissa not been forced to escape with her into the future and raise her there, she herself would still be a baby.

It was all utterly and completely just too strange to deal with, especially on little to no sleep.

Despite Belinda's continued protests, the group decided to put her in an upstairs room and post a guard. Aurianna felt bad they were keeping the girl prisoner, but she was a danger to herself and others at the moment. Belinda wasn't thinking logically, which would be a challenge under the circumstances, even without the pregnancy.

As everyone split up, some heading upstairs and others back to the far side of the room, Aurianna felt someone behind her. She spun around and came face-to-face with Mara.

The new Regulus. Or the old one resurrected, depending on how one considered it.

Pharis's sister leaned close. "So, have you thought about what I asked you?"

"Which thing would that be?"

"About joining us and going back to meet with my leader."

"I don't know. I need to consult a few people."

"Haven't you done that already?"

"Not the people here. I'm talking about... others."

"Didn't you just tell that girl she couldn't risk leaving the tower and endangering everyone? What makes you any different?"

"I can protect myself."

"I'm sure you can, from what I've seen. But that's not what I mean, and you know it."

"I don't need someone else telling me what to do. If you want me to even consider your offer, you'll step off and leave me be."

Aurianna walked away before Mara could respond, seeking out her friends.

Theron and Leon were gearing up. Sigi and Laelia stood between them, examining the weapons laid out on a table. As she approached, Aurianna whispered, "Where are you guys headed?"

Leon stole a look at Laelia. "Theron and I are going to check on Orion and Juliet. I haven't been able to find them since the Volanti attack. And with the baby . . . it just complicates things." He had to tear his eyes away from Laelia to continue strapping on weapons.

"Where did these weapons come from?"

Theron shrugged. "The Voids who clean the guard barracks. Ethan was able to get a few of them to help. Some are less than thrilled with the Magnus. Shocking, I know." He winked.

Sigi seemed more troubled than ever. "I don't like to think about people connected to us finding themselves in danger." Aurianna knew the quiver in her friend's lip had more to do with Hilda— Sigi's younger sister who was still trapped at the Imperium—than with the current conversation.

"So, you're all going?" Aurianna was surprised they would leave the tower to the resistance members. Sigi, at least, didn't seem to trust them.

"Yes," Laelia and Sigi replied at the same time as Leon and Theron said, "No."

Sighing, Leon rubbed the bridge of his nose. "Look, it doesn't make sense for all of us to go. Theron and I can handle it."

"So, you want the girls to just sit on our hands here?" The ire in Laelia's eyes burned with such intensity Aurianna thought she might incinerate Leon with the glare she leveled on him.

"What? No! That's not—"

"Well, I'm going whether you like it or not." Sigi continued picking out weapons as if nothing had happened. "I'm a guards-woman. This is what I do."

"Fine, Sigi can come." Leon threw his hands up in exasperation.

Sigi rolled her eyes. "Thank you for granting me your permission."

"And what about me?" Laelia took a step closer to Leon, and he stepped back when he saw the rage in her eyes.

Theron tried to calm the situation. "Some of us need to stay behind and keep an eye on things. I don't know what to think about the Order of the Daoine or Belinda, and honestly, I'm not sure how far we can trust your parents." He studied Aurianna with an apology in his eyes. "None of these people should be left alone here until we know more."

"But Aurianna will be here. And Pharis." Laelia had begun to pout.

Aurianna took a deep breath before replying, "Aurianna will not be here. Aurianna is going to speak with Simon."

Theron shook his head. "You can't go anywhere right now. We discussed this earlier. Wait until we get back, and then—at the very least—take Pharis with you again."

"I don't need Pharis to babysit me!"

"It's not—"

"Why does she get to go out, and I don't?" Laelia asked, pointing an accusing finger at Leon.

He wouldn't meet her eyes but continued to fiddle with his weapons, so Aurianna answered instead. "Because they know I'll blast them with Fire if they try to stop me." She was half joking, but the others appeared uncomfortable at her words.

"Fine! Whatever!" Laelia stomped off, heading to the upper levels.

The current argument aside, Aurianna marveled at the new-found relationship between Laelia and Leon. The two of them had done nothing but bicker and belittle one another since she had met them. Yet somehow, in the last few days, they had found a spark and blown on it until it was an open blaze.

She didn't want to admit it, but she was jealous of their freedom. No awkward feelings of guilt. No dead lovers. No desire to run away and leave it all behind.

She still thought everyone would be safer if she did what the brand on her back said and ran away. But no one was going to let her leave on her own.

Aurianna quietly holstered a weapon and tried to sneak off to the tunnel. She was halfway down the first length before she heard a voice behind her.

"Wait up." It was, of course, Pharis. The group had obviously alerted him to her departure and put him back on babysitting duty.

She faced him. "I don't need a chaperone, Pharis."

Instead of stopping in front of her, he put his hands on her hips and kept walking until he had her backed against the wall of the tunnel. "Maybe you do," he whispered, his voice raspy with need. His breath was hot in her ear. "You never know what some scoundrel might try to do to you in the dark when you're all alone."

Aurianna closed her eyes as he nibbled her earlobe. Then, instead of continuing his ministrations, Pharis edged back an inch or two and said, "Talk to me. What's wrong?"

Her eyes flew back open. "Nothing."

She felt his hair brush her cheek as he shook his head. "Something is bothering you."

"Really? You mean something like the fate of the world? Or the lives of my friends? Or maybe the fact that *your father* wants to arrest us?

"You don't have to take all of that on yourself. I'm here. Your friends are here. We can do this together. I love you, Aurianna."

A small part of her wanted nothing more than to melt into his arms, to let him erase all her doubts, her fears.

Her feelings of guilt and betrayal.

She had killed someone. And Javen's body had barely been cold before she had found herself in Pharis's arms. Javen's own betrayal didn't make her feel any better. That wasn't the point.

Disgusted with herself, Aurianna pushed Pharis away from her. "Shouldn't you be spending time with your long-lost sister?"

"Well, yeah, but I can—"

Without waiting to hear the rest of his reply, Aurianna stomped off in search of more answers to the never-ending questions bombarding her reality.

CHAPTER 5

AURIANNA

Aurianna strode at a brisk pace for a while before finally slowing. The silence continued for a while as she trudged along.

The sound of Pharis's approach reached her ears. "Have I done something wrong?" His question was soft, almost humble.

She had made herself as clear as she could, but he refused to listen. "No."

"Right. So why are you mad at me?"

Aurianna still felt impatient, but her irritation had subsided. "I'm not mad."

"Right." His tone clearly conveyed his disbelief. "Okay, well, what's the plan then?"

She drew in a calming breath. "The plan is to talk to Simon."

"Simon is the Arcane who's been helping you?"

"Helping? Talking, yes. Helping, not so much." Aurianna eventually stopped before the door to the Arcanes' sanctuary and pounded. When no one responded to her "knock" after a few seconds, she said in a whispered shout, "I know you can hear me. Open the damn door!"

A man who seemed oddly familiar opened the door a crack and eyed them. He scrutinized Pharis especially before widening the opening.

The small man was a surprise. Simon had always somehow known when she was coming, but this time he wasn't there to greet her. She had seen this man somewhere before, though she couldn't place where. Tentatively, Aurianna moved closer to the entryway. "Do I... Do I know you?"

Instead of answering, the man merely smiled. "Simon is waiting for you. Come this way."

She had no choice but to follow.

Pharis was gazing around as if he'd never been in the room before, even though she knew he had. But this was his first visit since learning the entire place was nestled within a time bubble. It was bound to be disconcerting for him. Aurianna had been on the verge of a nervous breakdown when she had discovered that fact. At least he had the advantage of knowing and preparing himself before walking in.

Simon was sitting at one of the back tables. A familiar book sat closed before him. He gestured. "Please have a seat."

Aurianna glowered at him in frustration. "I need you to answer my questions. No vague comments, no skirting around the truth—"

"I told you before, I am limited in what I can say. The Essence—"

"To hell with the Essence right now! So many things could have been prevented if you had only told me everything from the beginning."

In a nearby corner, a small group of Arcanes glanced up at the sudden outburst. The small man who had opened the door joined them. They seemed to be randomly taking books from the shelves and cramming them into new homes.

"Could they?" Simon's voice brought her attention back from the odd scene.

"What do you mean? If I had known that woman was my mother, none of this would have happened!"

"No? So, you wouldn't have gone to stop that train? Your friend wouldn't have kidnapped those Voids and used them as he did?"

"As for the train, if I had known that was my mother, I probably would have tried to speak with her." Sighing, she added, "Only problem is, she denies the whole damn thing. Is it possible she was under a spell?" Aurianna now realized how badly she wished for something like that to be true.

"I don't have an answer for that."

"But you *do* have an answer! You just refuse to give it!" Aurianna slammed her fist on the table between them. The Arcanes didn't turn around this time, but they stopped moving for a moment. Each of them seemed to be staring at the wall in anticipation. Of what, she could only guess.

Arcanes were, by their very nature, odd and mysterious in ways beyond her understanding. They held the mysteries of the world in these rooms, amid the tomes filled with histories and prophecies which may or may not have come true over the course of time.

Shaking his head, Simon contemplated her fist, which was still tensed against the wood of the table. "Just because I know and have withheld some things from you—because the goddesses directed me to do so, I will remind you—doesn't mean I have all the answers. For instance, I don't know why your friend was involved in the incident on the rooftop."

Pharis had been silent till then. Now he stepped around her to chime in. "He wasn't *involved*. He *instigated* the incident."

"Whatever the case, we don't have the answers. And we cannot see the end of this road you are on."

Pharis shared a side glance with Aurianna. "What do you mean?" His voice was shaky.

49

"We can only see what is and what has been. Not what may be. Our ability to walk into the future is limited to the futures that exist as of now, based on the actions you are taking right now." Simon spread his hands on the table before him.

Aurianna felt a rising panic—a tightening in her chest, her heart pushing against her ribcage in a staccato rhythm. "But Larissa said—" She paused a moment, scowling at the ground. "She knew. When you took me through the door to the future—she knew what hadn't happened yet. She knew the future. And she promised me she'd wait for me."

"Your Larissa will wait for you. But you shouldn't try to reach her while the future is still in flux. The danger is far too great, even for you."

"What are you saying? Has the future timeline been corrected or not?"

"It has not, not completely."

"So, what happened on the roof...that wasn't the singularity?"

Simon shook his head. "You misunderstand. That was indeed the singularity—"

Leaning over the table, Pharis got in Simon's face. "Then why the hell hasn't it changed anything?"

"It was never—"

"It was me." The room began to spin as she remembered the words—spoken with such clarity by a person she'd thought she could trust. "I caused the singularity. Not Javen."

Pharis's forehead creased. "Aurianna—"

"No, Pharis. On the roof, just before you ran over to me, Javen told me I was the reason the singularity occurs. That we had done this many times, over and over." She spun on Simon, making him lean back in his chair. "Simon, you told me I died every time I tried in the past to stop it. But...it wasn't just me who died, was it? I'm the reason Kinetics began fleeing this place and traveling to the future, just to be drained and killed and . . ." Sobs choked her.

Pharis attempted to put an arm around her shoulders, but she shook him off. No one could possibly understand the weight of that knowledge, of knowing something so horrifying about yourself and your failure. Glancing at the strange group gathered in the corner, Aurianna noticed they were now staring at her openly.

Simon's eyebrows crinkled with concern. "We don't know if it ever was him, or if it was always you. The details of how these things work are . . . complicated. I don't know if the Essence even know for sure whether our bringing you back in time created the singularity, or whether you were meant to stop it and things just went wrong. All I can tell you is that stopping it was required to stop the time loop. That has happened, but it is not the final step."

Words from Caendra, goddess of Fire, floated into her mind. "Yes. Caendra said the battle would be won, but the war would not be over. What did she mean?"

Simon nodded. "By stopping the singularity and learning to control your powers, you stopped the explosion and resulting catastrophe, which was always what sparked the civil war. But the entity behind it all will only try again. Preventing that is your next goal."

"What entity?" Pharis leaned forward, confusion in his tone.

"I honestly do not know. We have never gotten this far in the chain of events. I told you, we don't know the details of any future that hasn't happened before. And the future is now uncertain because you opened the time loop. Many paths are now possible. You must wait for instructions from the goddesses. I can't help you any further."

"Wait!" Aurianna cried. "But what about us? What about my

friends, my . . . parents?" The word was still awkward in her mouth, her uneasy relationship with them a heavy stone within her, weighing her down. "If we wait any longer, the Magnus will come for us. It's a miracle he hasn't before now."

"The Magnus is not searching for you. He is currently dealing with bigger matters."

"What the bloody hell is bigger than a dead Kinetic and a missing Regulus?" Pharis sounded indignant—or perhaps disappointed.

"Irate Consils breathing down his neck. What else?"

Aurianna pursed her lips then nodded. "So . . . he's playing politics right now?"

"The Consils are using this situation to make the Kinetics appear dangerous. The Magnus is on the verge of being physically removed from power. I think they've had enough of his scheming."

"So, a civil war is inevitable?" She was fuming.

Shaking his head, Simon folded his hands and rested them on the table. Choosing his words carefully, he said, "Well, the situation is different now. Before, the singularity would result in chaos. People revolted, a mass exodus from the capital ensued, and the Magnus was executed almost immediately."

Aurianna expected Pharis to be shocked by this news. But the only outward indications of deeper emotions were his face going pale and the slight bulging of the tensed muscle in his jaw.

She was staring at Pharis, unable to look away. "Because of me."

Pharis's nostrils flared as he inhaled sharply. "No, my father is the monster he is because of his own actions. I'm sure he deserved it, either way."

"But . . . he's your father!"

"And Syrena is your mother. Yet you yourself planned to deal with her despite that fact, back when you thought her a monster."

Point taken.

Aurianna addressed her next thoughts to Simon. "But either way, it's still a civil war."

"Indeed. Which is why you must speak with the Essence to determine what your next steps should be."

"It actually sounds like I need to go have a chat with the Consils."

"Not necessarily. You should find out more first."

"Why must I always wait for others to tell me what to do?"

"You know that isn't true, Aurianna. If anything, we've been waiting on you to tell *us* what to do. You've been in control the entire time, left to your own devices to make your own decisions."

She hated to admit it, but he was completely right. The lack of guidance had been . . . frustrating, to say the least. She chewed on her bottom lip as she thought through her options. "What about Larissa?"

"What about her?"

"I don't understand why I can't go speak with her right now. Through the magic time door thingy like I did before. She could—"

"You could try, yes." He nodded slowly, hesitantly. "But, as I said, that option is dangerous, and right now, it would be ill-advised. She can't help you right now. I promise you will have the opportunity when the time is right. Plus, there are consequences for bypassing the Aether to travel through time."

"And you're just telling me this now?"

"Your previous trip was preordained. I'm just saying you should think carefully before you make any hasty decisions going forward."

The Arcane librarians continued their seemingly nonsensical redistribution of the tomes. The intricate choreography of passing books back and forth, reshelving, and rearranging was all accomplished without discussion or pause.

Aurianna watched them with keen interest. She focused

especially on the man who had admitted them, the one who had seemed so familiar to her.

And suddenly she realized why. She remembered where she had seen him before.

Pointing at him, Aurianna let out a shaky breath. "You." The noise of her beating heart throbbed in her head, pushing out all other sounds. "I know you. You ran into me in the street. During my timeline. In the future, before I ever came here."

Out of the corner of her eye, she watched as Simon stood and walked around to stand in front of her, partially blocking her view of the other man. Simon took in her frightened expression. "And what of it? Knowing what you know now, is it so strange that this man was walking the streets a hundred years from now? As you just said, it would be a simple matter of walking through the time door."

She stepped right into his personal space. "But you just said it's dangerous to use it too often."

Disregarding her aggression, Simon said, "Not for us. Only for others."

"So, it's just a coincidence I bumped into this man in the future? And he wasn't dressed like you, more like something I'd expect the Consils to wear."

From behind Simon's back, the man spoke up. "I was tasked with keeping an eye on you. I was usually so careful, but that morning you were so . . . forlorn—I forgot myself for a moment and lost my focus."

Aurianna's raised an eyebrow, pushing Simon to the side as she spoke directly to the other man. "So, you've been spying on me? For how long?"

The man looked sheepish. "Basically, your whole life. That's all the Essence asked of us. We weren't to speak with you or interfere in any way. Just check in on you."

She stared without seeing for a moment, her mind trapped in thoughts of the past. Future. Whatever.

Time travel was complicated.

"What's your name?" she asked.

He gave her the barest of smiles. "Eber."

She tried her best to return the gesture, despite the mix of emotions swirling within her. She decided to change tack. "Eber, what are you doing? All of you, I mean. With the books."

"Arcanes are charged with keeping the histories and following the prophecies. Your prophecy is ongoing, but many others exist besides. We are following the rhythm of the Essence, who guide us in reordering the tomes."

"That's ... weird."

Eber drew his brows together and cocked his head. "Perhaps." He and his brethren abruptly resumed their odd dance with the surrounding books.

Puzzled by their behavior, Aurianna nonetheless shook off her questions as another thought occurred to her. "Simon, we know the source of the Aether Stones. We can just get a piece and go find Larissa that way."

Instead of showing surprise or concern, Simon's mouth twisted into a grim version of a smile. "You would have no luck in removing a single shard from that room. But you'll have a chance to speak with Larissa if you go to the Fae."

"The ... what?" Aurianna felt her insides deflate at the mention of that enigmatic legend. "The Fae? You can't be serious."

He shrugged. "Your decision, of course."

"But, the Fae are a myth." She sputtered in frustration. "No one believes they exist."

Pharis said, "The clerics in the temples scoff at the notion of even a remnant of them existing."

"My job is to guide you. The Fae will help you contact your aunt. That is all I can tell you."

"So, they can help me find another way home to Larissa?"

Pharis's incredulity was clear. "You aren't seriously going in search of the Fae, are you?"

"Well, Pharis, if there's a chance for another way back to my home, I'm certainly going to keep it in mind." She saw the hurt in his eyes and realized what she'd said. Did she truly still think of that place as home? "In the meantime, Simon, we're going to speak with the Order of the Daoine. Mara has returned."

He grew pale at her words but only said, "I think you should consider the Fae instead."

"I understand. Anyway, right now I think I should speak with the ones in charge."

Pharis stared at her quizzically. "The Consils?"

Aurianna laughed sardonically. "No. I mean the ones who are *really* in charge." When his puzzled expression continued, she explained. "The Essence, Pharis. I need answers only a goddess can provide."

CHAPTER 6

AURIANNA

Terra, goddess of Earth, was formidable.

Aurianna was somewhat prepared for the frightening ethereal nature of the Essence after multiple conversations with them.

Pharis, however, was not. And no amount of explaining could have prepared the poor man for what he was now experiencing.

On the night of Javen's betrayal, when Aurianna herself had manipulated the time stream and pulled herself out of the normal flow of time, everyone else—Pharis included—had been frozen in place. But being an active part of what the deities called *evanescence* was wholly different.

Evanescence was a sort of temporary oneness with time— outside the normal time stream. Everything and everyone else appeared to be stuck in place, but the reality was they were simply on a different plane of existence.

She and Pharis had left the Arcanes and skirted the town to avoid any patrolling guards. As dawn broke, they slipped into the temple of Terra, hoping to have a meeting and get the answers they sought.

Terra sat in the middle of the temple dedicated to her element of Earth.

Aurianna glanced sideways at Pharis to check how he was handling all this deity stuff then cleared her throat. "So, you can answer my questions now, right? Now the time loop is open?"

Terra leaned forward, and Aurianna could have sworn the otherworldly creature sighed. "We wish it were that simple. But the time isn't right yet for the final battle."

"Battle? What the hell are you talking about? What battle?"

"You've known all along a war was brewing—"

"Yes! Between Kinetics and non-Kinetics. And I *stopped* it, remember? I am the singularity—or I caused it—or whatever. I've accepted that. But I stopped the ball of Energy from destroying everything, which should have prevented the war. But I still don't understand why there's so much damage."

"The war of which I speak is no earthly war. The petty squabbles of humans are not my main concern."

"Then why did you tell me my job was to prevent the civil war?"

"It was, Aurianna. But the war is bigger and much graver than that alone. The war to which I refer does not only cause strife and pain for humans. Divine suffering affects us all. When the Aether is in trouble, all are doomed."

"And what is that supposed to mean? So help me, if you tell me you aren't allowed to say—"

"No, the time loop is no longer closed. We are freed from the chains holding us back."

"Then what—"

Terra held up a hand. "You should know by now, Aurianna— nothing is ever that simple. The battle I speak of is the battle for humanity."

"You just said it wasn't an earthly war!"

"Aye, it is not. But it *will* determine the fate of all who reside in Eresseia and beyond."

"I'm really tired of the melodrama. Who are we supposed to be fighting now if the villain's been stopped?"

Pharis hadn't spoken, but Aurianna could see him squirming in the corner of her eye. Her frustration mounting, she shouted, "What is it, Pharis?"

He opened and closed his mouth a few times, but he didn't make a move to step closer. "Melodrama seems to be the order of the day, doesn't it? I mean, everything we've been through recently has been over the top, right?"

"What's your point, Pharis?"

"I just think we should hear her out."

"Hear what, though? They never actually tell you anything useful. They just talk in circles and then use you however they see fit. She and her sister have—"

"What about the others?" Pharis asked.

"What?"

"The other Essence. There are five. You say you've also spoken to Caendra. You've still got Unda for Water, Fulmena for Energy, and . . ." His voice trailed away, but Aurianna knew what he was going to say.

Before she could respond, Terra spoke. "I can see in your eyes, Son of Air, that you wish to speak to your benefactor. But it is impossible."

"Why?"

"Because he was taken from us."

"Taken?" Pharis inched forward, his eyes narrowing, but he kept a safe distance from the ethereal being. "By whom?"

"By an entity who seeks to destroy us."

"That's why his power is diminished? Because he was captured?"

Terra nodded.

But Aurianna was confused. "Who could capture a god? I don't understand."

"You asked me about the villain. 'Villain' is the name we give to one we see as enemy, no? They may not even see themselves as such from their own point of view. The truth of the matter is never black and white. You fought against your friend turned enemy. But you do not yet comprehend why he did what he did."

Pharis stared at Aurianna, and she felt her cheeks redden under his intense scrutiny. Finally, he looked back to Terra. "Fine, then. I'll ask. Why did Ambrogetti do it? Why try to kill all those people? Why instigate a civil war? Why impregnate that girl?"

"The enemy you seek is ancient, and I am not free from his control. He is angry for things done to him a long time ago." She paused, and seemed to drift off for a moment, then shook her head and continued. "I will let others tell that story."

"What others? Simon isn't telling me anything I don't already know. He won't even let me through the time door to speak with Aunt Larissa. Why can't you just tell me?"

"Let Simon guide you to the right path. But remember, as always, the choices are up to you. The time loop might have been opened, but it doesn't change your destiny. The future is unknown, but it is not unknowable."

"Yet you're trying to control my life through a prophecy. A prophecy *you* created!"

But the ephemeral figure before her dissolved into a wisp of nothing.

Aurianna huffed in frustration. They left the sanctuary of the Earth temple as they made their way back to the tower.

* * *

By the time Aurianna stormed back into the tower—Pharis following in a daze—Sigi and the men had already returned with good news: Orion and Juliet had managed to sneak out of Bramosia and were going to stay with family in Menos for a while.

Mara wasted no time before approaching Aurianna. But before she could voice her invitation once again, Aurianna said, "Yes, Mara—Regulus—or whatever I'm supposed to call you. I'll go with you. But only to talk with them. I want more information about what we're up against here, and exactly who's on whose side. I'm not ready to pick one yet, so don't ask me to."

Pharis's sister shrugged. "Fair enough. Get some rest. We'll leave before dawn tomorrow."

Dawn. A name fit for a prophecy.

Realizing her friends likely had many questions, Aurianna gathered them into her room upstairs, away from the eyes and ears of the others. Before they set out on this journey into the unknown, she needed them to be aware of some things that had impacted her decisions, and which might also influence theirs.

Not wanting to burden them with everything, she filled in as many gaps as she dared. She shared the things she had learned from Ethan, Syrena, and Pharis about the Magnus's obsession with her mother, and the ensuing chase and imprisonment. She gave them the full story of how she had been taken away as a baby, and not seen again by anyone from this time until she was brought back by Pharis, fully grown.

None of them had any words of wisdom, only expressions of shock and pity, both for her and for Pharis when they realized how devastating it must have been for his mother to know her husband was so desperate for the attentions of another woman. Pharis himself looked mortified, but Sigi made a point to pat his shoulder and give him an encouraging nod.

The part of Aurianna that longed to protect her friends still suspected they would be safer and happier to be away from her. She wanted to live up to her brand and *run away* to face the inevitable dangers while seeking answers on her own. But they insisted on coming with her, whether she liked it or not, and no amount of arguing would change that. Sigi was already making plans.

After that, the tension broke, and everyone headed off to their respective rooms to rest before their early morning trip.

Much of the day was still left, but the fitful tossing and turning of the previous night had not been restful for Aurianna, so she really needed to try to get some sleep to be prepared for the journey ahead.

Pharis followed her to her—*their*—room, making it clear what was on his mind. He pulled her close, his hands cupping the sides of her face. Those three words she didn't need to hear—didn't *want* to hear—fell from his lips again as he gently pressed them to hers. He was trying to take her mind off the events of the day, and she allowed the temporary distraction.

For a time.

But her mind filled with a fog of angry whispers: *Traitor, murderer.*

They seemed to be falling into a relationship she wasn't sure she was ready for. She knew she cared for Pharis, but those confusing emotions conflicted with her guilt. And the guilt was multiplied by the others witnessing her new relationship. She was sure they must condemn her.

An hour later, as they lay curled together beneath the blankets, Aurianna stared at the door, her mind unable to rest. She knew Pharis, too, was still awake, as his hand traced circles on her shoulder blade. Her head lay on his other outstretched arm which was curled around her but tense.

Pharis's voice cut through the dark silence. "I'm trying to be patient." He sighed. "But I don't know what to do. You've put up a wall between us."

"I haven't." The lie sounded ridiculous even to her.

"Yes, you have. Maybe not intentionally, but you have. And it's really hard not to take it personally when I don't understand what I've done to upset you."

When she didn't reply, he buried his face in her hair, breathing in her scent. "I do love you. Nothing will change that, even the fact that you've never responded in kind. I'll give you time because I know you've been through a bloody nightmare with all this. But you've got to let me in."

"Don't tell me what I have to do, Pharis. I have quite enough on my 'must do' list right now."

"I didn't mean it like that." He leaned over, rolling her back a little so she could meet his eyes. "And you know it." He frowned, then pulled away and rolled to his back.

Pharis covered his eyes with an arm, and moments later was asleep.

The cold began to seep into her body almost immediately. Aurianna lay awake, dwelling on those thoughts which had plagued her incessantly since the night on the rooftop, the night she had killed the man she'd thought she loved.

* * *

"No, darlin', you can't go with us this time." Theron's tone was soothing, but Aurianna could tell leaving his fox behind pained him as much as it did Rhouth.

The two of them were practically inseparable. Hunter and companion. Aurianna wondered—and not for the first time—what it would feel like to have someone you were so vitally dependent upon and trusted so implicitly.

Rhouth continued to whimper, letting out a sharp yipping noise every few seconds as she rubbed her furry backside against her master's trousers.

Theron sighed, placing his thumb and index finger against the bridge of his nose. "Girl, I know. But it's going to get really wet, I'm told, and you don't take kindly to that sort of thing. Stay here for now, okay?" He crouched to pet her and indicated Syrena with a look and a nod. "They'll have food for you, and I promise I'll come back to get you once everything checks out."

Syrena nodded her agreement. She and Ethan, along with Belinda, were staying behind in the tower for now. They weren't happy about it, but everyone felt they needed someone on the outside in case things went badly with the Order of the Daoine.

The resistance team had arrived in an airship, and it was that same craft they took to leave the area. Aurianna had no idea how they had hidden it so well, but she and Pharis hadn't even noticed it when they had come upon the group at the secret door.

Of course, she and Pharis had been a little *busy* at the time as they floated through the Air on his Kinetic powers. The memory made Aurianna shiver, both from excitement and dread. She couldn't deny the man was talented. The rumors about him with a plethora of women were probably not as far from the truth as she would hope.

Hope was a poison, leading a person away from reality and setting them up for disappointment and heartbreak.

Aurianna gazed out across the expanse of Perdita Bay. The sunrise reflected off the water, mixing the translucent blues and greens with the bright richness of orange and red. They were keeping close to the surface of the bay, and Aurianna found herself lazily waving her arm back and forth above the water. She watched as the liquid swirled and eddied in time with the motion of her hand. All her

Kinetic powers seemed to be coming much more naturally to her now. She wasn't sure how she felt about that.

Her Water ability was allowing her to gather the spray caused by the bottom of the airship. Aurianna playfully waggled her fingers, forming long spindly rivers, which she directed at the back of Sigi's head when she wasn't looking.

Eventually, the airship began to slow, causing everyone to lean on the rails and peer around for their destination. They saw nothing but water and cliffs as far as the eye could see.

Aurianna recognized the area, however. Above them was the region of Eadon, the birth home of most Aerokinetics.

The resistance team handed each person a mask connected to a long tube. One of them announced, "These are breathing tubes for going underwater. You won't need it for long, and you'll have to hold your breath for the deeper part. But we'll show you what to do. This way."

The rebels proceeded to jump into the water and beckon to Aurianna and her friends. One by one, they followed, tentatively plopping into the bay. The water was uncomfortably cold but not as chilling as when Pharis had been sent to fetch her from the future, and they had appeared in this time right over the water. She looked over at him and grinned. That seemed such a long time ago. They'd been quite different people.

Then she thought back to the moment when she had watched Sigi plummet from the train to what she had thought would surely be the girl's death, and her smile faded.

At the base of the cliff, Mara halted the group and demonstrated how to put on the mask and use the breathing tube. She pointed to the rock behind her then reached for her brother's hand. Pharis took it and dove with her. After several moments, Aurianna began to panic. She made to follow, but firm hands restrained her.

Her instinct was to fight, but it was impossible. She panicked, losing her focus. She was unable to pull any power from the bay around them.

The large, muscular man from Mara's team who was holding her back removed his mask and explained, "He's fine. We have to take you one at a time or risk losing someone."

"I don't understand where they went! They haven't come back up. He's going to drown!"

"No, he won't. Not if he follows Mara. You just have to get to the other side of the cliff."

"Let me go!" Aurianna was still squirming in his grasp.

The man released her and gave her a bit of space. "My name is Sullivan. If you're that worried, we'll go next. Come with me. I'll show you."

"Your hideout...is underwater?"

"Not exactly. You have to go underwater to get there, but the place itself is in a hollowed-out area on the inside of the cliff. We warned you there'd be swimming involved." When Aurianna glared at the man, he added, "You'll just have to trust me until we get there. You don't think she would risk hurting her own brother, do you?"

"I don't know that woman any more than I know you."

Aurianna had no choice. She followed the man to the cliff face where he again took her arm and pulled her under the waves with him.

Once they swam under the front face of the cliff, the tunnel they followed had just enough clearance for an air pocket so they could use the breathing tubes. They swam through pitch darkness until Aurianna's fingertips could feel rock beneath her. She tried to stand and was thankful that the space above the water had risen several feet.

Aurianna removed the tube from her mouth and continued

to walk up the slope until she could hoist herself onto dry rock, gaping at the new world around her. It looked like a giant spoon had scooped out a great chunk of the rock, leaving a large open area. Every sound echoed in the cavernous expanse. The cave was dimly lit by crude torches on the walls which caused veins of an unknown material in the stone walls to glitter.

Sullivan motioned for her to help herself to a thick blanket. Aurianna did so and tried to work up a grateful smile despite the chills racking her body.

Voices to one side caught her attention. Mara and Pharis stood, similarly swathed in blankets, amidst a small group of people. Their quiet voices reverberated eerily off the walls.

She couldn't shake the anxiety that had seized her heart at the sight of Pharis disappearing beneath the waves of Perdita Bay. Mara was a stranger to her. She might be Pharis's sister, but Aurianna knew practically nothing about her. Plus, the woman was working with a group which, until recently, Aurianna had thought of as the enemy.

She and Sullivan joined the group, and she was greeted by a pair of familiar green eyes which shone in the torch light. Aurianna felt her body grow even colder, despite the warm blanket.

This was the third time she had encountered the man.

The previous time she had been at a pub with her friends. He, of course, had not recognized her, but his presence had startled and unnerved her. Dealing with altered timelines had that effect on a person.

They had met the first time on a day in a dark future where she had lived with Larissa, the woman whom she thought of as both aunt and mother.

On a day when her world had been shattered—replaced with something both exciting and terrifying.

On a day when she had discovered she might have Kinetic powers and be the fulfillment of a prophecy.

On a day when the man standing before her had recognized her and known she might become the cause of the singularity and the destroyer of worlds.

On a day when he had died in her arms, full of hope she would one day fulfill her destiny and be their savior instead.

CHAPTER 7

SIGI

The location of the headquarters for the Order of the Daoine was a bewildering secret that defied comprehension.

But Sigi was more concerned about her friend at the moment. Aurianna had been sitting on the ground inside the grotto wrapped in a blanket and shivering when Sigi and the others had finally surfaced. The place was a wonder, but Sigi had focused on her friend, worried something had happened.

Aurianna had refused to say what was bothering her, but it was clear to Sigi her friend was having some kind of breakdown. Sigi sat beside her and wrapped her own blanket around them both, hugging her and rocking her like she used to do with Hilda.

She thought of her sister, still stuck within the confines of the Imperium. The Magnus may have already decided to imprison the girl in retaliation for Sigi's treason. These were the crucial years in an Acolyte's training, and Hilda was stuck in the middle of a war she couldn't possibly understand.

Recalling memories of her years as an Acolyte, she wished they could be enjoying time together at the Imperium, planning shopping trips and fun activities on their days off. Sigi wished they had the time for a little frivolity now. She knew these thoughts were merely an excuse to avoid dwelling on the inevitability of what lay ahead, but memories of her childhood always made her feel safe.

Sigi had grown up in a large family—all boys except for her sister and herself . . . and her mother, before she had fallen sick and died when Sigi was young. Her mother's death had affected the entire family, but Sigi had been the only girl old enough to remember and feel the weight of her absence. When she had finally succumbed to her illness, Sigi had been nine years old, but Hilda had barely been a toddler.

Without a feminine role model, Sigi had spent the next couple of years trying her hardest to make her father proud. Even before then, she had always tried to be as good as her older brothers in everything. Her father taught her how to make and use armor and weaponry, and Sigi showed a natural talent for heavy weapons at an alarmingly young age.

But here . . . with her friend, she was out of her element.

She caught Pharis watching them, and she tilted her head toward Aurianna. He shrugged and mouthed *I tried* before going back to his conversation with a member of the resistance.

The whole experience was surreal, and Sigi wasn't about to trust any of these Daoine, even the new—old?—Regulus.

She begged Theron with her eyes, and he came over to help get Aurianna to her feet.

Aurianna seemed to come out of her trance. She squared her shoulders and walked over to a man who was, as far as Sigi knew, a stranger to them. Aurianna led him to the far side of the grotto. Though their conversation was clearly very emotional for them both, and their voices reached every corner, their words were too soft to understand.

After a few minutes, the man reached out and hugged Aurianna. Sigi saw the woman's whole body go rigid in the embrace. When the man pulled away, he was smiling. He nodded and walked off to join the rest of the group.

The more recently resurrected Regulus and her crew were ushering everyone into one of the smaller caves extending out from the open grotto area. They intended to give Sigi's group a brief tour on the way to meet the leader of the Order.

Several minutes of walking had Sigi immediately suspicious as to their intentions. No one was speaking, and there didn't seem to be anything but the long passageway before them.

"Where are you taking us?" She directed her question to the Regulus, but it was the man Aurianna had been speaking to who answered.

"Don't worry, friend. These people have been nothing but hospitable and gracious to me and the other Kinetics who came here seeking sanctuary."

Moving closer to the man as they continued walking, Sigi whispered in an effort to keep their conversation as private as possible, despite the echo. "You're a Kinetic? How *did* you get here?"

"The night of the . . . the night on the roof, we were placed on ships to get to safety. You and your friends, in fact, helped us get away."

"Yes, but how did you end up here?"

"Our airship landed in Eadon. We got off and wandered around for a bit, unsure where to go as none of us were familiar with the area. But the people there were . . . less than gracious, shall we say. They do not like our kind. Even the City Guard in Eadon is treated with little respect."

"You haven't answered my question."

"I'm attempting to explain. The Eadonites had basically cornered us down a side street, looking like they would stone us or something. Then the resistance showed up. The people of Eadon apparently listen to them, so they backed off. And we were brought here. They have fed us, clothed us, and provided us with rooms. You are safe here."

"I'm a guardswoman and a Kinetic. I feel the furthest thing from safe around them. If you yourself are a Kinetic, then what makes you think they aren't using you for some reason? They actively seek to destroy us."

The group had reached an area where side passages were finally visible, and the voice of the Regulus cut their conversation short. "Each of these caves to the left holds a separate set of rooms for training with the non-Kinetic weapons we use, including both guns and some non-projectile weapons we'll be happy to show you later."

Sigi perked up at the mention of weapons before the woman's words sank in, causing her hackles to rise. Sigi's family made a living from the creation and sale of weapons. "You never actually explained where you get the components for your guns."

The man they called Sullivan answered. "We make our own weapons here, with our own materials. Don't worry. We're not thieves."

"No, just terrorists."

"I think you'd be surprised at how little terror we actually instill."

"What is that supposed to mean?"

Sullivan kept to a swift pace, and the group struggled to keep up. "It means, *guardswoman*, that the people who you see as helpless victims are neither helpless nor victims, no matter what state your Magnus would like to keep them in."

"Yes, I'm sure they appreciate their homes being bombed." Sigi remembered the day in Bramosia with vivid clarity, and she knew her friends did as well.

Mara glared at her. "We have *never* caused damage to personal property."

"No, just people."

"We took out infrastructure. Bombed the irrigation system. No one was supposed to be near those explosions—"

"And yet they were."

Mara seemed uncomfortable—almost ashamed—but Sullivan responded. "Our spies were scouting that section for months. We knew their patterns."

"Clearly."

Sullivan started to speak again, but Mara cut him off with a sharp glance before replying. "Look, I won't make excuses for what happened, but I promise you it wasn't intentional. Thank the Essence the healers were able to help, and no one was killed."

"Ah, noble terrorists."

Aurianna put a hand on Sigi's shoulder, pulling her to a halt. "Sig, I think maybe—"

Shrugging her friend off, Sigi continued. "No, I'm not going to pretend our people aren't victims of their acts of violence."

Mara bristled with anger. "Our actions are only intended to decrease the people's dependence on your kind."

"Don't you mean *our* kind?" Sigi narrowed her eyes, waiting on a response. *This woman has some nerve, Regulus or no.*

Studying her brother, Mara directed her reply to him. "I...Pharis ...I don't...Can we talk later? In private?"

Before Pharis had a chance to respond, one of the members of Mara's group interrupted. "Fitz is waiting." He indicated a set of doors just ahead. He and the rest of their team departed down another hall, leaving Mara and Sullivan—who was clearly her second in command—to take Aurianna and her friends into the room beyond.

Mara slammed through the doors, leading everyone into a large audience chamber. The lighting was even dimmer than it had been in the passageways, so it took Sigi a moment for her eyes to adjust. A voice in the semidarkness echoed across the room, and she was able to make out a figure before them.

"So, you're the famous Storm Girl."

"Excuse me?" Aurianna responded with indignation.

The owner of the voice, a man, sat atop a fancy chair in the middle of the room. He threw his hands up in surrender. "Woman. Sorry."

Aurianna shook her head in confusion. "That's not what I—"

"I heard it was Fire," Sullivan piped up from behind.

"I think you're missing the point, Sullivan."

Sullivan merely shrugged, so the man continued.

"Some of our . . . newer members were there that night. They escaped on ships from the roof of the Imperium but were still close enough when the chaos started. They said that storm wasn't natural by any stretch of the imagination. It came out of nowhere. Our scouts said the sky grew dark as pitch, and it wasn't late."

Sigi threw a meaningful glance in Aurianna's direction, but her friend was finding her feet infinitely more interesting. *How can she keep pretending it didn't happen? I know what I saw. The lightning . . . when she kissed Pharis . . .*

Finally, Aurianna looked up and stared the leader of the resistance in the eye. "Storms do that."

Sullivan's voice rang out again, this time sounding more frustrated. "All the damage around the regions would suggest Fire. Don't lose focus, Fitz."

Sigi found it odd this "Fitz" was seemingly a leader who was not threatened by subordinates speaking to him in such a manner. But she saw that he and Aurianna were not actually paying any attention. Their gazes were locked in challenge.

"And who are you?" Aurianna asked boldly.

"Fitzgerald Kennedy, though you should probably just stick to Fitz. We like to keep things simple. No Magnus around here to complicate things." With this last statement, Fitz glanced between Pharis and Mara.

Perhaps Mara is not as well-respected as she would have us believe.

"And yet you share his love of throne-like furniture."

"No, our hierarchies work differently. I think you'll find quite a lot of things are different here. But don't take my word for it. Stay awhile. Make yourselves comfortable. Ask around. You'll see what I mean."

"Why have you brought us here?"

"I couldn't care less about your friends. But you, Storm Girl...we could sure use your influence to gain more traction in the regions."

"I thought the people just *love* you."

Fitz sneered at her—an expression that only accentuated his already menacing demeanor. "The people, for the most part, accept and even encourage our endeavors. But many of them are still too scared of the Imperium and the Kinetics. However, they look up to those who stand up for themselves. They respect you for being at odds with the Magnus, believe it or not. You could help us convince more to join our cause. Or, at the very least, to support us."

"And how am I supposed to do that?"

"Just by showing that lovely face of yours to the masses. Tell them you support us, and convince them to do the same."

"First of all, why would they listen to me? I'm one of the Kinetics, the 'enemy' from your perspective. And second of all, who says I do?"

"Who says you do what?"

"Support you."

Fitz smiled, but the emotion didn't reach his eyes. "I think perhaps you haven't been paying attention. They know what you did."

"They think I'm going around setting the place on fire."

"No, don't listen to Sullivan here. The Magnus might be thinking that. But not the people. They know that ain't you. And they know you saved their asses that night. At least the ones closest to the Imperium do. The people of Bramosia, Kinetic and non-Kinetic alike, are grateful they aren't currently a pile of ash in the street. The people—right or wrong—trust you."

"Trust me? Why?"

"Because you are something . . . other. You might be Kinetic, but you're something else too. How else can you explain what happened, Storm Girl?"

"Which would make me even less like them. People don't trust things they don't understand."

"Give them some credit. I think they understand more than you think."

"How can they? *I* don't even understand it. None of it! And while I might agree with a few of your ideas, I don't agree with how you've tried to implement them."

Sigi piped up. "She didn't come here to help you. She came here to ask for your help."

"My help? With what?"

"We need to find out what's causing the damage in the regions," Sigi continued. "And we need to come up with a solution back at the Imperium."

"Solution to what? The City Guard is none of our concern here."

"Yet you claim we have a common goal."

"We want the people of this land to be free from the rule of a madman. I believe your friend here agrees." He gestured to Aurianna. "Whether or not you agree is none of my concern. She is vouching for you, so for now I am tolerating the presence of a City Guard member. But do not think I would hesitate to take action were your loyalties to come into question."

"My *loyalties* are to the people first and foremost, and to my friends. Aurianna has my support. Whether or not you do remains to be seen."

"Why don't you and your friends allow us to show our hospitality? Stick around long enough to see for yourself what we do around here. Check out our training, get some rest, ask questions. Whatever you like. We don't have any secrets."

Sigi felt her nostrils flare at his words, but Aurianna spoke before she could. "Everyone has secrets."

"I knew I'd like you, Storm Girl." Fitz snapped his fingers. "Take our friends here to the rooms we prepared. Let them settle in, and make sure they're fed well. Tomorrow morning, show them around the training grounds. Let them see what we're about here."

Aurianna asked, "What about the people from the roof who ended up here?"

"Yes? What about them?"

"Will I be able to speak with them?"

"Of course. You can speak with whomever you like. Go wherever you like."

"What about Javen?" At Aurianna's question, Sigi froze. She felt the others do the same.

Fitz sat forward and squinted at her quizzically. "I'm afraid I'm at a loss."

"Javen Ambrogetti. He was one of yours, right?"

"One of mine?" He shook his head, pursing his lips. "No. Sorry, I'm not following."

"Look, if he went rogue, I just need to know."

"Could you perhaps give me some context here, Storm Girl?"

Aurianna visibly bristled. "The man on the rooftop. The one who created that whole disaster the other night."

Fitz raised his eyebrows. "And you think we were behind it? What would we have to gain?"

"Because you hate Kinetics and want to incite a rebellion."

"We don't hate Kinetics. We just don't like their policies and want to live independently." He leaned his elbows on his knees. "But we don't hate your kind. Not at all. Certainly not enough to cause that level of destruction." He gestured to Mara and Sullivan. "My friends here will escort you to your rooms."

Sullivan and Mara led the group back along the same tunnel and down a separate passageway. Mara kept glancing at her brother, trying to catch his eye, but Pharis was either ignoring her intentionally or was so focused on Aurianna he didn't notice.

When they arrived at a set of rooms, Sullivan politely excused himself after giving them directions to the dining area. Mara stuck around for a moment, but Pharis followed Aurianna into one of the rooms, despite there being enough for everyone to have their own.

Sigi tentatively chose one of the rooms on one end and shut the door behind her.

She washed her face and sat on the bed to think. What were they even doing here? Aurianna wanted answers, so Sigi would be there for her friend. But she didn't trust these people, and she didn't think Aurianna did either. Pharis was a complete question mark, and the others had been utterly silent throughout the earlier exchange. Theron was always observing, so Sigi hoped he had some helpful insight.

Leon and Laelia were never this quiet, so their silence completely unnerved Sigi.

A short staccato knock at the door interrupted her thoughts. She got up to answer the door, opening it just enough to peek out.

Theron was standing there, looking sheepish.

"What's wrong?" Sigi asked, worried something had already happened.

"There's...um...well, I just thought I'd come talk to you, seeing as how it's getting a bit...noisy at the other end of the hall."

Sigi stood, her mouth agape as his meaning dawned on her. "Seriously? We just got here!"

Theron shrugged. "Can I come in?"

Sigi ushered him into her room, blushing. "Which one?"

"Huh?"

"Which...couple?"

"Oh." Wincing, he asked, "Does it matter?"

"Yeah, I guess not. Have a seat." She gestured to the only seat in the room besides the bed.

Theron sat, his back rigid as he clasped and unclasped his hands, fidgeting nervously.

"What's wrong?" she asked again.

"Nothing."

"Then why do you seem nervous? You're never this jittery."

"Am I?" He was glancing around, as if he expected someone to jump out from behind a curtain at any moment.

"Theron." She tried to catch his eye.

Sighing, he tore his hands apart to lean his weight on his knees. "Sigi, I'm just thinking about the future."

"Future? Like, where Aurianna is from?"

He peered at her, a puzzled expression on his face. "No, I mean our future."

"Our future?"

"Well, not *our* future. No. Actually, yes, our future." Theron shook his head, exuding agitation from every inch of his stiffened frame. "I mean . . . But yeah. Our future."

Sigi just stared at him in confusion. "Are you drunk?"

"You know . . ." He shook a finger at her. "That is an excellent idea."

"What?"

"Let's go find a drink. Please."

"O . . . kay." Sigi didn't know how else to respond, so she got up and led the way out of the room, Theron following close behind.

CHAPTER 8

AURIANNA

Aurianna knew the dark shadow in her vision wasn't real, yet she couldn't pull herself out of the nightmare.

This was like her recurring dream, only now it was dominated by rings of flame and destruction she was powerless to control. She watched helplessly as those she loved perished.

Out of the inferno waltzed Javen.

He sauntered over to her as she stood amid the conflagration, surrounded by chaos and destruction, a smirk teasing the corner of his mouth. Without a moment of hesitation, without a word of warning, Aurianna lifted the gun that suddenly appeared in her hand and aimed it at his heart.

Tears streamed down her face, and the air crackled with lightning. But the lightning was coming from her, Energy radiated from her skin to float out in waves.

She pulled the trigger, the sound a more percussive rumble than the sharp, explosive sound she expected.

Aurianna awakened—her skin covered in a cold sheen of

sweat—to an insistent pounding which filtered through the dark recesses of her mind.

Pharis lay beside her, snoring softly into his pillow and completely oblivious to the noise outside the room he had decided to share with her.

When she cracked open the door Aurianna was treated to the sight of Laelia caught up in Leon's arms, her legs wrapped around the man's muscular torso. She had never seen Laelia smile as much as she had these last few days.

How nice it must be to have no worries or cares, no one expecting you to save the world one last time.

What a relief to not have the guilt of someone you love dying by your hand.

The thought made Aurianna groan inwardly. The feeling of resentment and jealousy was unfair, but there it was. Swallowing down the choking sob which threatened to overtake her senses, Aurianna cleared her throat and raised her eyebrows in question.

Leon saw her and detached the girl clinging to him, unceremoniously dropping her to her feet. Laelia glowered up at him with confusion and fury.

Aurianna saw this, but Leon had turned away by then, oblivious to or unconcerned about Laelia's wrath. He leaned his forearm against the top of the door frame. "Hey. Wanna join us downstairs?"

Aurianna's horrified disgust must have shown on her face because he immediately leaned back and added, "Don't be daft. For a drink. Sigi and Theron have apparently found somewhere to get a decent brew, and they came up and told us to join them. Must be good, because they were already a bit tipsy when they showed up at our door. I'm pretty sure Theron giggled."

"Theron . . . giggled?" Aurianna narrowed her eyes in disbelief.

Leon shrugged as he crossed his arms. "They told us to come ask you, then they ran back down. So, do you wanna?"

"Sure thing, friend." Groggy with sleep, the voice which answered came from behind her. When she wheeled around to look at him, Pharis had lifted his head a couple of inches off the pillow, his eyes still mostly closed.

"I'm not your friend." Leon's voice was tinged with irritation and something else. Aurianna plastered a fake smile on her face before facing the two at the door. Laelia was still fuming, but she was trying to tug Leon down the hallway. With his bulk, it was an exercise in futility. A frown replaced his earlier pleasant expression, and Aurianna wondered how long they had till this group imploded.

If she took off, it would solve some of those problems, at least the ones they had with her. But it wouldn't fix the awkwardness and bitter feelings between Leon and Pharis.

But Leon's reaction was completely understandable. Javen had been his best friend—even though he turned out to be an evil monster mysteriously bent on civil unrest, at best, and societal destruction, at worst. She supposed she still should not have allowed Pharis into her bed.

Or into her heart. But no one had to know that part of the story. It would stay hidden, tucked away for now. She had given her heart first to Leon's best friend, and he would probably never forgive her disloyalty.

No matter what Javen had done, Leon couldn't be expected to like having his best friend's memory smeared by her inability to walk away from Pharis's attentions.

But this thing between them wasn't a whim or passing fancy. What had passed between her and Pharis in recent months was powerful but private. Leon and the others weren't aware of most of it and couldn't possibly understand everything they had been through together.

But that didn't excuse her actions. She was impetuous and hotheaded.

Aurianna had killed a man whom she'd thought she loved, and she'd saved the man she realized she couldn't live without.

Maybe she had been wrong. Maybe arresting Javen had been possible. If only she had stopped to consider . . . But it had all happened so quickly, and she had felt so blindsided and betrayed by the stranger in the form of her lover.

Jumping straight into Pharis's arms had felt so right in the moment.

But now all she could think about were the brown eyes currently boring a hole in her heart as Leon stared at her with so much emotion on his face. He probably hated her. He had every right to.

An unbidden thought flashed through her mind, and she tried to push it back.

What if I hadn't inadvertently brought Pharis back to life? What if it were his *body left on that rooftop instead of Javen?*

Keeping the fake smile on her face, she said, "Sure. We'll be down in a minute." Aurianna closed the door and let the tears fall silently in the darkness.

* * *

Aurianna snatched the paper from Sigi's hands to read it again. The words were nice, but the sentiment was downright beautiful.

It was a poem. Short, but intense.

My heart is an aching chasm echoing the words I long to say.

Essence help him. The poor man.

Time is a cruel enemy, and I yearn to see you every day.

The note wasn't signed, but Aurianna knew it was from Theron. She shook her head for what felt like the hundredth time. What should she do? Sigi was her friend, but so was Theron. He had finally managed to express himself in this romantic gesture, despite his stoic nature. But things were never going to get anywhere if he didn't just come right out and tell Sigi he loved her.

That he was, in fact, desperately, unequivocally, head-over-heels in love with her.

Sighing, Aurianna flopped back on the bed. Somehow, she had ended up in Sigi's room after their night—day? afternoon? evening?—of drinking in the common area downstairs. The rebels certainly loved their liquor.

Leon had made himself right at home, but the others—herself included—had felt more than a little hesitant. They had no idea who these people were or what they were up to. But as is the case with these things, more drinking had led to less hesitation, and so the cycle had gone until everyone had forgotten why they had been so hesitant.

With no idea how they'd gotten there, or where the others were, Aurianna and Sigi had woken up to surprisingly mild headaches and a poem on the table by Sigi's head.

"What should I do?" Sigi furrowed her brow, leaning back against the pillow. "I mean, why would someone do this? Is it a joke? It has to be a joke."

Struggling with her loyalties, Aurianna chewed on her lip and shrugged. "Whoever wrote it needs to own up." Theron's choices—or lack thereof—were none of her business, but the whole affair was becoming ridiculous.

The gesture was sweet, and a part of Aurianna felt another stab of jealousy. It was immediately followed by a sudden anger at people who squandered their time instead of appreciating the fact that no one was expecting them to save the world or be a hero. No one would feel betrayed or angry if they got together.

"But . . ." Sigi's voice trailed off. Then she burst out, "It's ridiculous! None of these people even know me. This is someone's idea of a joke. Maybe Pharis left it here for *you*." She waggled her eyebrows suggestively.

"'I could lose myself in your *steel-blue eyes*'?"

"Okay, yeah, maybe not." Pouting, Sigi pounded her fist into the mattress. "So unfair."

"Excuse me?"

"You know what I mean. I'm just really curious now."

Theron should have just told Sigi how he felt, and he should have done it a long damn time ago.

Standing up and stretching, Aurianna yawned and said, "I think we should stay for a few days at least and see how this goes."

"I'll do whatever you think, but please be careful. I still don't trust these people."

"I'm going to head back to my room if that's okay."

"You mean head back to Pharis?" Sigi's waggled her eyebrows again.

Her smile was teasing, but Aurianna only felt irritation at her friend for making light of the fact she was suddenly with him. As if it were no big deal. As if Sigi and the others weren't feeling betrayed or angry with her. Javen had been their friend for a long time. And that sort of friendship wasn't something easily cast aside, no matter what he had done.

"Why don't you mind your own damn business?" Aurianna yelled before stomping out the door.

* * *

"So, do you just jab or slice, or what with this?" Aurianna turned the sword over in her hand.

"Either. Like this." Sullivan demonstrated a stabbing motion.

The edges were sharp, and she could imagine the damage it could inflict with the slightest bit of pressure.

When they had arrived at the training grounds, several of the rebels were there to run them through the basics of their weapons and training.

They claimed they made their own weapons from a material which could only be found in Eadon. They called it iron. Sigi had been livid no one had shared this information with the Imperium, but it was clear the Eadonites were not the biggest fans of the Kinetic community.

Sigi should have been livid with *her*, after the way Aurianna had shouted at her friend and stormed out of the room. But she'd only sent Aurianna a soft puzzled look from where she was being instructed on the other side of the training area.

Addressing the man holding the weapon, Aurianna asked, "And this is better than a gun how?"

"For starters, it isn't made of bronze. The iron is stronger but lighter. And it doesn't need to draw power from Kinetic power. So anyone can use it."

Desperate for information, Aurianna still hesitated before asking, "So, how are the people in Eadon doing... after the dragon-blood incident?"

Sullivan stopped his jabbing motions to eye her. "How do you think they're doing? Things were already tense, but that just solidified the issue. They blame Kinetics. It was a Kinetic who lived in that tower and who poisoned the water with the dragonblood." Hearing the words made Aurianna wince, but she refused to tell these people the truth.

Besides, what was the truth? Didn't she herself still believe her mother was in some way responsible—intentionally or not—for the train explosion, not to mention the dragonblood in the water supply? Syrena's dragon was just an image she could project, not a real dragon, but she still possessed the only known connection to one, as far as Aurianna knew.

"They truly hate us, then? But why? I mean, I get why they're mad about the dragonblood, but they hated us long before that, apparently." Aurianna held out her sword and swiped clumsily at Sullivan.

He jumped back, laughing at her awkward efforts. "Caelum is their representative deity within the Essence." He set down his weapon and stood at her back, clasping her sword arm and holding it straight out from her body. "His absence is felt keenly in Eadon."

Aurianna bristled slightly at his nearness and shuffled forward a few inches to widen the space between them. "But I thought no one really worshiped the Essence anymore."

Sullivan pushed her elbow down to bend it slightly. "Funny how the absence of a thing can move your faith in many directions."

"What does that mean?"

He retrieved his weapon and resumed his position in front of her, taking up a similar stance, bending his arm at the elbow and holding his sword up to cross hers. The sound of metal on metal was grating to her ears. "It means they want what they can't have. And they blame the Kinetics for his disappearance."

"I . . . that makes no sense. I thought he's been silent for as long as anyone can remember."

"Yes, but people need someone to blame. And sometimes those who stand to lose the most are least capable of judging right and wrong."

"Do you think any of them are capable of going outside the directives of the Order?"

"Like vigilantes? We do have quite a few Eadonites among

us—Fitz and myself, for instance—but our people are not who I worry about. We train them to focus on what's important."

"So, who do you worry about?"

"The ones who haven't joined us. Those in Eadon who are silently biding their time, waiting to exact revenge on either the Imperium or Rasenforst for what was done to them and their families."

"How do you know that?"

"Because I know people. It's kind of my job to study and observe human behavior."

"Then why don't your people go and talk to them? Try to stop it before something bad happens."

"We were, to a degree. But we can't leave the grotto right now, not since the curfew. We're grounded until further notice. The regions are locked down tight."

"We've gotten in and out a few times."

"There's a difference between sneaking in to take a look and going around to speak to people. Crowds always form no matter what we do, and they tend to attract the notice of the guards."

Aurianna failed to move in time. The edge of Sullivan's sword dragged across the side of her arm, opening a small gash. She stared at it in mute shock for a moment before glaring up at Sullivan.

Pharis must have noticed what had happened and hurried over to them. He glared threateningly at the other man.

Trying to calm the situation, she forced herself to smile through the pain. "Just a scratch. I should probably have it treated, though." She allowed Pharis to lead her over to the healers on duty in a corner of the large expanse.

They passed by Theron, who seemed to be getting the hang of the small crossbow he'd been messing around with all morning. It was strange to see him without Rhouth, and Aurianna thought he was probably missing his furry companion terribly.

The healers went to work immediately, cleaning and then attempting to bandage her wound. But the cut was stubborn, refusing to stop bleeding after numerous attempts to staunch it. As she sat in a chair, holding a large towel to her arm, Sigi staggered up with Theron draped across her shoulder.

"What the hell happened to you?" Aurianna noticed he was holding his other arm rigidly at his side, pain etched into his features.

Sigi answered for him. "The idiot dislocated his shoulder with that stupid crossbow."

Sweat was beading on Theron's forehead. "Shoulder got in the way." He sat with Sigi's help, grunting with the effort. The arm was hanging limply at his side, his body arched in an awkward position.

Two healers, one female and one male, came over to inspect the hunter's injury. When they began to poke and prod him, Theron let out several uncharacteristic curses.

Sigi gaped at him, startled by his outburst, but Aurianna found herself trying to smother her laughter. One glance at Pharis told her he was having a similar reaction.

The female healer suddenly gripped the injured man's arm and placed her free hand atop his shoulder while the male healer held his body back against the chair. Before he had a chance to react, Theron's arm was yanked down forcefully, causing a stream of expletives to flow from his mouth.

Despite feeling sympathy for the poor man's plight, Aurianna couldn't hold in her laughter anymore. She giggled hysterically, Pharis joining in a second later. Sigi seemed confused at first, but after a moment, she was laughing as well.

Theron's face was red, and not just from the pain. He was livid with anger. "What the bloody hell is so funny?"

Wiping tears from her eyes, Aurianna gasped, "Sorry, Theron!

I really am. But you never talk like that. I don't know why, but it was funny."

"Talk like what?" He grit his teeth as he spoke.

Sigi looked sheepish. "Yeah, sorry. Were you even aware of the words coming out of your mouth? I don't think even Leon at his most inebriated curses like that."

"I'm glad everyone can have a good laugh at my expense."

Pharis leaned in as if to clap Theron on the back but thought better of it just in time. "Sorry, mate. I guess we all just needed to let loose."

Aurianna started to speak again, but a wave of dizziness washed over her. She felt herself falling forward out of the chair, the ground rising up to meet her.

In the distance, a man's voice rose above the others, and a familiar pair of sapphire eyes danced across her blurry vision.

PART TWO

BRIARS AND THORNS

In the end, briars may sting, and thorns may bite;
The spell was cast, but death did not take me.

Chapter 9

AURIANNA

Aurianna cracked her eyelids. The room looked familiar, but it took her a moment to place where she was. They had only been with the resistance for a couple of days, and this was the room she had been sharing with Pharis.

A curious grating sound off to her left caused Aurianna to turn her head. She instantly regretted the motion, as it brought on a fresh wave of dizziness and nausea.

Pharis reclined in a chair, his head lolled back, and snores erupted from his sleeping form.

She sat up slowly, trying to combat the effects of the nausea. She felt a sharp pain in her arm. Investigation revealed dark lines zigzagging down a long, thin cut on her upper arm.

As she gingerly touched the wound, a stab of pain shot down to her fingertips, causing Aurianna to cry out involuntarily. The sound awoke the man beside her, who sat forward and grabbed her hand, pulling it away from the injury.

"Don't touch it."

"What happened?"

"You passed out. They think it was the blood loss. You were still bleeding, so they had to stitch it up to try to stop it."

"It hurts worse now."

It was painful, but she couldn't help comparing it to the pain she had felt the night the Consils had branded the word *effugere* on her shoulder, which meant "runaway" in the old language. In her village in the future, they had thought to teach her a lesson for trying to leave town, an act which was forbidden.

"Yeah, it's going to do that for a while." He smiled gently. "Can I get you anything?"

"I want to go back."

"Back?"

"To the Imperium. To check on everyone. We've been here for a couple of days, and we have no idea what's going on back at the tower. Your father could have already stormed his way into the place. My...my parents..."

"All right. We can do that. I've been able to spend some time with Mara. She showed me around the place, but really all she wants to discuss is Fitz and the Order. And to offer justification for her decisions and choices. I don't know if I can trust her, but I can't just leave and pretend I never saw her. She and I were so close, but now...now I don't know what to think."

"Yes, you should certainly stay. You don't have to come with me. I just need to check on everything."

"Of course I'm coming with you! Why wouldn't I come with you?"

"But you said—"

"I just meant I want to come back afterwards. I'm not letting you out of my sight. Apparently, even a few moments can lead to things like this." Pharis gestured to the wound on her arm.

Aurianna jerked her hand away. "I don't need protecting, Pharis."

"Of course not." His expression of hurt was unmistakable, but he didn't say anything else.

"I think Leon, Sigi, and I should return. We'll be back within a day or so, at most."

"I don't think so." Fitz was standing in the doorway, two men by his side.

"Excuse me?" Aurianna felt her blood begin to boil at the man's tone.

"None of you can leave right now."

Pharis stood up and made his way around the bed. "And why not? Who are you to stop us?"

Fitz's mouth curved up in an arrogant smirk. "Me? Oh, I'm just the leader around here. No one comes or goes without my say-so. You know our secret location now. What's to stop you from revealing it to our enemies?"

Aurianna winced. The nausea wasn't gone, and the pain in her arm was almost unbearable. Why did it hurt so badly? It was just a little cut. But she pushed herself out of bed. "I have no intention of telling anyone anything. I just want to check on our friends."

"And how do I know that?"

"Because I'm telling you."

"I'm supposed to trust the word of someone who keeps secrets from her friends?"

Aurianna stopped in her tracks. What was he saying? What did he know?

They were interrupted by shouting from the hallway beyond Fitz and his men. Leon's voice boomed with rage. "What is going on here? Get out of our room!"

Fitz glanced behind him, then back at Aurianna, his expression hard. "You don't leave this place until I say you do. Until I feel you can be trusted with our secrets."

"You can't keep us here!" Pharis shouted.

"I can, and I will. My people will be watching the exit." Fitz and his men left the room and shut the door.

A moment later, Leon and the others stormed in wearing matching expressions of bewilderment and outrage.

Laelia leaned against the wall, crossing her arms. "So, what are we going to do?"

Aurianna sighed. "They said they'll be watching the exit. What can we do?"

Laelia's face was almost puce with anger. "They can't keep us here. We were invited as guests."

Back in the chair he had just vacated, Pharis leaned forward, his elbows on his knees, head hanging in defeat. "I can't believe Mara would let them do this."

"Your sister is one of them. Don't you get it?" Laelia pushed herself from the wall to stand by Leon. "She's not going to help us."

"Then we find a way to sneak out."

"How, if the exits are being watched?"

They stared at one another mutely. Aurianna racked her brain for an idea. There was no way to get back to Perdita Bay, apart from those underground pools at the entrance. Unless...

"The cliffs." The words left her mouth before she could contemplate the sheer insanity of the idea.

The idea was stupid, absolutely crazy.

"What?" Sigi's tone was cautious.

"The cliffs," Aurianna repeated. When everyone continued to gape at her in confusion, she explained. "We can use Aerokinetic and Geokinetic power to make our way to the top."

Sigi shook her head. "Aurianna, that's not the problematic part. We can't even get to the cliffs if we can't get past the guards. They'll be watching the exit from the grotto to the bay."

"Who said anything about the grotto?"

Leon raised his eyebrows. "Darlin', you're not making any sense."

"The ocean side of the cave system won't be watched." Aurianna nodded at Pharis. "You said Mara showed you around the caves, right? You can guide us, at least well enough to make it out of here. No one will be in the rear tunnels or think to stop us."

When everyone turned to stare at him, Pharis shrugged as he searched for a response. "I-I guess so."

Aurianna watched as each of her friends, in turn, realized what she was suggesting.

"They won't." Sigi spoke slowly, as if to a child—or an idiot. "Because it's not a way out. We can't get through a solid wall of dirt and rock. Not that thick. On the other side is—"

"The Mare Dolor. The Sea of Sorrow. Yeah, I know. But we'd only be reaching it and then traveling straight up to the land above us."

"That is crazy."

"Yep. Do you have a better idea?"

The room was silent as everyone stared around, each of them probably thinking the same thing.

Did they have any other choice?

* * *

Simon's words echoed in Aurianna's mind: *Follow the path that draws you.* The repeated mantra had been a dark shadow in her thoughts ever since the night of the train explosion. Yet, despite her hatred of hearing them spoken aloud, she constantly found herself mentally chanting them when she felt sure of an action she was taking.

This was not one of those times.

Pharis was leading the way down tunnels Mara had shown him. As they tried to reach the back area of the encampment, Sigi kept casting pointed glances at Aurianna out of the corner of her eye as the group trudged along. The plus side to choosing these passages was the scarcity of Fitz's followers. The downside was when they did come across someone, they were hard pressed to explain why they were there.

Desperation had clouded Aurianna's judgment when the idea had come to her. But now she felt positive—the plan was going to fail. Her powers were growing at an alarming rate, but it wouldn't be enough. Besides, she was still struggling to shake off the effects of the wound on her arm.

The first couple of resistance members seemed to shrug off their explanations, and the third just waved politely as he walked past. But a few minutes later, a trio stopped the group in their tracks.

"Where do you think you're going?"

"I thought we were allowed to go wherever we wished." Aurianna assumed a defiant stance. "As long as we steer clear of the exit."

"There's nothing back here. You should return to your rooms."

"We have every right to be here. Fitz said—"

"Well, Fitz changed his mind." The gruff voice behind them caused everyone to whirl around. Aurianna glared at Fitz who stood with arms crossed and a smug grin on his face. "I'm not buying the 'we're just out for a midnight stroll' routine. I think we all know perfectly well what you're trying to do." He leaned forward, breathing into Aurianna's face. "And I don't rightly appreciate your lack of gratitude."

"Gratitude?" Pharis spat, his nostrils flaring. "For what? Keeping us prisoner?"

"Naw, that comes next. I tried being nice, but you've left me no choice."

Before she could respond, Aurianna felt someone enclose her wrists in manacles of cold iron.

* * *

Pharis gripped the bars and pressed his face close, yelling, "Hey! You can't do this! Let us out! I demand you let me speak to your leader. Take me to Fitz right this instant." His manacles clanged against the metal of the cell door.

Aurianna observed the scene with a vague sense of dizziness which was increasingly overwhelming her senses.

Laelia huffed, blowing a chunk of her bangs out of her face. "Chill, man. They aren't coming."

"Who the bloody hell are you speaking to? I *know* you aren't—"

"Seriously, Pharis," Laelia interrupted his tirade with a roll of her eyes. "Cut it out and help us find a way out of here."

"I'm the Regulus. Surely, he'll parlay, one leader to another—"

"Ex-Regulus. And nobody cares who you are. Least of all them."

Leon was repeatedly banging the back of his head against the cell wall with a nauseating thunk. "I sure do miss my hat."

Everyone turned to stare at him.

Aurianna squinted. She could see her friends, each in a corner of their shared, cramped space, but her blurred vision was making it difficult to focus on who was speaking. And to her befuddled ears they were just buzzing sounds with little resemblance to human voices.

"Something's wrong." Her own voice was a raspy whisper too soft to echo against the walls surrounding them. What kind of place was this?

"No shit, princess." Leon stopped his head banging just long enough to utter the words before resuming his monotonous action.

Aurianna tried to shake her head, to alert the others to her intended meaning, but the movement nearly crippled her. Crying out, she felt herself tipping sideways. Her cheek hit the floor as a numbness took over her senses and the fog within her mind tumbled her over the edge into unconsciousness.

Chapter 10

SIGI

Sigi watched in mute horror as Pharis tried to catch Aurianna before she hit the floor. He wasn't fast enough, however.

Her friend's cry had echoed in the stone cell they had been thrown into by the resistance as she toppled over onto her side with a thump. At least Aurianna had been sitting on the floor at the time. Was she still weak from her wound? The healers had said they were having issues stopping the bleeding, but the stitches should have closed the cut.

Just how badly had she been injured?

Sigi stooped to help Pharis roll Aurianna to her back as carefully as he could with shackled hands. Her eyes were closed, but she was clearly breathing.

"What happened?" Leon had scurried over on all fours, worry etched into his features.

"I . . . I don't know," Pharis answered. "She just fell over."

"And passed out, it seems." Laelia had joined the circle around their friend's unconscious form. "How deep was this cut of hers?"

Pharis shook his head. "It didn't seem that bad, but it wouldn't stop bleeding." He lifted her arm to inspect it. "It's not bleeding, but it looks like it's trying to. The skin around the edges is extremely red and swollen."

"She's got an infection then." Theron was squatting at the far edge of their circle, cradling his still-sore shoulder.

"No." Sigi stood up slowly, the softness of her voice belying the underlying wrath. "They poisoned her. That blade must have been poisoned."

"That's horrible." Leon sat back in stunned silence.

Sigi got up and started pacing. "I knew it. I said we shouldn't trust them. I knew they were up to something—"

"You were playing with their toys same as the rest of us." Laelia narrowed her eyes. "I saw three swords when we passed by your room earlier."

"That's not the point, Laelia! These people are our enemies. They *hate* our kind, remember?"

"But why would they poison her if they said they needed her?" Pharis whispered, his face ashen in the dim light. "They were going to use her powers for themselves. What good would it do them to harm her?"

"Speaking of powers—"

"Won't do you any good, I'm afraid," someone said from the darkness.

"Who's there?" Sigi ran over to the bars, seething with anger. "Let us out of here immediately! She's hurt, and she needs a healer right away."

A figure approached the cell. Mara. "No one poisoned her."

Sigi struck out with her hand in an attempt to grab the other woman, but she was too far away. Behind her, scraping sounds indicated the others were getting to their feet.

Pharis approached the bars, his eyes accusing. "You! How could you do this to us? To me!"

Mara shook her head. "I didn't, brother. I swear it. I had nothing to do with this. But she wasn't poisoned. At least, not by us. Fitz does want her to help us. Whatever is happening to her isn't our doing, not intentionally at least. And you won't be able to use your powers right now. Those manacles," Mara said as she pointed to their wrists, "are made entirely of iron."

"So?"

"Iron negates Kinetic powers."

The silence in the room lasted for several seconds before Sigi blurted, "What?"

"Which is one of the reasons they use it. With those on, you won't be able to summon so much as a pebble."

"Why did no one tell us this?"

"Why would they? It was leverage against you in case we discovered you couldn't be trusted."

"Is that what's wrong with her, why her wound isn't healing?"

Mara shook her head. "No. It doesn't work that way. The metal works by touch and by proximity, but it's not harmful. All it does it stop you from manipulating the elements."

"But look at her! She's—"

"And I've been cut loads of times. It's never affected me more than a normal injury."

"If you're Kinetic, why would they trust you? Don't they hate you too?"

"Fitz . . . It's complicated. I had to prove my loyalty, yes."

"By bombing towns?" Sigi's lips curled in a sneer.

Mara, clearly uncomfortable, couldn't meet any of their eyes. "I've never been okay with any of that, honestly. I never volunteer for those missions."

"Oh, so that makes it okay then—"

"I'm not asking for your forgiveness, lady! I'm here to help you, believe it or not."

Laelia pressed herself against the bars on the other side of Sigi. "How can you help us?"

"Yes, Mara. Do tell us how you plan on helping them?" Fitz and two of his goons—Sigi refused to think of them as anything else at this point—had slipped into the room so quietly none of them had noticed.

Mara's face had already gone white as she whirled around to face him. "Fitz, I—"

"Save it, girl. We all know why you're down here. You disappoint me. Just when I was beginning to think you'd make a good lieutenant."

Mara said, "If you thought so highly of me, why did you have me followed? Because let's not pretend you didn't."

"Aye, I did. What else can I do when I can't figure out who I can and cannot trust. And clearly, I can't trust you, my dear." He nodded to the man on his left. "Sullivan, arrest her."

Sigi recognized him as the one who had injured Aurianna. Accident or no, the man had wounded her friend, and her blood began to boil.

The man walked forward, shame suffusing his features as he placed a pair of the iron shackles on Mara's wrists. He made a show of making sure they were tight, but Sigi caught a brief wink aimed at Mara. Then Sullivan addressed his boss.

"What would you have us do?"

"Filena here can take her down the hall to the other cell. I want you back on patrol."

"Yes, sir." Sullivan nodded and left the room, Fitz following behind before any of them could get in a word. Filena escorted

Mara—none too gently—from the chamber. A few moments later, Sigi heard the unmistakable sound of another cell door latching down the hall. Then Filena went marching past, her job done.

The group slowly returned to their previous positions within the cell. Pharis sat slumped on the ground with Aurianna's head in his lap, looking utterly defeated.

Sigi had barely settled into her own corner when a booming clang of metal on stone resounded down the passageway, seemingly from the direction of Mara's cell.

What the hell did they do to her?

Less than a minute later, the unmistakable dark hair of the current Regulus came bouncing into the room.

Pharis nearly dropped Aurianna's head on the ground in his scramble forward, not bothering to get up from his knees. "What's going on?" he bellowed at his sister.

She held up an object, grinning as she waved it. "Oh, you know, just a key."

"Is that...?"

"The key to your manacles? Sure is."

"But how?"

"Sullivan slipped it to me when he put mine on. He and I ... I knew he was just as angry as I was over all of this."

"He's the one who stabbed my friend!" Sigi felt the words slip out as she fought to contain her ire.

"And he feels bad about that. But he didn't stab her. It was just a slice across her arm. It wasn't even deep. I have no idea what's wrong with her, but you've got to get her to a healer." Scrunching up her face, she added, "Not here, obviously."

"What was that explosion?" Laelia attempted to cross her arms over her chest with her manacled wrists before realizing the futility of the gesture. She gave up and let them hang limply.

"Unfortunate timing on the part of one of the guards, I'm afraid. He walked in just as I was escaping. I didn't hurt him too badly." Mara waggled her fingers and winked. "I am a Kinetic, you know. Aerokinetic, just like my dear brother. But unfortunately, that cuts short your head start as someone is bound to have heard that. So you need to get out of here." Throwing the key to them, she didn't realize everyone's attention had shifted to Pharis, who was glaring at his sister. Perhaps he'd planned on keeping that little secret to himself?

Interesting.

Leon finally reached down and grabbed the key from the ground.

Mara retreated at the sound of footsteps. Someone must have heard her explosive escape. "Hurry!" She ran back to the hallway and peered to her left, her eyes widening at what she saw. Sigi could hear voices in the distance as Mara paused long enough to be spotted by the resistance members who had come to check on the disturbance. She turned and ran back toward her cell room as they gave chase.

"Hurry up!" Sigi urged as Leon used the key to unlock his own cuffs and tossed it to her. Once released, she tried using her Kinetic powers to pull magma from the ground, but the floor of the cell appeared to be made of the iron material as well.

The lit sconces on the walls gave her an idea. Closing her eyes, she tried to feel for the flames, to pull the Fire toward them. She wasn't even sure what her plan was. Maybe they could get it hot enough to melt the metal.

But the Fire wasn't moving. "Damn it!" Sigi punched the bars in frustration. It was no use. The iron surrounding them was stifling her abilities.

"Move out of the way." Pharis stood beside her at the cell door. When Sigi just stared at him, he repeated, "Move, Sigi!"

She stepped back to check on Aurianna, who was still breathing but showed no sign of regaining consciousness.

Pharis was clenching his fists, as he concentrated. He pushed forward with his arms and a grinding sound echoed in the small space, but nothing more. Just when she was about to ask him what he was doing—and by the looks of it, so was everyone else—he leaned against the bar in apparent defeat, spinning his body and sliding to the ground with a look of utter bewilderment on his face.

Leon sauntered over with the key to the shackles and silently slipped it into the hole in the cell door. He was rewarded with a loud click. Turning to the others with a disarming nonchalance, he stated, "Sometimes the simplest answer is the best one."

Pharis got to his feet, nodding his thanks to Leon. He ducked back and, with Sigi's help, carefully scooped Aurianna into his arms, cradling her to his chest as he took off at a rapid pace. Theron used his good arm to slap Leon on the back as he exited their prison, followed by the others.

The resistance was bound to know of their escape at this point. They would have to fight their way out.

When they reached the hallway, Pharis hesitated as he peered down the passage to their right, emotions warring across his face. He didn't want to leave his sister behind, despite everything. And she had helped them to escape, Sigi had to admit.

She laid a hand on Pharis's arm. "She's doing this to help us. Let her. Don't waste this."

"Waste it? I can't just—"

Just then, his sister came running back down the hall, stopping in her tracks when she saw the group frozen at the intersection ahead of her. "Go, Pharis!" she screamed. "I'll be okay."

"No, you won't!"

To illustrate his point, the group of guards who had been chasing her came around the corner. They picked up speed when they saw the others had escaped as well. "Mara, behind you."

"Go, brother. I've got this. I'll be in some deep shit, but they won't kill me. I promise you. Trust me." With that, she pivoted to face her pursuers. A wave of Air slashed across the distance, knocking them off their feet.

Sigi ran left, yelling for the others to follow. She knew Pharis would come with them, if only to protect Aurianna. Mara's powers were dwindling, but she should be able to hold them off for a few moments at least.

As they reached the upper levels, more of the rebels came into view. They would have to try using their Kinetic powers; there was no way around it. Leon and Laelia were basically powerless here. The only source of Water was at the entrance to the hideout, and the resistance didn't have access to Energy.

Theron, however, could be immensely useful with his Earth power. But his struggle was due to his injury. As they ran along, Sigi reached out to the flames in the sconces they passed. These were closer and larger than the ones in their prison, so she had no trouble bending the element to her will.

As someone approached them from behind, Sigi threw a ball of Fire. She wasn't certain whether she was intending to hurt them, but the figure cried out and rolled away to dodge the projectile. Her anger had reached a whole new level, and she didn't want to think about what she might be capable of at the moment. Her friends were all that mattered.

But should they head to the front entrance instead? Would they have time to enact their original escape plan with the entire Order of the Daoine on their tails? If only Aurianna...

A moan behind her had Sigi glancing back, even as they continued to run in what she hoped was the right direction. Pharis was slowing as Aurianna tried to wriggle out of his grasp. He resisted her attempts, but she was pushing against his chest as she swung her legs down. His jaw was clenched as he fought to keep her in his arms. "Let me carry you! We have to get out of here, and you're too weak to stand, much less run."

Sigi and the others wanted to help, but none of them knew what to say or do.

Aurianna braced herself against the wall with an arm. "No. I need to help you."

"You can't. You're not strong enough right now."

She frowned, an emotion which Sigi couldn't quite identify washing over her features. "Just give me a second. I can do it."

"Do what?"

Instead of answering, Aurianna closed her eyes and began breathing heavily. Sigi worried the girl might pass out again. Just as Pharis reached out to lift her back into his arms, the area behind them lit up in wall of flames, Fire licking at the ceiling as everyone stared in awe.

"How...? How...?" Laelia couldn't form the question they all wanted to ask.

"Not now. Let's get out of here." Aurianna pulled her weight off the wall and immediately pitched forward into Pharis's waiting arms.

He scooped her up and took off running again, the others in close pursuit. At least no one could follow them for the moment.

But more rebels were up ahead. Just as one or two would close in on their group, one of Aurianna's balls of Fire would twirl around them, surrounding the enemy as it branched out into sizzling lines. The fiery spectacle would press its prisoner toward a side wall, keeping them from getting through the flames.

And in between the snaking lines of Fire, Sigi saw sparks of

Energy merging and twining together, an added layer to ensure no one could reach their group.

Sigi was both relieved and aghast at the power surging from Aurianna.

Just what the hell is she?

* * *

They reached the rear of the cave system, or as near as Sigi could guess. But the escape plan wasn't panning out as they had hoped.

Only two of them were capable of manipulating Earth. Theron was the only Duster in the group, but his Geokinetic power was hindered by his injury. Sigi doubted it would have made a difference anyway. Even on a good day, he wouldn't have been able to punch through the cliff to the open air. It would require a massive amount of elemental ability, more than any but Aurianna wielded.

But her powers were depleted after using them to stop the attacks from the resistance. And something else was at play as well. The wound on her arm wasn't just a normal wound. Sigi wasn't sure what was going on, but she was afraid her friend might be dying.

She kept her thoughts to herself, however, as they all stood with matching scowls, trying to figure out how to execute any sort of plan.

Pharis had set Aurianna on the ground. He gaped around in a panic as the sounds of pursuit grew louder, echoing off the cave walls and making it impossible to determine how close or how many.

Something had to be done. Sigi pulled from the illuminating flames and tried to form one gigantic ball. Javen had created something similar using the Voids on the roof that night, but the size of that Energy sphere was beyond the scope of her powers. Still, she might be able to slow down the resistance long enough for someone else to think of a better plan.

Theron was trying his best to create a hole in the side of the cliff, but exhaustion oozed off him in waves, and he finally sat on the ground in defeat.

They had lost. Nothing was going to change that.

Here she was, a former member of the City Guard. And a complete failure at protecting her friends when they needed her most. They were more than outnumbered here, but she needed to do something. The flames in her hands had grown, but it was hopeless.

A group rounded the corner, approaching with weapons raised. A few held guns, the majority carried drawn swords and other weapons these rebels liked so much.

Fitz elbowed his way through the throng to stand at the front of the pack, hands on hips.

The jackass was grinning from ear to ear. "Well, it looks like I was right. Kudos to your friends for their valiant efforts." He squatted by Aurianna, who had propped herself up on an elbow. "But you, my dear, are something rather extraordinary."

"I'm not going to be your prisoner, your poster girl, or your weapon. I will not help you, no matter what you say."

His smile widened. "I'm letting you go."

"You're—wait, what?"

Fitz shrugged as he got back to his feet. "I'm sorry for all the theatrics. It was the only way I could be sure you were giving it your full effort."

"What?" Sigi echoed Aurianna's earlier comment.

"We had to verify her power is genuine. And that it wasn't a fluke."

"Are you saying this whole thing was a setup? Holding us captive, poisoning her . . . It was all a ruse?"

"Nobody poisoned her. I honestly don't know why her body is reacting that way. And yet, she still practically annihilated my defenses."

"What were you trying to prove?" Pharis's voice was heated, the veins in his forehead bulging as he breathed heavily.

"That she can do whatever's necessary to stop the Magnus and his plans."

"What plans?"

Fitz threw his hands up in exasperation. "I don't know. Something is going around destroying the towns. It ain't us. Someone is out to get non-Kinetics."

"My father might be many things, but I don't see why he would actively seek to destroy what he considers his own realm." Pharis poked a finger into Fitz's chest. "You and your people stand to gain far more from that than he ever would."

Fitz had raised his eyebrows as Pharis was speaking. Now he batted away the offending finger before backing up. "Believe what you want. All we desire is a free world where we don't have to rely on your kind."

"All *you* want is my father's power." His eyes tracked movement in the crowd.

Mara stepped forward. "Pharis, you and I both know what our father is capable of." Her voice was soft but insistent.

"You know *nothing*, Mara! You left, remember? I was stuck with the burden of trying to keep him in line, knowing I would one day have to take on that role. You let us think you were dead just so you wouldn't have to be the next Magnus."

She shook her head, tears welling in her eyes. "You're right, Pharis. I never wanted to be the Magnus. I don't want a Magnus at all."

"So, you'd put this man here in power instead? Whatever, sis. I'm done. And if we're not actually prisoners, I guess we're leaving."

Mara opened her mouth to speak but closed it instead. She shook her head again and retreated into the crowd.

"If I can't convince you to stay, at least consider what we've said." Fitz's words were directed at Aurianna. Something haunted her eyes, the golden depths lacking their usual luster. Sigi was still concerned for her friend's health, but she did appear slightly better than she had earlier.

Aurianna said, "Give us a ride up top, and we'll think about it." She ignored the sharp look Pharis gave her.

Fitz nodded. "All right. Fine. Only to Eadon?"

"Yeah. I don't trust you any further than that, Fitz." Aurianna glared at him as she got to her feet, a darkness within the amber depths of her eyes. "And to be honest, I don't expect that to change."

CHAPTER 11

AURIANNA

Aurianna was too exhausted and ill to deal with all the anger surging within her. She sat in a chair in the tower and let it wash over her in small waves, knowing it would hit her once she had returned to full health.

After the rebels had delivered them to Eadon, they'd needed to rent an airship. And when they arrived in the town, Aurianna had spotted a familiar vessel.

Argo was more than happy to take them, even offering to transport them for free. But they had insisted on compensating him for his time and trouble.

Laelia knew a healer in Vanito she trusted, someone who had been her father's friend. Despite Aurianna's protestations that the risk of being caught or seen wasn't worth it, Pharis had insisted they take a detour to Vanito to have her arm looked at by someone who didn't have an agenda.

The Vanitian healer had been just as baffled as the rest of them. He did apply an ointment to stop the bleeding, and it seemed to speed up the healing process. But he couldn't offer any advice as to what had caused such an adverse reaction to a minor injury.

After that, Argo had dropped them off at the top of the tower, graciously accepting their pay and their gratitude.

Witnessing Theron's reunion with Rhouth was heartwarming. The fox jumped up, practically reaching the hunter's chest, and he cradled her in his arms.

Her parents, too, were overjoyed to see her, both pulling her into a hug. But Aurianna just felt awkward and unsettled.

Then a wave of dizziness had hit her. It was all too much.

As they helped her sit in the nearest chair, Pharis rushed over to check on her, but she waved him off. Hurt flashed in his eyes, but he left her to her thoughts.

Syrena, however, did not.

She sat across from Aurianna, leaning back as she crossed her legs. A small smile teased at the corners of her mouth, but she didn't speak.

Aurianna eyed her questioningly.

The woman was a stranger to her. These people were her natural parents, but they had not raised her and had no real relationship with her. And Aurianna wasn't sure how she felt about that changing. Still, wasn't this exactly what she had been searching for? Answers to her questions, truths about her past?

After a tense moment of staring, Aurianna finally blew out a breath she didn't realize she'd been holding. "What?" Out of the corner of her eye, she saw Ethan pause in his conversation with Leon to glance over.

Syrena flinched at the curtness of her daughter's voice. "Nothing, really. I just thought maybe we should get to know one another a little better."

"And what? Have a little mother-daughter bonding?"

"Is that a bad thing?"

"I've gotten this far without you—"

"Aurianna, you don't mean that." Ethan joined them, Leon trailing along behind.

"Who are you to tell me what I do or do not mean? You don't even know me!"

"Aurianna—" Leon started.

"No, Leon. This is none of your business. And I was the one on that train, lest we forget. Whether you really were under some sort of spell, or if you're lying, it doesn't matter. I almost died. Sigi almost died. A lot of people almost died. So, don't lecture me. I don't owe you anything."

Leon stepped around Ethan, his glare piercing her defensive walls. "It *became* my business when *you* asked me to find out about them for you. And here they are, ready to provide the answers you claim to want. What you choose to do with it is up to you. But keep in mind, many don't have the opportunity." Leon walked away, taking Laelia's hand on his way to the stairs.

Huffing, Aurianna folded her hands in her lap. "Fine. Talk then."

"No one's going to force you to talk," Syrena whispered, glancing around the room as if suddenly aware everyone might be watching and listening. "But I would like to get to know you, get to know the woman you've become. I lost out on all your childhood. Those years were stolen from us by that horrible Fae—"

Aurianna sat up, her heart hammering in her chest. "Did you say *Fae*?"

Syrena frowned. "Yes. The one who cursed you, remember?"

"That was a . . . Fae?"

"What else could it be? Only they can cast spells or do illusion magic like that."

"They're real?"

"Real? Aurianna, did Larissa never explain any of this to you?"

"Any of what? I don't understand what's going on!"

"The Fae are absolutely real," Syrena said. "Larissa should have explained all of this to you. She helped take care of me when I was younger—before I was sent to the Imperium—and taught me a bit of the old language. We lived in Menos, but it was just me and Mom and Larissa. I never knew my father. Larissa also taught me how to project the dragon you saw."

"It wasn't real. Up close, I could tell it was just an illusion."

Syrena nodded. "Yes, a Fae spell. I used to get harassed by the local kids when I was younger. She showed me how to scare them off—to protect myself. I could show you?"

Aurianna chews on her lip. "I'm not interested in tricks. I want to know what this has to do with the Fae."

"Larissa told me stories of the Fae and how she used to visit them as a child. She learned some of their spells, and she taught a few to me. You've seen how I get food in here. Larissa got an earful from my mother when she caught me conjuring food right out of her kitchen. Unfortunately, Darius saw me doing it one time, and I'm afraid that may have spurred his infatuation with me and my powers."

"I thought he was in love with you?"

"I wouldn't call it that, though maybe others might. Going to the Imperium was both the best and worst thing to happen to me. When my Kinetic powers manifested, my mother tried so hard to keep me out of the Imperium's sight. But she was also terrified of what they would do if I didn't go and we got caught."

Aurianna hesitated. "What happened to your mother?"

"I told you what happened the night you were born. About the Fae who used a glamour to appear to be Amara, one of the midwives who attended me along with Larissa and Hermia. The Fae killed Hermia. She was my mother. Your grandmother."

119

Silence descended between them like a heavy blanket. Her grandmother was yet another casualty of her destiny. Another senseless death. Finally, Aurianna said, "Do you believe the Magnus was behind it?"

"Darius? Why in hell would he do that?"

"He locked you in a tower."

"Yes, to keep me from running away again. Not to kill me. The man was obsessed."

"The lock on the tower was also Fae magic, I'm now realizing. Doesn't that connect him straight to the murderer? How would he have gotten something like that?"

Syrena narrowed her eyes. Leaning forward in her chair, she placed a hand on Aurianna's knee. "Darius wouldn't have risked harming me, but he might have tried to harm *you*."

"The Magnus also tried to kidnap you." The words came from behind her. Aurianna spun around. In the corner sat an exhausted-looking Belinda. She was nibbling on a piece of chocolate cake, both hands covered in icing.

"What are you talking about? How do you know that?" Aurianna slowly rose and went to the girl. She assumed an intimidating stance as she loomed over her. Belinda didn't cower. She simply licked the frosting from her fingers, finally interrupting her grooming to say, "He told me."

"The Magnus *told* you he hired the kidnappers," Aurianna said with more than a hint of skepticism.

"No, not him. Javen. He told me it was the Magnus who did it."

"Why would he tell you that?"

Belinda glared at Aurianna even as her eyes filled with tears. "How the hell am I supposed to know? Why did he do *this* to me?" She pointed at her enlarged stomach.

Aurianna shrank back in shame. She had no reason to threaten the poor girl. "Belinda, how *did* you get pregnant? Weren't you drinking the water?"

"Yeah, I mean I was. I thought I was, at least. We spent a lot of time in my room, especially at mealtimes. I don't know where he got the water."

Aurianna shook her head in disbelief. Javen had managed to live a double life for so long.

She heard footsteps and glanced up to see Pharis and Theron coming down the stairs, conversing in hushed tones. Turning back to Belinda, she asked, "And he told you he knew for a fact the Magnus was behind the whole thing with the train?" Aurianna cast a glance at her mother, who was still sitting across the room, watching and waiting.

"Well, he said he knew the guys who were hired, and the Magnus was the one who hired them."

At this declaration, Pharis and Theron paused in their descent, mouths open.

Aurianna exhaled loudly, baring her teeth in a semblance of a smile. "Well, I guess we know what we're doing next."

* * *

This was not what she had planned on doing next.

She had envisioned storming the front doors of the Imperium, marching up to the Magnus's sleeping chambers, and dragging him out of bed to interrogate him.

Painfully.

But no, instead, she was—

Aurianna lost her focus and plummeted to the water below.

"Ohhhhhh shiiiiiiit!" she screamed into the dark.

She curled her body and scrunched up her face, her muscles braced for impact.

But abruptly, she was no longer falling—just hovering above the water's surface. Peering over, she could barely make out three figures sitting on the edge of the cliff. Laelia and Leon had come to watch her practice her Aerokinetic powers with Pharis.

Pharis was probably glaring at her. She was supposed to be quiet to avoid attracting the attention of the patrolling guards.

It wasn't late, but the night sky was darker than usual. Only a small amount of moonlight glinted through the clouds overhead. The entire scene felt odd and left Aurianna with a cold sense of dread. The scene was far too reminiscent of her childhood and the all-too-familiar sensation of the Darkness as it crept in and stole the joy from the world.

She was transported across the expanse, past the tower, and up to the cliff top, her body riding the crest of a wave of Air.

Pharis was indeed fuming. He set her down away from the other two, evidently so he could rebuke her in private. "What happened?"

"I'm sorry. I panicked. Screaming was sort of involuntary."

"Not *that*. I mean you completely zoned out and broke your concentration. If I hadn't slowed you down in time—"

"I was just thinking about what I want to do to your father."

He raised his eyebrows dramatically. "Excuse me?"

She punched him in the shoulder. "Don't be crass. I mean I want answers. *And* I want to see him squirm. I always knew it was him."

"I thought you always knew it was your mother."

Aurianna's gaze was piercing as she took a step toward him. "Syrena was there, no question. But if he put her up to it, either by putting her under a spell or—"

"Spell? Aurianna, do you hear yourself?" Pharis reached out and stroked her shoulder, just above her wound. It still throbbed with a sickening intensity, but she was almost used to it. "My father doesn't know any spells. He has no connection to the Fae . . . if they even exist."

"Yet he placed a locking *spell* on the tower with that pendant."

Pharis was silent for a moment. "Point taken." He dropped his hand and sighed. "Look, you'll get no argument from me about what a nightmare the man is. But I don't get why he would plot to destroy his own city. It doesn't make sense. We should—we should just keep working on this so we can find out."

"Pharis, this is pointless. Why can't we just walk in the front door?"

"Because the second we do, the guards will have us thrown into prison before we even get a chance to speak to him."

"Then you should just fly me up to his window. Wouldn't that be simpler?"

"How are you ever going to learn if you don't practice?"

"Not everyone is like you. Most of us only have a little Air ability to work with."

Pharis rolled his eyes at her then pulled her closer, his eyes focused on her mouth, lingering there as he spoke. "I've seen firsthand that's not the case for you, haven't I?" He trailed off as he leaned in and caught her lip between his teeth, breath hitching at the contact. Then he crushed her lips, pushing her back against a tree.

His mouth was warm. The world was spinning, and her wound felt fine.

"You know, she could probably use some help with her Hydro powers as well," Leon called, irritation lacing his words.

Aurianna startled and pulled back, taking a deep breath as she pushed Pharis away.

Leon continued. "And since I'm the only Hydron in the group—"

Aurianna walked over to where he and Laelia sat, arms entwined. Trying to sound casual and business like, she answered, "I think I'm doing okay with Water, Leon. I made those bubbles to stop the fire and the Volanti. Plus, when I first went to the tower—"

"Well, excuse me. I guess you don't need us anymore." Leon stood, pulling a whining Laelia up with him. Aurianna started to protest, but he cut off her words with a forestalling hand. "We'd best be heading back to the tower."

Laelia yanked herself away from his meaty grip. "Don't pull on me! And don't tell me what to do."

Leon glared at her for a moment. Then, he shrugged. "Fine. Suit yourself." He walked off before realizing his predicament. Turning around, he said grumpily, "I'll need a ride."

"How about I take both of you back?" When Laelia started to protest, Pharis added, "Just until tomorrow. I don't think it's a good idea to confront him in the middle of the night."

Aurianna protested, "Wasn't that the point? To take him by surprise?"

"Either way, he won't be expecting it. But the guards seem to be on higher alert during curfew hours, and he's bound to have a heavy entourage outside his door right now."

She frowned, pouting. "Fine."

"But you and I should continue practicing. You never know when you might need to use the skill."

"Fine," she repeated.

It was going to be a long night.

* * *

The next morning, Aurianna groaned as they prepared for their journey to confront the Magnus. She ached all over, and not in a good way. Her wound was still on the mend, but the nighttime

Aerokinetic practice had all but done her in. When she thought about it, she had basically been cliff diving for most of the night.

Pharis and Leon were going through the small stash of non-Kinetic weapons they had gotten from the resistance. Guns would be helpful, but daggers could be concealed much more easily.

Leon hesitated before placing a delicate but intricately carved knife in Laelia's outstretched hand. "I wish I were going with you." A meaningful look passed between them, but Aurianna couldn't decipher it.

Laelia returned his stare before rolling her eyes. "I won't be alone. I'll be with them." She gestured to Aurianna and Pharis, who shrugged at Leon when he glared over at him.

"You can't do what they do. Someone will have to carry you." He was still glaring at Pharis.

Aurianna raised her hand. "I'll do it."

Pharis leaned back from perusing the weapons and shook his head. "I don't think so. You might drop her."

"I. Will. Do. It." She gave him wide eyes and cocked her head meaningfully at Leon. "It'll be fine. You can stay close. It's not like we're going far. Just straight up."

Flaring his nostrils, Pharis reached back and picked up a pair of daggers. He handed one to Aurianna before hiding the other in his boot.

She followed suit then looked over to Laelia. "Ready?"

"Yes." She gazed back at Leon one last time, some deep understanding passing between them. "Let's go."

They walked through the tunnels under the bay and up to the secret side door. Pharis propped the door open and levitated up to the greenery roof above the door. He made it look so easy.

Tall Laelia locked her arms around Aurianna's neck. Aurianna grasped her around the middle with her good arm. Concentrating on what Pharis had taught her, she inhaled once then exhaled slowly, allowing her body to rise as if it were made of Air.

Laelia gasped, then giggled. Aurianna scolded her. "Don't do that. I'm trying to focus."

The other girl nodded and, to her credit, didn't make another sound.

The three of them slowly drifted upwards. Aurianna held on to Pharis's shirt to help maneuver as she felt unwieldy with the extra body in tow.

Suddenly, Aurianna felt an inexplicable rush of power fill her, and her speed picked up to a dizzying degree as she struggled to control her ascent. Laelia cried out, tightening her hold until Aurianna regained control.

When they reached the Magnus's audience chamber windows, they peeked in and stared at the unexpected scene. The Consils had assembled, and they did not seem happy. The focus of their attention was Darius Jacomus, Magnus of Eresseia. But he was not holding court from his not-a-throne as usual.

He was on his knees and trembling.

Whether it was excitement or anger which spurred her action, she wasn't sure. But Aurianna gestured to Pharis and whispered her plan in his ear. He nodded hesitantly, backing away and gesturing for Aurianna to do the same. Laelia had her eyes closed the whole time, like she was going to be sick.

He gathered his power and directed the Air around them at the window. It exploded inward, shattering on the not-a-throne-room floor.

Aurianna followed Pharis through the opening, and everyone whirled around to face the intruders.

When they touched down, Laelia released her death grip, and the three uninvited guests moved further into the room.

She knew why she was here. It was time for answers. All the merrier if they had an audience for the spectacle. The only issue might be the guards, but if they could convince the Consils to hear them out...

Consil Giana Rossi of Vanito didn't display any surprise at their unorthodox entrance. She smiled and addressed Laelia specifically. "It's good to see you making friends, dear."

Laelia's typical feline grin held more than her normal blend of tactless humor and innuendo. It contained a heavy dose of cynicism and rage as well.

"Hello, Mother."

Chapter 12

Aurianna

"What?" Pharis spun around, almost knocking Aurianna over as she, too, did an about-face to stare at Laelia.

"I see you've been keeping things from your friends."

"Like mother, like daughter, right?" Laelia said through gritted teeth.

"I have no secrets."

Aurianna tore her gaze from Laelia and found her tongue. "Everyone has secrets." Her attention swung back to the Magnus, who still cowered on the floor. "Like blowing up a train, for instance?"

Darius Jacomus, Magnus of Eresseia, trembled with fear. He seemed more afraid of her than he had been of the Consils.

Good.

He shook his head. "That was you, my dear," he said in a poor attempt at his usual pompous tone.

"I may have triggered the explosion, but you're the one who hired those men to kidnap me and rigged the train to take out Bramosia."

"No, I..." The Magnus's eyes darted around.

Aurianna realized something was missing from this scene. "Where are the guards?"

Anson Glaeser, the Consil for Rasenforst cleared his throat. "We have our own guards keeping watch over those loyal to you lot. They're just outside the doors, so don't even think—"

Aurianna's arm flared with Energy, the sparks of electricity weaving across her skin. "Or what? You'll hurt us?" She glared menacingly at the group of Consils.

"There's no need to threaten us. We aren't the villains here." Consil Glaeser gestured to the broken window, the shattered bits of glass catching the dull light of the afternoon sun peeking through the cloud cover.

"Yes, they are!" cried Darius, pointing an accusing finger at Laelia's mother. "She's the one who convinced me to hire those goons in the first place." He closed his jaw with a snap the moment he realized what he had admitted.

"Giana, what is he talking about?" Margery Rigas was the Consil for Menos, Theron's hometown. The woman's usual cheery demeanor was gone, replaced with an icy stare directed at the Vanitian Consil.

Laelia's mother's expression bore not a shred of concern or fear. "Oh, please do shut up, Margery. We can't all sit around guzzling wine, expecting the world to fix itself."

The other Consil's face went bright red. "Excuse me?" she said, sputtering. "Who the hell do you think you're talking—"

"Please spare us your protestations. We both know how much you want the Kinetics to be put in their place. You sit back and let others get their hands dirty so you can claim no involvement." Giana was now inches away from the other woman's face. "But you wanted a war just as badly as the rest of us."

"Us? What are you talking about?" Jonn Etling, Consil for Ramolay, asked. His face showed his confusion as he regarded each Consil in turn.

Aurianna found her voice again. "Why would you want war?"

She noticed Consil Lowe of Eadon sidling along the edges of the assembled group, attempting to slip from the room. But before she could alert the others, Consil Rossi beat her to it. "Cormick, so help me, if you take one more step, I'll let this girl do as she pleases to you."

Aurianna bristled at the woman's words but bit her tongue. Pharis had barely taken his eyes off his father, but now he walked over and placed a hand on Aurianna's shoulder, a silent gesture of solidity.

The Eadonite Consil was slinking back. But he wasn't looking at Aurianna. His wide eyes were focused on Giana Rossi.

Laelia hadn't moved since they'd entered the room. Now her shoes crunched on the broken glass as she strode forward. "Mother, why don't you stop with all the cloak-and-dagger bullshit and just admit to whatever nefarious plot you're involved in now?"

Pharis regarded her quizzically. "Laelia?"

Laelia affected a pout. "Mother dearest here, well . . . She's not exactly winning any mommy-of-the-year awards. Or wife-of-the-year either, for that matter."

Consil Rossi sighed and shook her head reprovingly at her daughter. "Child, I taught you better than to spread rumors."

Laelia's eyes narrowed and her voice took on a chill. "You taught me nothing except what not to do and what not to be. And they're not rumors, as you and I both know."

"Liar."

"I saw it with my own eyes! He was lying there on the floor, and you were standing there with the bottle in your hand." Her voice shook as tears of fury and grief spilled over and rolled down her cheeks. "You might have fooled the rest of them, but not me."

"What is she referring to, Giana?" Consil Etling asked hesitantly.

"Just going on about things we've been over before. She was a child. She has no idea what she saw."

Margery Rigas whispered, as if in a daze, "Is she talking about your husband?"

Laelia huffed and said, "Of course I am. He never stood a chance, married to this conniving pile of garbage."

"Laelia!"

"No! I will not be silent any longer. I tried to tell the City Guard when they came to take away his body, but none of them would listen."

"Because you were a—"

"A child? What does it matter? I know what I saw." Laelia sobbed before adding, "You killed him. I wasn't supposed to be there. I wasn't supposed to see. But you took him from me, and I can never forgive you."

"This is ridiculous. Why are you even here?" The woman sounded more bored than concerned by the accusation or the hate in her daughter's eyes.

Hate so deep it sent a pang through Aurianna's chest. *Why did Laelia never tell us about this?* Aurianna recalled the nonverbal communication between Leon and Laelia before they'd departed. Perhaps Laelia had confided in him, at least.

"We are here . . ." Aurianna began and cleared her throat, "to question the Magnus regarding his involvement in certain events. The plot to kidnap me and blow up Bramosia is only one of them, but let's start there." She addressed the Magnus. "You admit hiring those men. Why did you do it?"

The man started to rise, but Pharis's menacing step forward had him sinking back to his knees. "I-I-I only needed you out of the way for a while!" he protested. "And I planned on letting my son find you eventually."

"You son of a bitch!" Pharis had his hands around his father's throat before Aurianna could process the man's words. The Magnus's face was turning purple.

"Why did you need me *out of the way*?"

He couldn't answer, of course, so his only response was a strangled gurgle.

Aurianna sighed. "Pharis, please."

For a moment, it seemed as if the former Regulus would refuse to listen, but he eased his grip. He didn't move, however, but retained his threatening stance over his father.

Darius Jacomus rubbed his neck and sucked in a breath. When Aurianna loudly cleared her throat, he finally responded to her question. "The other Consils were on my back about the engagement between you two."

"There was no engagement. You just wanted to keep my power to yourself somehow."

"And yet, look at you two now." The Magnus wore a leering grin as he gestured between Pharis and Aurianna.

Pharis didn't waste any time before clutching the man by the throat again.

Aurianna spoke calmly to Pharis. "He's just riling you up. Don't forget we came here for answers."

"Fine." Pharis released him and backed away, continuing to scowl.

The Magnus loosened his collar and stared off into the distance as he regained his composure. "As I was saying, the engagement business was becoming a problem, so Giana suggested I have you abducted to take the focus away from all of that. This was before the dragonblood issue really took off. I had no idea that was going to happen. And *she*"—he gestured to Laelia's mother with a sneer—"even recommended the kidnappers to me."

"And why would she help you? Wasn't she just as angry over your plan to marry me off to your son?"

"She and I had an agreement."

"Darius." Giana's threatening voice sliced like a knife through the conversation.

The Magnus shook his head. "No, Giana. Our deal is over. I know it was you who ordered those explosives."

"You're saying it wasn't you?" came Aurianna's shocked reply.

"Of course not." Laelia called from across the hall where she'd been leaning quietly against the wall, arms crossed. "That has my mother's name written all over it."

"I did arrange the kidnapping." Darius actually sounded indignant. "But why would I blow up my own town? My own home? That was meant to be a catalyst. I don't want war. She does!"

As he finished, Giana Rossi bared her teeth and leaped toward the Magnus where he still crouched on the floor. Pharis grabbed the woman and yanked her arms behind her, holding her immobile.

Aurianna's curiosity took over, and she asked the Vanitian Consil, "What *did* happen to your husband?"

"My husband had a heart attack and died in the middle of his dinner." The woman appeared bored with the conversation. "Laelia blames me for it. She was grief-stricken, and I think it has colored her memory of the event."

"I was there," Laelia said through gritted teeth as she marched back over to her mother's side. "I saw you pour poison in his drink!"

"You were a child, dear. You needed someone to blame."

"Enough. I'm sorry, Laelia." Aurianna shook her head, cutting off Laelia's reply. "But we didn't come here for this. We need to discuss the events of the other night."

"You mean the roof?" Consil Etling asked. "What happened up there?"

"You mean you don't know?" Aurianna was incredulous. Is that why no one had come after them?

"We've heard rumors concerning a lightning storm on the roof of the Imperium. But we've found no explanation for what happened, just plenty of damage."

"What did you do with . . . with the . . ." Aurianna couldn't bring herself to form the rest of the words.

Consil Rigas narrowed her eyes. "With the what?"

Pharis finally pulled his eyes away from the Magnus and answered her. "The body. Javen Ambrogetti's body."

Aurianna winced but remained silent.

The faces of each of the Consils bore matching expressions of confusion. "Body?" Anson Glaeser said with uncertainty. "No one mentioned a body. Just rubble and scorch marks."

The room began to spin. Aurianna, already weak from the wound on her arm, felt herself falling.

But Laelia caught her and supported her around the waist.

Aurianna tried to focus on the girl's face, but she finally had to close her eyes to allow her balance to find its center once again.

Pharis, meanwhile was staring at the assembled group, his mouth agape. "How is that possible?" His jaw clenched spasmodically. "He was there when we left."

"You were there?" Giana asked, suddenly interested in the conversation again. "So, the Regulus himself was involved in this." She studied her fellow Consils and seemed to invite them to join her efforts to shift the blame, even as her arms were trapped behind her in Pharis's grip. "It seems the resistance may not be solely responsible for the damage to our towns."

"The resistance had nothing to do with that. Because of the

curfews, they can't even get into the towns right now." Aurianna snapped her mouth closed the moment she realized what she'd said.

"And how would you know this, dear?" When Giana's smile turned feline, Aurianna saw the woman's unmistakable resemblance to her daughter. "Tell you themselves, did they?"

A strange expression came over Pharis face. He froze, his hands falling limply to his sides.

"I...I..."

Consil Rigas demanded, "Have you been speaking with the resistance?"

"The girl must have made a deal with them," the Magnus said with a raspy voice. "They're traitors!"

"I did no such thing." Aurianna's voice was coldly furious. She faced her accuser, pulling the dagger from her boot as she stalked toward him. Even as she did it, she knew how it would look, but she didn't care at the moment.

The Magnus squirmed away, flinching as she brandished the weapon in his face.

Pharis moved a few slow steps closer.

Aurianna spoke clearly. "But the Order couldn't have done that damage any more than I could."

The Magnus locked gazes with her. His expression was so intensely furious she had to look away, but he yelled, "I should have killed your bitch of a mother when I had the chance. Then you'd both be out of my—"

Strangled sounds rather than words finished his statement, bringing Aurianna's focus back to the man on the floor. A dagger protruded from his throat, rivulets of blood snaking between his fingers and down his neck as his hands clutched the wound in vain.

Aurianna, trembling in confusion and fear, stared dazedly down to her hand where her dagger still glinted, unbloodied in the light from a nearby electric sconce.

She gaped up at Pharis, now looming over them.

He looked down to his hands, and her eyes followed.

Specks of red marred his right hand. He frowned in confusion and held up the trembling appendage. He stared at it with a detached scrutiny, as if the hand had moved of its own accord.

A voice behind them floated through her foggy mind. "Guards! They've killed the Magnus! Arrest them!"

CHAPTER 13

AURIANNA

Laelia sighed. "I want a more comfortable bunk in our next cell."

Aurianna stared at the woman, incredulous.

Seriously?

Laelia simply shrugged—her mask of indifference back. It was as if she hadn't just accused her mother of murdering her father, or witnessed a son murder his father.

Aurianna could see again the dagger sticking from the man's neck, blood gushing out in crimson waves of hot, hard finality.

Pharis had stabbed and killed the Magnus.

Was he dead? How could he not be?

They had all been too stunned to resist when the guards had taken them away, and now here they sat . . . in another cell.

The *Magnus* was dead.

The Magnus was *dead*.

Pharis had killed his father?

Her gaze shifted to the man who sat in another corner of their cell, holding a blood-splattered hand with his other. He continued to stare at it with a hint of accusation. Aurianna wasn't sure who exactly he was blaming.

Sure, he hated his father. But enough to kill him?

When Simon had described the future that would result from Aurianna's failure on the rooftop—the future in which the Magnus always ended up dead—Pharis had seemed upset, despite his words to the contrary and his condemnation of the man as a monster.

Not once had Pharis implied he wanted the man dead. So why?

Desperate for answers, yet also dreading to hear them, Aurianna forced herself to go to Pharis and sit on the floor beside him. He didn't acknowledge her, so she sat in silence, trying to come up with the right thing to say. But her thoughts kept circling back to wonder how the Magnus had known she would be on that train. How could he, or anyone, have predicted her actions that night?

Gradually, however, the reality of their situation settled in, and Aurianna knew they needed an escape plan.

Before she had a chance to comment, his quiet words cut through the silence between them. "It was a threat."

"What was?" she asked.

"What he said, about killing your mother."

Aurianna shook her head at him even though he wasn't looking at her. "He was being an asshole. He was trying to upset me."

It was Pharis's turn to shake his head, but the motion was barely visible in the dim light. "But he wasn't threatening *her*, not directly anyway. And he wasn't trying to upset *you*. He was trying to get to me, by implying a threat against you."

"I don't understand."

"By saying he should have killed her, what he was really saying was he should have killed her before you were born," Pharis continued. "When you glanced away—you didn't see it, but he looked me dead in the eye." He winced, presumably at his poor choice of words.

"He was baiting *me*. He could see how I feel about you, and he was goading me into reacting." Letting his hands fall to the floor, he leaned forward slightly and hung his head. "So, I guess that's what I did. Only he probably just thought he'd have me arrested for punching him."

The Magnus. The Magnus was dead. Long live the Magnus.

"Mara...?"

Pharis nodded in resignation. "Yep." Then he closed his eyes and leaned his head back against the wall.

Mara is the new Magnus.

"Would that even be allowed?" she wondered.

"They don't have a choice. It's the law. But they don't know she's alive yet. I considered telling them, but somehow it doesn't seem like my secret to tell." His eyes suddenly opened, and the desperation there nearly broke Aurianna's heart. "How am I supposed to tell her? She helped us escape. I mean, I was still angry at her, but she helped us. And she doesn't want this. And now I've..." His words trailed off into the silence.

Aurianna placed a palm against his cheek, the skin there cool and clammy. Bringing her face closer, she leaned her forehead against his. "Pharis, she has no love for that man. Even less than you. I know she'll understand. And now she has the power to fix the problems in the system."

Pharis was shaking his head again, the motion causing his mouth to inch closer to hers, and her gaze was drawn to his lips. "I can't let that happen, Aurianna." His words surprised her so much she leaned back so she could read his face and comprehend his meaning.

"Why?"

"Because she's one of them."

Them. The Order. The resistance.

The enemy.

They had imprisoned her and her friends, and they were responsible for her injury, even if the "accident" had truly been just an accident. Definitely the enemy.

Right?

"Then..." Aurianna floundered around in her whirling thoughts, trying to settle on something definitive. They had enough questions. They needed answers.

And a plan.

"Then," she finally continued, "you'd be the Magnus."

A bitter laugh escaped his throat. "No. Not me. I think we need a third option."

"But you'd be able to do so many things for this land, for its people."

"I can't, Aurianna. Not me." A sudden light shone from his eyes, his shoulders relaxing as if a weight had been lifted. "No, not me. You."

"Me?" she squeaked. "I think you're in shock, Pharis."

Laughter reached her from the other side of the cell. Laelia's amusement was plain in her oh-so-familiar feline grin.

When she didn't speak, Aurianna finally asked, "What's so funny?"

"What's so funny?" Laelia rolled her eyes. "Seriously?" She stood and stretched her back. "The heir kills his father, refuses to take his rightful place, and now he wants the girl from the future who just happens to be the *love child* of the woman his father was obsessed with—to take his place." She raised an eyebrow. "What's *not* funny about that?"

"His father is dead, Laelia."

She shrugged again and said somewhat bitterly, "So is mine."

Aurianna felt as if she had been punched in the gut. "Laelia, I'm so sorry. I've been so focused on the immediate situation, I wasn't even thinking about that. Why didn't you ever tell us? Consil Rossi is your mother? And it was your father's grave you visited on your birthday?"

"Yes. But that woman isn't my mother. She's the woman who killed my father, and she gave birth to me. That's all."

"Still, I'm sorry."

"It's fine." When Aurianna raised an eyebrow at her, Laelia sighed and added, "Okay, no, it's not fine, and I guess I needed that confrontation. But it happened a long time ago. So, you're right. We need to focus on the here and now so we can get out of this place." She turned her attention to Pharis, her expression full of compassion. "Like she said, your father was a horrible man. Don't lose sight of that."

"You're not wrong—I'm certain he caused more pain and suffering than I'm even aware of—" His lips began to tremble. "But I didn't have enough reason to . . . That doesn't make what I did right."

"Pharis, you—"

He had gotten to his feet, his legs unsteady beneath him as he gazed down at her. "I don't actually remember or understand why I did it."

"You said he threatened me."

"Yeah, but Aurianna, do you really think I could be a cold-blooded killer? I know I have a temper sometimes, but—" He hesitated before continuing. "I don't remember it."

Laelia was frowning. "Pharis, you *did* kill him. I don't think it's healthy to try to deny it right now."

"I'm not saying I didn't do it. I'm telling you I don't remember. I mean, I remember doing it. I just don't remember deciding to do it. It was like my body was acting of its own accord."

Aurianna stood as well. "You were in shock."

141

"No. I mean, yes, I was—after. But it was like I couldn't stop myself. I got angry when he said what he said about your mother, but I really wasn't in control of what my hand did."

"That sounds—" Laelia started.

"Crazy? Yeah, I know. It does. But I'm telling you, that's what happened."

Aurianna studied their surroundings, narrowing her eyes as she contemplated their predicament. "It doesn't matter right now. We need to get out of here."

"So why haven't we?"

"Because my powers aren't working again. Whatever they did to me back at the resistance hideout is still affecting me."

"But you were fine last night when you were cliff diving and playing tongue twister with daddy-killer over here."

Pharis bristled, then reconsidered and avoided their eyes, frowning in consternation.

"Like I said, it seems to come and go. What about you? The electric sconces are close enough aren't they?"

"Maybe. What exactly do you have in mind?"

"I want you to pull Energy and put it into the bars of our cell. Concentrate on the ones in front."

"And then what?" Pharis was staring at her with trepidation, leaning against one of the bars for support. When he realized what he was touching, he yanked his hand away.

"And then I have a sudden change in my health situation." Aurianna smiled grimly, obviously not happy or amused in the slightest.

Once Laelia had the cell bars as electrically charged as they could be, Aurianna—without warning—collapsed into a heap on the floor. Pharis barely managed to catch her before she hit the ground.

Laelia began screaming for the guard on duty. The man came running around the corner, stopping just before the cell as he tried to ascertain what had happened.

Pharis held up Aurianna's wounded arm and started shouting about her stitches and how she was losing blood again.

The guard, thankfully, didn't seem to question it once he realized what was being explained. The three of them literally held their breath as the man reached for the door to their cell, his other hand shoved in his pocket to bring out the key.

As his palm gripped one of the bars, what started as a tiny jolt of electricity shot through the man's arm and down his side. The guard's entire body went rigid, then he seized up and fell to the floor.

"Now what?" Pharis asked as Aurianna got back to her feet, frowning with concern at the man on the ground.

"He'll be okay, right?"

He frowned at her question. "You're asking this now? Yes, he'll be fine in a couple of hours. Unemployed. Possibly in a shitload of trouble. But physically fine."

"Now we get out of here. That was the only guard on duty. I checked as we came in, and no one's entered the place since we got here."

"But how do we get out?"

"Uh . . . You're an Aerokinetic. I'll let you figure out the specifics. But keep the theatrics to a minimum. We don't want to attract any more attention."

"Theatrics? I'm not the one who wanted to bust in through—"

"If you two love birds want to have a go at each other and work off some of this"—she made a face and waved a hand between them—"whatever this is, fine by me. But right now, we're short on a little thing called time."

Aurianna huffed out a breath. "Look, Pharis. I know you don't like demonstrating your powers and all, but we need you right now."

He stared at her for a moment. Then, without looking away from her, he slowly exhaled.

And blew the doors right off their hinges.

Chapter 14

AURIANNA

The door to their cell flew a few feet before toppling to the ground with a reverberating clang. The women gaped at the sheer power he had demonstrated. Laelia appeared frozen, her mouth hanging open, her customary quips absent.

Pharis glared at her intently, probably trying to convey a warning not to share.

Laelia cringed but tried to cover the involuntary reaction by rushing through the now-open cell door, but it was too late.

Laelia was frightened of him. Aurianna had to admit to herself she might have felt the same way had she not already witnessed his power previously. But she also had to admit this was different. Rawer, somehow. Perhaps, like her, his emotions were fueling his abilities.

A conversation for later, considering the sounds she could hear from down the hall. They were already losing precious seconds, so Aurianna took Pharis's hand and ran out into the passage with Laelia following close behind.

Too late. The approaching sounds were far too close, the voices almost...

Familiar.

Running ahead of the others, Aurianna rounded a corner and found herself face-to-face with the last person she had expected to see.

Simon was gesturing behind him to two figures who were scurrying along in the dark. Beside him was Eber, the Arcane who had been spying on Aurianna in the future. They seemed relieved to see her.

Simon nodded to her. "We thought we might have to get creative in breaking you three out of there." He threw a meaningful glance at Pharis before adding, "But it appears you've managed."

"Simon," Aurianna whispered, "what are you doing here?" As the words left her mouth, an excited squeal erupted just behind Simon, and a small person launched herself into her midsection. "Hilda!"

Aurianna pulled the girl into a tight hug and glanced beyond to the dimly lit hall where Hilda's friend Sebastian, another young Acolyte, lingered. She reached out and included him in the embrace, closing her eyes. She opened them to observe Simon and Eber, her puzzled expression communicating the confusion in her heart.

Eber responded to her unspoken question. "These Youngers might be in danger. Until now, you and your friends were not the Consils' biggest concern." He glanced at Pharis, an apology in his eyes. "The Magnus is dead. And you are now the number one enemy of the land. The Consils will be searching for you in every region, every bar, every home from here to Vanito. You must not let them find you."

"Any suggestions where we can go then?" Pharis's voice was gruff, full of grief and fear. And something else Aurianna couldn't quite place.

"You must seek out those whose very existence the Consils would never even consider."

"And who might that be?"

Simon shared a grimace with Eber, deep lines etched in his forehead as he frowned at the rest of them. "You have no choice but to go to the Fae. They alone can guide your next steps on this journey."

Aurianna shook her head. "You said this before. And it's true my mother claims knowledge of their existence, but I don't know if I can trust her any more than I can you."

"Aurianna—"

"You say you can do nothing to help me. You talk in riddles—"

"Aurianna—"

"Then you suddenly show up to help me escape from prison, and you tell me to go visit a mythic group of . . . of . . . I don't know what they are, but they certainly aren't going to just help a group of strangers!"

Simon sighed, rubbing his thumb against the bridge of his nose. "Aurianna, I understand how you feel. But you have been complaining about no one helping you, about me not being helpful, and now I am trying to help."

"Yes, Simon. And why is that?"

"Why am I helping? Because the timeline is no longer in a loop. The future is unknown, and my hands are no longer tied as they were. However, the irony is . . . now I have no idea *how* to help because this part is unwritten."

"So basically, you are still no help to me."

"Well, Eber and I are here to bring you your young friends. This seemed important to us. But we do not know anything for certain beyond this moment."

Pharis practically growled as he spoke. "Then why do you keep insisting she visit the Fae? Seems oddly specific."

"It is not specific to a timeline, and it can be better explained once you get there. We are still concerned about meddling too much. But the Consils are looking for anyone connected to you, and these children are in great danger if they stay here."

Aurianna felt a burst of impatience. "All right. We need to get out of here. Someone is bound to have heard us by now."

Eber seemed grimly self-satisfied. "We have taken care of the guards on duty for this level. Eventually, however, someone will discover what has happened."

"Taken care of?" Laelia narrowed her eyes at the little man.

"They are merely asleep, I assure you. But you must hurry. We will show you the way through the tunnels to avoid any others who might come upon us."

Eber and Simon went back the way they'd come. The others followed, Aurianna bringing up the rear to keep a look out.

The Arcanes led them through a series of tunnels, most of which were familiar by now. However, at a few key junctions, she could hear far-off voices, and she knew Simon and Eber were leading them into less frequented tunnels. Aurianna suddenly realized how lucky they were never to have been caught if their usual routes were so well traveled.

Luck was no longer a concept she took lightly. Perhaps the Essence were already playing a bigger role than Terra would admit.

They reached an intersection Aurianna recognized near the tower. Without a word, Simon bowed and fled back into the dark passageways. Eber followed after locking eyes with Aurianna and nodding.

His cryptic gesture was forgotten in their rush to return to their friends. Aurianna and Pharis led the others into the entrance to the tower where Sigi stood with her weapon drawn.

When she saw her little sister among the group, Sigi let out a gasp and ran forward to throw her arms around the girl.

Sebastian stood awkwardly to the side.

Sensing an unease within the boy, Aurianna sidled up to him and whispered conspiratorially, "I bet you never thought you'd be getting mixed up with a group like this, huh?"

He attempted a smile, but the halfhearted effort ended with a pensive frown instead. "I don't really understand why I'm here. I mean, Hilda is Sigi's sister. I'm no one."

"How much do you know about what's going on, Sebastian?"

The boy shrugged. "Simon told us enough. But I still don't understand what it's got to do with me."

Aurianna tried to sound calm and reasonable. "Sebastian, the Consils are looking for us. And that's just the start of it. You're close to Hilda, and Hilda's close to Sigi. I don't think it's any more or less complicated than that. The Consils might use anyone close to us to try to hurt us or hunt us down, so I think you're better off getting away from the Imperium."

"Wait, what?" Hilda's higher-pitched voice broke the relative quiet of the room. She had clearly been listening to the conversation while embracing her sister. Hilda pushed out of Sigi's arms and confronted Aurianna. "We came here to help. I'm not going to let you send us away."

"Not let us?" Sigi cried. "No, ma'am. This isn't even up for discussion. You and Sebastian are going home."

"But Simon said the Consils will be searching everywhere for you. Which means home isn't any safer for us than here." Hilda crossed her arms mulishly, looking like a miniature version of her sister. "All our families could be in danger. You have to warn our father."

Pharis was leaning against a nearby chair, his face pale and grim. "She's right. We must warn everyone we can. Right away."

Sigi tilted her head in confusion. "What are you talking about? What's happened?"

Aurianna traded glances with Laelia, who had been watching silently up till then. No one seemed inclined to answer. Sigi huffed in impatience, glaring at Hilda until she blurted out, "The Magnus is dead."

Sigi blanched. She clenched her fists then whispered, "What?"

Aurianna hung her head and sighed. "It's a long story, Sigi, but the Magnus is dead. And the Consils are after us. So, we need to get out of here as soon as possible."

Theron and Leon had been descending the stairs, but at Aurianna's announcement, they stopped in their tracks. Theron raced back to the upper level as Leon joined them downstairs.

Sigi shook her head. "I don't understand. How is the Magnus dead? And what does that have to do with—" Sigi's face and voice reflected her horror. "Aurianna, did you kill him?"

"No," Aurianna replied softly.

"Then how...?"

Pharis cleared his throat. "I killed him."

The room was silent. A chill in the air sent shivers up Aurianna's spine. She glanced back to Pharis. Was he...?

Just then, Theron came back downstairs followed by Syrena and Ethan, who wore matching expressions of concern and confusion. Then everyone began to ask questions as once.

Aurianna held up a hand and was rather surprised when everyone grew quiet. "I need everyone to trust me. You'll get the full story as soon as possible, but please understand that right now we need to get out of here before the place is swarming with guards."

"But where can we go?" Leon asked, finally finding his voice and staring at Pharis with a calculating look as he spoke.

Aurianna glanced at her mother.

Syrena simply nodded as if somehow reading her daughter's

mind. "I don't know what kind of trouble you're in, but if you're looking to hide where you'll never be found, it's the only way."

Leon frowned. "What are we talking about here?"

Aurianna chewed on her bottom lip. "The Fae."

"I'm sorry, what?"

Theron shook his head as if not hearing her correctly. "You can't be serious. The Fae are just—"

"A myth. Yeah, I know. Only ... maybe they're not. Syrena has a bit of secondhand knowledge, and the Arcanes keep insisting I go see them, and—"

"The *Arcanes* told you to go talk to the Fae?"

Aurianna could feel Pharis silently encouraging her. He knew her secret now, and she owed it to her friends to tell them as well. She looked right at Theron and said, "I guess it's not any more far-fetched than speaking to the Essence."

Laelia, Sigi, and Leon all burst into nervous laughter.

Not Theron. He simply stared at her in wonder. His lips moved as if he wanted to say something, but no words came out for several seconds. Finally, he blew out a breath. "Aurianna, why would you say that?"

"Because I have." She returned his gaze, refusing to look away.

He squinted at her and waved a hand vaguely. "You're saying..."

She nodded. "I have spoken to the goddesses—well, two of them. Yes." Her lip curled in a sardonic smile. "Several times."

Syrena and Ethan gaped at their daughter. Everyone remained standing except Theron, who sank into a chair next to Pharis, his movements slow and deliberate. He rested his face in his hands. "I knew it." His words were muffled, but the tone was unmistakable.

He was relieved.

"What?" Pharis asked quizzically, unaware of the import of the situation.

151

Leon nodded at Theron. "When he was little, Theron was almost taken by the Volanti. He's always been convinced he was saved by the Essence."

"Well, I can attest to what Aurianna is saying," Pharis said. "I was with her just the other day when we went to an Earth temple and had a brief conversation with Terra."

"You what?" Sigi was indignant. "How could you keep something like this from the rest of us?"

A twinge of irritation crept into Aurianna's voice. "Would you have believed me?"

"Of course."

"Really? Because it sure seemed like you didn't believe me when I told you about the Enchantress still being around." Out of the corner of her eye, Aurianna saw Syrena bristle at the moniker. She amended her statement. "The truth might have ended up being a little off, but all of you guys were willing to dismiss and ignore what I had to say."

"Aurianna, what are you talking about?" Laelia asked, a note of concern in her voice. The sentiment was out of character for the girl's typical blunt attitude.

Sigi was also frowning at her in confusion and concern.

Aurianna felt sobs threatening to erupt, the emotional impact of everything bubbling up to overwhelm her senses. But this was not the time.

"Look, we can discuss all of this later. Right now, we need to leave."

"But how do we find the . . . the Fae?" Sigi was staring at her sister as she spoke. "And what do we do about Hilda and her friend?"

Aurianna started to answer, but Theron interrupted. "We need to warn our families. I suggest we head straight to my parents' house and let them know what's coming. That's the first stop from here geographically. Then we can—"

Leon piped up, "First stop? We can't just take the train, Theron. They're hunting us."

Theron nodded in agreement. "True. But I was thinking horses would be a better option, and more flexible." Theron laughed at the crestfallen look which washed over his friend's face. "Just until we get to Menos. I think we can reassess the situation once we get there. But your family would be next, and then Laelia and Sigi—"

Leon's concern became something much darker at Theron's words. "No one's contacting my mom. I can assure you she would hand us over to the authorities in a heartbeat."

Laelia nodded. "Yeah. I don't think mine is going to be giving us any assistance either."

Aurianna realized they hadn't discussed that piece of information with the group yet. She gave Laelia a pointed look, urging her to continue.

With a huff of frustration, Laelia blurted, "So, my mom is the Consil for Vanito. She's a murderous bitch, and she's the one coming after us, so yeah. There's that."

Leon came to stand behind her, wrapping his arms around her. He didn't seem surprised by her statement, verifying Aurianna's earlier supposition that Laelia had probably confided in him at some point.

Everyone seemed to be taking all the shocking truths in stride. Aurianna snorted. At that point, she could have told them she was half-Fae, and she doubted anyone would have batted an eye. She continued, "And we need to get Hilda and Sebastian to safety at some point as well."

When the two in question began to whine in protest, Sigi held up her hands. "I'm going to warn my father. That's my first priority right now." She pointed at the Youngers who were glaring at her, arms crossed in mirror displays of indignation. "You two are coming with me whether you like it or not. Everyone else head to Menos. I'll meet you . . . where exactly is it we're going after that, Aurianna? You haven't clarified that point."

Theron's eyes widened, his hand reaching up before falling in defeat. "Sigi, I don't think you going off on your own is wise right now."

"You don't think I can handle myself?"

Theron flushed. "That's not what I meant, and you know it. I know you're capable. But Rasenforst is a long way from Menos, and if you run into trouble, we wouldn't even know."

Hilda repeated. "We can help!"

Sigi rolled her eyes and ignored her sister's outburst. "Then someone else come with me."

Theron's shoulders slumped. "I have to go warn my parents. I have to go to Menos."

"I'll go with her." Leon sighed—probably at the prospect of more time on a horse—but stuck to his offer. He gazed down at Laelia with raised eyebrows. "If that's all right?"

She nodded, laying her hand over the one he had placed on her shoulder. "But Aurianna still needs to tell us where we're heading after that. How do you find something that nobody believes exists?"

Aurianna chewed her lip in thought. "I don't know." She looked over to Syrena. "Did Larissa ever tell you anything about the location of the Fae?"

Syrena shook her head. "No, not really. Larissa was secretive when it came to specifics like that. She always said they could only be found when they wanted to be."

Aurianna sighed. "I just thought maybe it would come to me like everything else. Follow the path that draws me, as Simon says. The answers usually find their way to the surface."

"How very nonspecific." Leon started rubbing Laelia's shoulder as he spoke. The gesture was both intimate and jarring. Their new-found relationship was going to take some getting used to.

"I know, I know. One step at a time though, okay?"

Theron stood up. "Then it's settled. Horses, then on to Menos and Rasenforst. We can figure out specifics later, but it's probably safest to meet back in Menos for now. Everyone's going to need supplies—clothing and other necessities. My parents can help with a good deal of it."

A sound from the top of the stairs brought everyone's attention to the girl standing there, rubbing the sleep from her eyes.

Aurianna sighed and felt a collective echo of her sentiments from the others.

What the hell were they going to do with Belinda?

Chapter 15

AURIANNA

Menos was a land of lush greens and vibrant life. Aurianna suspected she could feel right at home in such a place. The rolling hills, the soft breeze lazily drifting across sun-kissed skin, and a plentiful supply of wine from the local vineyards pared well with a table spread with homegrown vegetables.

But this was not the time for relaxing or enjoying the company of friends and family. Nor for appreciating the lives she had so recently saved.

Had she, in fact, done that—saved them? Or had she merely protected them from her own mistake?

In other timelines, she had been unable to stop Javen's massive ball of Energy from exploding, killing untold number of people, and sparking a civil war.

No, that wasn't right either. It wasn't that she had been unable to stop it. Aurianna had *caused* it to expand into a weapon of destruction on a massive scale. In every other version of the timeline, she herself had created the world of her childhood. She was responsible for the brutality, the cullings, the deaths, and the depression of the small community which managed to survive into the future.

It didn't matter how Simon tried to present those facts or avoid the question entirely. He couldn't change the truth. Aurianna knew it was her fault, her failing.

Standing on the back porch of the Panago home, she stared off into the distance at the expanse of vineyard before her. Syrena and Ethan sat nearby, while Pharis and Laelia were inside with Theron, talking to his parents about Mara and about the death of the Magnus.

Jerry and Nerina Panago had been more than a little flummoxed to be hosting the Regulus—former or no—in their humble home, but they were as gracious and accommodating as ever. Before arriving, Theron had been adamant they could be trusted implicitly and wanted Aurianna to relate her experiences with the Essence to them.

If anyone would believe her, it would be the Panagos. They were devoutly religious and had raised their son to be as well. And the incident in his childhood had thoroughly sealed the deal for the three of them, particularly Theron. He had once shown her the necklace he always wore, featuring a symbol which represented the five Essence. Five as one, he had called it.

Thinking of that piece of jewelry brought her mind to the one she'd lost, the necklace which had once belonged to her mother. Ethan had recognized it on her when she first arrived in the past, but Aurianna had never mentioned it to Syrena. Considering the reason she had lost it, she wondered why she felt any guilt at all.

She focused now on Syrena and Ethan. She had peripherally been aware of them staring at her the whole time they'd been outside, but neither had spoken a word.

Aurianna cleared her throat, gathering her nerve. "I think I should tell you something. I had a necklace. Larissa gave it to me. She said it belonged to you, and Ethan confirmed it."

Syrena nodded. "The one with the dark stone in it."

"Yes, well. See, I was wearing it the night we were on the train, and one of the kidnappers the Magnus hired—"

"I told you, I wasn't on that train, child."

"Stop calling me *child*!" Aurianna felt her temperature rise. Out of the corner of her eye, she noticed her raised volume had captured the attention of the people inside. "And I know what I saw. You *were* on the train, whether you remember or not. I lost the necklace because I was trying to stop you." In her agitation, she had to stand. "It doesn't really matter now. I just thought you should know."

Without waiting for a reply, she stormed off into the house, almost colliding with Laelia. The other girl stopped her and wrapped her hands around Aurianna's upper arms—careful to avoid the stitches. She forced their eyes to meet. "What's wrong?"

Aurianna dejectedly shook her head, unsure of how to respond. What *wasn't* wrong?

Laelia continued. "Well, I just checked on Belinda. She's napping on the couch now. I don't trust her not to run away if she gets the chance, so we'll have to set a watch on her."

"Do we have the right to keep her?"

"What do you mean?"

"I mean, she's practically an adult. And she's pregnant, which kind of bumps the whole argument up a notch. What she does is her business, isn't it?"

Laelia clenched her jaw. "Normally I'd agree with you, but this isn't *normal*. That baby isn't *normal*, and for more reasons than we even know, I'd guess. I think it's important we get answers first. Maybe it's not fair, but it is what it is. The Panagos are gathering clothes and food for us." She watched Aurianna for another few seconds before relaxing her grip. "We need to start loading everything up. I'll let them know." She nodded to indicate the couple outside and passed Aurianna to join them on the porch.

In the main room, Theron was showing Pharis something on the wall. Rhouth lay curled up like a baby in his arms.

As she got closer, she realized what it was. "This is the *arrrgh* map you were telling us about?" She smiled at the memory.

Pharis furrowed his eyebrows. "The what?"

"You know, like pirates and such? We were poking fun at Theron when he mentioned it one day. He'd been drinking a good bit, so I wasn't sure if he was being serious or not."

Theron pouted a bit. "Well, I was. This is it. Framed and all, just like I said."

"And you have no idea where it came from or what it is?" Aurianna glanced over to where his parents were busy pulling down storage trunks from an attic overhead, sifting through the contents. "Should we be helping—"

A gasp behind her interrupted her question. Aurianna turned to see Syrena standing with a hand covering her open mouth and eyes wide in shock. Beside her, Ethan and Laelia seemed just as confused as the rest of them. Rhouth jumped down from Theron's arms and ran over to Syrena, eager to join in whatever the excitement was.

Syrena pointed at the map accusingly. "Where did you get that?"

Nerina dropped the pile of clothing in her hands and walked over, confusion clear on her face. "My mother said she bought it from someone a long time ago, and my father had it framed for her. It's been in my family ever since. Why?"

Syrena's face looked ashen. "I've seen it before."

Nerina shrugged. "I'm sure the peddler had loads of copies. But they claimed it was 'one of a kind' or whatever. My mother was the type to fall for something like that, I'm afraid."

"Mom, what's wrong?" Aurianna awaited an answer to her question then realized everyone, including Syrena, was staring at her. A second later, she realized what she had said and blushed profusely. Amending her statement, she said, "Can you tell us what it is, Syrena?"

Her mother nodded, shock giving way to excitement and wonder as she looked at her daughter. "I can tell you exactly what it is. And you were right. Things do seem to fall right into your lap, don't they?"

"Excuse me?"

"I mean this is exactly what you were searching for, Aurianna."

"What?"

"A map."

"Yes, I can see it's a map. But a map to where? It doesn't look like anything."

Syrena shook her head and beamed at her daughter. "Because it's not to any place you've ever seen." Leaning forward, she dropped her voice to a whisper. "It's a map to the Fae."

CHAPTER 16

SIGI

The neighs and whinnies from a riled animal echoed around the clifftop.

That horse is pissed off.

As Sigi approached her friends, the strident tones were enough to get them all caught and imprisoned.

Again.

Since her departure from the others, a plan must have been put into place because an airship was hovering just below the edge of the cliffs. Theron was standing within the edge of the forest, waving her over, but Sigi had slowed her horse to a walk to better take in the scene.

Oracle was standing in the middle of the ship as Aurianna attempted to soothe the frightened animal. Argo, the same Aerokinetic who had helped them in the past, was trying to help her pull a blanket over the horse's eyes, but Sigi suspected it was a little late for that.

Sigi and Leon had been riding nonstop since Rasenforst. She

had left Hilda and Sebastian with her father and brothers, and they had decided to visit a distant relative. Hilda had been livid at being left behind, but Sigi needed to be certain the girl was safe. That her family was safe.

Once plans had been finalized, they had agreed to meet at a discreet location behind the stables in Menos. Since they'd had no idea where they would be going next, or how they'd get there, the forested area which jutted up to the back of stables seemed the safest bet for a meetup spot.

"You think we could maybe hurry on over there so I can get off this damn creature?" Leon's voice in her ear made her jump. As she sped the animal's pace, she heard him chuckle. "Did you forget I was here or something, darlin'?"

"Perhaps I did for a moment?"

"I'm hurt." Sigi could hear the pout in his voice, but it was laced with amusement.

Now that they were closer, Sigi could see Laelia and Pharis standing against a rail of the airship. Syrena and Ethan, who were watching over a disgruntled and pregnant Belinda, had yet to board.

As Leon dismounted, Theron hissed, "Some locals told my parents that guards have been sent to the regions. At this point, they could be anywhere."

"Where are we going then?" Leon asked.

"I'll explain when we're all aboard. We need to go before someone spots the *Minya* and Argo gets into a lot of trouble for helping us."

Sigi returned their mount to the stables. By the time she returned, Argo had brought the airship up to the edge of the land long enough for them all to board. As soon as everyone—including Oracle—was settled, he steered them away from Menos and off across Perdita Bay.

Sidling up to Aurianna, Sigi stared at her friend until the other girl finally spoke. "Yes, I realize it's a bit ridiculous. But I wasn't leaving without Oracle. You warned your family and got them to safety. She's all I have. I couldn't leave her behind."

A pang of sympathy washed over Sigi, and she dropped her voice to a whisper. "But you do have family now, Aurianna."

"No, I—"

"It's just a fact. You don't have to accept them or have a relationship, but you do need to be honest with yourself."

They stared at one another for a moment before Aurianna nodded. "Yeah, you're right." She gestured at Oracle. "Blanket seems to have calmed her down a little, but at least it's not a long ride."

"What's the plan? Theron wouldn't tell us anything back there."

"Theron's right here. Ask away." The hunter's deep voice was just behind them, Leon at his side. "It's a long story but, suffice it to say, we know where the Fae might be located."

Sigi narrowed her eyes. "How?"

Aurianna sighed. "I mean, you've always known where Fae territory was, mythically speaking. Javen—" The word left her mouth before she realized. Pausing a moment to clear her throat, she continued. "He told me the forest behind Vanito was unofficially called Fae territory."

Sigi leaned against the railing of the airship, disbelief lacing her thoughts. "Yeah, but surely if something were beyond Vanito, someone would have found it. Although it is a huge area."

Theron beamed. "Well, it helps we now have a map."

"What map?" Leon stared about as the others formed a semicircle around them.

"Remember when we were at the pub in Bramosia?" Aurianna asked. "And Theron mentioned his parents had a pirate map or something?"

"You're saying a pirate map leads to the Fae?" Skepticism dripped from Sigi's words.

"No, I'm saying a Fae map leads to the Fae. It's not a pirate map. In fact, it doesn't really look like a map. More like a bunch of random landmarks. There's writing as well. Syrena's trying to decipher it."

Leon's eyes had widened further as the conversation progressed. "What do you mean?"

"It's written in the old language—which apparently is Fae."

"And your mother can read it?" Awe transformed his face as Leon glanced over his shoulder to a corner of the ship where Syrena and Ethan sat cross-legged, staring at a piece of paper spread out in her lap—presumably, the map in question.

"I mean, my people were able to read a few words of it. I told you about my brand. Surely someone—"

Sigi grimaced and shook her head.

"You're telling me no one else can read the old language?"

Sigi shrugged and pushed herself off the railing to stand back beside Aurianna. "I guess maybe the Arcanes? But it's not taught to anyone."

"She said she grew up with Larissa, and Larissa taught it to her."

Laelia pursed her lips, tapping her finger against them. "Did your aunt ever mention it?"

"That she watched my mother grow up? I mean, I kind of assumed something along those lines, or else why would Larissa give up everything to save me?"

"No, Aurianna. I mean about reading the Fae language. Did she ever mention it?"

Aurianna shook her head. "But it's not the sort of thing to come up very often."

Lost in thought for a moment, Laelia finally shrugged. "I don't know. It's all just incredibly weird."

"Welcome to my world, where weird happens every day."

Sigi scanned the group and grinned. "Happy to be along for the ride."

Aurianna frowned at those words.

Before Sigi could inquire what was wrong, Ethan called over to tell them Syrena had deciphered part of the map. They crowded around the woman. Argo pretended to be focused on steering the ship, but it was obvious he was curious too.

Was it possible—truly possible—the Fae actually existed? Syrena seemed so sure, and yet...

She had been on the train with Aurianna. Aurianna was sure of it. No matter who the woman was, they still didn't know enough about her to be certain they could trust her.

Ethan was holding the map up against his body so everyone could see while Syrena pointed out a large section of text. "This part is what I've been focusing on, since it seems to be the most important message."

"What makes you think that?" Pharis asked.

"Well, for one, it's the largest block of text on the page. Also, it's prominent, like it represents the map as a whole, as opposed to some of these other, smaller phrases. Most of the rest are just that—small phrases or even single words. You'd think those would be easier to translate, but none of them make any sense to me. I don't recognize most of the words, so maybe they're place names or something. But this part"—she jabbed a finger at the larger section again—"I was able to translate. It's a poem of sorts."

The group held their breath, waiting for the woman to continue speaking. After a moment, a voice from the left called, "Well, what does it say?" Argo had crept over while Syrena had been explaining. His eyes glittered with curiosity.

Syrena's eyes crinkled with amusement and warmth. Argo had

that effect on people. "The old language doesn't always have exact translations, but roughly it says: *Moonlight upon the trees. Bells toll the circle round. Lost inside to time. Invisible to an outside face.*"

No one spoke for a moment. Finally, Leon blurted, "What the hell does that even mean?"

Syrena shrugged. "No idea. Something to do with Fae magic, perhaps? Moonlight is important to them. Not sure about the bells or the rest of it. I'm hoping we'll figure it out when we get there."

"Sure. Yeah." Leon sauntered off with Laelia. The rest wandered away one by one, lost in their own thoughts.

A group of young Kinetics was cliff diving in the distance. Sigi once again thought of what her life should look like, all the things her sister too should be experiencing in her final years as a Younger.

Sigi wanted to teach her so many things—about boys, and makeup, and how to fire a weapon properly. Sure, others could show her how to choose the correct color of eyeshadow or how to breathe—*just so*—when finding your target. But she wanted to be there for Hilda's first crush, her first heartbreak, her first Yule Ball.

Sigi had loved her job, loved being a member of the City Guard. But that life was dead to her now. No matter what happened next, nothing would be the same again. She couldn't even truthfully promise her father she would be okay.

Even if they managed to make it through this alive, her life would be different. She had never had time for anything outside friends and work. Romance wasn't exactly forbidden for Kinetics, but the idea of starting a family intrigued her. When all of this was over, would that still be forbidden?

Sigi was used to being among men who admired her ability to shoot better than any of them. Yet no one admired her in other ways. The closest she had come was that ridiculous poem, but that had obviously been a prank on the part of a resistance member. Evidently, no one who truly knew her ever thought of her in that way.

As a guardswoman, her fellow male guards had always treated her like one of them, a fact for which she was normally grateful.

And yet...

* * *

The path wound through the strange forest in a seemingly endless pattern of curves and straightaways.

The group had landed on the far side of the landmass on which Vanito was typically the only destination. Argo had flown off after leaving them on the outskirts of the vast woods, an area usually left unmarked and unlabeled on maps.

Except for the one in Theron's hands.

Only it didn't even look like a map. No paths or directions were indicated. It just had vague drawings of landmarks, which seemed like they'd been drawn by a small child and which could refer to any number of the trees or rocks they'd passed.

None of it made any sense.

"This doesn't feel right at all," Laelia whispered. "I think we might be going in circles." She waved her hand vaguely then dropped it with a sigh.

"Can't be. We haven't left the path since we found it," Sigi replied matter-of-factly.

"Why does that matter? Don't you get it? We are in Fae territory here, sister. There are no rules. At least, not the kind we're used to."

"Yeah, okay. Point taken." After a pause, Sigi added, "But I still don't think we're going in circles. This seems... tactical."

"What do you mean?" Aurianna asked.

The group halted to stare around and up to the canopy through which only a glimmer of light could penetrate. The last tendrils of sunlight attempted to snake their way through the overhanging green to display a rainbow assortment of flora. Large blossoms interspersed with delicate buds in red, pink, violet, lavender, yellow, and impossibly bright white.

Sigi tore her eyes from the sight and the overwhelming desire to touch the beautiful petals. "I mean, look around us. All of this is meant to keep us—humans—out. If we were going in circles, at least one of us would recognize something familiar. At least, I know I would. Being observant is a big part of my job. But it doesn't mean magic isn't at work here. The Fae could be leading us through an illusion."

Aurianna seemed to consider this for a moment, then asked, "You suggest all of this could be meant to keep us out. How?"

"I don't know. I just . . . Well, aren't you getting an unsettling vibe?"

With a huffed laugh, Leon sarcastically agreed. "Yeah, we are in Fae lands. It's all kinda unsettling."

Sigi shook her head. "No. I mean yes, that's true. But that's not what I meant. Not exactly. It's more than just an aura of magic. It's..." She trailed off as she glanced around them again.

"The forest," Syrena said knowingly, gazing about at their surroundings.

Leon raised his eyebrows, eyes wide and questioning. "Yes, we are in a forest."

Syrena continued after a moment's pause, trying to find the right words. "It's the forest itself. It almost seems alive, don't you think? Like we're intruding, and it wants to keep us out."

Sigi nodded her agreement. "Exactly. Can't everyone feel it? Like it's trying to get into your head."

Pharis hitched his bag up on his shoulder irritably. "Okay, so maybe something doesn't want to let us in. What in the name of the Essence do we do about it? We can't turn around, for multiple reasons. If we can't continue forward, and we can't go back, what can we do?"

Sigi could sense his growing frustration—everyone's frustration. It mirrored her own. But she had no answer.

Aurianna stomped over to Theron who was trying to make sense of the map for the hundredth time. Rhouth lingered by his feet, weaving in and out between his legs impatiently. The fox had been sticking even closer than usual to her master as they made their way through the forest.

Oracle had been intractable as they'd approached the outer edge of the forest, sweating, shying, and rearing. They'd had no choice but to leave her in a nearby meadow to graze. Aurianna was sure the horse wouldn't run off, but Sigi wasn't convinced. At least they knew she wouldn't follow them into the forest after the fit she'd thrown.

"Let me see it." Aurianna took the paper right out of his hands, causing Theron to gasp in surprise. As he started to protest, she hushed him. Despite their current situation, Sigi giggled, hiding her smile behind her hand before anyone noticed.

Pharis walked over to Aurianna. "What is it?"

"I don't know." She was squinting at the map and gnawing on her bottom lip. "I think I've seen this rock formation before."

"We haven't seen any rocks."

"Not here. Somewhere else."

"You're telling me we're in the wrong place?" Leon snapped. Tempers had been flaring for a while, but things seemed to be reaching a breaking point.

Aurianna shook her head. "No, that wouldn't make any sense. The rocks I'm thinking of are—"

"Does anyone else hear that?" Pharis's voice had taken on a sense of wonder.

169

"Hear what?" Sigi asked.

"The music. It sounds like—"

"I don't hear anything." Aurianna sounded as apprehensive as Sigi felt. What was he talking about?

Laelia's eye widened. "I hear it too. Someone singing."

Aurianna shook her head. "Laelia, no one is singing. I think you're hearing things."

But Pharis and Laelia had already started wondering off the path, faces lifted to the canopy above them. They weren't even watching where they were walking.

"No!" Aurianna yelled. "Both of you need to stay with the group. Please don't do this now." She shared a look with Sigi and the rest of her friends.

"You don't hear it?" Ethan asked Syrena in a dreamy voice.

Syrena was too late to stop him before he took off after the other two. "Not you too." Syrena huffed as he disappeared into the dark forest.

"Where's Belinda?" Aurianna asked suddenly.

Sigi spun around. "She was right here a moment ago."

"Define *a moment*, Sigi."

"I don't know! This whole damn place is making me think I'm losing my mind."

As Theron's eyes began to glaze over with the same starry-eyed expression as the others, Syrena clutched his arm. Rhouth snarled at the woman, her teeth bared, but Syrena ignored the little creature. "I don't think we can question this being Fae magic at this point."

Sigi agreed. "Maybe we should just follow them and see where they go."

"I thought leaving the path was a bad idea! And what about Belinda?" Aurianna shrieked.

"She must have followed the others before we noticed. They

went through there." Without hesitating any longer, Sigi led them through the dense underbrush between the trees. The branches scratched at their exposed skin like otherworldly fingernails, giving Sigi chills. Ignoring the sensation, she pushed on, peering back occasionally to make sure the others were still behind her.

Theron was trying to pull ahead, but Syrena had a lock on his wrist. Sigi felt a twinge in her gut at the intimacy of the contact. Rhouth kept jumping up trying to get her master's notice, but when he didn't pay attention to her, she just followed behind the group, whimpering.

When they reached a large open clearing, their missing group members were nowhere to be seen. In the middle of the space was a ring of lush green. The last rosy glow of sunset was gone, and the canopy had opened to reveal a full moon, its light shining down on the circle of grass.

At the edges of the circle were small footprints that could not have belonged to anyone in their group. They were small, bare, and had longer toes than those of a human.

Sigi threw her hands up in despair. "I don't understand. Even if they were running at full speed, we should have caught sight of them here. There's plenty of moonlight. But it's like they disappeared."

Aurianna was spinning around in a circle, clearly agitated. Sigi regretted her words, wishing she felt more optimistic about their situation. "I'm sorry, Aurianna. I didn't mean to upset you. I'm just not sure what to do now."

Aurianna shook her head emphatically. "No. I think I understand."

"Huh?"

"The poem. The one Syrena translated."

Syrena furrowed her brow. "What about it?"

"*Moonlight upon the trees. Bells toll the circle round. Lost inside to time. Invisible to an outside face.* Don't you see? Moonlight!" She pointed up to the sky above them.

"Yeah, but moonlight isn't just in one place, is it? It's everywhere."

"Not in here. We haven't seen the sky beyond the trees since we entered the main part of the forest."

"Yes, I think you're right!" Syrena exclaimed, releasing Theron's wrist in her excitement.

Sigi grabbed his hand before he could get far. Frustration and impatience were building within her chest. "Great. Okay. So what? What do you mean?"

"Let him go." Syrena was regarding her expectantly.

"Excuse me?"

"Let him go, Sigi." Aurianna repeated her mother's words.

"Is that code for something?" Frustration morphed into anger. "Are the two of you under some kind of spell as well? What are you talking about?"

Aurianna bit her lip and gestured to Theron. "Let go of him, Sigi. Let's see what he does."

"If I let go of him, he'll take off."

"I don't think so."

"And why is that?"

"Because, like you said, if the others were still on the move, we would have seen them heading into the woods on the other side of the clearing."

"What?"

"Just ... Just trust me, okay?"

At the note of pleading in Aurianna's voice, Sigi's irritation deflated. She dropped Theron's hand.

Eyes still wide and glassy, but with a hint of a smile on his lips, Theron advanced into the circle of grass as if drawn by an unseen rope. Rhouth followed at his heels.

And they...vanished.

"What just happened?" Sigi cried in confusion and shock.

"The words on the map were a warning as much as a clue, I think," Syrena reflected pensively then quoted the poem. "*Lost inside to time.* Time could mean so many different things. But *bells toll the circle round.*" She shook her head. "I'm betting the bells are part of whatever it is they are hearing."

"Okay, but why only them? Why not us?"

"I have no idea."

"Where did they go? How do we find them?"

"I don't think they went anywhere. I think they're right in front of us."

"Wait, what? Nothing's there." She looked confused for a moment then continued to quote the poem. "*Invisible to an outside face.* You think they're—" Sigi stopped midsentence. "You think they're invisible. Do you think they can see us?"

"I don't know. If they're 'lost inside to time,' there's no telling what might be happening to them."

"Then we need to follow and help them!"

Aurianna took her mother's hand tentatively, followed by Sigi's. "Agreed. It's all or nothing."

With a deep breath, the three of them stepped into the ring.

Everything shifted. The trees grew closer. The moonlight faded.

And their friends were standing on the far side of the glade. They must still be under the spell, as they all stood frozen in place. The clearing and the forest had changed a bit, but their location was basically the same.

Sigi, Aurianna, and Syrena ran up to the others. Sigi approached Theron, who stood near the back of the group. Walking around to face him, she knew something was wrong. His glazed look had been replaced with fear. What could terrify Theron so?

Sigi slowly turned around.

On the hill just ahead, amid a copse of tall trees, stood a moonlit figure.

Impossible. The moonlight could barely reach through the thick canopy above. Then Sigi realized the light around the form was, in fact, emanating from within. It was glowing.

Impossible.

She looked over to Aurianna, who stood on the other side of Theron, gazing up at the same hill.

Forcing her gaze back to the impossibility before them, Sigi watched as the creature came closer, the light growing brighter as it moved.

Then she noticed five others on the hill, standing in a line. Suddenly, all of them lit up the forest with their ethereal glow, allowing Sigi to distinguish their features. She gasped.

They were shorter than any adult person she had ever known, even shorter than herself. Their arms and legs were somewhat spindly, their glowing skin a coppery hue. Much of that skin was exposed, as the creatures wore little clothing compared to the humans. The females wore short pants with a sleeveless top, their midriffs bare. The males wore similar short pants but were shirtless. All of them—male and female—were barefoot. But none of that was what made her gasp.

Every one of them had flaming red hair. The intensity of the color made Syrena's appear almost dull by comparison.

Sigi had barely registered these details before the creature in the middle—who appeared to be female—spoke. The words were foreign but musically mesmerizing.

When no one responded, the entity spoke in the common language. "The queen wishes to speak with the trespassers. You will place your hands above your heads, and we will escort you to the palace. There you will be made ready for an audience with Her Majesty." With a nod to their right, the female added, "Except for that one. She will not be allowed into the sacred city."

Glancing past Theron and the others, Sigi noted Belinda standing off to the side of the group. It was she who the entity had indicated. The girl was beyond frightened, tears rolling down her cheeks. She held a hand over her swollen stomach.

Sigi found her voice and asked, "Why? Why would she not be allowed?"

The Fae—for indeed, what else could these creatures be?—turned to Sigi, eyes alight and intense. The golden glow of her skin also shone from her eyes, a terrifying yet familiar sight which brought everyone's attention back to Aurianna.

Pharis looked dazed, his mouth slack and eyes a bit too wide. Syrena was nodding as if a great mystery had been solved. The others were looking back and forth between their friend and the Fae before them.

Aurianna seemed too stunned by everything to realize everyone was gaping at her and her mother. She remained completely focused on the Fae.

Sigi refocused, and when the female spoke again, Sigi saw her teeth. They were sharp, which was more than a bit disconcerting.

"She carries that which should not be. And it will not be allowed within our borders."

Aurianna's voice rang out. "Well, we're not coming with you unless Belinda comes as well. I'm not leaving her here. You can lock her up somewhere and keep a guard on her. Just don't mistreat her."

The Fae's smile widened, exposing more of her teeth. "I think you misunderstand, child of the dirt. You are *all* our prisoners."

Aurianna swallowed audibly. "Fine." The rest of their group

gaped at her words. Pharis opened his mouth to speak, but she cut him off. "But she comes with us, or we don't go."

"Again, you're confused about your options here."

Another voice from the hill cut into the conversation. "Aurianna."

Sigi watched as her friend's face went deathly white. Her mouth opened, but no sound came out. She pushed her way past the others to stand at the bottom of the hill.

Finally, she stammered, "La-Larissa?"

Chapter 17

AURIANNA

As they were escorted through another portion of the forest, Aurianna pulled her power up from the depths, closing her eyes in concentration as she tried not to stumble.

But it was no use. Something about this place kept their powers in check. The attempt was enough to unbalance her. Dizziness and nausea, which had plagued her since she was injured at the rebel's hideout, continued to well up from time to time. The wound was no longer swollen or red, but the healing was a slow process.

The trees they passed were illuminated by small orbs that clung to the branches, the source of the light a mystery to Aurianna. It was neither Fire, nor Energy. Nothing about any of this was normal, but the soft glow emanating from all around them brought more questions than answers.

The Fae had confiscated their weapons, leaving her feeling vulnerable and exposed to this dreamworld they were walking into.

"Larissa" had not met her eyes again after speaking her name. Aurianna was confused and devastated.

This couldn't be her Larissa—the woman who had raised her. This Larissa was one of *them*. Her form was Fae—her limbs lean and thin, red hair flowing behind her as she led them through the forest. She also looked quite youthful. *Her* Larissa had been middle-aged—slightly soft in the middle, of average human height, with brown hair that was starting to gray. And her eyes had been nothing out of the ordinary, nothing spectacular.

Yet the voice was the same. The look she had given Aurianna and Syrena made it clear she knew who they were.

But how?

How could Larissa be here? How could she be Fae? None of it made any sense.

Looking over, she saw the wide-eyed and shaking form of Belinda. Aurianna had refused to follow the Fae unless they brought her along. Every Fae weapon was trained on the frightened girl as they made their way, but at least she hadn't been left behind in the maze of forest.

They reached another open area surrounded by trees. These trees were different, however. They were broad and strong, their branches far above and loaded with what appeared to be dwellings. Their Fae guards took them past these trees to a much larger structure on the ground.

This must be the palace. Aurianna squirmed as they approached, both anxious to meet the queen of the Fae and desperate to get away. These woods gave her an eerie sensation which ran though her whole body.

They entered the large building through the main entrance. The guards then directed them to an archway which accessed a long dark tunnel.

One of the Fae stopped at a door and said, "These rooms are where you will prepare yourself for an audience with the queen.

Males to the left, females to the right. The one with the spawn will be taken to a cell."

Aurianna heard a gasp behind her. She scowled. "You can't put a pregnant woman in a cell. When I said lock her up, I meant a room not a prison."

"She will not be mistreated."

Aurianna noticed her friends all seemed to be in a daze. She shrugged, allowing herself to be escorted through the door.

Once Sigi, Laelia, and Syrena had joined her, the guards closed the door. Aurianna studied the space before her. Multiple rooms branched off to either side, with a main sitting area in the middle. The benches for seating encircled a massive tree trunk which dominated the middle of the room. The sight was a wonder, but she didn't have long to admire it.

A soft knock at the door announced visitors who promptly entered without waiting for an invitation. Eight tiny female Fae filed into the room, one after the other, carrying buckets, brushes, clothing, and other items Aurianna couldn't identify.

One of them spoke. "We are to prepare you to meet the queen. She insists you be scrubbed clean before entering her chambers."

"What, does she think we're dirty or something?" Laelia was indignant until she scanned herself and the others. "Okay, maybe we are."

Each of the women was led into a separate bathing room. Aurianna assured the two females who had followed her, "I can bathe on my own, thanks."

Both shook their heads, one of them replying, "No, you must strip down and be scrubbed. Then we have been instructed to bring Larissa in to see you."

"Who instructed you to get her?"

"She did."

179

"Oh." It didn't seem worth a fight, and she really did feel a bit grubby, so she allowed them to help her bathe and dress. When they were finished, they left to get her aunt.

Or whoever she was.

Stepping over to a mirror in the corner, Aurianna admired the gown the attendants had given her to wear. Considering the diminutive frames of the Fae, she wondered where the human-sized clothing had come from.

A moment later, Larissa—this version of her—poked her head through the door. "Can I come in?" Without waiting for an answer, she closed the door behind her and stood staring at Aurianna's reflection, her arms crossed. "I can't believe it."

"Can't believe what?" Aurianna whirled around to face her. "I think that should be my line, don't you think?"

"I thought I'd never see you again."

"You've never seen me before. You are not my aunt, no matter what you're doing to try to look like her."

"I am she, child. Just not the one you knew."

"What does that mean? There's more than one of you?"

"Yes. Let me explain."

"Please do." Aurianna sat on the edge of the tub.

"I failed you. Or another version of you, I guess. You were unsuccessful in stopping the singularity, and I finally realized what needed to be done. But I broke a cardinal rule in the process. I was never supposed to interact with another version of me, let anyone try to influence the timeline. But I intercepted myself—the next version of myself—who was set to take off with you into the future. You were just a babe in her arms, but I warned her of what you would become, of what we all stood to lose. And why you would fail."

"And why exactly is that?"

"Because you could not control your emotions. You were always emotional—too emotional. You were angry all the time, and you failed to control it. I knew part of you could not be changed, as it is a vital part of who you are. But you did need to learn to control it. Had it not been for a particular conversation I had with Simon in the future, I might never have realized this."

"Simon?"

"Yes. Simon has always kept a close eye on you, and he became one of my closest friends. He was telling me about one of your outbursts with him, and I recalled how certain things would always trigger an emotional response, more than was often warranted in those situations. You had such a temper, always going off before you had a chance to think things through. And I realized I had failed to teach you patience."

"My temper is the reason for all of this?"

"I'm not saying that. I'm just saying—because I hadn't instilled them in you—you lacked the tools to deal with certain situations effectively. Believe it or not, I'm not exactly a role model for patience and calm, Aurianna. My sister was the kind one. I was always a bit of a hothead."

"You?"

"Yes, indeed. I can't imagine how difficult it was for my other self to learn self-control while also trying to teach it to you."

"You—She hid it well. Auntie was always so composed. Even when she was fussing at me about something, her emotions always seemed unruffled."

The Fae Larissa laughed until tears formed in the corners of her eyes. She wiped them away and continued her story. "So, I told my younger self to focus on that, to do whatever she could do to ensure you grew up with those checks in place."

"Where exactly are we? How did *you* get here? Why aren't you in the future?"

LISA M. GREEN

"I am. Well, she is. Your Larissa is still in the future, waiting on you. I crossed the timelines. Fae do not need Aether Stones to travel through time, and we do not forget. Like the Arcanes, we know of every failure, every change to the timeline and every alternate version of it. But this is not my version of the timeline. In my version, you did not stop the singularity. But the queen gave me permission to live out the rest of my days back here among my people. I admit, despite my warning to . . . myself, I had little hope things would turn out differently. Yet here we are."

"But who, exactly, are you?" Aurianna asked, indignation rising to the surface. "And how are you a-a . . ."

"Fae?" Larissa smiled, the gesture familiar and yet terrifying with those razor-sharp teeth. "I always have been. You and Syrena only ever saw me in my other form. We are shape-shifters."

"Why did you never tell me?"

"What? Tell you I was Fae? Do I really have to explain that to you?"

"You lied to me!"

"I withheld a truth." She raised a hand as Aurianna started to protest. "I didn't tell you a number of truths, actually. But it was always for good reason. You trusted me because I took care of you and always did what I thought best for you. I may not be *your* Larissa, but I was there for you in another time. Right now, I need you to trust me and let me help you."

"Help me how?"

"You are Syrena's daughter."

"So I've been told. What's your point?"

"Syrena has two distinctive traits." Larissa peered at her meaningfully.

"Is someone going to explain why her hair looks like all of yours?"

"It's not just her hair."

"That's not an answer."

"You don't want it to be true, but that doesn't make it false. Her hair is only part of the story. You both have eyes the color of honey amber. Your skin might not glow, but your eyes certainly do."

"Pretend I'm stupid for a moment because right now I'd rather just hear you say it."

"Syrena is part Fae."

"Which means..." The dizziness was threatening to engulf her again. Somehow, none of this was a complete surprise, but hearing it confirmed was almost more than Aurianna could take.

"You are as well, though to a lesser degree. But you are also something more."

"More than what?"

"I was Syrena's nursemaid because her mother was my sister. Syrena believes she's from Menos because that's where she grew up and was raised. Her father was a human from Rasenforst, though she never knew him. So, *you* carry the genetic material of both human and Fae."

"How does that make me more? She's only half-human. If what you say is true, I'm three-quarters human, and that..." Larissa was shaking her head slowly as Aurianna trailed off. "Are you saying Ethan isn't my father?"

"No, I'm saying he's special in his own right."

"Voids are still human."

"Right. But how many Voids have fathered children?"

"It's not because they can't. Only because the Imperium forbids it."

"And why do you think that is, Aurianna?"

"I... don't know." She narrowed her eyes in suspicion. "What is it you want from me?"

"It's for your benefit I offer this. I need to color your hair."

"Why? The Fae queen isn't likely to fall for a cheap trick like that."

"It's not a trick. We're not trying to deceive her. But she is aware you are Syrena's daughter, and she is aware of who her mother was. She will expect your appearance to be more like ours. The queen will respect you more if you look like one of us."

"I'm not going to start this meeting off with a deception."

"It's not a deception. She will know full well it's not real."

"Then why?"

"Because it will allow her to speak to you of things which aren't spoken of outside our people."

"Then let Syrena do it. She already looks the part."

"The queen knows you, not Syrena, are their leader. She will not speak to anyone else. The others may join you if you are careful and they remain silent throughout the audience. None of the Fae will object to your friends' presence if they can clearly see that you, their leader and spokesperson, are Fae."

"I don't feel like playing political games right now."

Larissa snapped, "This *isn't* a game, and no one is playing. Either you do as I say, or you might as well have never come here in the first place. You won't get your answers." She squeezed her eyes shut before lowering her voice again. "It's not about games, Aurianna. It's about you demonstrating a respect for our customs and traditions. It doesn't matter that it's only for show. The show is what's important."

Aurianna stared at the door then huffed. "Fine. How permanent is this stuff?"

Larissa grinned. "A week. Maybe two."

Aurianna spun to face the mirror again, holding up a lock of her hair before sighing in resignation. She glanced back down at her gown, dropping her hand to stroke the soft fabric.

"Do you like it?" asked Larissa. "It was my sister's. Your grandmother's. Back when she lived in Menos in human form."

Aurianna smiled. "It *is* pretty, but I brought my own clothing."

"If you want to be seen as a leader, you must dress like one. For now, this will do. But I will have our seamstresses make you enough gowns to see you through your stay."

"And how long will that be?"

"As long as it takes, child."

* * *

Her friends couldn't stop staring at her, and it made her uncomfortable.

Aurianna had explained the plan to the girls as Larissa escorted them to where the men awaited them.

Pharis's expression was something between shock and interest, but he didn't comment.

Leon, however, had no such restraint.

"You heard I like redheads, didn't you?" he drawled as they followed the guards. He couldn't see the murderous glare Pharis was giving him behind his back.

She whispered, "Leon—everyone—I need you trust me on something. You *cannot* speak while we're in there. I don't care what they say or do. You have to let me be the one to interact with the queen. Larissa explained this is just protocol—the way things are done, and if we want help, we have to follow the rules." She didn't mention anything further from her conversation with her aunt.

"Is that why you look like that?" Pharis's voice was tight and strained.

Aurianna ignored him and continued to stare at the floor. They were ushered out the front of the building and around to the back.

The path continued through the looming trees, which grew closer together the farther they went.

Finally, they reached a small opening in the foliage. Up ahead, a tiny female sat regally upon a large throne framed by two tall scepters arising from the ground at her feet.

The tops of the scepters were each adorned with a giant purple stone, slightly rounded and smooth but still unmistakable.

Aether Stones.

The Fae queen, unlike the Magnus, wasn't playing games. Running up and down the back of the Fae queen's luxuriously carved throne were lines of small triangular stones of various colors. At the top sat another Aether Stone, lodged within a six-sided carving.

Unlike the other Fae, the queen was dressed in a long, flowing gown in a rich shade of emerald. She was royalty. She reveled in the power her position gave her and wanted there to be no doubt in anyone's mind that she was queen. She wore an elaborate tiara adorned with a dark-blue stone in its center.

Aurianna stumbled as they approached the throne.

A pair of guards stood with crossed spears but swung them to the side to allow the group entry.

The space was filled with Fae, all with bright-red hair. Apparently, their arrival was a bit of a curiosity to these beings.

The queen's gaze locked with Aurianna's as she came to a stop at the foot of the dais, their eyes telling one another a story before either spoke a word.

"You come before me today seeking answers."

The Fae's words didn't sound like a question, but Aurianna answered anyway. "Yes. We need your help, but I have so many questions. I don't even know where to start. I—"

The Fae queen interrupted her with a raised hand. "My name is

Treasa, and this is my domain, Ayshetha. We Fae are exceedingly long-lived, but we are not immortal. I have been queen of the Fae for a long time, but I know the ancient stories because, unlike your people, we are careful never to forget."

"What do you mean?"

"Eresseia was once much, much larger. A divide stirred up among the humans, and so, this world was sundered from the rest. The Fae were already living here as a group when that occurred, so this did not impact us greatly. But the humans who stayed were disconnected from much of the knowledge and history of the world."

"The others just left? Where did they go?"

"The world you know was once a part of a greater whole. Your human ancestors were in a great disagreement over many things, and they used magic to divide the land and separate from one another."

"You're saying parts of Eresseia exist elsewhere?"

"Perhaps." Treasa looked past Aurianna as she spoke, refusing to meet her eyes. "I do not know if it still exists, or if anyone still lives on a remote piece of land on the other side of the world. It would seem unlikely, and you'll soon understand why."

"Why would our people allow this history to be erased from the history books?"

"I do not know. Nor do I know the details of why they fought. I only know what happened before. Long ago, five deities known as the Essence ruled over the world."

"Do they not still rule?"

"Their powers are diminished, which is part of my story. In the beginning, the world was empty. What started as a point of light in the void of darkness became a vast planet, filled with vegetation and every manner of walking, crawling, swimming, and flying animal the five of them could conjure.

"Caelum, god of Air, created the winged creatures that used his winds to soar through the skies. From Terra, goddess of Earth, came all the beasts that walked on the ground or crawled beneath it. Unda, goddess of Water, filled the seas and lakes with all manner of swimming creatures, large and small.

"Caendra, goddess of Fire, and Fulmena, goddess of Energy—of lightning—were left with no clear domain in which to create and rule over life." The Fae queen sat back and closed her eyes. "So they conspired together to create a creature beyond any of those the other deities had made. Caendra gave the creature a piece of her power, the element of Fire. Fulmena used the pure power of lightning to imbue it with not only life but also sentience. And so, the first intelligent being beyond the gods themselves was created. Or so they thought."

"So they thought? It wasn't sentient then?" Aurianna could sense the unease of the others.

The queen shook her head. "No, it was. It was a strange entity, with the power of Caendra's Fire. And something else as well. In what they had thought was its normal form, it looked and spoke like the gods themselves, having limbs and smooth pale skin, eyes clear as glass and a tall, thin torso like Caelum's, the only other male at the time. But upon seeing the animals roaming the world, this new creature displayed an ability to morph into the shape of any one of them, much to Caendra and Fulmena's surprise, for they had not given it this power."

"Then where did the power come from?"

"Hush, child. I am speaking." Treasa's skin took on an ethereal glow. "All things will be answered in time."

"I do not have time! And I don't understand what this has to do with me or anything that's going on right now."

The queen leaned forward again, eyes blazing. "It has *everything* to do with you, and everything to do with what you have unleashed on this world."

Aurianna froze, stunned into silence. She had seen it, felt it—but hoped she was wrong.

"The Darkness," she whispered.

Ignoring her, the Fae queen continued. "The other deities were furious with them, especially with Caendra, who had given the power of Fire to the creature, a power meant only for a god or goddess. The Essence fought, and Caendra and Fulmena were eventually cast out from the Aether, the dwelling of the gods, to live among the animals and beside the being they had created. Over time, the two goddesses fell in love with the creature, whom they named Drakon. He convinced them to create more of his kind instead of fighting over him. And they did. In their zealous desire, they made two more like Drakon. And the result of their union with these creations was the race of beings you see before you."

The Fae.

The female nodded at Aurianna, as if she could read her thoughts. "After a long period had passed, the other gods sought to make amends with the outcast deities. They had seen the Fae and become desirous to create their own sentient race, one which would not have any of their powers but would have their likeness. Humanity was created from the elements of this world, a mixture of all five of the gods and their creative powers.

"Now that the Essence were reunited, the Aether was at peace, as was the world they had created and filled with so many beings. They named the world Eresseia. Caendra and Fulmena soon forgot about Drakon and his brothers, having become obsessed with the humans. All the deities began to spend more and more time in the world with their new creation, enthralled with its ability to create new and wondrous things with its immense imagination. Their dreams drew

189

the gods in, and eventually all of them fell in love with humans. The Essence never meant for humans to have powers like their own. But the offspring of these unions inherited a small measure of their powers, and the bloodlines were irreversibly intertwined."

Aurianna suddenly realized the queen was waiting on her to speak. "Kinetics."

"Yes."

"So why do some of us possess powers and others don't? And where do the Voids come into it?" Aurianna glanced behind her and saw her friends watching and listening in rapt attention to this story of the origin of their species.

Treasa replied, "These entities, the so-called Kinetics and Voids, are two sides of the same source—the Essence. When the Essence procreated with humans, they begat beings who were either wielders or wells of elemental power. Wielders of this power are now referred to as Kinetics. Wells, who contain bits of elemental source, are referred to as Voids.

"Over time, these beings interbred with the original creations of the Essence, who had been given none of these powers. These unions produce progeny who may be born a wielder or a well or neither. Humans who are neither wielder nor well you call a non-Kinetic."

"You say the Essence didn't intend for their creations to possess these powers. Is that why it is forbidden for Kinetics and Voids to procreate?"

"Your leaders did, at some point, realize the outcome," Treasa said. "But whether the Essence manipulated them into creating those rules prohibiting such unions in order limit the strength of these powers, I do not know."

"So how does that relate back to the other creatures—the ones created by Caendra and Fulmena?"

"The Fae had long since retreated to the depths of the forest. Meanwhile Drakon and his brothers saw the Essence's new obsession and became enraged with jealousy. They and their offspring had been forgotten.

"But even the gods themselves did not know the whole story. Caendra and Fulmena believed they had created Drakon when, in fact, they had merely opened a rift in the veil between worlds, allowing creatures from the Nether—the realm of demons—into Eresseia. Drakon and his kind were in fact demons brought over and imbued with the power of Fire by Caendra. Fulmena's lightning accentuated this power and provided other . . . interesting abilities for their children." She held up her arm and a soft glow began to hum across the female's skin. "Shape-shifting was their natural ability, one all demons possessed. In anger, they shed the form they had used to trick the goddesses and took on their true forms, exposing what they were to the gods and unleashing their power on them. The five deities fought back, killing all of Drakon's brothers with the help of the Fae."

"You helped them?"

"Drakon and his brothers may have been our fathers, but they were demons. My predecessors were horrified by their parentage. Their wrath brought out their innate powers, for the Fae retain the powers of both the gods and the demons. Having the ability to control the elements as well as shape-shift allowed them to defeat all but one of the demons, Drakon himself. They did this by sending the other demons back through a Nether rift. They created this rift—this passage—by combining forces with the gods to steal the stone Drakon wore upon his brow."

"Is that what we call the Aether Stones?"

Treasa shook her head. "Aether Stones were created when this world was formed. Like I said, the Essence became obsessed with

191

the humans and wanted them to travel back and forth from their realm. They weren't originally intended to be used for time travel. A Nether Stone is similar, but they are not of Eresseia. Drakon was wearing it when he was pulled from his home world."

"You have Aether Stones here now. Where did you get them?"

"They were gifts from the Essence, though we do not need them for time travel. The magic we possess from our Essence heritage suffices."

"Why do you keep them here then?"

The queen sneered. "As a reminder of what we stand to lose."

"What *do* we stand to lose?"

"Everything." Treasa gestured broadly to the gathered assembly. "But you must know the whole story in order to realize what that truly means."

"You were speaking of the Nether Stone."

"Yes, the stone opens a Nether rift, a black void. It is a one-way gateway to the Nether which is opened with a Nether Stone and the power of the demons themselves, power the Fae inherited from them. Drakon escaped by flying far across the ocean to an island. The ocean you know as the Mare Dolor.

"The gods followed him, leaving the safety of the Aether. Again they fought him, but Drakon managed to capture Caelum, the god of Air, temporarily absorbing a small amount of his power and locking him in a cage crafted of all of the elements. This severed a piece of the bond between the deities and trapped the four goddesses in the Aether, unable to return to Eresseia to save their brother. It also diminished Caelum's power within the world, drastically reducing the number of humans born with Aerokinetic abilities."

"But I've seen the Essence. Here. In this world."

"No, child. You have seen their likeness. A piece of themselves they are projecting—not their true form."

"So that's why everyone is at odds and why so few Aerokinetics exist?"

The queen inclined her head. "And thus it shall remain. Until the prophecy is fulfilled and the demon is defeated, Caelum will remain imprisoned and the world divided."

"Demon, you call him. This word means nothing to me. You mentioned their true form. What is their true form?"

"Legend holds the story of where it came from, just as I am telling it to you. Drakon's world is one of fire and ash, the sky blotted by smoke and soot. In their true form, he and his brethren were capable of spewing fiery storms of destruction down upon their enemies. Humans would call it a dragon."

Ice inched up Aurianna's spine, and she was dimly aware of her body and breathing, but it felt distant and fuzzy. Finally, she whispered, "Why are you telling me this?"

"You asked for answers, child."

"But what does any of this have to do with me or everything going on right now?"

"You're asking me how a dragon has anything to do with the fires popping up all over Eresseia? The destruction you have witnessed?"

The queen's sardonic smile, with her sharp teeth, unnerved Aurianna. Even knowing it was intentional, Aurianna couldn't help her reaction, regardless of the Fae blood running through her own veins. "You're saying this Drakon is responsible for all of it?"

"And more, I imagine." Treasa looked at her meaningfully. Aurianna glanced at her friends, all of them probably thinking the same thing.

The dragonblood in the water supply.

"Why?"

"Why is he doing it?"

"Anger. Betrayal. He was yanked out of his own world and into

193

ours, only to be tossed aside when the Essence got bored. Now he has no way to return, and all he wants is revenge. He wants havoc and chaos. He is in a war with the goddesses, and he holds their brother hostage. He wants to create a war between Fae and humans as well, but we refuse to get involved in a conflict between our parents."

"Yet you did before. In fact, it almost sounds like you started it."

"We Fae live a long time, but not that long. My ancestors made that fatal mistake. I have no desire to fight your enemy for you."

"Is he not also your enemy?"

"Ayshetha lands have not been touched, nor have our people. We have no reason to get involved."

"You're getting involved by telling me all of this."

"I am giving you your answers. That is all."

"And for what? Not out of the goodness of your heart. You want something."

"What makes you think that?"

"In my experience, everyone wants something."

The queen nodded. "True enough. But just because we refuse to get involved doesn't mean I don't want to help you."

"What do you want?"

"For you to win this war."

"But I thought—"

"I will not fight. But I will show you the way to win."

"Okay. Tell me then."

"We will speak further on it. In private. I think you and your friends might benefit from some nourishment, no?" Treasa clapped her hands. Several guards appeared behind them. "Take them to get food and drink. Bring Aurianna to my chambers to dine with me." She narrowed her gaze back on Aurianna. "We have things to discuss."

CHAPTER 18

SIGI

Sigi tried to remember why she had a snake around her neck.

She knew it wasn't the sort of thing she would normally do. In fact, it was exactly the sort of thing Leon would do. Or even Javen.

The name darkened her mood, but she knew it should feel worse than in did. Something wasn't right. Yet she couldn't figure out what. Rhouth jumped up on the table and growled at her.

Swallowing the lump in her throat, she asked, "Leon, did you put this thing on me?"

Across the table loaded with mounds of food, Leon squinted at her. "What thing?" he asked, a note of confusion in his voice.

Sigi gaped down at her chest again. It was a strange-looking snake, flat and skinny with oddly square-shaped head. The head appeared to have a hole in it, but she couldn't be bothered trying to determine what sort of snake had a hole in its head. Pointing to the area in question, she repeated herself. "This. Did you put this on me?"

"Why would I do that?"

"Well, how did it get there then? Where did it come from?"

The fox expressed her agreement with a yip, demanding an answer. Seconds later, she lost interest and bounded back over to Theron, tugging a leftover piece of meat along the way. Rhouth made herself comfortable at his feet and began to gnaw on the bone.

"I imagine from around your waist." Leon answered with a giggle and took another sip of the wine they had been served along with the assortment of foods.

The table was covered with platters of every delicious food one could imagine—meats, cheeses, fruits, breads, cakes, pies—and far more than they could eat.

Laelia was going to be disappointed she had missed the feast, but she hadn't been feeling well and had gone to lie down. Ethan and Syrena had also slipped off early to the sleeping rooms prepared for them.

At least they weren't sitting in a prison cell like Belinda.

Remembering how much she had eaten, Sigi placed a hand on her stomach and moaned. Stuffed was an understatement.

What had Leon said about her waist?

She patted around her waist. Her pants had been loosened. When had that happened? And where was her belt?

When her brain finally caught up, the others were in hysterics at her predicament. Theron had tears streaming from his eyes, and the former Regulus was grinning from ear to ear. Leon slapped his thigh and roared with laughter.

A belt. She had a belt around her neck.

"I'm glad you find this so funny," she snapped, "considering you boys all have food on your faces."

"Just means we—" Pharis started to say before wiping his hand across his mouth. It came back covered in grease and other residue of their meal. He looked down at it frowning. "I don't eat like an animal. What is going on?"

"Probably from when you were gorging your face with an entire leg of meat." Sigi sat back and stared at the man who would have been the leader of their world, shaking her head at the incongruity.

"I don't *gorge* on anything. All of you were stuffing your faces. It was quite disturbing to watch."

"Who ya calling disturbing?" Leon stood, towering over Pharis. To his credit, the smaller man didn't flinch or cower under Leon's reproachful stare.

Theron slowly rose and went to stand beside his friend. Placing a hand on Leon's shoulder, he said, "Why don't we sit and just relax?"

Leon whirled and shoved Theron into a nearby wall. Rhouth immediately started yipping as Leon stalked toward the other man with his fist raised. Leon swung out and missed the hunter, plunging his fist into the wall to the left of Theron's head instead. The fox clamped her teeth onto his pant leg and began thrashing back and forth.

"Hey!" Sigi shouted, jumping up. "Calm down, Leon. What's wrong with you?"

"What's wrong with *me*? You're—" He shook his leg, trying to detach the animal, but she held on. "You're the one with a damn belt around your neck!" He reached down and picked Rhouth up, but she immediately snapped at him. He dropped her and jumped back before she could attack him again. Theron picked her up.

"I didn't put it there!"

"Well, darlin', I didn't touch your pants. I love ya and all, but not like that. Maybe His Royal *Handsiness* over here did." He glared back at Pharis, who still sat on the far side of the table observing the scene with caution.

Pharis started at the comment. "His Royal—What the bloody hell are you talking about, you daft bastard? You're the one who can't keep your hands to yourself." Pharis gestured to Theron, who hadn't moved. "Clearly."

"You know exactly what I mean, Your *Highness*. You think we don't see what you're doing, slithering your way into this group, into Aurianna's life. Putting us all in jeopardy, like we didn't just lose—"

"Leon." A familiar voice on the edge of the room grabbed their attention. Aurianna had entered the room, her hands balled into fists as she took in the scene. Shaking her head, the girl fought to hold back unshed tears.

Leon lowered his eyes, looking almost sheepish.

"What's going on in here?" Aurianna asked.

No one spoke.

Sigi decided she should take charge since the males were obviously experiencing a shared delusional state. Maybe it was the wine. Maybe the Fae were trying to get them drunk. Leon was always drinking too much.

Clearing her throat, she murmured, "We were having dinner, and Leon got a little upset is all."

"About me, I see. As if I am anyone else's business." Turning to Leon, she added, "And I know what you think of me. About what I did. That I'm a traitor." Leon's eyes widened as he shook his head emphatically at her accusation. "But I have bigger issues to deal with right now."

Leon said, "Aurianna, I don't—"

"I know who cursed me, who tried to kill me when I was born."

"Who?" Pharis asked. He motioned for Aurianna to sit in the chair beside him, but she ignored him.

"The same being the queen spoke of. Drakon."

"You're saying you were attacked by a demon?" Sigi was dumbfounded. "Why though? Why would he care about you?" Aurianna visibly flinched. Sigi amended her statement. "Why would he care about a random baby when he's trying to start a war?"

"I don't know. Azel was there with the prophecy, but how would this Drakon have known about it before the Arcanes? I mean, he must have planned how to get into the tower in advance. He killed the other midwife and took her form. He would have been planning all of that before Azel was given the prophecy, so . . . I don't know. And I can't ask Azel about it because Drakon burned him to cinders."

"So, what are we supposed to do then? We don't know how to stop him."

"I can do better than stop him. I know how to destroy him."

"How?"

"The Fae queen told me about two objects. One she mentioned back in the throne room. The Nether Stone she called it. They allow travel to the Nether realm where Drakon is from. She says she has a piece of one, and we can use it to send him back. We must send him back. The Essence brought him here, and he must be returned for the world to right itself. To bring balance. But not before we make sure he can't possibly return."

"And how do you propose we do that?"

"By stabbing him with the second object she mentioned to me in private. An ancient sword, lost long ago. She says it's the only thing that will kill a demon."

Sigi narrowed her eyes. "Then why didn't they use it before now?"

"They tried, a long time ago. But the sword needs the stone attached to it in order to harm him. Otherwise, he is impervious to it. And then the sword was lost at the bottom of Perdita Bay. Over time, it's probably floated out to sea."

"And she thinks you'll be able to get it?"

Aurianna nodded. "I told her about the prophecy and what it said. Remember the line 'Beware the silent knife'? The queen believes the long-lost sword is the knife from the prophecy."

"A knife and a sword aren't the same thing."

"Yeah." Aurianna waved her hand in the air. "But you know how this prophecy stuff is. They use a bunch of confusing words just to make it harder to decipher the damn things."

"I don't know, Aurianna. Seems a stretch."

"Well, we'll find out tomorrow. A group of Fae will take me to the edge of the sea to retrieve the sword."

"And what? You're just supposed to say some magic words, and it'll leap up into your hands?"

Shrugging, Aurianna smiled. "Maybe. Guess I'll find out."

"But where did this sword come from? What makes it special? I don't understand why we're just trusting this queen."

"I don't know its history. And I have no doubt she knows more than she's telling. But I think it's worth a shot, even though I don't completely trust her."

Pharis shook his head. "Never a dull moment with you." As the words left his mouth, he glanced from the side of his eye at Leon, who was glaring at him again.

Did Leon blame Pharis for what happened to Javen? Surely he could see the only one to blame was Javen himself. Right?

Blowing out a breath she didn't realize she'd been holding, Sigi gestured to the food still left on the table. "Help yourself to something to eat. Don't drink the wine though. I think it's a bit stronger than what we're used to."

Theron was petting Rhouth, who had been whimpering in his arms. "That's an understatement."

Aurianna shook her head. "I've already eaten. And I had wine. Nothing was wrong with it. I'm actually about to go check on

Oracle. Treasa said I can bring her back here. They have a potion that will help her calm down. And they'll put up a makeshift fence to keep her from wandering." She sighed, combing her fingers through her bright-red hair. "We have to figure out what to do about Belinda. The Fae won't let her out under any circumstances, but she'll need medical care. And I don't know if anyone here even understands human anatomy."

Sigi hesitated before asking, "Don't you think she's better off locked up, considering how weird her pregnancy is getting?"

"It's a baby, Sigi. We can't let anything happen to her or her child, no matter how obnoxious she is."

"I didn't mean it like that. I was just wondering... If the Fae are as scared of it as they seem to be, maybe we should be too?"

* * *

Sigi scrunched up her face against the blazing midday sun. Hands on her hips, she switched her focus from Aurianna to the water at their feet.

They were near the back edge of Vanito's landmass, facing out over the ocean beyond. The Fae had a set of stairs carved into the cliff face, much like the ones around Eresseia used for cliff diving into the bay. Sigi wondered if the Fae also used it for recreation, or if another purpose existed for the stairs or for the dock-like platform at its base upon which they now stood.

No one was certain where exactly Perdita Bay ended and the Mare Dolor began. The waters here in the strait between Rasenforst and Vanito were much choppier than they were in the lagoon. The bay's name meant *lost things*, a fact which was not lost on Sigi as she contemplated what they were here to do.

She had never been this close to the ocean before, though they were not that far from her hometown of Rasenforst. Vanito was far beyond the trees up above and behind them, but Rasenforst was somewhere off to her distant left. Nothing but miles and miles of ocean lay straight out from where they stood.

And somewhere out there, if the Fae queen were to be believed, Drakon sat on his lonely island.

Aurianna was still staring at the water in concentration, but the others had lost interest ages ago. Laelia snoozed on Leon's chest as they leaned against a boulder. Theron lay flat on his back on the shore, Rhouth curled up on his stomach. Ethan and Syrena were practicing her powers by the water's edge on the other side of a rocky outcropping.

Sigi shook her head in disbelief. He was allowing Syrena to draw from his elemental Water substance to boost her Kinetic output. It didn't appear to matter that her affinity was with Fire, a different element altogether. The act required a level of trust Sigi wasn't sure she could ever understand.

Pharis was skipping small stones across the water, clearly bored. Every now and then, Aurianna would glower at him, but he didn't seem to notice.

Two Fae guards stood with their backs to the cliff and waited with arms crossed in irritation. Neither of them seemed happy to have been assigned this duty.

Walking over to Aurianna's side, Sigi silently observed her efforts.

After a moment, Aurianna raised a brow. "Can I help you?" Her tone oozed with frustration.

Sigi shrugged. "I'm just not sure what's supposed to happen. She didn't give you any clear instructions."

"I'm doing my best, Sigi."

"I know. But who says this sword is even down here? It probably got swept out to sea a long time ago."

Aurianna shook her head. "No. According to the queen, it shouldn't matter. If I'm the one chosen for this destiny, then I should be able to summon it."

"Only, that's not what's happening, is it?"

"So I'm not the one in the prophecy? Maybe I should just go home then."

Sigi felt the blow from her friend's harsh words. "I thought this was your home now. And I'm not talking about the stupid prophecy—"

"So it's stupid?"

"Aurianna, *you* were the one screaming about it being bullshit, were you not?" Sigi was fuming now. "You told everyone it was nonsense, and you wanted nothing to do with it. And what? Now you're suddenly all in on the prophecy business?"

"There's a difference between—"

"Shut up, both of you!" Pharis's voice cut through the conversation like a knife. When the two girls wheeled on him with matching expressions of fury, he added, "I hear something." He was pointing to the water. "Something's out there."

"Yeah, I hear it too," Syrena said, moving away from the water's edge, Ethan following.

Everyone was on their feet now, moving back from the waterline. Rhouth was yipping with abandon, the sound echoing against the rocky cliff. Theron picked her up and attempted to comfort the animal.

"What did you do?" Leon asked, his gaze accusing.

"What did I do? I did exactly what I was asked to do. While the two of you have been back there cavorting in the sun, I've been working over here."

"Cavorting?" Laelia snorted. "Are you serious?"

Pharis interrupted their bickering. "Can all of you please *shut the hell up*? Something is coming!"

Ethan and Syrena stood beside him, the three of them staring into the frothing waves at their feet.

Syrena shook her head. "Something isn't right. The sound seems distant, yet almost as if it's already on top of us."

Ethan tried to pull her back to safety, but the woman wrenched herself free. He said, "Syrena, I don't think you need to be standing so close. In fact, none of us—"

His words were drowned by a sudden screeching sound.

Everyone covered their ears in a futile attempt to block the pitch reverberating painfully in their heads.

Everyone but Aurianna and Syrena.

The two women moved away from the others, toward where Aurianna had been standing only moments before. They inched closer just as a gigantic wave crashed on the shore, and a monstrous creature emerged from the depths of the ocean.

It shot up above the water's surface, then seemed to hover in midair. Though somewhat humanoid, the lower half of the figure seemed half-aquatic, half-Volanti—covered in scales with a fish tail instead of legs and feet. And its upper half was Fae-like, with bright-red hair.

In its hands was a sword.

The monster held the object out as if presenting a gift. Aurianna tentatively reached for it as Pharis rushed over to stop her. But the being had already yanked the sword back, and two more creatures—almost identical in form and size—crawled up from the water and each took hold of one of Aurianna's legs.

She screamed. Sigi ran forward to try to help Pharis pull her back. The others had been stunned and immobile, but now they too began to move. Everyone held on, resisting the incredible strength of the two beings trying to drag Aurianna down to the depths of the sea.

Pharis was shouting at the Fae guards to help, but Sigi could only focus on trying to keep her grasp on Aurianna's right arm. She remembered the night the situation had been reversed, and Aurianna had been trying to hold on to her. Had it not been for divine intervention, or whatever had saved her that night, Sigi would have drowned in the waters of Perdita Bay.

But there seemed to be no hope for Aurianna. The girl's legs and torso were already submerged, and the sea creatures were inexorably pulling all seven of them closer and closer to the water's edge.

Sigi felt someone let go of her arm. Before she could glance back, Syrena was coming around to stand before the monster with the sword. She reached out, palms to the sky, and the sword was placed gently in her hands.

The two creatures holding Aurianna abruptly released her, and all three swam away.

Sigi stared open-mouthed into the distance. Pharis hauled a soaked and breathless Aurianna back to dry ground, and Sigi helped lay her on her side. Aurianna was shaking, whether from the cold water or fear, Sigi couldn't be sure. But she held her friend as the trembling subsided.

Her arms still around the other girl, Sigi looked over at Syrena, who hadn't moved since receiving the sword.

She felt Aurianna pushing against her arm, so she relaxed her hold, and Aurianna propped herself up on an elbow. No one spoke as she stared at the woman who had given birth to her. Finally, Aurianna pushed to her feet and trudged over to her mother.

Syrena pulled her gaze from the weapon in her hands—eyes wide with wonder and confusion—to stare at her daughter. The sword was surprisingly small, not much bigger than the daggers they had used when training with the resistance.

Then Aurianna did the last thing any of them expected—Syrena most of all. She pulled her mother into her arms and hugged her tightly. Sigi teared up as she thought about her own mother. Although Aurianna's Aunt Larissa had been like a mother to her, she really was so fortunate to have this opportunity for a relationship with the woman who gave birth to her. Sigi knew it to be a gift without price.

Aurianna was smiling when she pulled back. After a moment, she said, " 'Beware the silent knife, for she will be your end.' It was never about me." She actually seemed relieved.

"I don't understand." Syrena shook her head. "I really don't. Why—"

"That part of the prophesy was never about me. I'm not the 'she' it's referring to." Aurianna's smile widened. "You are."

"No. No, you are the red sky at morning, dear."

Aurianna nodded. "Yes, I am. But the prophecy had three parts, remember?" She led her mother over to a rock so they could sit as they spoke.

Bewildered but mesmerized, the rest of them listened attentively. Even the Fae no longer looked bored.

Aurianna asked, "Why did you take the sword from those creatures?"

"What do you mean?" Syrena's eyes widened in confusion. "They were trying to drag you down. They would have killed you."

"Yes, but what made you walk over and take it? What made you think that would work?"

"Well, I—" Syrena started, then stopped, her eyes glazing over in thought. "I don't know. Something in me just told me to do it."

"Like a pull, right? Like something was guiding your actions."

"Yes," Syrena said slowly. "Yes, I guess it was something like that. To be truthful, I really don't remember."

Aurianna nodded. "That's how it feels for me as well when I'm following my instincts. Anytime something related to the prophecy plays out, I have this feeling deep within me that seems to draw me in a certain direction."

Syrena took Aurianna's hand and, for the first time, Sigi's prickly friend did not pull away or rebuff her. She just smiled in a sort of bemused way and continued. "The first stanza said, 'When the red sky at morning bursts forth to cleanse the land, beware the dragon's warning, for the end is close at hand.' That part is clearly talking about me." She glanced back at Sigi with a sheepish grin. "As much as I didn't want to admit it, there's no denying I'm a part of this. But it's not *only* about me."

"What do you mean?" Syrena asked.

"Even the last bit is moving on to a new topic. Ever since the dragonblood incident with the water supply, I had always thought the 'dragon's warning' had to be a reference to, well, to you. But I think it must be referring to Drakon. If he is indeed a dragon."

Theron scratched his chin in thought. "You know, I've been thinking about the whole dragon thing. Have you ever noticed how the Volanti look a lot like what we think of as dragons? But maybe our lore has it wrong. I don't know."

Sigi found a rock to sit on. "True. But the Fae queen said only one was left."

Theron shrugged. "What about those nightmares that just tried to drown our little Aurianna here? Hybrids are certainly possible."

Pharis had been staring at the ground, his jaw clenched. He regarded Aurianna steadily before interrupting. "I had hoped I was wrong, but I've been thinking about the prophecy too, and I believe my father may have actually considered you an enemy. I don't think he was originally in favor of the Arcanes' plan to bring you here."

"What?" she gasped.

"He sometimes spoke of the prophecy as if, well, almost as if he feared it coming true. Like you were going to stop *him*. 'Rising up to heights unknown' had him more than a bit worried for his own position. I don't think he ever really stopped to consider the other parts. And I always assumed that was the reason behind our engagement—just another power grab and a way to keep you under his thumb."

Aurianna blushed at the memory of the Magnus's schemes to marry her off to his son. "Sounds like he had a guilty conscience."

Pharis nodded. "Indeed. But this is so much bigger than him. Who exactly is the enemy here? The Order? The Consils? This Drakon the Fae claim exists?"

"I don't know, but I think the entire second section may also be referring to Drakon. If he can indeed 'scorch the sky' in his natural form, it would make sense. But 'beware the infernal stone' sounds more like a warning for him, not against him. It doesn't make any sense."

"Unless we're supposed to be wary of it as well," Sigi whispered, aware of the Fae who were pretending not to listen to their conversation. "Who says we can trust the Fae, anyway?"

Aurianna dropped her volume to match Sigi's. "Well, Simon did. And the Essence. They told me to come here for answers."

Sigi raised her eyebrows. "That doesn't mean they thought we should trust them."

"Good point." Aurianna chewed on her bottom lip, throwing a glance at their guards. She cleared her throat and continued to speak in a soft voice. "But my original point remains. The final part of the prophecy must refer to my mother. There's no other explanation."

Syrena let out a nervous chuckle. "Just because of a sword?"

Comprehension widened Aurianna's eyes. She smiled grimly, no amusement in her tone. "I think I understand it now. 'She will steal your life, for the world to burn and bend. Beware the silent knife, for she will be your end.' It doesn't matter which of us is which within the prophecy itself. It was never about the Magnus, or the Consils, or any of them. It was always about this Drakon. The entire prophecy is a warning for him." Aurianna's eyes glowed with excitement, but she kept her voice low. "Don't you see?"

The gentle lapping of the waves against the edge of the platform was an odd accompaniment to their turbulent thoughts.

"The prophecy was never meant for me or Syrena. Azel was there to warn Drakon."

CHAPTER 19

AURIANNA

Treasa shrank back, and the guards rushed forward, crossing their spears in front of Aurianna the moment she revealed the object of their quest.

Aurianna stared blankly at the Fae queen, the small sword in her outstretched hand. "I don't understand. You asked me to get this for you."

She lowered the weapon, letting it dangle at her side.

The queen's golden gaze tracked the movement.

She had convinced the others to allow her to confront the Fae queen on her own. As far as Treasa knew, Aurianna was destined to wield the weapon against the dragon in the prophecy. Whether she was right or wrong about the true meaning of the prophecy, Aurianna wasn't prepared to start trusting the Fae just yet.

"Do you know what that thing is made of?" The queen's eyes were wide, her hand trembling as she pointed at the weapon from behind the safety of her guards. "Aye, I sent you to retrieve it. But you march in here pointing it at me as if to threaten."

"I'm not pointing anything at you. Yes, it's made of iron. I know firsthand what it does to Kinetic power, but simply touching it isn't harmful."

"Not for *them*!" Treasa hissed, baring her teeth. "But for Fae, it is deadly. One cut is enough to kill us. Just touching it is painful."

Aurianna thought of her arm where dark stitches still marred the skin beneath her shirt. The wound she had incurred with the resistance had never really healed. Mara had insisted they weren't trying to harm her, not lethally at least.

They probably wouldn't have known any more than Aurianna had. Why would they? The Fae were a myth lost to history.

They were also her people. A part of her, at least. "I didn't know." Her voice was hoarse. "I didn't realize it was that serious, but it explains why my injury has refused to heal." Aurianna rolled up her sleeve to display the wound.

Treasa motioned for one of her guards to take the sword from Aurianna and waved the rest back to their normal positions. She leaned forward, taking in the angry wound.

The Fae queen shook her head. "How did you get that? How are you not dead?"

"I almost was." Aurianna started to tell her about the Order of the Daoine, but something warned her not to divulge that bit of information. "I was accidentally cut by an iron sword, and the healers tried to sew me up, but it never would heal. We couldn't figure out why."

"Your Fae blood is both a blessing and a curse to you," Treasa observed with a simper. "As is your human blood, it seems. Were you fully one of us, you'd have been dead within minutes."

"Is there anything you can do about it?"

"We have the blood of gods and demons within us. It is the demon who gave us this weakness. The Essence are the only ones who might be able to help you. But we can try to ease the pain. Our healers have far more experience with this sort of thing."

"What is so special about this sword in particular? Wouldn't any iron sword kill him?"

"The sword was a gift from the Essence, used long ago in the wars against Drakon and his brothers. In a final attempt to defeat him, the bearer of the weapon fell, dropping the sword into the bay. That is how Perdita Bay gained its current name. That is all I know."

Aurianna was skeptical, but she asked, "What are you going to do with the sword?"

"It . . . requires the stone within my crown to work properly. Do you see the indentation in the hilt?" She pointed to a small divot Aurianna had failed to notice. "I must affix the Nether Stone with Fae magic. Then it will be ready for you."

Aurianna squinted at the hole. It was perhaps the size of a coin. The stone upon the queen's brow was much larger.

Aurianna glared. "You sent me to retrieve an item with the potential to kill me—and failed to warn me. Nor did you mention the creatures who guarded it."

The female sat back on her queenly seat, shrugging. "I naturally assumed you knew." She avoided Aurianna's gaze and flared her nostrils in distaste. "And we had no idea those things would have it."

"See, I think you did. I think you knew precisely what I was getting into. What are those things? I've heard others speak of them, but only as legend."

"Like the Fae are legends? They are the unfortunate result of Drakon and his brothers' . . . wanderings within our land."

"Are you saying . . . ?"

"Yes. They are the offspring of demon and Fae. Remember, our people live long lives. This was before the war, but our race was well established at the time. The families of the females were shamed by these dalliances outside our race."

"What happened to them?"

"They were banished from our lands. We never knew what happened to their children until those creatures were first spotted."

Aurianna shook her head at the warring thoughts within her mind. "So, when will I get the sword back?"

"As soon as I affix the stone to the hilt. Tomorrow, we will discuss plans to move forward."

* * *

Almost two days had passed since they recovered the sword, and Aurianna had made a decision.

Her talk with the Fae queen had cemented the anxiety already tearing her apart. This mission was dangerous. If the prophecy were to be trusted, bringing everyone along would only serve to put them at risk.

She would speak with Syrena and come up with a plan. The prophecy, if Aurianna's speculations were correct, dictated Syrena's involvement. So having her there was unavoidable. But the idea twisted her insides into knots since, despite everything, the woman was her mother, and Aurianna had no desire to put her in harm's way.

Her friends, however, were better off staying here. She didn't want to endanger their lives further. She considered just leaving without telling anyone else. At least then no one would try to stop her.

But she was done running. This was her story to end.

Aurianna hesitated before the door to the room she shared with Pharis. She looked down the passage, wishing she could avoid this.

She peeked into a dark and empty space. Now what?

Pharis and Theron had been spending a lot of time out in the open-air garden lately. Aurianna wondered at their newfound friendship, but she was happy Pharis had found his place within the group. They would need each other when she left.

She wandered through the intricate maze of the dormitories out to the courtyard in the middle. The explosion of brightly colored blossoms did nothing to calm her soul or ease her terror.

But as she'd hoped, Pharis was sitting in the gazebo, reading something.

She sat beside him. "Can you read that?"

"Excuse me?"

"I mean, I thought everything here would be written in the old language."

"They actually have four libraries, with plenty of books in the common tongue. I'm reading about a type of fishing they do here. Theron and I were talking to one of the males, and he invited us to join them one day soon."

"Fishing? I didn't think they had boats."

"They don't."

"You and Theron, huh?"

Pharis cocked his head. "Yes?"

"I'm glad you're making friends."

"So glad you approve." His rolled his eyes and went back to reading, as if to dismiss her and any conversational topics she might broach.

"I have to do this alone, Pharis." The words spilled from her mouth.

He immediately set the book down. "What? Why?"

"It's best for everyone."

"Why? Says who? You?"

"Yes, me! I'm the one in charge of—"

"In charge? What the hell? Nobody put you in charge!"

"Somebody has to be! Just because you're used to getting your way with everyone—the kingdom, women—"

"You're not seriously on that again, are you? Who I was with before you shouldn't matter—"

"Why? Doesn't it bother you that I slept with him first?"

"You think that's . . ." Pharis gaped at her in confusion, his mouth hanging open. He jumped to his feet and stomped a few paces away. He raked a hand through his hair before turning around. "I meant what I said to you that night."

"What night?"

"What night?" His jaw muscle flexed, and his cheeks flamed. "Are you just trying to—" He closed his mouth without finishing the sentence.

"What, Pharis?"

"Nothing." His voice was low as he tried to remain calm. "Even after, I tried to accept things as they were. And I did. I bought you that dress as a peace offering. I just wanted things to be right again."

"For the Yule Ball? You bought the gold dress?"

Pharis looked confused. "I thought it was obvious. It was really expensive. But I wasn't doing it to show off. I just thought it suited . . ." He trailed off, nodding in sudden understanding. "You thought he gave it to you."

"Well, naturally. We were together at the time." At those words, she saw a flash of pain in his eyes. "Why would I have assumed it came from you?"

He opened his mouth but didn't respond. Closing it again, Pharis shook his head. "You are unbelievable. Why am I surprised you have a misguided sense of duty? The whole world is burning alive, and Aurianna wants to go play superhero."

"Like I said, someone has to be the hero! I thought that was why you brought me here!" she shouted.

"But why do you insist you have to do it alone?" His volume rose to match hers as he stalked across the gazebo toward her.

"Because I'm the one with the prophecy!"

He froze, tilting his head. "Are you?" Pharis huffed out a laugh, glaring at her across the gazebo. "The prophecy isn't about you. It barely even mentions you. Didn't you yourself just tell us that?"

Aurianna glared back. "I've been the one pulling us along this entire way. I've been the one who got us where we are."

"And look where we are."

The slap shocked both of them. Aurianna gazed at her hand, red from the impact. She wasn't even sure when she approached him.

Pharis stared at her hand then back to her face, his emotions unreadable. Finally, he said, "What gives you the right to decide the destiny of the rest of us? I gave up everything to be here with you."

"You gave up . . . You gave up? I gave up everything to avenge your death when I thought he'd killed you!"

A deathly silence filled the space. Not a sound echoed for what felt like miles to Aurianna.

"What?" came his whispered reply.

"I killed him . . . because of you."

And there it was. Her hand came up to cover her mouth, but the words were already spoken.

"Regretting it now, are you? And here I thought I was the good guy." Pharis marched across the garden, stopping with his hand on the doorknob leading back into the inner hallway. Without looking back, he added, "Goodbye, Aurianna. Good luck on your own." He didn't need to raise his voice to be heard. She could read the farewell in his eyes.

She tried to find the words.

But none came.

Aurianna ran to the door and peered down the passage, but he was gone.

Closing the door, she stood frozen with her hand on the knob. For a few moments, Aurianna stood in the silence left behind by his farewell. This was real. It was raw. And her heart ached in the emptiness left behind.

She was alone. Wasn't that what I wanted?

Instead of running from her problems as she always had, Aurianna had chased them away instead.

Was there a difference?

She didn't try to stop the flow of tears. Instead, she welcomed the salty warmth they brought to her skin. The floodgates opened, months of anguish and bitter resentment pouring out.

An explosion of emotion hit Aurianna full force. A storm raged within her, a screaming siren beating against her ribcage, desperate to get out.

A keening wail erupted, and she dropped to the ground, crushing more than a few flowers as she hugged her knees, leaning against the wall.

The sky darkened above her. Lightning crashed and the air sizzled—all reflecting her inner turmoil.

Her wailing intensified, and she knew someone was bound to hear her soon.

Then a soft voice penetrated her misery. "Come over here, child."

Larissa was standing in the doorway to the gardens, her arms outstretched. Without thinking, Aurianna went to her, stumbling and collapsing into the woman's welcoming embrace.

Not woman. Fae. Aurianna felt her isolation deepen. This wasn't even her Larissa.

She pulled back, wiping her face on her arm. Her sobs were

easing, the wetness on her cheeks already drying up into a desert of cold and sorrow.

Aurianna felt empty and numb inside. Larissa studied her for a minute then gestured to the gazebo. "Let's chat, shall we?"

She followed Larissa to the bench and sat, waiting for her to speak. But Larissa was silent.

Aurianna leaned back and closed her eyes, her thoughts churning. After a moment, a curt "What is it?" registered through her filtering fog.

She opened one eye. "What is what?"

Larissa's face was unreadable. "Why do you do that?"

"Do what?"

"Push everyone away. Refuse to accept help when it's freely given."

"I don't need help, Larissa! I need everyone to stay away from me."

The female-who-looked-like-her-aunt smirked. "Liar."

Aurianna sat up and glared. "Excuse me?"

"It's not true, and you know it. You forget, I know you better than anyone."

"You've never even met me. How could you know me?"

"I know you'd like to think other versions of you weren't you. But you're exactly the same."

"If that were true, we wouldn't be having this conversation. I would have failed again, and the singularity would've started a war. Everything would have started over again."

"Yes, you have managed to control yourself better, but who you are is essentially unchanged. No one can truly change who they are at their core."

"And who am I?"

"You are a scared little girl trapped in a big world, and guilt is eating you alive. You don't think you deserve happiness."

"What do you know about my guilt?"

"I know something is tearing your heart apart, and it isn't the boy who just left. You might blame him, but it's not his fault."

"How the hell do you know what is or isn't his fault?"

"I don't. But as I said, I know you. And I know when you're consumed by a thing. It won't help anyone if you lose control again."

"He expects me to pretend everything will one day be okay."

"And won't it?"

Aurianna stood and paced the floor. "Larissa, you know it won't. I think you've always known it. That's why you kept so much from me."

"No, child. It was just my stubbornness and the instructions from the Arcanes."

"The Arcanes told you to lie to me?"

"To hold back certain truths, yes. But you have a destiny."

Aurianna shook her head. "That damn prophecy is the reason we're in this mess. I can fix this myself, without the Essence, and without help."

"How?"

"I have the sword needed to kill Drakon. I know where he lives. Sort of. And I can use my Aerokinetic powers pretty well now."

"And you don't need any help with your plan?"

"They all despise me anyway."

"Do they now?"

Aurianna spun on her. "Yes! I killed their friend. A man they had known for half their lives."

Larissa gave her a knowing look. "They don't despise you, dear. You despise yourself."

"Of course I do! Look at what I did!"

"And what did you do that was so horrible?"

"I killed him, Larissa!"

"Did you have to kill him?"

"No! I should have made sure he was tied up and had him arrested. I had the ability, the upper hand, and I let my emotions take over." Aurianna stumbled back to the bench and collapsed in a heap. "You're right. That's exactly my problem. I was so worried about Pharis, I didn't stop to think about my actions. And I had all the time in the world." She leaned her head back and let out a wail. "Why? Why did I do it?"

Larissa tsked, a wry expression on her face. "Pharis should never have put you in that position, huh?"

Aurianna's head flopped forward. She stared at Larissa. "Why would he sacrifice his life?"

"To protect the one he loved."

"I guess so."

"Like you did."

"What?"

"You were protecting the ones you loved as well."

"Don't try to justify—"

Larissa shook her head. "I'm not justifying anything. You might have been in the wrong."

"Wait, what?"

"Maybe you shouldn't have killed him."

"I thought—"

"But you did it, child!" Larissa exclaimed. "You made a mistake. Or maybe you didn't. Maybe it was the only way. Maybe it wasn't. Does it matter?"

"Does it matter that I took someone's *life*?"

Larissa shrugged. "Can you change what happened?"

Aurianna turned her gaze to the ground, staring at her feet in silence.

"Listen to me." Larissa lifted Aurianna's chin with a finger, forcing her to make eye contact. "We're always faced with choices.

To move forward, sometimes we must choose between two very different paths. Those choices are like sunrises and sunsets. On the surface, they look similar, but one leads to darkness, and one leads to light. A beginning and an ending. But the thing about sunrises and sunsets is that no matter which one you're looking at, there will always be another opportunity tomorrow. As long as we're still breathing, anything is fixable."

Aurianna pulled away from Larissa's touch. "So you think I made the wrong decision?"

"No, I think you made the right decision in the moment, but perhaps for the wrong reasons."

"That's just as bad."

"Maybe it feels that way to you, but there are a lot of people alive right now who wouldn't be if it weren't for you, child."

"But I'm supposed to be the savior! I'm supposed to *follow the path the draws me.* I'm supposed to trust my instincts. How can I do that when my instincts are wrong?"

"Your instincts weren't wrong. Just clouded by emotion. You still made the choice you felt was needed to save the ones you loved. Do you think any of your friends would have been able to take that path, to make the hard choice?"

"That doesn't make it okay."

"No one said anything about 'okay.' You did what you thought was right at the time. But you can forgive yourself."

"It's not that simple."

"Yes, it is. You're the only one who hasn't."

"Hasn't what?"

"Forgiven. No one else blames you."

"How do you know?"

Larissa smiled. "The way they follow you. They wouldn't respect you the way they do if they blamed you for what happened."

"Leon definitely does."

"Leon is grieving. They were best friends, right? His heart is aching the same as yours. You must work through it together. Deep down, he knows what happened. He just doesn't want to think of his friend as the enemy."

"They were very close."

"And you've found your place among them. Pharis, especially, loves you."

"Pharis loves too much. It doesn't make sense sometimes."

"I think you have a lot to discover, my dear."

"What do you mean?"

"You're still on the path of discovery. I've known you longer than anyone."

"So, the other version of you, the one I grew up with . . . She's still in the future?"

"Yes, she is. Her—my role is to prepare you for your journey and see that you succeed. When you didn't, I broke away from that role and came here. But the queen refused to allow me back at first. She knew what I had done, what I had been involved in with my sister and with you. I convinced her I needed to detach myself from the world of humans."

"Why would Treasa not allow you back? Because of me?"

"Because of my sister, Hermia. By involving herself with a human, she became a source of shame for the Fae, at least in Treasa'a eyes. And, owing to my involvement in her life and that of your mother, so was I."

"Syrena told me she was also my grandmother, which I guess means you really are my aunt. My great aunt, at least. Or the other version of you is. It's very confusing."

"True."

"What did your sister do to anger the queen?"

"She fell in love with a human from Rasenforst. Hermia found out she was pregnant, and he found himself no longer interested."

"That's terrible."

"A half-Fae child isn't an easy thing to explain. She begged him to come back here with her. But the queen wouldn't allow it. He was never going to follow her anyway. He was already married. My sister was merely a fascination for him. Once his curiosity—and lust—had been satisfied, he lost interest. The baby simply sped up the process."

A flicker of light in her peripheral vision startled Aurianna. She turned and saw a glow in a corner of the garden. Larissa reached out and clutched her hand as the two of them stood.

The blue light intensified until an almost transparent figure emerged. It was Terra, goddess of Earth. "Dry your tears. You must prepare for a journey."

"What?" Aurianna cried. "You think you can show up whenever you feel like it and expect me to do whatever you ask?"

"I do not expect anything. But what is destined will surely happen, whether you will it or not. You must be ready."

Larissa's eyes were wide.

"Ready for what? I have the sword the Fae queen asked me to get. The one from the prophecy. She's going to combine it with a Nether Stone so I can defeat Drakon. Notice the pieces of information you failed to give me. At least I'm getting answers now."

"The queen of the Fae will not give you what you seek. You must seek it on your own. Go. Prepare for a journey. Meet us in the main conservatory by the back wall. We will discuss everything there in one hour."

"No, we will discuss it here. And now. Tell me what's going on."

"We will not speak of these things until it is time for you to go."

"Look—" Aurianna spat, but the goddess was already evaporating into nothingness. "Hey, come back!" She rushed to the space where the Essence had appeared, but Larissa pulled her back.

"She's gone, child. I suggest you do as she says."

"How can I trust you won't tell Treasa about this?"

Larissa sighed. "Because you are the only family I have left. And I think she's lying to you."

"Who? The queen?"

"Yes. But we'll talk later. Go to your room. A hot bath would do you good. I'll have water brought over."

"But if she's lying, I need to—"

"This is your path, Aurianna. You are about to embark on the most important quest of your life. Embrace it or walk away."

CHAPTER 20

AURIANNA

Aurianna thought a bath and a nap sounded quite wonderful.

Alas, she had no time for the latter.

The water arrived within moments. Aurianna took her time bathing then dressed in a fresh gown.

She made her way through the maze of passageways to the conservatory. When she arrived, the room was already occupied by several of her friends.

"Why are you here?" she asked in confusion.

Sigi was pale. "It seems we all had a similar visit." She rubbed her hands over her crossed arms.

"Visit?"

Leon was smoking a cigar, which Aurianna was pretty sure wasn't allowed. He pulled it from his mouth to speak. "Yeah. From your friends. You know, the Essence."

"Wasn't creepy or anything. At all." Laelia looked like she had seen a ghost, which was understandable if they had been visited by the goddesses.

"So, where's everyone else?"

Sigi glanced at her askew. "I, uh . . . Theron and I were messing around with a bow and arrow. Pharis came by the training yard and asked if he wanted to go fishing with him." She glanced away again.

"What's the matter?"

"Well, he was pretty upset. Honestly seemed like he was on the verge of crying. Did the two of you—"

"It doesn't matter."

"I know it's none of my business—"

"You're right. It isn't. So, what did they say to you? And where are my parents?"

"I haven't seen your parents. The goddesses—I still can't believe we just saw them—said you would need our support. What were they talking about?"

"They? Two of them? Together?"

"Four actually," Leon muttered.

Aurianna scowled. "I've never seen all four of them."

"Well, here we are, and now you have."

Aurianna turned toward the speaker and saw four ethereal figures standing on the dais. She moved closer—fascinated and terrified at the same time.

The one who had spoken was Caendra, goddess of Fire. Aurianna also recognized Terra, the cooler-headed goddess of Earth. The other two were new, but they were obviously Unda and Fulmena, goddesses of Water and Energy, respectively. Aurianna could tell which one was Fulmena by the electricity sparking from the edges of her semi-transparent form.

And she looked pissed, pouting like a petulant child who has just been scolded.

Terra said, "Thank you for your expediency. Time is of utmost importance."

"Funny, because, besides the elements, that's one of the few things we do have control over."

"Do not presume to elevate yourself to the level of a god!" Fulmena fumed at her.

"Hush!" Terra turned on her sister. "You have no right to judge, considering what you've done. The entire world hangs in the balance because of your blatant disregard for the rules of nature. You are the reason we are here."

Aurianna didn't hesitate to address Terra. "Why didn't you just tell me the truth about Eresseia and how this world began?"

"I did not trust myself to tell the story without bias. My sisters are at fault for all of this, and we seek to right their wrongs.

"Exactly! You started all this mess. Drakon is our mutual enemy because of what others did long ago. You may not have made him, but he's a monster of your own creation."

"That is why we must do what we can to fix what has been broken."

"And what of the other part of this world? The ones who separated from our ancestors. Are they in danger as well? Do they still exist?"

"That is another story. But the ones in danger are yourselves and your people."

"What is it you need from me? Haven't I given enough?"

"You must retrieve the Nether Stone."

"You want me to steal from the Fae queen?"

Terra shook her head. "No. The trinket she has is a forgery. It will not fit within the sword."

"She told me her magic could fix it."

"She lied. Did the stone seem familiar?"

"I thought . . . I thought it looked like the stone in my mother's necklace."

Terra nodded. "Indeed. *That* is the stone you need. The real Nether Stone."

Aurianna felt a heat rise within her as her fury unleashed. "Then why in the bloody hell didn't you tell me that before I lost it?"

"We needed it to remain safe and out of the hands of those who would take it."

"So, in order to protect it, you made sure I lost it? That makes no sense!"

"The necklace had to be out of reach until it was needed. Otherwise, it would have gone into the wrong hands."

"Which hands might those be?"

"Drakon's. He was preparing to take it from you."

"I've never even seen this Drakon. Why couldn't you have just had me hide it somewhere? Wouldn't that have been safer?"

"No, he would have searched all of Eresseia for it. It had to be presumed gone forever until the time was right."

"Well, it's a little late for that now. The necklace is at the bottom of Perdita Bay. And I don't expect those sea creatures to be bringing it straight along to me anytime soon."

"It is lost to the waters now, yes. But that has not always been so."

"What do you mean?"

"You said it yourself, Aurianna. Time. One of the few things we can control."

"But I lost it the night of the train explosion. Before the singularity. Before the time loop opened. Simon said nothing could change within the loop and things always happened the way they happened."

"You must go back. You cannot change anything that has already happened, but you must find a way to bring the necklace back. Queen Treasa is correct in what you need to do, but she is lying about her intentions. She has no desire to allow you to complete your mission."

"Why? What are her intentions then?"

"Treasa wants power. She wants control. She will have you deliver the sword with the fake stone to Drakon. She seeks an alliance with the enemy."

"And how am I supposed to stop that? We are in her domain, and we are outnumbered."

"You have developed so many powers, yet you doubt your abilities."

"Since you mention it, why are my powers different from those of other Kinetics? How am I able to create flame when all they can do is control what already exists?"

"You can create any of the elements if you wish. You are the daughter of unity. All the pieces of the puzzle in one. Your mother was half-Fae, but your father is key to this as well. He is what your people call a Void. Simon and the Fae have told you what they really are and what they do."

"Yes. They contain a piece of their element, though they can't control it."

"Imagine a child who holds the elements within and has the power to control them. Then imagine that child being descended from the Fae, who wield all the elements because they are the progeny of deities. Essence, demon, and human beings combined. No matter what my sisters did"—Terra glanced at Fulmena and Caendra in disgust—"the fact remains you are an amalgamation of every sentient being tied to this world."

Caendra appeared almost bored. "You should thank me and Fulmena." She sneered arrogantly. "Without us, you wouldn't exist."

Terra ignored her sister. "You absorb what you touch. The night of the singularity, you absorbed the Energy into yourself. It would otherwise have killed you."

"It *has* killed me, according to Simon!" Aurianna shouted.

"Keep your voice down unless you want the Fae to know what we're doing. Yes, it has. But you managed to stop it this time. You can absorb what you touch, but you can also be drained like a Void."

A gasp behind her reminded Aurianna others were in the room. She pointed a thumb over her shoulder and murmured, "And why are they here? I should be doing this alone." She hesitated then asked, "What exactly am I doing?"

"Your friends are here to support you. You need to remember what you are fighting for, Aurianna." Terra pointed an ethereal finger at her. "Remember, you cannot change anything. You must follow the path that—"

"The path that draws me. Yeah. I get it. But I don't understand how I'm supposed to get the necklace without yanking it from my own neck. Pretty sure that would be forbidden."

"The right path will come to you." Terra motioned her forward. Aurianna stepped onto the dais and stood before the goddess. "But you must hurry before the guards find out you have left. Your friends will be waiting here for you."

"But I don't know how to travel back in time. I've stopped time before, but nothing like this. And those Aether Stones the queen has are under constant guard."

"You have been preparing for this day for a long time, Aurianna. You already have the ability and the means. You just need to call on it." Terra gestured to her sister Caendra, who approached and laid a ghostly hand on Aurianna's shoulder, pulling back the fabric to expose her branded skin. The Fire goddess flicked her wrist, and Aurianna's skin began to heat.

She cried out, "What are you doing?" She tried to pull away from Caendra's grasp, but she couldn't move.

Just as the heat became almost unbearable, she peered over her shoulder at the tattoo and nearly collapsed in shock.

The branding was lifting away from her shoulder, the word *effugere* floating in the air, the edges of the design glittering as Caendra waggled her fingers at it.

Runaway.

"What did you do?" Aurianna whispered, no longer trusting the strength of her voice. She could sense the puzzlement of the others as they stared at the hovering word. The skin where it had been was now smooth, as if the word had never been there.

"This was given to you long ago. A way out. A way back. The old language is powerful. It was originally from us, a gift to the Fae, who used it almost exclusively until recent years. This word is now our gift to you."

"What am I supposed to do with it?"

"It is an incantation in written form. It has been tied to your life ever since you were touched by it."

"I still don't understand."

"It works just like an Aether Stone. You touch the word and recite it. It will take you where you wish to go."

"But I'm sure I've said it plenty of times. And it's always been touching me, technically." The word drifted down in front of her, and Aurianna stared in wonder as it landed in her palm.

"But now you know where and when you need to go."

Aurianna's friends' faces were full of concern and amazement, but no one spoke. A sound at the entrance startled her reverie, and she looked up, expecting a group of Fae.

Instead, Theron and Pharis burst into the room. They skidded to a stop when they saw the goddesses but didn't seem surprised. Terra and the others must have contacted them as well. A surge of emotion welled within her. They had come back to show their support...for her.

Words welled in her throat, but Aurianna could not voice them.

She just stared at the man who had given up everything for her, who had loved her long before she had ever known she felt the same.

It didn't make any sense, but it didn't matter. He was here, and he was staring at her with a longing that nearly broke her.

But she knew she must do this first. The necklace had to be retrieved. Stealing the sword back from the queen would come later.

A strange sensation on her arm brought Aurianna's attention to the skin there. Her wound was disappearing before her eyes—stitches and all.

When she met Terra's eyes, she started to ask the question. But she knew it didn't matter. The Essence had healed her, and now she must begin her mission.

Staring back at the branding in her hand, she said the word which would bring her back to the second-worst night of her life.

"*Effugere.*"

CHAPTER 21

AURIANNA

Reality faded away. The room and its occupants fading from Aurianna's clouded and confused mind. Instead she was traveling, bodiless, through the swirling colors of the Aether. Aurianna took a moment to observe, something she had never been able to do. The Aether was the unknown, the domain of the sacred. Only now, she was a part of it—or as much as a mortal could be.

A part of her felt relief knowing she was in this alone—no one to chase or follow her, no one to chatter incessantly about nothing in a misguided attempt to distract her from her feelings. No one to help. No one to guide her.

Alone.

In the hazy distance, a blurred image of a woman holding a bundle of blankets emerged from the kaleidoscopic display. Barely distinguishable from the dancing lights around her, only the jagged edges defined where the Aether ended and the vision began.

"Do not grieve, little one," the figure crooned. *"You will not die. I cannot undo what has already been done. You will indeed be lost to this*

world for a time, but your curse shall be to linger in the future a hundred years from now, safe from the evil in this land. At the end of that time, the one you are destined to love will find you and awaken you to your true calling. I will be your salvation, girl, but in time ... in time, you will be ours."

The vision was dream-like, a manifestation of the Aether as she found her way back through time. But there was no mistaking that voice. Larissa. Aurianna also knew she was the infant Larissa was comforting in her arms. Despite currently lacking corporeal substance, she could have sworn she felt tears prick her eyes.

This was a gift, a reminder of why she had been saved from Drakon's curse. And she would treasure it along with memories of her dear Aunt Larissa.

The spinning was coming to an end. The swirling colors were rearranging themselves into strange shapes.

She briefly wondered if she might one day be able to do more than stop time. The ability to fly back through time without assistance from the Essence could solve so many problems. Ease so many regrets. Erase so many mistakes.

And perhaps that was exactly why she would never be allowed to do so.

A strange pressure was pushing in from all sides, knocking the glowing particles into more and more complex forms, the colors combining and warping as time itself began to close in on her.

"Yeah, yeah, I get it. I'm going," Aurianna muttered as she let herself fall through the portal to her destination.

She had expected to land somewhere familiar, a dark corner where she could hide in case someone she knew happened to be near.

In case she herself were near.

The idea made her shiver for half a second before she crash-landed into something hard and—from the sound of things—breakable.

The impact made her curse the Essence to a thousand hells as she struggled with the material of her voluminous gown.

A floor. She was inside somewhere. She couldn't begin to guess why or how the Essence had chosen where to plop her down.

"Aurianna?"

One word pronounced by an achingly beautiful voice. It was a question, a statement spoken in a hopeful tone, but spelling disaster for her.

At least now she knew where she was. And the realization made her grind her teeth and curse the Essence anew.

A dim light shone through the enormous window on the far wall, the moon threatening to expose her before she even set off on her night's journey. The giant glowing orb was as big and bright as she had ever seen it. But the moon wasn't what held Aurianna's attention.

Sapphire eyes.

Shit.

Barely daring to breathe, Aurianna remained perfectly still, hoping Pharis would think he was dreaming and remain where he was, tucked into the covers on his...

Bed. At the Imperium. I'm in Pharis's bedroom. Correction: I am in the Regulus's *bedroom.*

It wasn't like she could just explain away her presence—sprawled out on the floor *in his bloody bedroom*—without raising a teensy bit of suspicion on his part. After all, if she was correct that this was the night of the train explosion, Pharis practically hated her at this point in time. He would be calling for his guards any moment. Time for a bit of quick thinking.

"Uh, yeah. Yeah, it's me. Don't panic. I-I was just leaving." *So much for quick thinking.* She winced at the utter stupidity of her remarks. Yep, he would definitely call the guards on her now. She sounded like a raving lunatic. And her backside hurt something fierce.

Aurianna scanned her immediate vicinity and realized she had landed on a small dresser. Her fall had knocked it over onto its front and several—possibly valuable—trinkets lay about her in a sad circle. How the guards hadn't heard the sound was beyond her.

Pharis had propped himself up on an elbow and was squinting into the darkness on her side of the room. Now he sat up on the bed, reaching for—

"No!" Aurianna yelled, much louder than she should have. When Pharis looked up, startled, she whispered, "I just mean, um . . . I'd rather you didn't turn on the light. I'm, uh, not properly dressed."

Not properly dressed? And standing in his bedroom? Bloody hell, what is wrong with me?

His look of confusion morphed into barely concealed amusement as he threw back the blanket and stood. Thankfully, he did not turn on the lamp.

Pharis approached with a small smile and his head cocked to the side in puzzlement. "Are you all right?"

No, no, bloody hell of hells, I am not *all right!* But she said, "Yes, I'm fine. I just need to get out of here." *I need to get out of here like Leon needs a drink on any given night.*

"Are you . . . lost?" The amusement had drained from his face.

"Yes!" *Why didn't I think of that?* "That's it! I'm lost."

The Regulus's expression had darkened, his shoulders slumping forward. The man appeared almost . . . disappointed.

Guilt and regret for how she had treated him washed over her with the force of a tidal wave. It wasn't his fault. None of it had been his fault, as Larissa had reminded her.

Javen was gone because of the choices *Javen* had made.

Ever since that fateful day, she had been feeling guilty for finding happiness after what some would see as a devastating betrayal. Javen was dead, and Aurianna had jumped into bed with the next man to come along.

Only Pharis wasn't the *next* man. He was *this* man, this figure in front of her who had been a complete ass to her throughout much of their relationship, yet she could forgive all of that because...

Well, because she loved him. Had loved him since before Javen had died, but because of a displaced sense of loyalty to a man she had *thought* loved her, she had never acted on it.

But this man in front of her *did* love her. He was a good man. Not his father. Not his failures. Pharis's character and sense of duty were the foundation of his convictions and the dreams he held for his people.

As the wild thoughts rampaged through her mind, Aurianna had been slowly inching forward across the great expanse of the bedchamber. Pharis no longer appeared crestfallen, but his puzzled expression had returned, mixed with a hint of trepidation.

Without stopping to consider the consequences, Aurianna rushed forward to close the last several feet between them, pressing her lips to his as she snaked her hands around the back of his neck. Lips to lips, chest to chest, they stood frozen in the center of the room—her hands in his hair, his body stilling at her touch.

Time stopped. Not in the evanescence way, but in the normal way it does when two people have no idea what to expect from each other, and one of them goes and does a thing neither of them anticipated.

The bubble burst as Pharis took the kiss to a whole new level, gripping her waist and pulling her closer. Her moan echoed in the space, spurring Pharis on.

Before she could come up for air, he was walking her backward until she hit a wall.

Crushing her—in a good way—with the weight of his body, Pharis wasted no time. His hand was already slipping slowly up the side of her thigh, pushing the material of her gown higher and higher as he made his way up and around to the curve of her backside. When he squeezed, she cried out, whether owing to pain from her fall or pleasure from the unexpected touch, even she wasn't sure.

Either way, he took the noise as encouragement, wrapping his left hand up the side of her other leg. He hoisted her up against the wall, never pulling his lips away, totally focused on *the kiss*.

He created the smallest of gaps between their lips and whispered, "I love you," repeating the mantra a few times before capturing her lips again.

Aurianna heard the words, but her mind couldn't bring them into focus. She'd lost herself in the moment. The two of them fit together perfectly—no beginning and no end—just one shattered soul, finally united and entwined for eternity.

Only she didn't have eternity. She didn't even have tomorrow.

And this wasn't *her* Pharis.

As the realization of what she was doing hit her full force, Aurianna practically knocked Pharis over as she pushed him away. Their breathing was ragged, and she could tell he was fighting the urge to rush forward again.

But . . . she was endangering the entire mission. And possibly the entire future of the world, including the man who stood gasping for air in front of her.

His eyes still filled with lust, Pharis stared, waiting for an explanation. But she had no explanation to give. Telling him the truth of how and why she was here was absolutely forbidden.

But messing with the past was also forbidden. They had warned her that everything had to play out exactly as it had the previous time. The goddesses hadn't specified what the repercussions would be if it didn't, but Aurianna didn't want to find out.

What the hell have I done?

Needing time to think, she allowed the feel of the Aether to surround her, hoping she could concentrate enough to make time bend to her will. The air in the room stilled—Pharis's loud breathing suddenly silent, so she knew she had been successful.

Brushing her fingertips across her swollen lips, Aurianna determined not to let this one mishap derail the plan. She could salvage this, as long as she played it right. The Essence might annihilate her when she returned to the future, but right now she was on her own.

After all, it wasn't her fault she'd been dumped straight into the bedroom of her soon-to-be but-not-yet lover. The Essence could have dropped her off right by the train station, so she could snag the necklace and be away before anyone was the wiser.

But no. The goddesses had an odd sense of humor, it seemed.

She took a few extra minutes to calm her breathing and assure herself she was in no danger of jumping him again. A thought brought reality spinning back into the world, time marching on at its usual pace once again. Her Chronokinetic power was becoming almost too easy to control.

Pharis was still staring at her like he wanted to either yell at her or throw her on his bed.

Probably both.

Aurianna cleared her throat. "I'm . . . I'm sorry about that. I think I've had too much to drink."

Pharis stared at her like she had grown an extra head. "Bullshit."

Well then.

"No, I-I shouldn't be here. I got confused, and I thought . . ."

Pharis was shaking his head. "Don't. I get it." Without another word, he went to stand in front of the giant window overlooking the fields which led to Menos and beyond.

She sighed, knowing she couldn't leave things this way and not have everything ruined between them later. "Wait," she whispered urgently. When he didn't respond or turn back, Aurianna went to the side of the room in shadow, clinging to the dark as much as she could.

Looking past him into the moonlit world, she could make out the stables in the distance. Aurianna thought about Oracle and wondered how she might pull this off. She would need the horse to get to the train once it took off. Yet her other self would come to take the horse to chase down the train as well.

She had no guide, no answers. No way of knowing the right thing to do. But everything that had already happened needed to happen again, and in the same way.

Pharis kept throwing her side glances, his crossed arms and scowl reflecting his frustration.

She beckoned him over. He refused at first. But after some coaxing, he huffed and approached the corner where she stood.

Aurianna pulled his face close, careful to keep her forehead touching his to avoid thoughts of . . . other things. She gazed into sapphire-blue depths that held so much raw emotion they practically consumed her.

Shaking her head to clear those thoughts, she whispered, "I'm so sorry about all this. I really shouldn't be here. Promise me one thing?"

"Yeah, what's that?" Pharis mumbled reluctantly.

"Don't give up on me. Just give me time."

"What the hell is that supposed to mean?"

She had meant it to be a talking point for when she returned to the future. Obviously, his memories would be all mixed up now. Or maybe not. Perhaps he would only remember this version, or perhaps *her* Pharis would only ever remember things the way they had already happened between them.

Either way, she had no more time. The fate of the world rested on her.

Aurianna noticed a door to the left of the window, in front of the bed. A quick glance told her it led to a small balcony.

Could she somehow manage to avoid the attention of the entire Imperium by escaping via Pharis's balcony? Could she sneak out without him seeing where she went?

Time for Chrono magic once again.

When the edges of the room became blurry and ethereal, Aurianna went out to stand at the balcony rail.

She couldn't help noticing the view was spectacular from this high up in the Imperium. The dorm levels had offered no windows of any kind, much less a balcony. Closing her eyes and offering herself to the night breeze until her heated skin cooled, Aurianna decided she would hide among the rocks behind the stables until she could sneak in.

Then she climbed over the railing and let the Air carry her— quite ungracefully—to the rocky base of the Imperium, but she did manage to slow her fall before landing.

Aurianna sighed. Flying was never going to come naturally to her, so she would have to settle for strategic high jumping instead. She took a leap once again, this time landing in the middle of the fields. Jumping once more, she managed to land roughly at her destination.

Peeking around the edge of the rocks, Aurianna tried to see into the back of the stables. Two grooms were talking and laughing as they put away equipment.

While she waited for them to leave, her thoughts turned to the events of a few moments before. Pharis was probably wondering if he had dreamed the whole thing. Either that, or he was royally pissed at her right now.

But he hadn't even blinked, hadn't even questioned her bold move. Pharis—the Regulus, the man-who-would-be-ruler, his high-and-mighty broodiness—had kissed her back without hesitation. And he seemed not to hate it.

Yet he had hated her. Well, maybe hate was too strong a word. But he certainly was still being an ass to her at that time and even admitted later he had resented being sent to fetch her like an errand boy.

And she understood, now. But back then, they barely tolerated one another. In fact, the day she left to go back home to the future, she had tried to mend that bridge, had tried to thank him for every-thing he had done for her, but all he said was . . .

The air around her seemed full of noise, tiny whispers clawing at her consciousness, trying to crawl inside her mind and leave their truths like unwelcome gifts.

Her heart had momentarily stopped, but now it sped up in time with the whispers, which in turn grew incessantly louder and more frantic.

Oh my bloody hell.

The world was spinning. Yet this was not magic—just realization sinking in.

"Everything must happen as it happened before. Nothing can be changed."

She had thought it a warning of the danger of messing around with the timeline inside the closed loop.

The Essence weren't telling her she *shouldn't* change anything. They were telling her that she literally *couldn't* change anything.

The kiss she had just shared with Pharis, those moments of heady passion in his bedchambers . . . had already happened.

Her legs threatened to give out as her brain processed the weight of that revelation.

It explained why Pharis was so angry at her the day she left, why he was upset when he saw her holding Javen's hand the day after the train explosion. That would have been the day after she showed up in his room and kissed him.

No, not would have been. Was. It *always* was. All of this already happened.

So many things began to click into place as she remembered all the times he had tried to tell her.

Yeah, pretty sure it was you who kissed me. Not like there was anyone else there.

At the time, she had written off his words as him being weird or cocky or something. She had been talking about their first kiss, the incident in the tunnels when he had grabbed her in anger and kissed her roughly.

Only that wasn't their first kiss. Not for him.

I mean, it was dark, but I feel pretty confident in my assessment.

All this time, he'd been waiting for her, as she'd requested. And she had had no idea. The poor idiot thought he'd fallen in love with her that night. *Tonight.* Whatever.

Bloody hell.

But what a relief she hadn't screwed everything up!

Her head was pounding, and Aurianna wasn't sure which way was up when she noticed the two grooms heading toward the front of the stables, away from Oracle's stall. At least something was working in her favor. She would have to focus on the mission and deal with the life-altering realizations later.

Careful to avoid making any noise, she crept along until she reached the beautiful black-maned horse. Oracle shook her head and whinnied, but Aurianna quickly quieted the mare, stroking the soft mane as she whispered a song her aunt used to sing to her when she was little. The memory panged as she thought about home, about everything she was risking, everything she stood to save.

Lifting the tack from nearby hooks, Aurianna worked feverishly to get her horse ready for the journey ahead. Two journeys, in fact. Oracle would have to take her to Menos to be ready to sneak on board the train from the opposite end as her former self. Then Aurianna would have to send the horse back for the second trip to Menos, the one that stood out clearly in her memories.

She heard voices and peeked around the stall door only to see . . . herself, walking straight toward them.

Too late.

She was too late. It must be later than she had thought. Why had the goddesses not given her more time? Sure, she had taken a detour—not her choice—but she hadn't been there *that* long.

Had she?

Skirting down the back aisle, Aurianna weaved her way over to a side door on the right. Once outside, she leaned against the wall that faced away from the Imperium as she contemplated what to do.

The woman on the train—her mother, an impostor, a figment of her imagination?—would be showing up soon. Her other self was currently trying to figure out why Oracle was already tacked up. Any minute now, the ghostly figure would float across the grounds, heading for the train with orbs of Fire in her hands.

She needed to try to get on the train another way. But no stops existed between here and Menos, where her earlier self had boarded the train. She couldn't get to Menos in time without Oracle, and she obviously couldn't board.

Oh. No.

Noooooooo.

No. What the hell? No.

Aurianna closed her eyes. She was too tired for any more revelations.

And yet this one slammed into her, and she could do nothing but accept it—along with the reality that the Essence really were some sick, twisted ladies.

Aurianna vaguely wondered if their brother was this abusive to mortals.

She wanted to shake her fist and yell obscenities. They were probably back in the Aether, laughing it up over the tantrum she was trying not to throw.

At least one good thing had come from what was going to be a nightmarish evening. She now knew that her mother had been telling the truth all along.

Syrena wasn't the woman on the train.

She was.

PART THREE

AWAKENED

Fumbling, stumbling, crumbling mind.
In death I'll not be someone's rotting corpse.
In sleep I lie in dreams that do not die,
Awakened by one who knows my true name.

CHAPTER 22

AURIANNA

The white gown and hood glowed in the moonlight. She had been so intent on her meeting with the Essence she'd just picked something and put it on without recognizing the garment.

The red hair. Why hadn't it occurred to her before? The Essence had known all along, of course. Did Larissa know?

She had no time to sit and cry, to curse her fate, or to shake her fist at the Aether and curse the Essence. There was no time left at all.

The irony was not lost on Aurianna.

She sighed and hung her head, allowing herself a second to prepare for the hell she was about to experience.

Again. And this time from the losing side.

Aurianna held her head high while making sure the hood of her pale gown was pulled down to hide most of her face. She made a wide arc around the front of the stables to avoid anyone else noticing her.

Not that she needed to worry about it. Clearly, she wasn't changing anything. All of this had already happened. This was her mission to fulfill, her destiny from the very beginning. There was no turning back, no choice but to go on.

Vaguely, she wondered how badly it hurt to have the power drained from your body. She had never been on the receiving end before and was not thrilled by the prospect.

Quite a few things about this night had never made any sense to her, but now it was all quite clear. Chronokinetic power would be essential to pull this off. It was the only way the "Enchantress"— correction, *she*—had been able to reach the train so quickly and without alerting anyone at the station. And it was the only way she could have avoided the men lying in wait to kidnap . . . her.

I'm a tricky little bitch, she thought sardonically. If she had to do it, she might as well play up the role of "evil Enchantress."

Gliding across the field, Aurianna conjured an orb of flame in her palm, making sure she was holding it in plain sight. The wind picked up the edges of her brightly colored hair, tugging it out to dance in the breeze. She risked a quick peek behind to make sure her other self was paying attention.

The other Aurianna had stopped petting the horse and was gaping at the red-haired woman in the field.

Making her way to the train depot, she kept to the edges of everyone's vision, using her Chronokinetic ability to freeze time as needed. The front of the train was closest to her position, so when she reached it, Aurianna peeked into the engine car. No one was there. A sense of relief washed over her. Where were the Pyros who ran the train? Why had they left when it was clear it was supposed to leave any moment?

It was late, the moonlight dim, but even if few people were about, the men inside the train—the ones intent on kidnapping her—would still be an obstacle. And this time she was aware that the "woman on the train" was not their ally. She would have to avoid

250

them, but she also needed to do a sweep for any Pyro engineers who might be somewhere else on board.

Aurianna edged down the length of the train with her back practically flush with the outer wall. Sneaking onto the final platform, Aurianna used her Chronokinetic ability to skirt past the kidnappers in the back car. She was still baffled by how they had known she would get on this train. Someone in the chain of events had known what she would do before she did it.

And it frightened her beyond belief.

Aurianna cleared her mind of those thoughts to focus on the task at hand. Her first job was to make sure any innocent Pyros left on board were spared from the explosion. The necklace would come after.

But how was she to save the necklace if she wasn't able to change anything?

Inching forward, one train car at a time, Aurianna manipulated the Aether to suit her needs. She slipped into a state of evanescence as she floated through each car, slipping back into the normal flow of time as she traveled to the next compartment.

When she reached the coal car near the front once more. Aurianna was satisfied that the engineers were not on the train. What that meant, she didn't know. But the coals were primed, and the boiler was already full of steam. She drew the power of the flames into herself, molding it and making it stronger before letting it seep back into the firebox. She opened the throttle, then pulled the lever which sounded the train's whistle, the noise jarring in the stillness of the night. The wheels began to turn, and the train took off down the tracks.

Through the window to her right, she saw the advancing horde, reduced to near-mindlessness by dragonblood. The immediate threat would be dealt with this night and into the following morning, but the tragic effects of their actions would be lasting.

Meanwhile, she had to keep the train going, while also taking care not to blow up the engine too early. And she also had to get the necklace. Once she had it, she would have to double back to the engine room, since the showdown with her former self would begin in this very spot. The timing would be crucial. And yet, if she truly couldn't change anything, was it possible for her to fail in any of this?

All these questions made her head hurt. She realized her focus was slipping, and each time it did, the train would slow down and speed up in a reckless fashion. A sudden thought occurred to her. It was the jerky movements of the train that had made Sigi fall that night.

Dizziness and nausea washed over her in a tidal wave of guilt. The Essence—or whatever it had been—may have saved her friend, but Aurianna had been responsible for nearly killing her.

Aurianna felt the train's movement slip once again. She cursed and forced her attention back to the coals within the firebox. As they neared the station in Menos, she yanked on the braking mechanism, allowing the train to slow almost to a stop. She had no choice. This was what had happened—how Aurianna had managed to get on board the first time. After a moment, she stoked the fires and released the brake. The train began to move once more.

A sound just behind her made Aurianna jump. As she spun around, someone hissed, "Who the hell are you?"

One of the kidnappers had made his way to the engine room, probably to check on why the train was moving so erratically. The train lurched once again as Aurianna focused on removing the threat.

"Just whatta ya think yer doing? Where's the men what's supposed to run the engine?"

Still refusing to speak, Aurianna inhaled slowly, summoning her Air power. She needed to keep the train running, rescue her necklace, and not lose her mind in the process.

Exhaling sharply, Aurianna rushed forward, a gust of Air propelling her as she clasped the man's arms before he could react. In a blink, she pulled him through the open side of the engine room. She released her hold on the henchmen, and they fell.

The man screamed.

Aurianna scooped Air around herself and landed back inside the train, leaving him to his fate. She got the train moving again, much quicker this time, the speed increasing even as her emotions boiled.

She remembered the horror she'd felt that night at the death of these men, despite their intentions. Her heart had hardened since then. It had started the day she'd discovered that the man who had claimed to love her had deceived and used her—had ultimately betrayed them all.

And the one who truly had been in love with her had stood by and watched the entire chain of events—while she blindly followed the source of so many evils. He had even given his life to save her.

Her goal now was to be worthy of so great a love, so grand a destiny. To hell with the Essence and their schemes to use her in their cosmic games. Her destiny was aligned with his, to save the people and the world in which they lived.

So yes, her heart had hardened, but Aurianna still wept, choking back a sob as she grieved for the men who would die this night. In addition to kidnapping her, their orders had been to blow up the train once they came back around to Bramosia, possibly killing hundreds or thousands of innocent people. They deserved punishment, certainly, but did they deserve death?

Whether she had the right to decide their fate or not, she knew the fate of the world rested on events playing out as they had.

She could blame the goddesses for putting her through this, for involving her in their nonsense. But she had more immediate issues to deal with. Through the open door, screams of terror floated to her on the night wind.

Sigi!

Aurianna raced up the ladder to the top of the train and ran along its length, stopping just before she reached the two women at the back. Her past self was leaning over the edge of the back platform, a desperate grip on Sigi's arm as she struggled to hold on. But this story already had an ending. If the Essence were ever going to interfere, this was the...

But...the Essence never interfered.

They had told her multiple times that they simply *couldn't*. Not in this closed part of the timeline. Drakon had held power over the world until Aurianna had opened the time loop. They were forbidden from doing anything to aid her.

The train had a good momentum going. With clenched fists, Aurianna reached down to the waters below. She heard a horrified gasp from her other self as she lost her grip on Sigi. In the moment Sigi began to fall, the younger Aurianna had turned away, unable to watch her friend die.

The girl tumbled through the air.

Her thoughts started to return to the man who'd just experienced the same fate.

No. That wouldn't help anyone right now.

Aurianna heard a crashing sound, like thunder, just below them. She knew it was working. The waters of Perdita Bay were bending to her will, rushing up to meet the falling girl and save her.

Aurianna used her Hydrokinetic power to continue moving Sigi to safety. She dropped the girl off on land, and the train left her behind in the shadowy distance.

Now her other self was battling with the kidnapper. The man was leaning out of an open train car door, attempting to strangle her younger self as she dangled by her neck. Her fingernails were digging into the man's arm as he lifted her.

Aurianna shivered as she remembered the panic, the sheer terror of knowing she was going to die. Her body was lifted higher as the man grabbed hold of her necklace and her hair. She knew what would happen next.

And then she remembered.

In just a moment, she would pull back from the pain, and the chain would break. This had caused the man to lose his balance— his weight pulling him out of the compartment—and he'd tumbled to his death.

But her younger self had been too scared, too horrified, to watch the man fall. She had pulled herself back into the car before looking back. By then, the man and the necklace had both disappeared into the water.

Or had they?

The man was already pitching forward through the door, the broken necklace still in his grasp. Aurianna waited to act until the moment the pendant flew out of his hand.

Time seemed to stop, swirls of Aether surrounding her, as she lightly jumped off the side of the train, her Aerokinetic powers cushioning and taking her to the necklace where it hung in midair. When her fingers closed around it, she carefully let go of her Chronokinetic power.

Once she was back in sync with the normal temporal flow, Aurianna could move with the necklace. She used Air to push herself back to the top of the train, collapsing into a heap while she caught her breath.

In a few moments, her younger self would discover the explosives on board and come to what she now knew were outrageously incorrect conclusions about the "Enchantress."

She felt horrible for blaming Syrena.

Aurianna tucked her mother's necklace into a pocket inside her gown. She summoned her Aerokinetic ability again and floated swiftly down to a compartment near the front of the train where she knew she must make an appearance.

She climbed down the ladder to the open platform and peeked inside the car. Three men were within, and she knew what she was going to do.

Because she had already done it.

Adjusting her hood to hide her face and cover most of her red hair, Aurianna took a deep breath before stepping into the space. Instead of evanescing herself, she removed only the three men from the timestream, essentially freezing them from her perspective. And she waited.

She held the men in stasis as her other self entered the far end of the compartment and stared at her in awe before asking, "Who are you?"

Aurianna didn't answer. She held up her hands, palms up, igniting a small orb of Fire in each. The flames changed colors from blue to orange to red.

The younger version of her moved closer and repeated her question.

But Aurianna wouldn't answer. The memory of this night was burned into her mind, and she already knew the outcome. What she wasn't sure about was when the Essence would bring her back to her own time.

She began edging her way back to the door behind her. She called the Air outside to slam the door open. She spun around and left the car, expanding the evanescent cocoon with the three men in the car to include her other self just long enough to get through the next compartment, where the coal was stored, to the engine room. There she did an about-face to again confront her inevitable attacker. This was the part she had dreaded most of all.

And she saw the moment when the anger and frustration within her past self began to pull from the heat of the burning coal. She remembered the feeling, remembered the fear and the turmoil.

But what she felt next was new.

Pain.

Pain worse than anything she had ever felt. The power she had grown accustomed to was slowly, excruciatingly, being sucked out of her to light another flame. And she was weakening.

This was what being drained felt like. She thought of the Void she had injured that day in the tunnels during Fire training. She thought of the Kinetics who had suffered through this at the hands of the Consils of her childhood in the future. Those men and women had been forced to endure this, again and again, until they died—a slow torture at the hands of those greedy for power, yet ignorant of its true potential.

Her senses muffled, she felt her body lean against the wall for support. The heat within the small space was suffocating. It took all her willpower not to fall to the floor. Aurianna reached out a hand to guide herself to the ladder.

The draining continued, almost bringing her to her knees.

She had to get out before *she* killed *herself*.

But she had to let it happen. It was necessary in order for her younger self to move forward after this night. Without it, things wouldn't have played out as they had, and she might not have succeeded in stopping Javen this time around.

But allowing it to happen didn't mean she couldn't fight back a little. The first time around, Aurianna had been confused as to why the woman on the train—who was clearly more skilled at using her power, even possessing powers which had seemed impossible—hadn't done more to fight back.

Tears began to well, but Aurianna willed them away. *Later.*

She had a job to do. The girl before her was scared but persistent, and Aurianna needed to get to the top of the train. She gripped the ladder and pulled herself up before she collapsed completely. As she began to haul herself up the metal rungs, she concentrated, forcing her other self's movements to slow and her feet to feel stuck to the floor. It would only last for a moment, but it would be enough to allow her to reach her destination.

Only a little longer and the Essence would pull her back. Aurianna's mission was to return with the necklace. Actually being in one piece hadn't been specified, but she had thought it a safe enough assumption.

Perhaps she was wrong.

The wind blowing across the top of the train was frightening in its intensity. The force of it was enough to make Aurianna feel small as she straightened and walked along the top of the train away from the locomotive before turning to face her enemy.

Herself.

She had to keep her head tilted at an uncomfortable angle so the wind wouldn't knock her hood off. She again manifested the orbs of Fire in her palms. All her actions felt natural, yet she remembered watching them in confused amazement.

Her past self inched closer, so Aurianna struck out with her hand and shot a warning flame in her direction, causing the girl to stumble and land hard on her knee. Aurianna winced with the memory of that pain.

She edged further away, and her other self gave chase. They both picked up speed.

Wrath boiled in young Aurianna's eyes, the anger flooding every inch of her. Aurianna remembered it with keen fascination, how the moment had taken over and unleashed a part of her she hadn't known existed. Any moment, the train would explode with that girl's unfettered fury. Aurianna had to escape, but how?

She patted the pocket which held her mother's necklace, whispering a plea to the Essence to get her safely back to the future.

Nothing happened.

Then she was blinded by a vision: flashes of images flooding her mind. Places she had been, people she had met. The Order of the Daoine, the resistance hideout. The enchanted forest. The Fae. None of it had made any sense the first time.

Their minds were melding, creating a mental bond, past and future. They would do this together. As one.

Her other self was draining her again without realizing it, so Aurianna helped by focusing their power on the coals, the firebox, the train cars themselves as the other Aurianna advanced. The explosives themselves would be the final defining moment, but Aurianna knew it would be too late by then. The Essence must retrieve her before the train exploded entirely.

Pieces of the train—both large and small—flew by as each car was decimated just as the other girl passed them. The heat was almost unbearable.

Young Aurianna began to run. So she pivoted and fled too. The power was about to take over the other her. The train would be obliterated. And her younger self would be floating in the waters of Perdita Bay.

What the hell are you waiting for? she screamed in her mind at the goddesses, tears once again blurring her vision as she fought down her panic and anger.

A lightness took over her being. Behind her, the girl was losing her grip on her powers. The deafening sounds of explosion grew.

In a moment of panicky inspiration, she shouted the incantation word, her voice lost within the blast. In that instant, the lightness expanded, and she felt herself being pulled through the Aether.

CHAPTER 23

SIGI

Aurianna's departure left behind a stillness and a dread. Anticipation kept them all rooted in place.

Sigi felt her friend's absence like a punch to the gut, as if she were well and truly gone. Aurianna hadn't just popped around the corner to get a snack or take a nap. She was gone from this world. Or this time?

She tried to wrap her head around the idea of time travel. Both occasions when Aurianna had arrived from the future, Sigi had accepted it without thinking. But now, when she had ample opportunity to think about it and what it meant, her mind couldn't handle the complexity of it all.

The moment Aurianna had gone, the Essence had gone as well. They were there, and then they weren't. Sigi had no idea where the goddesses were, or when they would return.

One by one, the others got antsy. Leon stood behind Laelia with his arms wrapped around her waist. But Laelia seemed uncomfortable with the gesture. Sigi wondered if they had been fighting.

When she glanced at Theron, he was looking straight at her as he absentmindedly stroked Rhouth, who must have scurried over at some point since Aurianna was sent through the Aether. His smile was awkward, but genuine. Sigi wondered what he was thinking.

Pharis stood beside him, just as horrified as when he'd walked into the room to find the woman he loved evaporating into the Aether. Since then, he hadn't spoken, hadn't asked what she was doing. His mouth was set in a firm line, his jaw clenched with every bit of anxiety Sigi herself felt.

Ethan and Syrena hadn't shown up yet, but it was probably for the best. If Syrena knew what Aurianna was doing, why she had gone back to the past...

Sigi wrinkled her nose and sighed. She should suggest that everyone rest or eat or something. She opened her mouth to speak but was interrupted by a brilliant flash of light that shook everyone from their collective stupor.

Sigi heard a gasp but was focused on the trembling, ash-covered form standing before them.

Aurianna had reappeared exactly from where she had left. Had it only been moments before? It felt like years. When she lowered her hood, the room took a collective step backward. The girl's face was haggard, her skin pale and covered in a sheen of sweat. Her eyes were haunted, and she seemed about to collapse.

Sigi abandoned her impulse to rush in and support her friend when Aurianna shook her head.

Aurianna swept her gaze around the room until she spotted Pharis. The haunted look melted away, and her golden orbs were riveted on Pharis's sapphire-blue ones. A charge electrified the room, invisible yet unmistakable.

The two shared a look so fraught, so intense, Sigi felt like she was intruding on an intimate moment. Despite the shared look, they were expressing two completely different emotions. Pharis seemed wary and confused, but he stood his ground resolutely. Aurianna, on the other hand, exuded fire.

Pure, all-consuming fire.

That, more than anything, unnerved Sigi and unlocked the fear in her chest she'd been trying to suppress or at least hide, ever since Aurianna had displayed such intense Fire power in the halls of the resistance during their escape attempt. She had also caused an entire train to blow up and somehow absorbed the sphere of Energy on the rooftop. Sigi hated to admit it, but she feared what Aurianna was capable of, especially considering everything they now knew about her heritage.

Swallowing the lump of dread in her throat, she started to speak but was silenced by what happened next.

Aurianna rushed past Sigi to throw her arms around Pharis, locking her mouth to his and causing the man to stumble back until he came to rest against a wall.

Sigi sidled toward the door, whispering, "Maybe we should give them a minute."

The others were also edging toward the exit. All except Laelia, who stood watching with a grin on her face. Sigi tried to pull her away from the spectacle, but before they reached the door, Aurianna gently leaned back in order to gaze into Pharis's eyes again. She lovingly traced his features with her fingertips. Somehow, the gesture was more intimate than the kiss.

Sigi froze, unsure what to do. Aurianna had gone through a major ordeal. Her friend had changed in some deep and meaningful way, and Sigi didn't want to abandon her.

Pharis's eyes were wide—passion and confusion alternating in his expression. He huffed a shaky laugh, and his voice was raspy with lust when he asked, "What was that for?"

"For being patient. For giving me time like I asked. And for not giving up on me."

"So, we're doing this *now*?" he asked.

"Doing what?" Aurianna's fingertips grazed his lips.

"I've begged you to talk about that night. You just disappeared into thin air."

Aurianna pulled away, her eyes dropping to the floor. "I...I know. I wish I could have done it differently. But all this time...I didn't know what you were talking about."

"Didn't know...what?"

"Until I went back just now, I didn't understand what you meant."

Pharis gaped at her. "What? How could you...? You said you'd been drinking, but—"

"No, I wasn't. I know I said that, but I panicked. I thought I was messing everything up. But it did happen. It just hadn't happened for me yet."

"What hadn't happened yet?"

"That night." Aurianna sighed. "Pharis, I wasn't aware of that night until just now. I wasn't there until today."

"You weren't where? What the bloody hell are you going on about?"

"Please don't get angry." Tears welled in her eyes as she pleaded with him. "I'm trying to explain. That night only just happened for me. I know you went through it a long time ago, and *now* I understand why you were so hurt and angry. I understand why me being with Javen was so hard for you."

"Hard? I told you I loved you, and you couldn't get away fast enough. You vanished! And the next day, there you were, hand in hand with that bastard. It was a slap in the face, Aurianna." Then he blinked as he realized what she'd said. "Wait, what?"

She drew in a deep breath, seeming to center herself. "I know you. I've always known you."

"What do you mean?"

"When I was born, Larissa told me the one I was destined to love would one day find me and awaken me." Her smile was tender as she explained. "You set me on my path. You awoke me from a dream I didn't even realize I was in. I walked with you in that dream, and you brought me into the sunlight, Pharis. The way you look at me, the way you've always looked at me . . . It was always there, always familiar, the gleam that told me you loved me. Nothing has turned out as it seemed it would. So many truths I thought I knew are just ashes in the wind. Look at me now, tell me you love me. I know you do. You've loved me ever since you brought me out of that dream."

Pharis stood frozen, his face unreadable. "I do love you. Of course I do. But it doesn't change the way you've been acting."

"You're right. I've been a beast to you. To everyone. I got it in my head that everything was my fault, and I felt so bad about . . . I've never killed anyone before! I convinced myself it was the wrong choice, that I could have found another way, and that I only did it because I was angry over losing you. When he shot you, I lost a part of myself I've been struggling to get back. All this time, I thought I was punishing myself. But really, I was only punishing you and everyone around me. I let my guilt take over. But that's no excuse for my behavior."

Sigi was slowly backing away again. They should have left before. This moment wasn't meant for an audience.

But Aurianna spoke, not taking her eyes from Pharis's face. "Please don't leave, Sigi. All of you. I'm sorry for making you uncomfortable, but I need all of you to know what happened."

Sigi stammered. "I-I just thought maybe—"

Aurianna took in the group, meeting each of their confused expressions with confidence. "When I left here, the Essence took me to a moment just before my past self left the Imperium for the stables. And I landed in the Regulus's bedchamber."

Leon muttered something, and Laelia punched him in the shoulder, snickering. Theron hadn't spoken, but Sigi knew he was as shocked as she was. Why would the Essence do that?

Pharis sputtered. "What? I would have remembered if there were two of—" His words cut off abruptly. His face paled. "Oh," he whispered, pointing a shaking finger at Aurianna. "That was *you*? In my room that night? I thought . . . I thought you were just scared to tell me why you were there."

"I *was*. But not for the reasons you thought. When I ran up and kissed you—"

Sigi interrupted, "What? Are you insane? You were told to avoid everyone!"

"What the hell was I supposed to do? I was already *in his room*, and he was . . . Well, it was complicated." Her cheeks reddened at the memory.

"Complicated?" Sigi spat. "You could have changed everything!"

"Yeah, that's what I thought too. Which is why I ran away, Pharis. I thought I had already messed up the timeline. The Essence warned me I couldn't change anything. But they didn't say I *mustn't*. They meant literally—I *couldn't* change anything. It had all happened before, the same way. See? This whole time, Pharis has been thinking I abandoned him that night, probably that I was leading him on or something. But it wasn't *that* me. It was *this* me."

Theron scowled. "My head hurts."

Aurianna huffed. "Yeah. Mine too, friend. But the part I need to tell you—" She paused, scanning the room. "The part I really need to tell you is about my mother. Where is she? Did anyone ever find my parents?"

Sigi shook her head. "No. In fact, you haven't been gone long. I mean, it was long enough to make us worry ... but probably only a few minutes. No one's had time to look for them or anything. She's most likely in her room."

Sighing, Aurianna sank to the floor and hugged her knees to her chest, her long white gown cascading around her. Pharis knelt down and put a hand on her shoulder, encouraging her to continue her story.

Placing a hand over his, she beamed up at him, a love shining in her eyes Sigi had never seen before. Their gazes clung to one another as if no one else in the world existed. Pharis mouthed the words *I love you*. Then he grinned.

Aurianna returned the grin and whispered back, "I love you too."

She's always been so afraid to open her heart. Sigi was filled with joy for her friend's happiness.

Suddenly, Aurianna's face fell. "And where are the Essence?"

Theron cleared his throat. "They, uh, they left." The poor man was still reeling from his second encounter with the cosmic beings.

"They left?" Aurianna gritted her teeth. "Oh, of course they did! Send me out, use me, then disappear. She healed my wound just to get my strength up for what they were about to do to me."

"What did they do?" Pharis's voice was a deep, wrathful rumbling that echoed in the room. They were all feeling defensive for their friend.

"I wanted Syrena here for this, but I guess I'll have to tell her later. My mother wasn't on that train." She waited for that to sink in before adding, "It was me."

"What was you?" Leon asked.

"The woman on the train. The one in the white gown"—she

267

plucked at her skirts—"with the red hair"—Aurianna pulled a strand of her hair—"was . . . me."

Laelia snorted. "Wait. It was you, but you didn't recognize yourself?" She laughed, the sound high-pitched and wheezing.

"I didn't see a face, remember? It's not like you expect to see *yourself* walking by . . . with different hair!"

Sigi sobered. "Aurianna, I almost fell into the bay." A cold chill washed down her spine. "Something, someone . . . Oh my Essence!" she exclaimed in a whisper, clutching her head. "That was you, wasn't it?"

Aurianna nodded. "Yeah. It was me. This me. And everything that happened—which had happened before—happened again. Only this time, I was on the receiving end of my powers. She drained me. Me, I mean. I drained myself, only I wasn't aware of what I was doing the first time. That's what caused the explosion."

No one spoke for a solid minute, enraptured with the impossibility of the story.

"I'm the one who boarded that train," Aurianna whispered. "I'm the 'evil Enchantress' I was searching for all that time. No enemy but myself."

Pharis blanched. "You're not evil, Aurianna. How could you say that?"

"I don't know what I am. And I know I didn't intend for things to go that way, but I can't help thinking—"

"You're *not evil*," Sigi said, echoing Pharis's words. "And you're not the enemy." She placed a hand on Aurianna's shoulder and squeezed. "Did you get the necklace?"

"Yes, I did." Aurianna smiled and seemed grateful for the subject change. "I had to use my Aerokinetic and Chronokinetic power to be there at just the right moment before it fell into the water. *And* not be seen by my other self while doing it." Aurianna got back to her feet and studied the group, tears in her eyes. "I felt so alone. None of you were there. I mean, no one was there to help me, to tell me what I should do. I missed all of you, and I'm sorry I pushed you away."

Sigi hugged her friend. "Everything's fine. We never doubted you."

Against her shoulder, Sigi felt Aurianna shaking her head. "No, you did. When I went back to the future after the train and then returned, none of you believed me. You were ignoring me, but—"

"Aurianna, we weren't ignoring you. Javen said you wanted to be left alone."

"What?"

Laelia came over and took a turn hugging Aurianna. When she pulled back, she said, "Yeah, he told us you were upset and needed time to cool off. He said you wanted space."

"That's not what . . . I can't believe he lied to all of us."

"Really, Aurianna?" Leon said from behind her, and she faced him. "That's the hardest part for you to believe in all of this?" He opened his arms, and she fell into his embrace with a sob. The tears which had been threatening to spill over finally fell in rivers. Leon patted her head as he rocked her.

"I thought you hated me." Aurianna sniffed.

"No, of course not. But I—" Leon pulled back and ran a hand through his hair. "Oh hell. That's my fault, I know. I was being an ass. But I wasn't really angry at you."

"Yes, you were." Aurianna's voice was flat.

He nodded. "Okay, I was. But only because I thought you were being cavalier with the—with Pharis here."

"I know. I felt guilty about it, but . . ." Aurianna scowled. "I'm sorry."

"No need to apologize. Javen's the one who messed us up. Not surprising we took it out on each other a bit."

LISA M. GREEN

"Why though? That's what I don't understand. What could he have gained from putting a divide between us?"

A sadness flashed in Leon's eyes. He pursed his lips in thought. "And why the whole drama on the roof of the Imperium? What was he trying to prove?"

Laelia swooped in, placing her hands on Leon's chest. "All I know is, his attempts at pulling us apart certainly didn't work." She pressed her lips to his. He didn't shy away from the affection, grabbing her by the waist to pull her closer.

Sigi cleared her throat.

The two ignored their audience until Theron cupped his hands around his mouth and shouted, "*Ahem.*"

Laelia pulled back with a lazy motion and pouted. "If we didn't want anyone watching, we would have gone to our room." She lightly punched Sigi in the arm. "Don't be such a spoil sport."

"Spoil sport? We have bigger issues right now, may I remind you. And—"

"Just because you aren't getting any doesn't mean you have to ruin it for others."

"Excuse me? How the hell would you know what I'm getting or not getting?"

"Well, I know you sure haven't taken up the—admittedly subtle—offers from a certain mutual friend of ours."

Theron started coughing. Leon was glaring at Laelia.

Sigi was simply confused. "Laelia, what are you—"

"Don't move!"

A group of Fae stood blocking the main exit, and a female guard continued, "You are all to come with us and present yourselves to Queen Treasa!"

Sigi's instinct was to fight, but for once she had no weapon to hand. She spun around, searching the room, only to realize why no one else had moved. Another group of Fae were poised just outside a glowing circle on the floor, its edges lined with symbols.

This was Fae magic. The circle wound around their small group, enclosing them in its magical borders. Sigi tried to use her Fire ability, but the spell was blocking her powers.

They were helpless.

One of the Fae spoke. "You will keep your hands visible and follow us."

"What the hell do you think we did?" Sigi snapped.

The female looked irritated by the delay and said, as if stating the obvious, "You stole the Nether Stone from the Fae queen's quarters."

Chapter 24

AURIANNA

Aurianna nodded at the Fae. "Lead on, then." Meanwhile she was running through a dozen possible scenarios in her head.

The queen obviously knew she had the necklace.

At the moment, she wasn't sure who she was more upset with: the Fae queen for lying to her, or the Essence for manipulating her.

The nullifying circle moved with them as they were ushered back to Treasa's personal quarters. They entered the suite which held a large dining table at the near end as well as several seating areas.

The room was empty. The guards prodded them to sit around a table laden with what could only be described as a feast. Aurianna's stomach rumbled, and she realized it had been ages since she had eaten. Leon stared at the table with both trepidation and longing.

One of the guards said, "Eat. The queen wishes you to make yourselves comfortable before she comes to interrogate you."

"Ah, dinner before imprisonment. Excellent!" Leon remarked caustically as the Fae left the room and closed the doors. They heard the distinctive click of a lock.

Aurianna jumped up and ran to check the other exits. She was not surprised to discover them locked as well. She was dismayed, however, to see the Fae circle stretching to encompass her movements. She rejoined the others at the table.

Sigi shrugged. "As long as we don't drink the wine, right?"

Leon nodded and began to dig in before anyone could question the wisdom of the action. Laelia ate with tentative nibbles. The others soon succumbed as well, from boredom if not hunger.

Aurianna couldn't bring herself to eat, despite her earlier hunger. Her thoughts ran rampant, her ire building to a crescendo. The greed and selfishness of so many had led to the ruination of their world. Did the Essence not even care? What did they really want?

Leon and Pharis were trying to whisper, but their voices were far too loud for any sort of confidential communication.

Pharis hissed, "I know, and it's so hard to explain to people what it's like living in your father's shadow. It's not like I asked to be related to the bastard. Do you know he tried to force me to marry Aurianna?"

A look of confusion crossed Leon's face. "But I thought you loved her?"

"I did. Do. Yeah. But see, he was doing it for all the wrong reasons. Selfish reasons."

The Magnus was just one of many who thought only of themselves, and Aurianna wondered if positions of power inevitably created the desire for more power, or if that was just how certain people were. If Pharis had become the next Magnus, would he have been corrupted as well?

"Yeah, my father was a right asshole too," Leon mumbled around a mouthful of food. "Stayed out all night drinking, whoring. Never there for us. Good thing he's dead." He slapped the table with a meaty fist then giggled.

Her trust in others had been broken time and again. But now she knew who her friends truly were. And she was grateful—

"Mine too. I killed him." Pharis said, also with a strange giggle.

Aurianna looked up, startled by the sound. That wasn't like Pharis at all.

Leon finished chewing, nodding and suddenly serious. "The night my father died, I had slipped out of bed and followed him to the pub. I was seven years old, but I sort of had an idea of what he was doing. He was in there a long time, so I sat by the edge of the water—a ways off but close enough to see when he came back out. I planned to tell him off, let him know we wouldn't stand for it anymore. But when he finally stumbled out of that place, he was so drunk he didn't even notice me or the storm that had blown up. He crossed the narrow street and took a few stumbling steps toward the canal. Didn't even see it."

A feeling of dread began at the base of Aurianna's spine, but it had nothing to do with his words. Something was wrong.

The entire table was listening now, enraptured by this story that, apparently, none save Laelia had ever heard. She remained focused on the plate of food in front of her, occasionally patting Leon on the arm as he spoke.

"Struck by lightning!" Leon shouted. "He got zapped and fell right into the channel. Drowned before anyone could get to him." Leon leaned forward and whispered conspiratorially, "But what they didn't realize was . . . the Water damn near swallowed him up before he even hit the surface." He pointed at himself. "I did that. Didn't realize it *then*, but I know it was me what done it." He shrugged, but his expression did not match his flippant words.

The room was stunned into silence, apart from the sound of Laelia smacking her lips and licking her fingers.

Something was definitely off. Aurianna snatched the plate from in front of the other girl. Laelia whined and tried to grab it back, but Aurianna shook her head. "No, stop eating. Everyone. Right now. Stop eating. Something is wrong with the food."

Sigi cocked her head. "But you said the food was fine. You ate it the other night too. And we've eaten it plenty of times since. It's the wine—" She scanned the table, suddenly realizing no wine had been served this time.

Aurianna shook her head. "I know what I said. But they're obviously doing something to the food when they want us off our guard. Like when we're about to be *interrogated*?"

"What do we do?" Pharis looked like he was attempting to sober up, but this wasn't the result of alcohol. This was Fae magic.

The door to the hall burst open. Larissa waltzed in, followed by a group of Fae. None of them seemed like guards, but Aurianna was wary.

"What's going on?" She stood, and the others followed suit— some rather unsteadily.

Syrena and Ethan pushed their way through the crowd.

Aurianna rushed forward to embrace them. "I was worried something might have happened to you—that the queen had already taken you captive. Or worse." She beamed, relieved and eager to share her discoveries. "We have a lot to discuss."

Her parents stood frozen, confused by her sudden display of affection.

"Indeed," Larissa declared. "I'm sorry it took me so long. Treasa has a good many of the Fae fooled." She grinned, looking all the more Fae as she did. "But not all of them."

"I don't understand."

"First things, first." Larissa pointed to the glowing circle on the floor. "That's got to go." Two of the Fae behind her walked over and placed their hands on the circle. The bright lines turned an intense shade of yellow before fading and finally disappearing. "That's better." Larissa gestured to another of the Fae, who held out a tray filled with potions. "Take and drink. It'll help."

Pharis shook his head and crossed his arms belligerently. "I'm not eating or drinking anything a Fae offers me ever again."

Larissa huffed. "Well, I guess that's fair enough. But we don't have time for nonsense. I'm trying to help you. The potion will reverse the effects of the spell she put on the food."

Aurianna stared at her aunt for a moment before nodding. "We can trust her. Everyone, drink." They each took a vial and downed the contents. The effects were almost immediate.

Larissa instructed the other Fae to station themselves at each door.

Then she gestured for them to sit back down, and she joined them at the table. With a wave of her hand, the food disappeared.

Ah! Now she saw where Syrena had learned it.

Laelia rested her chin on her hands. "*That's* the magic I want to learn."

"I'm afraid it is not a skill which can be taught to a human, my dear. Fae magic is much different from your kind. We inherit what we have from our parentage, as twisted as that parentage might be." Larissa grimaced. "Syrena was taught a little as a child. In time, Aurianna might learn it. But this is untested waters, I'm afraid. Never before has this world seen a being born of all the sentient races."

The others stared at Aurianna, a mix of wonder and fear on their faces. She hadn't divulged this part to them. She braced her hands against the edge of the table and said, "My father is a Void. Remember I told you how Simon described Voids as holding bits of the element inside them? That's why their Kinetic power never comes to fruition. But Kinetics are conduits of the elements who

276

can tap into that elemental substance, even draining a Void if we're not careful. And Treasa, if she is to be believed in anything, told us the origin story of how the different beings came to be. Fae are the children of the Essence and demons, or dragons." She preferred that word to the other, for some reason. "So, my grandmother was a Fae, my mother is a Kinetic, and my father is a Void. I'm literally a little of everything. Which is why my power works the way it does."

Aurianna's explanation was greeted with silence. Syrena seemed a little dazed, but Leon slapped his knee and burst out laughing. "Well, I'll be damned. No wonder I had such a hard time tracking your family down."

Larissa said, "Our heritage is no laughing matter. Drakon and his ilk are not something most of us wish to be associated with."

"I don't exactly have warm feelings for the Essence either," Aurianna muttered.

"What happened?" Syrena asked. "What did I miss?"

Aurianna explained once again what had happened when she went back in time to retrieve the necklace.

Larissa, however, didn't seem the least bit bemused. "It seems we are beset on all sides. The queen and those who follow her have been going down a dark path for quite some time. She has been in league with both the Consils of your world and Drakon himself. Treasa knew about the necklace, Aurianna. She knew about the train. She set the whole thing up with two of your Consils—"

"My mother," Laelia spat.

Larissa nodded. "Giana Rossi of Vanito and Cormick Lowe of Eadon. Consil Rossi led the Pyros away from the train, and Lowe set the explosives."

Pharis pounded his fist on the table. "And my father. He was involved in the kidnapping as well. He's guilty, same as them. Or was." His ire faded, and his eyes looked haunted.

Larissa reached out and covered his hand with her own. "Your father was responsible for hiring the men who were to kidnap Aurianna, but he was a pawn as well. His intentions were never pure, and I'm not going to justify anything he has done. Your father and his predecessors created a system where someone like Aurianna would have never existed. They refused to allow any power higher than their own, so they forbade Kinetics and Voids the right to procreate. They couldn't risk losing their control, so the birth control was introduced into the water supply many, many generations ago."

"He always chased after more power."

"Aye, yes he did. He was given the information on the kidnappers by Laelia's mother, who in turn, got it from Treasa."

"Where did she get it from? Who were those men, and where did they come from?"

"She's been working with Drakon for a long time, and that's where all of this originates." Larissa sat back and placed her hands in her lap.

"But why?" Aurianna asked. "Why would the queen agree to that?"

"I don't know, but I'm guessing she was offered a deal. More power."

More power. Always more power.

Her aunt continued. "Drakon has been using Treasa, and she's been using the Consils, and they've been using the Magnus. As well as the Order of the Daoine. All of them wanting something. All of them far too easy to corrupt, I'm afraid."

"The resistance is working with the Consils?" Aurianna shook her head. "That can't be right. Fitz was obviously up to something, but he wanted me to work with them."

"He wanted you to go off and blow something up. He desires a war against the Kinetics, as do the two Consils. By the way, it seems only those two were aware of any of this."

"How do you know all of this?"

"Fae are blessed—or cursed, depending on how you look at it—with a knowledge of many things. We know every instance of the timeline being restarted, and what you had or had not done. Fae exist outside the constraints of time, outside the timeline variations themselves."

"Like the Arcanes?"

"Their ability is a result of the magic within their rooms. The Essence set that up long ago. Ours is an innate power. That power and foresight is, once again inherited. Both sides of our parentage have this ability."

"They have the knowledge and the ability, and yet the Essence do nothing about any of these issues."

"To be fair, child, until the time loop was opened, they were just as imprisoned within it as we were. Drakon made sure of that when he captured their brother Caelum. The time loop was connected to Drakon's power, so when you opened it, you loosened some of his hold."

"But they sent me to get the necklace and never told me what was going on. They could have warned me."

Larissa screwed up her face apologetically. "Perhaps a warning might have altered your destiny."

"Destiny is just your heart following what it desires." Aurianna gazed into Pharis's eyes, and he warmed her with his smile. "Simon always told me to follow the path that draws me. The path was always something deep within my heart telling me what I needed to do."

"Perhaps. But we're here now because of those decisions, both yours and those of the enemies we now seek to defeat. All of it is part of something bigger than us. Even Syrena's exile in the tower.

My sister and I—and poor Amara—were allowed in to help with the birth. Treasa made sure of it when she gave the pendant with the locking spell to the Magnus."

"I knew it had to be Fae magic. I just didn't understand why I was able to remove it."

"Exactly what Treasa intended. As was the death of the Magnus." She addressed Pharis now. "Treasa foresaw your visit to the Imperium. Consil Rossi allowed herself to be touched by you, Pharis. It was the only way to pass on the spell Treasa had given her."

Pharis gaped at her. "Are-are you saying," he stammered, "I was poisoned?"

"Not exactly. The power of suggestion through an incantation, combined with something she rubbed on her skin. When you restrained her, she passed it to you."

"I remember feeling odd, like the room had gone all foggy. Then I couldn't remember what happened. Then, when I did remember, it was like it happened to someone else."

Larissa nodded. "She put you under a Fae spell."

Pharis sat back, deep in thought. Aurianna reached over and threaded her fingers through his, squeezing. He squeezed back, but he wasn't looking at her.

"I still don't understand how you know all this, Larissa." Aurianna contemplated this other version of her aunt. "If you could see all of it before, why only tell us now?"

"Treasa holds the knowledge. It is like a shared mind. She allows the rest of us to see what she wills. Many of these things were being hidden from us, but after you left to meet with the Essence, my friends and I decided the time was right to confront her. There are far more of us than she realized. She and her guards, including the ones she sent to arrest you, are now locked up. Dozens more Fae than you see here are helping us. Most are ignorant and innocent of her greed and actions."

"So, what now?" Theron asked quietly. He had been listening and watching, the workings of his mind spinning in ways Aurianna could only guess. "Do we take the fight to this Drakon?"

Larissa stood and looked at each of them in turn. "Both the sword and the stone the queen was planning to give Aurianna are fake. She hid the real sword, but the stone was never real. She has fooled our people into believing the stone in her crown is a Nether Stone for a hundred years."

Aurianna said, "I noticed the stone was the wrong size as soon as I saw the sword. So how did you get the real one?" she asked Syrena.

But she seemed just as perplexed as Aurianna was. "I-I really don't know. My mother gave me that necklace. Larissa?"

Larissa shook her head. "I have no idea. It was passed down through our family, but I never paid it much attention. Our mother never wore it, just kept it in a box. She gave it to Hermia when she came of age and told her to keep it safe." Larissa paused to consider then said, "The sword is now in our possession. And you have the stone, the real one. We will combine them and use them to stop the enemy."

"How?"

"The sword *was* designed and forged from iron long ago to kill a demon. That wasn't a lie. When combined with the stone, it has the ability to open a rift into the Nether realm. You must stab him with the sword, but only when he is in his true form. It is the only way to send him back and the only way the iron will harm him. The sword, once it is embedded within him, should hold him in that form long enough for you use a combination of your powers to activate the stone."

"Wait," Aurianna insisted, frustration lacing her words. "I have

Chronokinetic power. Why can't I just use that? I would have all the time I needed."

Larissa regarded her sadly. "I'm afraid it won't work, child. The Aether is the realm of the Essence. When you enter it, even for just a moment, you are connected directly to the Essence. The Nether Stone will not respond to anything within that state. And like the Fae, Drakon knows when the timeline has changed. As long as you avoid traveling back into the time loop before the singularity, events could conceivably be changed. But if you attempt any changes, he will immediately know what you've done."

Aurianna chewed on her bottom lip furiously. The task ahead seemed impossible. But now she could accept that this quest was bigger than she could handle alone. It always had been. She didn't need to ask. Her friends would come with her.

"And there is one more thing," Larissa declared. "You have more allies than you previously suspected. At least, I hope so."

"What do you mean?"

"We have a group of prisoners Treasa kept hidden from all but her personal guards. Seems they followed you to Ayshetha."

"Who?"

"Some from the resistance who claim they are defecting. Including a woman who says she is Pharis's sister."

Chapter 25

AURIANNA

The figure slumped against the cell door was almost unrecognizable.

Pharis stood back, not yet speaking, but Aurianna knew he was angry. The muscles in his jaw stood out as he stared at his sister.

Her appearance no longer held much similarity to her twin's. Mara's hair and skin were dirty, her clothes disheveled and her face pale, and she was far thinner than Aurianna remembered. The man slumped just behind her was the one who had given her the wound on her arm, the wound she no longer had. His face betrayed a deep sadness. Aurianna almost felt sorry for him. Maybe it had been an accident. He couldn't have known she was part Fae. She hoped.

The others in their group appeared just as dingy and malnourished. Part of her wanted to give Pharis the opportunity to speak first, but time was in short supply. "What are you doing here? Why did you follow us?"

Mara lifted her eyes to Aurianna, tears welling in them. "Sullivan and I—and some others—we haven't been too keen on the way things have been going in the Order. And when Fitz started getting all obsessed with you—" She coughed. "Pharis, I'm sorry. I really am. The boys and I don't want anything to do with whatever he has planned. We—I just wanted to stop the things Father was doing, not get involved in an all-out war. Especially not with my own people. You were right, little brother. You are my people. I should never have gotten mixed up with the order. And I'm sorry."

"How can I ever trust you again, Mara?" Pharis shouted, causing her to jump back. "You disappeared, you let me think you were dead, and now you act like it was all just a misunderstanding?"

She regarded him forlornly. "I came to tell you I'm sorry. Plus, I-I heard what happened to Father. Everyone's saying you killed him, but I can't believe that." Mara's eyes begged Pharis to deny it.

His smug expression was only a pretense, Aurianna knew, but she sort of felt sorry for his sister. "Why? Because I'm not capable of murder, unlike your friends over here?" He waved a hand at Sullivan and the other resistance members. He sneered, goading her. "Yes, Mara. I did it. I killed our father, and honestly, I'm not even all that sorry."

Mara shook her head in horror. "He was a terrible person, Pharis, but do you really think he deserved to die?"

All the anger seemed to leave him, and he hung his head, leaning his forehead against the bars. "No," he whispered. "No, I don't." He slid to the floor. "It was an accident. Well, not an accident. But I wasn't in control of my actions."

Mara knelt on the other side of the bars and reached through to stroke his hair. "What do you mean?"

"One of the Consils put me under a spell. A damn Fae spell."

His sister's tone expressed pity. "The Consils and our dear Magnus have never seen eye to eye, but that seems extreme."

"Two of them have been plotting. They were in league with the Fae queen *and* with your precious leader."

At those words, Sullivan shot up. "I knew it. I knew he'd cut some kind of deal with one of those slimy, plotting assholes. I *told* Fitz we were better off standing our ground on our own side, not joining someone else's. And he went behind all our backs and sold us out."

Pharis grabbed Mara's hand and clasped their fingers together. "I'm sorry, too, Mara. I was just so angry over losing you. You let me think you were dead. It gutted me. I felt like you'd betrayed me."

"I never meant to hurt you. And I want to help you now. That's why we're here."

"You are in no shape to be heading off anywhere with us right now. It appears they've been starving you. Though, considering the fare we've been given recently, it may be for the best."

Aurianna addressed Mara, "Larissa gave the choice to Pharis whether to let you out." She looked at him affectionately. "If he doesn't unlock your cell, I'll have some food—*real* food—brought down to you as soon as possible."

Pharis stood back up, wiping his hands on his trousers. "We're leaving in the morning. But I'll ask them to prepare rooms for you."

Mara had been shaking her head emphatically since her brother's curt dismissal of her offer to help. "No. I mean, yes, we need to get our strength back. Food and warm beds would be wonderful. But I do want to help with whatever you are doing. My men can stay behind, but I'm Kinetic, same as you. I can help you, brother. Let me do what I can to make this world better. It's all I've ever wanted."

Pharis regarded his sister's pleading eyes with indecision. Finally, he said, "Okay. Eat and rest, and if you're fit to travel, you can come. I'll need to explain everything to you first, though, because you might just change your mind when you hear what we're doing." He brought his attention to her team members. "The rest of you, listen to me carefully. You are not to leave this place or try to contact anyone outside. And you are to do exactly as the Fae named Larissa says until we get back. Is that clear? If you don't cooperate, I'll let them douse you in Fae magic. The nasty kind."

He waited for them to voice their consent before unlocking the cell. Then he beckoned Mara to follow. "Come with us, and we'll fill you in on everything we've learned. Father was involved in a lot more than you even know, but this is far bigger than him or us."

Pharis clutched Aurianna's hand, and they led the others into the forest outside. He met her eyes. "We've got a world to save." He spoke with a confidence and determination she hadn't seen in a long time.

But as they walked, Pharis kept looking down at her legs, the skin of her thighs peeking through the slits at either side of the long white gown. She remembered the feel of his hands on her skin during those heady moments in his bedchamber.

As they strolled along the path, he leaned close again and murmured, "You know, I do love that dress." Winking, he squeezed her hand.

* * *

The Mare Dolor stretched out below them in endless glassy waves. Nothing broke the surface of that blue expanse.

While Mara rested and ate untainted Fae food to build up her strength, Aurianna and Pharis had taken Oracle to the ferry near Vanito in search of the Aerokinetic pilot, hoping Argo would be available and willing to help them in their quest to save Eresseia. The man needed no coaxing, as his loyalty to Aurianna and the former Regulus was unquestionable and sincere.

So it was the Minya, Argo's airship, that ferried them in their quest to find Drakon's island. They skimmed atop the waves for a time before gliding far up into the sky to search from above. All they had to guide them were a general direction and Larissa's description of "sharp, jagged rocks" gleaned from Fae lore.

Argo—perhaps bored with decades of ferrying folk around in the relative safety of the unchanging bay—evidently had the heart of an explorer. He was undaunted by the risk and eager for the opportunity, even though he had known a few shipmasters in his time who had braved the Mare Dolor in search of what lay beyond. And no one had ever returned from those forays into the unknown.

Aurianna had tried to explain to her group of friends that by coming on this quest, most of them would needlessly be putting themselves at risk. But her friends insisted they would not abandon her. They would see this through.

In pairs, they took turns watching for any sign of the mysterious plot of rocky land amidst the endlessly undulating waves of the "Sea of Sorrow"—the translation for Mare Dolor, named in reference to those adventurers who never came back.

Squinting into the bright distance behind them, Aurianna could no longer make out the landmass which consisted of Vanito and Ayshetha. Larissa would be busy trying to bring order to their corrupt leadership. The Fae queen would hopefully never be permitted to meddle in the affairs of human or Fae again.

Her parents were currently on lookout duty from the bow of the airship.

Syrena's fate was irrevocably entwined with this quest, but she had tried to convince Ethan to stay behind. He had merely laughed at her attempts. He had watched her from afar for so long and would not be separated from his love for anything.

Aurianna understood the feeling. Beside her stood Pharis, tall and powerful, ready to brave the end of the world by her side. They were a team, united in their goals, and she could finally be honest with herself and admit she wouldn't have it any other way.

A very serious-looking Sigi had joined Mara as she rested in the stern, and they were deep in conversation. The events of the past weeks had been hard on the former guardswoman, who was searching for her place in a world where she no longer fit. At least not in the way in which she was accustomed. Perhaps Mara could relate.

Theron was fiddling with a small piece of rope in his hands, tying it into intricate knots before releasing them and starting anew. He hadn't wanted to leave his furry companion behind once again, but their destination was no place for a small animal. The fox was safe back in Ayshetha. Between Rhouth and Belinda, the Fae would have their hands full until their return.

A shout from the front had everyone straining to see the black dot above the blue of the ocean.

Here they would say their goodbyes to Argo, a true friend and confidante throughout their journeys. The group would rely on the Fae potion Larissa had offered to convey them the rest of the way.

Despite her recent success with Aerokinetic power, Aurianna decided to rely on the Fae potion as well. Even Mara and Pharis opted to save their Kinetic strength.

As she swallowed the sweet concoction, Argo stared at her with brimming eyes. She reached out and embraced the large man, whispering her thanks in his ear. Neither of them wanted to think about it possibly being their last goodbye. He repeated his confidence in them and his assurance that he intended to wait for their return.

Climbing over the rail of the airship, they all pushed off, some more tentatively than others. Laelia was clinging to Leon's arm to keep from floating away. Everyone waved one last time to Argo as they floated down to the island far below. The Minya was their only hope for escape, assuming they made it out alive. Aurianna had given Argo strict instructions to stay as far away from the island as possible but to maintain a lookout for their return.

Aurianna was barely able to see their destination with the sunlight glinting off the water's surface and nearly blinding her. As they drew closer, she was able to perceive jagged spikes around the edges of the tiny landmass.

They aimed for a relatively clear stretch of shoreline, and each landed with varying degrees of gracefulness. Pharis didn't even pause, just performing a smooth crossover from flying to walking. He tried not to look smug but failed miserably.

Disgruntled that she still felt clumsy, Aurianna frowned and playfully stuck out her tongue.

Shrugging, he smirked and went to help the others. Laelia almost hit the water, but Pharis helped Leon grab her and pull her inland.

They turned their attention to the prospect before them. A giant structure was built into the middle of the island, a castle-like building which looked oddly like a twisted version of the Imperium. It was formed of dark stone and exuded a primal sense of foreboding that made the hairs at the nape of Aurianna's neck rise.

"Well, whoever this Drakon is, he sure knows how to decorate." Leon quirked an eyebrow and attempted a smile.

Sigi rolled her eyes. "Yes. It's quite lovely."

Laelia chuckled ruefully. "It certainly establishes the 'I'm an evil villain' vibe quite nicely." She winked at Leon and took his proffered hand.

The rest of the group ignored them as they drew closer to the hulking edifice. They'd taken only a few steps when they were startled by the thrashing sound of large wings beating the air.

Aurianna and the others whirled around to see three Volanti landing on the jagged spikes that formed the outer edge of the island.

She gaped, wild-eyed, at the monsters. "Anybody got any ideas?" she finally managed to squeak out.

They all had weapons, but Kinetic powers had proven to be of little use against these creatures, and guns were even less so. But that was all they had, and at the very least they could distract and harry them until a better plan was conceived.

They drew their weapons and began to fire at the winged monsters. One raced forward and snapped with its massive jaws, the razor-sharp teeth narrowly missing Sigi as she jumped out of the way, rolling against the relative shelter of a spike.

Drawing on her power, Aurianna conjured Fire balls and launched them at the enemy. Then she ripped open the ground beneath two of the Volanti. She pulled a bubble of magma up from the depths and unleashed boiling globules on them, searing their skin and the membranous wings at their backs. But the creatures healed quickly.

Sigi borrowed some magma, trying to repeat Aurianna's display, but she finally gave up and focused on smaller, sneak attacks.

Leon had slipped behind the creatures, summoning the waves at the shoreline to rise up over the heads of the Volanti. His efforts were also failing, so Aurianna reached out with her power to aid him. When he realized what she was doing, Leon grinned and gave her a thumbs-up with one hand as he guided the now massive wave with the other.

Syrena stood beside her daughter, working to boost the efforts of the others just as Aurianna was.

Theron was busy trying to widen the crack at the feet of the monsters. Pharis and Mara were shooting from the cover of one of the spiky outcroppings, the Air chilly with their combined exertions. Laelia and Ethan had taken cover as they were not much help at the moment. If only Aurianna could call up a lightning storm to give Laelia something to work with. Her attention was already too divided, however.

Aurianna pointed to the magma-filled crack, and Syrena nodded. They needed to help Theron open the rift wider. Magma was the only thing that stood even a chance of stopping the Volanti.

They concentrated their efforts on the gash, the opening slowly growing. The sound of cracking rent the morning air as the gap widened. As the sun beat down on them, a bead of sweat rolled down Aurianna's temple.

Sigi had come over to help, but there wasn't much she could do. Everyone else was trying to distract the creatures as they built their graves just beneath their towering frames. By the time the Volanti realized what was happening, it was too late. The two monsters fell into the boiling magma below. They could not heal from that.

But one Volanti still remained. It watched in fury as its brethren were boiled and burned within the liquid rock. Then it trained its beady red eyes on the spot where Aurianna and Syrena had been standing.

They were already on the move, however, running back to the comparative safety of the giant saw-toothed rocks. The same trick wasn't going to work a second time.

Aurianna racked her brain for inspiration on how to defeat this third Volanti. It had spotted their hiding place and was now running straight at them.

She raised her hands in panic, hoping to pull from her Geokinetic power and create a shield like she had that day on the rooftop of the Imperium. She grimaced with the effort of trying to alter the topography of half the island. A sound behind her broke her concentration.

The sharp sound of hand striking against hand reverberated across the stone surrounding them.

Immediately, the Volanti broke off its attack and veered off into the sky.

As one, the scattered members of their group turned to discover the source of the mocking claps.

Aurianna hoped and prayed it was a nightmare, and she would wake up to Pharis sleeping peacefully beside her. The alternative was not a reality she was ready—or willing—to face.

Silver-white hair framed a pale face in which a familiar smirk and bright-green eyes twinkled at them mischievously.

Javen looked anything but dead.

CHAPTER 26

AURIANNA

Javen continued to clap, while obviously enjoying the expressions of stunned disbelief on their faces.

Aurianna couldn't bring herself to speak, waiting on the moment to correct itself. Surely she would wake up any moment now.

Only she didn't.

Finally, Javen dropped his hands with a mock display of hurt. "What? You didn't miss me?"

"Miss . . ." Sigi began, but her voice trailed off as she shook her head in mute horror.

Leon's look of anguish was almost too much to take. "Just what in the actual *hell* is going on here, Javen? How?"

Javen only smiled with fake benevolence. "My friends, you must be tired from your long flight."

"Like you care." Pharis's eyes narrowed. Hatred oozed from his tone. He had hated Javen long before, but now . . .

"This lot would have needed some serious Fae magic to get here, wouldn't they? Or perhaps some other assistance. Ah, I do see our good friend way up there. Hello, Argo!" Javen waved, smirking at the ship far off and well above them.

Aurianna's heart sank. The airship pilot had been spotted. Javen whipped his head in Pharis's direction, the smirk growing wider as he said, "But I'm sure *you* didn't need any help."

Pharis gritted his teeth. "What do you know about it?"

"Your little Aerokinetic 'secret' that's not exactly a secret? Same as anyone who knows anything about it. The Magisters sure like to talk when they don't think anybody's listening. And we all know Voids are nobody, right? They say all kinds of things around Voids."

"You're one to talk!" Aurianna screamed, marching forward. An invisible wall blocked her path. She stopped but continued yelling. "Those Voids weren't telling you secrets out of the goodness of their hearts. You had them under a spell. And you tried to *kill* them!"

"I was merely borrowing their power."

"Borrowing. Yeah. *Draining* them is what you were doing."

"Unlike yourself, of course? You would never do something like that, now would you?"

"What I did," Aurianna said through gritted teeth, "was an accident."

"And yet you chose to keep that little secret to yourself for so long. Seems we all have our secrets. Don't we, *Regulus*?" Javen swiveled back to Pharis and furrowed his brow. "Or should I direct that moniker to the current holder of the title?" He regarded Mara briefly, who glared at him but didn't speak, before continuing to taunt Pharis. "I told you I had nothing to do with her disappearance."

Aurianna bristled at his flippant tone. "Because you're incapable of kidnapping? Of murder?"

Javen tsked her. "Aurianna. Dear. Sweetheart—"

"Stop!"

His smirk became a leer and his eyelids drooped suggestively. "But haven't you missed me? After everything we shared? Our night of passion—"

A sound behind her made Aurianna glance back. Pharis had tried to run at Javen but had run into an invisible barrier with enough force to knock him back on the ground. When he sat up and rubbed his forehead, Aurianna turned back to Javen.

"You and I had nothing." Huffing out a breath, she asked, "What are you doing here? Is this who you were working for?"

"This?"

"Drakon. The Fae told us everything."

"Well, perhaps not everything. But, I'm glad you're here. I was beginning to wonder how long I'd have to wait till they sent you on your way over."

A chill washed over her. "You knew we were coming."

"Of course! I know everything. Even more than your Essence and definitely more than those bumbling Arcanes ever could."

"How?"

"How do I know everything?" Javen sighed. "*Before the Darkness comes to stay, the child will grow upon the day. And when the years have come and gone, touch the thorn and die at dawn.*"

As Javen recited the words that had almost become Aurianna's death curse, Syrena gasped behind her, and a strangling sob caught in the woman's throat.

Aurianna was too wrapped up in her own thoughts and emotions to do more than reach back a hand to comfort her.

The "midwife" who had cursed Aurianna, the creature who had killed the real midwife, Amara, and taken her place when Aurianna was born...

That was Javen. And Javen was...

"Drakon," Aurianna whispered. Dizziness pulled at her, tempting her with the oblivion of its depths. Refusing to succumb, she drew in a slow, deep breath and straightened her spine, balling her fists at her side. She would not be intimidated anymore, not even by an ancient fire-breathing dragon–demon.

Javen applauded again and inclined his head. "Standard point awarded. Considering I basically gave you the answer and all."

"Why did you try to put that death curse on me? I was a baby!" Aurianna cried.

He furrowed his brow. "Yes, you were a baby. Easier to stop you then than later. Or so one would think." The group flinched in horror at his words, but Javen continued as if oblivious. "But, alas, that Fae woman undid all my work by stealing off with you. Azel spoke the prophecy, but I knew what you were destined to become long before that night. I told you. I know everything."

Sigi couldn't resist trying to appeal to her old friend. "I don't understand. How are you . . . ? Why would you . . . ? You went to school with us, Javen. Why would you bother?"

A menacing look flashed in his eyes. "You have no idea what a burden time is. How slowly it passes, how completely mind-numbing it is to watch the passing of eons with no end in sight. The Essence took my family from me. They took away my ability to go home. They left me here to die." A sardonic laugh escaped his lips. "Only, like them, I can't die. I've been many people and many things over many centuries. Past, present, and future. I have been more, and I've been less. I can feign a small affinity for Kinetic power— enough to get myself into the Imperium. The illusion is enough to be accepted, but I cannot master those abilities. I have vented my fury on the toys they created—you humans—who have no idea who you're even worshiping in your little temples. Those damn goddesses have you all fooled. They are conniving and manipulative. I finally broke their connection to most of the people, for what little satisfaction it gave me. And I took their brother." Javen scrunched up his face in disgust. "He never shuts up!"

"You started this war." Aurianna inched her way around the wall before her, but another one popped up wherever she tried to go. Giving up, she clarified, "Against the Kinetics."

He shook his head. "It wasn't against the Kinetics. I don't give a damn who wins. I want all of humanity to pay."

"Why not take it out on the ones who did this to you?"

"The Essence? I am, at least in part. By hurting you, I'm hurting them. Humans are so easy to manipulate. They do it. I do it. All I had to do was promise a little power to those Consils of yours, and they did whatever I asked."

"My mother hardly needs any coaxing from you," Laelia spat. "She does just fine at corruption and greed all on her own."

"Yes, she was more than eager to aid me. But those aren't the only Consils I'm speaking of."

Aurianna furrowed her brow. "You mean . . . in the future? You've been to the future? My future?"

"I *am* the future!" The midday sun vanished in an instant behind a sudden blanket of dark clouds. The sky turned black as night. Lightning crackled in the distance.

Aurianna stumbled back a step. *The Darkness.*

"I used to think the Darkness was just the result of the war." She mumbled, mainly to herself. "Then that night on the roof, I . . ." Her voice trailed off.

"You felt it." Javen's smile was gleeful, and he actually rubbed his hands together and leaned forward eagerly. "I could feel you inside it with me. Even though you stopped the singularity, you still set the Darkness free. It was your destiny after all." Javen looked arrogant now, all traces of friendliness gone. "Just like that piece of metal you have hidden at your back."

Aurianna peered around at the others. Sigi stared at her in confusion. Pharis was beating on invisible barriers that now surrounded him completely. Most of the others were staring up at the sky. None of them had ever seen the Darkness before, except on the night they thought Javen had been defeated.

"Your Consils were even easier to corrupt, Aurianna. I whispered in their ears, told them when and where a Kinetic would fall. And they didn't even question it."

Leon had fallen to the ground, his knees caked with dried mud. He hadn't spoken in a while, but now he found his voice. "Why didn't you just transform into a dragon and burn us all to ash that night on the rooftop?"

For the first time, Javen directed his attention to his former best friend. "I'd already expended most of my energy fighting with you all. The singularity has become a bit of a game between us now, so when Aurianna here managed to stop the explosion, I wasn't quite prepared. Plus, at that point, it was better for you to think I was dead."

"Better for who? Certainly not for me, *friend*!" He emphasized the last word, his voice raw with emotion. "We were best friends for almost ten years, Javen! Why would you go to the effort of fooling me, fooling all of us? Because you were *bored*?"

Javen shrugged. "Pretty much."

Leon jumped to his feet and leaped for the monster before them. Another wall sprang into existence in front of him. Leon bounced back from the impact. He sat up and glared at the creature who had once been his friend.

Javen rolled his eyes to the heavens. "Look, it doesn't really matter. Your gods imprisoned me in this world. Blame them. Like I said, you have no clue what an infinite amount of time does to a person. I've been working on my revenge since the beginning of this world, and now you've brought me everything I need. So all is forgiven."

"Forgiven? I don't forgive—" Leon sputtered as Laelia helped him back to his feet.

"No, I mean I forgive you. And your entire miserable species, now that I have what I need. Guards!" Javen clapped one time and half a dozen men stepped from the shadows. They carried long pointy weapons sizzling with Energy. An inheritance from Fulmena, perhaps? Looking up, he considered the ominous clouds covering any suggestion of the sun. "I like it better this way." His gaze slowly dropped to fixate on Aurianna. "I think you do too."

"What?" she gasped.

"That night on the roof. You were inside the storm with me, but I could feel your own darkness within you, bursting to get out." His smile grew. "You liked it."

He gestured, and the guards sprinted forward, weapons raised. Aurianna and the others raised their hands in surrender. They had become rather good at the whole prisoner thing, sadly.

After their weapons were confiscated, the guards handcuffed them—with iron, Aurianna noted dejectedly but without surprise. They were marched up broad stone steps and into the dark structure. The interior was just as bleak as the outside. Nothing adorned the walls, no tapestries, no ornaments. No furniture to speak of, not even a throne.

Aurianna was astonished. It seemed like every other powerful being in this world wanted a throne. Why not Javen?

The group was hustled through the huge and echoing chamber to a flight of stairs in the corner. They started to go down, but the guards indicated the upper floor instead.

Interesting.

Aurianna scanned the area for an indication of what Javen was planning, or even who these men were. She wondered where they came from and why they would work for a demon intent on destroying the world. Something about them seemed familiar, but she couldn't pinpoint why.

She had many questions, but they needed to stay focused on the main goals. Stopping Drakon and rescuing Caelum.

Her head was already spinning from the iron rubbing against her skin. She had expected it, but the sensation was more than a little terrifying considering a tiny cut had nearly killed her. It made her appreciate the leather scabbard protecting her back from the sword hidden there.

Their destination was, unfortunately, not a single prison cell this time. Each of them was ushered into a small individual cell and locked behind iron bars. Without ceremony or a spoken word, the guards left. Two of them were left at the end of the passage, at the top of the stairs.

The cells had one window each, also blocked with iron bars. This would normally have let in a good deal of light, but the Darkness outside was impenetrable. Peering out, Aurianna saw sharp spindles of rock below that would make anyone reconsider before trying to exit that way, if they could bend or break the bars.

Sigi's voice echoed from across the hall. "So, what's next? He obviously knows about the iron. Makes sense if it affects him as well."

Aurianna came back to the barred door of her cell to whisper, "It doesn't just *affect* him, Sig. It's deadly to him. Just like it is to Syrena and me."

Her friend's face fell as she realized the full implication of those words. "I know. I'm so sorry. What can we do?"

Aurianna leaned against the wall and slid to the floor, sitting cross-legged and resting her manacled wrists in her lap. "Nothing.

I'll be fine. It's not as bad as before. My wound is fully healed now. Just feeling dizzy is all." A lie, but . . . "How's my mother doing?"

"Your mother has seen better days, I'm afraid." Syrena's voice was strained but carried as much humor as she could probably muster.

Javen had made it clear he knew about the sword she wore in a sheath under the back of her shirt. But he hadn't bothered to take anything other than their weapons from them. All of it had been a gamble, but why would he allow her to keep the sword if he knew the prophecy?

Aurianna couldn't see most of the others, but she knew they were there. Lowering her voice even further, she said, "Just give me a minute."

She reached into her boot and—trying not to clang her manacles together any more than necessary—took out the tiny stone vial Larissa had given her. Taking out the stone stopper, Aurianna held her hands, palms facing inward, out to the side and away from her body, and poured a few drops of the magma onto the underside of each shackle.

The timing couldn't have been more perfect. Another hour or so, and the substance might have cooled too much to melt the iron. But she watched as it slowly ate into the thick metal, creating a small opening.

Aurianna eased her hands out of the manacles to be certain her plan had worked. The opening was just large enough to squeeze her wrists through without touching the burning iron against her skin. She smiled fondly. Larissa thought of everything.

The next part was a bit more difficult. She placed the stopper securely back in the bottle and, from the front corner of her cell, held it out until the person next to her—Theron, by the looks of the jacket—could take the tiny bottle of magma from her.

They passed it from person to person until whoever was across from Syrena's cell received the stone container. Then the vial was rolled over with a swift but gentle motion. If they missed...

But Syrena snatched up the bottle easily. Aurianna watched down the hallway to ensure their guards weren't looking. Both men were engrossed in a quiet conversation, not paying much attention to their prisoners.

A moment later, Syrena sighed and said, "That's better."

Sigi was staring at Aurianna across the walkway between them. "Why do you think he's stalling? Why even bring us up here if he's just going to kill us?"

"I don't know, but he's not stupid enough to think we came here without a plan. He's trying to keep me on my toes, do the unexpected so I can't predict his next move. Don't worry, though. Syrena and I will take care of the next bit. We just have to wait until he decides to bring us to wherever his plan is going down. I don't know if he'll take all of us at once, or what, but it stands to reason he'll want as big an audience as he can get."

"Audience for what? Aurianna, what does he want?"

"To destroy our world before returning to his. To go home."

"Home?"

"His real home is the Nether realm. I think I understand him better now."

"Underst—what are you talking about? How could you possibly understand that level of evil? If he wants to return home, just give him the stone."

Aurianna shook her head. "It's not that simple, Sigi. He won't leave until he has his grand finale. He intends to desolate this world before he leaves it."

"How do you know that?"

"Because otherwise he would have tried to take the Nether Stone already."

"The . . . You have it." It wasn't a question.

"It's here, but he's not getting it. Not like that anyway."

Sigi hissed, "But what is the *plan*, Aurianna? You haven't told the rest of us anything."

Aurianna could hear the frustration in the woman's tone. "I know." She flopped her head against the hard wall then winced. "We're going to wait until Javen decides to get this show going."

Theron said, "That's *not* a plan." In his irritation, he was probably far louder than he meant to be because he then lowered his voice. "That's just letting things happen."

"Maybe that's what we need to do," she whispered back.

"Is this your stupid destiny bullshit again?" Laelia sighed from a few cells away. "Haven't we had enough of that already? Why can't you use your fancy powers to get us all out of here?"

Aurianna rested her temple on a bar of her cell door. "I did suggest you stay behind, didn't I?" When Laelia didn't respond, she added, "We need him to think we're all powerless. Surprise is the only thing we have going for us right now. And believe me when I say, you don't want to know any more."

The past felt like a dream now. Every word that had passed between herself and Javen echoed in her mind. He had once remarked on her amazement at the sunlight in this world, so different from the Darkness in her own time. Before she had even spoken the words to describe the world of her childhood, Javen had already known. He had seen it, had lived it.

I am the future.

But she was going to change all that. Once and for all.

CHAPTER 27

SIGI

Though it was only hours, it felt like weeks before the guards made any move to bring them to Javen.

Sigi had no idea what his plan was. She couldn't even fathom what Aurianna was going to do.

When the guards were coming for them, Syrena whispered a warning. Sigi watched as Aurianna slipped her wrists back into the cooled shackles.

As they were being led from their cells, Pharis fell to his knees, crying out. Almost simultaneously, Mara gasped and hung her head, collapsing against the wall.

Sigi thought perhaps it was part of the plan, a ruse to distract the guards so they could escape. But Pharis immediately stood up, breathing so loud she thought he might be having some sort of attack. Mara pushed herself off the wall. They beamed at each other, then Pharis met Aurianna's gaze. After that, he allowed himself to be ushered out.

Sigi shook her head in confusion.

They were taken down the stairs, past the main floor, to a lower level. The stairs to the lowest level went on for ages, their journey winding them down into a subterranean area. As they walked, Theron pushed his way to the front of the group, colliding with her in the process.

"Careful," Sigi muttered. "You knock us over, it's not easy to get back up." She forced a smile.

But Theron wasn't smiling. The expression on his face was something exceedingly un-Theron-like. She started to ask him what was wrong, but he began to whisper—the words gushing forth.

"Sig, I appreciate we've been friends for so long. So many years I don't want to take away. And here we are, in the bowels of hell"—he gestured to their dank surroundings—"about to embark on a . . . well, I don't rightly know what we're about to embark on 'cause they won't tell us—"

"Theron, what in the world is wrong with you?"

"Well, I'm just saying we might be near the end here and, seeing as how I might not ever get the chance to tell you . . ." He jostled into her again, but this time it felt deliberate as he pushed her against the wall of the narrow hallway, nearly knocking them both to the ground again. But before Sigi had a chance to push back with her manacled hands, warm lips met hers, and her world began to spin. The touch was gentle but insistent, and she was too shocked to move.

After a moment, he pulled back and whispered, "I love ya, Sig. Always have." And then Theron smiled at her.

She was too dazed to speak. She just stared at the man who had just confessed his love, unable to respond in any meaningful way.

The corner of his mouth quirked up further, and he winked, then pulled away.

The guards were staring, but not one had interfered. They had, in fact, seemed fascinated by the exchange. But now they gestured for the group to continue.

The guards prodded them with the scary-looking weapons down another long corridor and into the main chamber.

Her mind still reeled from Theron's unexpected kiss and revelation. *Did he say he loved me?*

The room was massive. The ceiling had to be five or six stories high. And waiting there to greet them was the being who looked like their friend but wasn't the Javen they'd known.

Javen had been her—their—friend since he'd come to the Imperium just a few short years behind the rest of their group. He and Leon had been inseparable for many years.

But the truth she'd refused to think about or accept was sinking in. This being before them was, in fact, Drakon.

Aurianna was speaking. "Why did you get Belinda pregnant? And how? Everyone takes the birth control. It's in the water."

"*That* is the burning question you chose to lead with?" Javen—*Drakon*, Sigi had to remind herself—asked derisively. "Same way Leon's friends did. We simply stopped drinking from the main supply."

"Why in hell would she agree to that? You're telling me she wanted to get pregnant?"

Drakon looked smug. "She would have done almost anything I asked of her. But I did entrance her a bit just to be sure. Same way I did with those Voids. Fae potions work marvelously well."

"The Fae queen was helping you."

"Of course." Drakon smirked. "Same as your Consils. All of them want the same thing. Power. It's so easy to manipulate people who salivate that hard for something they desire." He raised an eyebrow lasciviously. "And Belinda was really salivating for it."

He must have thought that would upset Aurianna, but if it did, she didn't show it. In fact, there seemed to be little emotion at all behind her words or her expressions. She responded slowly, as if carefully measuring her words. "You haven't answered my question. Why impregnate her?"

"You already know the answer." With a deliberate motion, he ran his tongue across the tips of his teeth—sharper than Sigi remembered, but strangely familiar.

And suddenly Sigi knew.

Oh, my Essence. No. No.

His scoffing answer came whether she wanted to hear it or not. "Belinda isn't the first human I've procreated with. I have many, many descendants born of human mothers."

"The Volanti," Sigi whispered in horror.

Drakon inclined his head. "Indeed. But they are a work in progress, although certainly better evolved than the disastrous results of mating with those stupid Fae females. Only some Volanti develop my"—he grinned toothily—"more dashing qualities." He shrugged dismissively, rolling his shoulders. "They serve me well. Some have my shape-shifting ability, but they lack certain aspects of humanity which I have come to appreciate. They aren't exactly the greatest conversationalists, for one thing."

"Then what's the point? Why do you need them?" Sigi yelled from across the room.

"What can I say? I'm lonely. They are the closest thing I have to brothers since mine were killed by your allies."

Leon's face had gone red, tears spilling onto his cheeks. "*I* was your brother! *I* was there for you! How can you do this? How can you act like you weren't my friend?"

"Because I wasn't." A twitch near Drakon's eye suggested this might not be entirely true, but he moved on. "You think you're the first of your kind to think of me as a friend? I have entered Kinetic training in many forms, at different times. You were nothing more than a diversion."

"Then why interact with us at all?" Sigi yelled, rattling her shackles. "Why pretend?"

"I'm bored." He flung his hands up in the air in exasperation. "Plus, you are mildly interesting. My kind are always born male. We have no mothers, no sisters, no mates."

"How is that possible?" Sigi was losing steam.

"In my world, we are born from a pool of magma, our bodies shaped as we crawl from the liquid depths. There has never been a female born in my dimension."

"You were lonely," Aurianna whispered. She raised her voice with her next words. "You wanted a female for companionship. You thought I might have been the one to give you that." As one, the group regarded him in horror.

Drakon chuckled condescendingly. "Not in the way you think, Aurianna. I simply wanted to further my species. And I am tired of this existence with no way to return home."

She tilted her head and asked, "You could have taken the stone at any time while I had the necklace, but you didn't. Why?"

"I wondered if you noticed my fascination. Yes, I recognized it immediately and could have taken it. But it won't work for me. It will only work for the Essence or someone directly descended from their power. Someone with Fae blood. Like you."

"Perhaps if you had simply asked," Aurianna said in a dry tone.

"Let's not pretend it would have been that easy. First of all, I already knew the path you were headed down. I had played this game so many times, watched you blow up half of Bramosia, over and over. Like your Essence, I have lived through each and every iteration, wondering when something would be different."

"Plus, you were enjoying the destruction of Eresseia."

"Yes, I was indeed. Still am."

"The dragonblood was you."

"Oh, yes." He rubbed his hands together like a true villain, a gleam of malice in his eye.

"And the explosives on the train. I thought your guards seemed familiar, and now I'm sure of it. The Volanti are shape-shifters. You sent some of your 'brothers' onto the train that night, even knowing they wouldn't make it out alive."

"I have plenty more where they came from."

The room filled with silence.

Sigi scanned the room, her eyes resting on Theron, who shrugged at her. They needed to do something, anything. Drakon was obviously not going to let them out alive.

She turned back to see that Aurianna had spun around and was looking her dead in the eye, shaking her head ever so slowly.

Turning to face the demon, Aurianna asked, "Why didn't you take the sword and the stone from me earlier? And why keep us imprisoned? You could have brought me down here and forced me to use it to send you home."

"I'm not done with your world yet. Besides, the sword at your back isn't the one I need to be worried about." Drakon took a step toward them, the sound echoing in the cavernous expanse. "It's the one behind me I'm more concerned with." In a flash, he whirled around, blocking the sword a figure just behind him was trying to plunge into his back. He captured his attacker's arm and squeezed.

Sigi recognized the high-pitched scream, but she couldn't understand what was going on.

The person Drakon was holding looked exactly like Aurianna.

CHAPTER 28

AURIANNA

That was her cue.

Seeing herself again was disturbing, even though Aurianna had anticipated it. Expecting it and being faced with it were quite different things.

Under cover of the distracting confusion playing out before them, she slowly retreated until she felt the warmth of the body at her back. Slipping one wrist out of the manacles, she reached to the Aether Stone hidden in her collar under her hair and whispered the now-familiar incantation under her breath. The sizzling heat was intense, and the glow would be noticed before long, even under her hair and clothing. She waited a moment, allowing Syrena time to remove her own manacles and place her hand on the purple stone.

In the crack between seconds, they were whisked into the Aether.

Syrena's fear was palpable, though they could not see each other in that space. Their bodies were without form or substance until they reached their destination.

If any part of this plan failed, there would be no second chances. A single change to the timeline would be immediately discovered by Drakon, and they would lose the upper hand. Every step had to be taken with the utmost care.

Drakon hadn't forced her to turn over the sword with the stone, which meant he anticipated she would try to use it, and he had a plan of his own.

Good. His attention would be on his own schemes instead of hers.

Using the realm of the Essence was a necessary part of the plan, despite her fury at the way they had used her. Her incantation had been both a promise and a request. She intended to keep that promise, but they would have to comply with her request if she had any hope of succeeding.

When they finally left the Aether, they were transported to a dark, dank tunnel smelling of rot. Peeking out through the cave-like opening, Aurianna saw the cavernous room they had just left, but it was now empty.

Syrena's voice came out in a wheeze. "That was not pleasant."

"You get used to it. Come on."

They followed the wall leading around the cave until they reached another opening. If they were to find him here, they needed to hurry. The others, presumably, would soon be leaving their prison cells.

With no idea where they were actually headed or whom they might encounter, Aurianna felt her way around in the dark, exploring room after room. No one appeared, neither Drakon nor the Volanti.

Finally, they came to an abrupt halt. The door before them was closed, but they couldn't detect any kind of spell or seal. Aurianna pushed against it, and the door opened without a sound.

In the middle of a large room sat a small, forlorn cage.

Within it sat a small, forlorn man. Though, he was not a man, Aurianna knew.

He was a god. *Caelum.*

The Essence were tall and mighty beings. Or at least that was how they had presented themselves. How had he become such a small version of his former self?

She approached the cage, wary of traps or enemies who might attack from the shadows. But the room was empty save the lone prisoner.

Caelum's eyes bored into her. His form was still ethereal, like his sisters, but the glow was weak, his power drained. His voice was hoarse when he spoke. "You are late."

Aurianna was taken aback. "Excuse me?"

"I have been expecting your arrival for quite some time. Maybe it is ... I do not know. I have seen you coming." Caelum reached up and rubbed his head. "I have seen it over and over, but you never arrived."

"Time has been caught up in itself for a long time," Syrena explained, placing a hand on Aurianna's shoulder. "We are here now, though. Your sisters sent us to rescue you."

Caelum nodded. "I cannot help you fight him. The demon visited me recently, and I have no strength. He siphons off my power over and over. He lets me refill then drains me again. He placed a spell on this cage. It keeps my power in check, even when he isn't here. Only he can remove the spell, and only he can release me."

Aurianna fumed. "But you said you've foreseen us coming. So what did we do in this vision? How did we open your cage?"

He shook his head, his pale form shaking, whether from shock or starvation or something else, she wasn't sure. "It was unclear. You touched the bars, and it opened."

With a tentative hand, Aurianna reached out and touched part of the cage. She was greeted with a spark of electricity.

"How in the hell is that not shocking you?" she hissed at him. She spun around to Syrena. "The whole damn thing's laced with Energy."

The corner of Syrena's mouth quirked up. "So are you."

Aurianna thought for a moment, remembering the night on the roof and how she had been boiling over with the storm raging within her and how the Energy had escaped from her and jolted Pharis's heart back to life.

Focusing on the cage, she let the emotions well up to the surface of her skin. She could feel the current within her as she braced herself to take hold of the Energy racing along the metal lines of Caelum's prison.

But the shock never came. The first thing she felt was a rush of Air, pushing against her and trying to force her away. She refused to let go, and instead she pushed back against the element blocking her attempts at rescue.

A blast of heat hit her as the Air dissipated and let her through to the next layer. The metal began to heat up, glowing like a flame, and she realized her hands were also on fire.

Burning bright against the dark room, her whole body lit up, like the sun at midday. Fire and flame, Energy and lightning. She was all things blazing and wonderful, and she could feel the elements seeking release. A dazzling intensity flowed through her—a euphoria that became relief as she emptied herself of the pent-up power.

The metal glowed white-hot, the edges melting, as piece by piece the cage was reduced to nothing. What had once been there, no longer was.

Aurianna stood back, a little shaken by the experience. Syrena reached out to steady her. Caelum stood with a slow, deliberate motion, flexing his limbs as he stared around him in wonder.

"I'm free," he whispered.

A light filled the room, forcing Aurianna and Syrena to shield their eyes. When they looked back, Caelum was no longer alone.

Beside him stood his four sisters. The five of them embraced, oblivious in the moment to the two humans.

Aurianna cleared her throat. "I hate to break up the party, but I have other priorities here as well."

Fulmena glared at her. "Your priorities, *human*, should be us, your creators."

Caelum's voice rocked the walls. "Your actions, *sister*, are what brought us to these dire straits in the first place. Do not think I will so easily forgive what you have brought upon all of us."

Unda turned away from Fulmena and Caendra in disgust and addressed the two humans standing before them. "We thank you. You have saved not only our brother, but all of Eresseia." Terra joined Unda in a brief nod of appreciation.

"Not yet, we haven't," Aurianna spat. "And your actions are not so easily forgiven either. You manipulated me, you used me, you—"

"We did what needed to be done. You are right, though. You must continue your journey. We will leave you to it."

"Wait!" Aurianna was incredulous. "You aren't going to help us? After what I just did?"

"We will help in the best way we can. Drakon still holds power here. It is his domain for the moment. Now that our brother has been freed, all of our gifts will be stronger to share with you and your friends."

Aerokinetics everywhere would soon feel that strength. Pharis was already so powerful . . .

Before she could respond, the light of the Essence faded, and they were gone.

"Seriously?" Aurianna whispered hoarsely into the empty room. "You use me to rescue your brother then just run off?"

Silence.

No matter. It was time to join the people she *could* count on and complete her quest. Drakon would be waiting for the others in his lair, and they would need to be ready for him.

They crept back to where they had landed when they'd traveled back in time. They heard voices before they saw anyone, and Aurianna noted they'd caught up with their earlier selves.

She peeked out into the massive cavern. This time, the room was occupied, Drakon gloating over his many betrayals.

She heard her own voice saying, "*The Volanti are shape-shifters.*"

They were running out of time.

Aurianna reached a hand back to Syrena. Her mother squeezed her encouragement and pointed to her goal.

The demon just beyond the opening of the cave.

His back was to them, his attention focused on the prisoners Aurianna was sure he planned to kill. She quietly drew the sword at her back from its leather sheath. As Drakon's next statement echoed across the room, she slipped from cover and inched up behind him.

This was the moment. She held the sword over her head, poised to strike.

Drakon continued speaking to the girl before him, but his next words were her cue. "*Besides, the sword at your back isn't the one I need to be worried about. It's the one behind me I'm more concerned with.*"

She braced for his reaction just as he spun around to face her.

He pushed aside her raised sword and grabbed her arm. He squeezed hard, making her scream in pain.

Chaos erupted.

Her other self disappeared in a blink, taking Syrena with her and confusing her friends even further. It was a calculated risk, leaving them unaware of the plan. They needed to look on and be dismayed by her failure. She just hoped they wouldn't, in their ignorance, try to do anything to stop or impede what would happen next—what needed to happen next.

Drakon wrenched her arms behind her, holding her still as the sword clanged to the stone floor. A strangled gasp escaped her lips as he wrapped one hand around her throat.

He trapped the sword beneath his foot. He had anticipated she would do anything she could to embed that sword in him. He had known, but the air throbbed with the heat of his fury.

She could feel his wrath pulsating off her flesh, feel the heat ignite beneath his fevered skin, and hear his frantic breathing in her ear.

He was angry, but he still thought he had won.

Her friends gaped in horror and confusion, their mouths open but their bodies unable to move. Drakon had them under a spell, but it had come a fraction of a second too late. She and Syrena had already disappeared into the Aether.

Pharis's and Mara's powers had been building since that moment when they were coming out of their cells—which had coincided with Caelum's release—and the power surge had nearly overcome them.

Now Mara's immobile form was vibrating with suppressed power, though whatever power Drakon was using to freeze them forced her into stillness. Both that and the manacles kept her from fully tapping into the wellspring of Aerokinetic power.

Aurianna could sense Pharis's erratic breathing, could see his pale skin slick with an icy sheen. Perhaps he didn't know what she had done, but he could feel the power's desperation to be released.

He was straining to hold it back, even with the binding spell and iron.

He was the wild card—always had been. If he could just hold it in a few seconds longer.

Meanwhile, Drakon refused to release her, but his emotions were taking over.

Time seemed to slow. It was like being inside the evanescence. But this was just a trick of her mind. Drakon's entire form stretched out. She could feel the sinews flexing. He released Aurianna as he grew, rising to tower over everyone.

Javen's human skin was replaced with Drakon's dark green scales, and wings grew out of his elongated spine. This was his true form— the one from her dreams.

Her nightmares.

As in one of her recurring dreams, a monstrous dark form stood over them. Massive and scaled, with wings black as night. His mouth opened to reveal a long green tongue, forked at the end. Wisps of smoke seeped from between row upon row of razor-sharp teeth which jutted out at all angles. Aurianna could imagine flames spewing from that wicked mouth and destroying towns.

The stuff of legends and nightmares stood before them.

Dragon. Demon. Drakon.

An inky blackness filled the room. The Darkness was suffocating, blinding, filling them with a despair which longed for oblivion.

He ground the weapon beneath his massive, clawed foot.

"I am the Darkness." The voice emanating from the demon's mouth sounded like Javen, yet not. It was more grating, less charming. "You cannot prevent this. I know all. I see all. I am one step—"

His words were choked off, becoming a keening wail when a flash of silver erupted from his chest.

Aurianna could only imagine what that pain felt like—pure iron, straight through the heart. A simple cut had nearly done her in. Now Drakon had a sword—the real sword this time—protruding from his body.

Syrena stood poised with her hands still gripping the weapon. Her arms shook as she released it and slowly backed away from the monstrous creature.

Beware the silent knife.

She would be his end.

Syrena was breathing heavily, the anxiety finally letting go and allowing her to exhale. The queen's fake sword with the fake Nether Stone lay discarded on the ground.

Larissa had warned them about changing the past, that Drakon would know if they changed anything in the timeline. But nothing was stopping them from doing it all the first time. Everything had to happen exactly as she and Syrena had planned, exactly as it would have always happened. No room for mistakes.

Drakon made a choked gurgling noise. He floundered around as he sought to make sense of what had happened. He spotted Aurianna on the floor, murder and hatred burning in his red glowing eyes.

Aurianna jumped to her feet, blasting the manacles off every pair of wrists in the room with a thought. Iron was metal, and metal was Earth, same as rock and stone. Every inch of her felt awash with power.

Pharis grinned at her.

She couldn't deny him the moment. Aurianna grinned back and nodded.

She saw him exhale, like blowing out a candle.

The force of a winter gale toppled the colossal form of the dragon. Pharis, still bursting with unspent power, approached the thrashing beast.

She could not stop time for this part. The Nether Stone would only work in real time.

Pharis exhaled again, this time his breath a slow leak which landed gracefully along the length of the dragon's prostrate form. Immediately, Drakon's convulsing body froze face down under a layer of ice.

Aurianna placed a hand on the stone—the *real* Nether Stone— in the sword jutting from Drakon's back. As she had done when releasing Caelum, she summoned the storm within her. Charging up the spark igniting in her chest, she let the Energy flow from her body and into the stone.

Its blue black became a bright light as the stone expanded, wrapping itself around Drakon as he lay helpless. The circle grew larger and larger until they had to back up to avoid falling into its depths.

She saw an ashen world within, fogged with grays and blacks and covered in a haze. Drakon's home world. The Nether realm.

The vision pulled Drakon and the Darkness into itself, his body disappearing into the inky fog as the fissure contracted. Behind them, shrieking sounds erupted all around the room. Drakon's children had rushed in to save their father. Those that could had already shed their human forms. Some ran toward the darkened hole in terror of being left behind, throwing themselves into whatever lay beyond.

The shrinking rift eventually glazed over, leaving only a dark circle on the stone floor. The sword was sticking up from the middle, its silver sheen blackened along with the now-useless Nether Stone.

Aurianna gasped in horror as she peered about. The remaining Volanti had surrounded them, blocking their escape.

Dealing with them was never part of the plan. But the others spread out immediately, blasting the creatures with everything they had, which for a few of them was quite a lot.

Evidently the Essence were keeping their word. Pharis and Mara were already at work trying to knock the creatures down so they could freeze them.

Theron used his Geokinetic power to pull at the stone floor. Small barriers began to pop up, temporarily providing an obstacle against some of the approaching monsters.

Sigi had Fire from the sconces to work with, but most of the group had nothing in the way of weapons down here. They would need her help.

Aurianna closed her eyes and pulled from deep within, drawing up the emotions she had felt the night that Pharis had died then come back to her. The storm within her raged into a cyclone that beat against her breast, longing to be set free. She opened her eyes and released the tempest.

Thunder boomed while lightning sparked a brilliant white, lighting up the dark.

Laelia wasted no time before pulling from the storm's Energy, aiming it directly at the approaching Volanti. Sizzling lines arced and pierced the heart of the nearest monster.

Next, Aurianna balled her fists and willed the mighty waves of the ocean to crash over the spikes of the island and surge inland at a ferocious speed. She felt its roar as it burst into the building, heedless of casualties as it cascaded through the tunnels and into the room.

She threw up her hand to pause its advancement so they could all get out of the way Then they would let the Energy already present work in conjunction with the Water to their advantage. Shouting for the others to follow her out a side tunnel, Aurianna focused on keeping the Water at bay. She nodded at Leon, who would help her direct its course once they were all safe.

A scream punctuated the chaos. Aurianna tried to stay focused, but Mara's cry for help pulled her attention. She was in the path of one of the Volanti. She was slumped, stumbling along, her power clearly drained.

Pharis had been fighting off three of the creatures but was also distracted by his sister's crisis. As he blew Air at the monsters to push them back, he edged backward toward his twin. Mara, in turn, was backing toward him as she retreated from the Volanti stalking her.

Laelia, Sigi, and Syrena were the only others capable of helping, but they were each involved in their own fight.

Aurianna was holding the Water back while also keeping the storm going. She could do nothing to help Mara without losing their only chance of escape.

She shouted again for everyone to join her in a tunnel that led to daylight and—hopefully—freedom. Aurianna glanced around to see that Laelia was battling four Volanti alone with her Electrokinetic power while Leon steered her toward safety. And Sigi, Syrena, and Ethan were making their way over as well.

Pharis finally felt his twin at his back, and he spun around to aim his Aerokinetic power at the beast stalking her. The Volanti seized up, its wings flapping for a brief second before toppling, frozen, to the ground.

Mara reached out to take his proffered hand. In the next instant, her shriek joined the warning screams of the others.

When Pharis had turned to face her attacker, one of his own had taken the opportunity to rush forward—its jaws open wide.

Mara threw out her hand and used the last of her power in a concentrated blast at the creature poised to sink its razor-sharp teeth into her brother.

The creature flew back, toppling another as it fell. And then—

A Volanti jumped from the shadows of a tunnel, pouncing on

Mara before anyone could react. Its sharp claws dug into her sides, and she wailed in agony.

Pharis cried out in anguish, trying to freeze the creature with his dwindling powers.

Ethan called out, "You can use me!"

Syrena screamed "No!"

But Pharis, looking fiercely determined, reached out with both hands. He squeezed his fists.

The Volanti froze.

And Ethan fell to his knees with a groan.

Pharis scooped Mara's limp, bleeding body into his arms, retreating to join the others before any more of the monsters could reach them. Tears streamed down his face as he shared a look of anguish with Ethan, who was being supported by Syrena and Sigi.

Aurianna didn't have time or energy for words. Making sure everyone was assembled in the elevated passageway, she nodded at Leon and Laelia then unleashed the Water. It flooded the room, crashing against the walls. With Leon's help, Aurianna directed its path, forcing it to stay within the stone chamber.

As the sea continued to churn in the center of the room, Laelia and Aurianna lit up their surroundings with a crackling web of lightning. Thunder boomed as the Energy chained the creatures in a writhing circle, the lightning stabbing repeatedly through their bodies.

Their shrieks resounded until they were cut off as, one by one, they fell. The greedy ocean waters claimed them, and the lower level of what had been Drakon's seat of power became their watery tomb.

Chapter 29

AURIANNA

The Panago family was never one to hold back on hospitality. Every manner of food, drink, and comfort could be found within the walls of their home—the home which had made Theron into the man he had become.

Theron, however, appeared more uncomfortable than Aurianna had ever seen him. He was trying to make small talk with Leon while sneaking peeks at Sigi but avoiding her eye. For two weeks they had been tiptoeing around each other, exchanging shy glances when they thought no one was looking. According to Sigi, the poor man had professed his love on the eve of battle, thinking they might not make it out alive.

Yet, they had made it out.

Aurianna sat rocking in the shade, a cool breeze wafting around her, and the afternoon sun beaming down on the world that almost wasn't. And she remembered.

This was how she had felt the first time she had glimpsed this new world.

A new world. A new home. A new life.

Pharis reached out and squeezed her hand from the rocking chair beside her. "What are you thinking about?"

"You."

He narrowed his eyes. "Right."

"Seriously. I was thinking of the first time you brought me here. You set me free, and I didn't even know it. All I could think about was everything I had left behind." She frowned at the memories flooding her heart. Those things no longer existed, save the one that mattered most.

"Part of you misses it?" He brought her fingers to his lips for a kiss.

"Not really. That world, as I knew it, no longer exists. And I feel guilty for that, but the Darkness was devouring it. So I didn't really—"

"Have much of a choice."

She sighed. "But what I lost is nothing compared to . . ." She looked at him anxiously.

His eyes held a familiar grief, but he squeezed her hand again. "I have you."

She squeezed back and whispered, "I love you."

Losing Mara all over again had affected Pharis in subtle but profound ways. He was more affectionate than ever, for one thing. But whenever the topic of his sister came up, he usually changed the subject. The healing would take time. Ironically, this was time they now had because of Mara. When the Essence had sent Aurianna back to retrieve the necklace, she had pondered the idea of one day being able to go back in time and erase the mistakes of the past. But the Essence would never allow it. Part of her understood, even if it was hard to accept. They would honor Mara's selfless act by making the most of this fresh opportunity, and Aurianna would always be grateful.

Sigi, oblivious to the conversation they were having, settled into the chair on her other side and leaned in conspiratorially. "Help me," she pleaded.

"What is it?" Aurianna dropped Pharis's hand to lean closer.

Pharis pouted for a moment then kissed her on the forehead and went to join Theron and his father who were discussing and enjoying the "fruits" of the vineyard.

Aurianna watched him go with an indulgent smile then turned back to her friend. She couldn't contain her exasperation. "I swear, if this is about Theron—"

"No! Belinda is trying to get me to babysit." Sigi glanced over to where the girl was sitting on the grass holding her infant son. She had given birth a week ago, and so far, he seemed to be a normal baby—sleeping and eating and doing all the things that normal babies did.

"That's actually a great idea, Sigi. We need to be as involved as we can in their lives, without making it seem like we're spying."

"But we *are* spying," Sigi deadpanned.

"Yes, but she doesn't need to know that. She's a pain in the ass, sure, but her parents aren't speaking to her. She needs us as much as we need to make sure her kid doesn't try to eat anyone."

Sigi and Aurianna giggled, causing the others to turned inquiring eyes their way. But they just sat back in their chairs, rocking contentedly.

Syrena and Ethan were huddled on the other side of the porch, leaning in to whisper and laugh together. Her mother and father—terms she was slowly but happily adjusting to—deserved every moment they could steal for themselves. The love that shone in their eyes for one another was impossible to miss.

"Things are going to be different." The words were her new mantra. "I know the Fae will never completely trust us—"

"The feeling is mutual."

"Yes, well, but most of them had no idea what Treasa was up to. She was selling out her own people for the power Drakon promised. A new queen will need to be crowned, someone outside Treasa's inner circle. Larissa is working on things over there. She'll be a good liaison between Ayshetha and humans."

Aurianna looked up when she heard Theron's mom shouting. Through the open doors she watched the woman chase Rhouth out of the pantry with a broom, her face ruddy with irritation as she swatted at the fox. Rhouth yipped as she darted between legs and out the door. The fox jumped up on Theron, who set down his glass and picked her up, petting her soothingly.

They watched him for a moment, then Aurianna gave Sigi a meaningful look. "You know, everything is changing in the rest of Eresseia too. Kinetics will be able to be together now, start a family..."

Sigi squirmed in her seat. "Yeah, you and Pharis—"

"I'm not talking about me and Pharis, and you know it." Aurianna waggled her eyebrows.

They both looked over at the hunter who continued to sneak glances their way.

Aurianna huffed. "For all our sakes, will you please just tell him already, so he'll calm the hell down?"

"I-I just need some time, is all."

"Bullshit. You don't need time. You've moped for as long as I've known you about how no man would ever see you in that way. Now, I kept my mouth shut, but that ridiculous man is in love with you. I saw it the first time I observed the two of you together. Please. Tell. Him. The. Truth. That you love him too."

"How do you know?"

"I can tell."

Sigi continued to sputter as Aurianna rested her head against the back of the chair. She closed her eyes and let the breeze cool her face. When she opened them again, Laelia was waltzing across the grass from the vineyard behind the house. Leon's face was pale as he stumbled along behind her.

They were headed her way. Not good. The two of them were beginning to get on her last nerve.

"So . . . we have news," Laelia announced grandly. She glanced back at Leon. "Well, come here, dummy, while I tell them." Leon looked like he was going to be sick.

"What news?" Theron asked. He and the rest of the group wandered closer to hear Laelia's announcement. When Theron started walking, Rhouth jumped from his arms and took off after something small and appetizing at the edge of the vineyard.

"Weeeelllll," she began, drawing out the tension. "Turns out, me and dummy here are gonna have a baby."

A baby. Aurianna closed her eyes to keep the happiness from leaking out.

When she opened them, everyone was hugging a beaming Laelia and a stunned Leon—who must have been told right before.

"Congrats, my friend!" Theron embraced Leon but pulled back when he remained unresponsive. "You okay there, buddy?"

"Yeah," Leon whispered, his voice hoarse. He cleared his throat. "Yeah," he repeated. "I'm just a little shocked is all. I never thought I'd . . . Yeah, I'm fine."

Laelia spun around on Pharis. "Now, *you two*," she said, pointing a finger first at him then at Aurianna. "Your kids are gonna be something else. Something out of this world entirely. In fact, warn me beforehand, all right?"

Everyone laughed, except Pharis. He was staring at Aurianna, a look in his eyes that promised perhaps more than she was confident she could handle.

He came over to stand by her chair, placing a hand on her

shoulder. She reached up and covered it. He leaned down to whisper, "We'll have plenty of time to practice now."

Aurianna felt her face heat. Yes, they would have all the time in the world, Essence willing.

Fitz would stand trial for his crimes, as would Giana Rossi and Cormick Lowe. The three Consils not involved in the plot had met with local leaders within each region in an attempt to forge a new path. The regions would work out how to govern themselves, but they needed laws to protect Kinetic and non-Kinetic alike while Eresseia found a new equilibrium.

Acolytes would still need to be trained, but the Imperium would no longer steal children away from their families for months and years at a time. Visits home would be encouraged as frequently as the curriculum would allow.

It may have been true that the head that wore the crown was always heaviest, crushed beneath its burdensome weight of responsibility. But there would no longer be a crown, even figuratively speaking, as there would no longer be a Magnus.

Pharis would help establish a new role for the Consils, stronger than before. Bramosia would also have a Consil, equal in power to the other regions and separate from the Imperium and the Kinetics.

Pharis had agreed to fill the post for a short time, but he was more than eager to relinquish the responsibility. The other Consils were initially hesitant to trust a Kinetic, but once the truth about Laelia's mother had been brought to light, they had to admit that their own ranks had also been compromised. Everyone would have to get used to a new way.

A new world.

A fireworks display began at the crest of a distant hill, celebrating a new season.

Aurianna sighed. She couldn't be happy while something so

important to her was missing. The Darkness was gone for good, but she still had a hole in her heart. And it was time to make things right again.

She stood and whispered in Pharis's ear. He nodded solemnly, leaning in to place a gentle kiss on her lips. "Back in no time, huh?" He winked.

Syrena and Ethan approached, and Aurianna motioned them to follow her out into the vineyard. She remembered her first time getting a tour of the place, and how wonderous this new world had seemed to her. The memory was tainted, however, by the man who had walked by her side, pretending to be everyone's friend.

No. She refused to let the Darkness back in.

This was her life, her world, her home. She just needed one thing to make it whole.

Stopping between two of the rows, Aurianna spun around and threw her arms around her mother.

The woman returned the embrace, seeming not to want to let go.

Then Ethan put an arm around Aurianna's shoulder and pulled her close to his side. He kissed the top of her head.

With a twinkle of understanding in her eye, Syrena said, "Are you going?"

Aurianna looked determined. "I am." She titled her head up at him and grinned. "The Essence are the only ones with the power to stop me, so if they let me through, then I'll consider that permission enough. I think I've done enough for them. All that's behind us now. We can now look forward to the rest of our lives. You and Syrena can maybe even..." Her voice trailed off, and she shrugged to cover her embarrassment.

Syrena narrowed her eyes. "Maybe even what?"

"Well, I mean, I've always wanted a sibling."

"Aurianna! You're twenty years old."

Aurianna shrugged again. "Sigi and her sister are close, and they're like ten years apart."

"Ten isn't twenty."

"Then don't do it for my sake. Do it for yours."

"What do you mean?" Ethan pulled his arm away and moved to face her, grasping Syrena's hand.

"The two of you are still very young. I mean, you gave birth to me less than a year ago, Mother. You're only a few years older than I am. Plenty of time."

Syrena huffed out a laugh. "I'm twenty-eight, child."

"That's nothing. And calling me *child* doesn't magically make you older." Aurianna smiled fondly at her parents, who gazed at one another with a question in their eyes.

"We missed out on everything, Ethan. Her entire childhood." Syrena's voice was low and rough. She swallowed back a sob as she held Aurianna's hand and looked back at her sadly.

"I'm sorry I missed out on that too. But Larissa took great care of me. She wasn't perfect, but she was exactly what I needed. Larissa saved my life, and now I want to return the favor."

Her mother nodded, her eyes brimming with tears. "I would like that. I want to thank the woman who saved my daughter's life so that she, in turn, could save mine."

* * *

As she touched the Aether Stone in her pocket that Simon had given her, she whispered the familiar words. Her view of her parents was replaced with swirling colors.

Light interlaced with dark in dizzying patterns. The sensation was both foreign and familiar, and she allowed herself to be pulled in whatever direction the Aether took her. The experience was still unnerving and frightening, yet the thought of seeing Larissa eased her anxiety somewhat. She was no longer running away. She now ran toward something—someone—who mattered.

Aurianna felt herself being pulled apart. The light intensified, then darkened, and she felt her feet first and then the solid ground beneath them. Slowly she opened her eyes.

Her aunt sat in a chair in the small familiar living space. She stood immediately but walked with halting steps toward Aurianna, her arm outstretched as if reaching to see if the apparition was real.

Aurianna beamed, extending her hand to the woman who, for so many years, had been her only family. The Larissa she had left back with the Fae was similar in many ways, but it was this face—smile wide and eyes crinkling at the corners—this woman who Aurianna held in her memory and her heart. She was *home* to Aurianna.

And Aurianna wanted nothing more than to bring all the elements of home together. Everything she loved and cared about. Everything she had sacrificed in order to save. Everything Mara had given her life for.

Aurianna grasped the woman's hands, holding tight.

Were she to look out the door, Aurianna knew she would see the sprawling town of Bramosia—albeit a new future version. Kinetics and non-Kinetics, living together without fear.

But she had no desire to see it. It was enough that it simply existed. This was no longer her home, if it ever had been. She didn't belong here any more than Larissa did.

"It's done?" Her aunt's voice was barely a whisper in the stillness of the new world they had created.

Aurianna nodded and smiled. "Let's go home, Auntie."

Explore more books
by Lisa M. Green

Discover your next favorite fantasy read at *lisamgreen.com/books*. You can find information and links to retailers for each book.

* * *

Expand the world of Eresseia
with a free ebook

Sign up for a free ebook copy of *Daylight Burning*, an Awakened prequel novelette starring Leon Bouchard. You'll also hear about new releases and other updates from Lisa M. Green. Go to *lisamgreen.com/newsletter* for your free copy.

* * *

Enjoyed the book and want to
show your support?

You are an amazingly awesome person! Thank you! Please take just a moment and post a review of the book on Amazon, Goodreads, Barnes & Noble, or anywhere you normally post reviews.

Once again, THANK YOU!

Glossary for the Awakened Series

Kinetics: those born with the ability to control or manipulate the elements, usually with an affinity for one element in particular based on their region of birth

Arcanes: a group of men who oversee the records and history books for all of Eresseia; they advise the Magnus on a multitude of issues but are loyal to the Essence (deities) above all

Consils: political delegates and representatives for the six regions of Eresseia

Magnus: leader of the Kinetics and the sixth Consil (representative for Bramosia); the other Consils are elected officials, but the title of Magnus is always a hereditary position

Regulus: the eldest son or daughter of the current Magnus and heir to the title

Magisters: teachers at the Imperium who specialize in training Acolytes in different elements

Acolytes: Kinetics who are still in training and haven't yet reached their twentieth birthday

Voids: those who are sent to the Imperium to train Kinetic powers which never manifest; they are shunned by others and end up working at the Imperium after failing to show any power

Praefects: people in Aurianna's future timeline who are chosen to do the bidding of the Consils (do not exist in the past)

Carpos: a special group of Praefects charged with tracking down, detaining, and torturing Kinetics who manage to travel to the future

Order of the Daoine: a resistance group that opposes the Kinetics

Volanti: nightmarish creatures who attack the towns and take captives every few moons but are impervious to Kinetic weapons; they are as tall as several humans, with spindly talons for hands and feet, sharp fangs and claws, long pointed ears, a wide yet angular head, and membranous wings

Fae: a legendary race of beings whose history has been lost to time

Drakon: enemy of the Essence

Aether Stones: amethyst-colored stones of unknown origin that allow the bearer to travel through time via the Aether

LOCATIONS

Eresseia: the known world

Bramosia: one of the six regions and the capital of Eresseia; home to Kinetics and non-Kinetics alike

Imperium: school and home for Kinetic Acolytes, as well as home to some other Kinetics who work nearby; located in Bramosia

Consilium: political building for the Consils, located in Bramosia

Rasenforst: one of the six regions, connected to the element of Fire

Menos: one of the six regions, connected to the element of Earth

Ramolay: one of the six regions, connected to the element of Water

Vanito: one of the six regions, connected to the element of Energy

Eadon: one of the six regions, connected to the element of Air

Ayshetha: the territory of the Fae

Perdita Bay: the body of water within Eresseia's inner coastline

Mare Dolor: the ocean surrounding Eresseia (*Sea of Sorrow*)

The Aether: the realm of the Essence (the deities)

KINETICS/ELEMENTS

Fire: Pyrokinetics (nickname Pyros)

Earth: Geokinetics (nickname Dusters)

Water: Hydrokinetics (nickname Hydrons)

Energy: Electrokinetics (nickname Sparkers), the name for electric power

Air: Aerokinetics (nickname Zephyrs)

DEITIES

The Essence: the collective name of the deities

Caendra: goddess of Fire, one of the collective group of deities known as the Essence

Terra: goddess of Earth, one of the collective group of deities known as the Essence

Unda: goddess of Water, one of the collective group of deities known as the Essence

Fulmena: goddess of Energy, one of the collective group of deities known as the Essence

Caelum: god of Air, the only male sibling among the collective group of deities known as the Essence

The Prophecy

When the red sky at morning
Bursts forth to cleanse the land,
Beware the dragon's warning,
For the end is close at hand.

Rising up to heights unknown,
Burning forth to scorch the sky;
Beware the infernal stone,
For the end of all is nigh.

She will steal your life,
For the world to burn and bend.
Beware the silent knife,
For she will be your end.

Acknowledgments

The Awakened series was a long time coming. No one knows that more than I do.

I began the first inklings of this story back in 2014. Then life threw me quite a few curve balls. But my mind never left the world I had begun to create.

Writing amidst the chaos of life was easier on some days, near impossible on others. I would spend a lot of time getting back into the story, only to have to stop again.

Things improved dramatically when I became a full-time writer and no longer had to juggle my day job with my writing time.

Now that Aurianna's journey is over, I almost don't want to let the story go. I've grown close to these characters over many years now. Letting go is difficult and bittersweet.

But alas, here we are at the end. The end of a series, at least. Perhaps not the end of this world I've created. We shall see what the future holds for Eresseia.

I want to thank everyone who picked up a copy of the very first book and decided to stick around for Aurianna's entire journey. Without you, I wouldn't be able to continue writing these crazy ideas that rattle around in my brain.

I'm currently working on my next series. It promises even more intriguing adventures, and of course, plenty of my unique brand of plot twists to keep you on your toes. I'm excited to share this new story with you.

If you'd like to keep up with me and my writing adventures, consider joining my mailing list for updates and special offers—and, occasionally, pictures of the woodland creatures that visit my home. You can sign up at *lisamgreen.com/newsletter*.

Thank you, once again, from the bottom of my heart. Happy reading, friends!

THE FIRST

A standalone novel for lovers
of mythic and dystopian fantasy

An ancient secret could hold the key to their salvation. Or their destruction.

Rinni and her brother Mori have been raised by their grandmother ever since the violent death of their parents. The Shadows, creatures who lurk beyond the walls of their village, kill anyone who attempts to leave.

But the biggest threat lies within their own village. Everyone and everything is dying, slowly and without hope of salvation.

The most vital beliefs of her people begin to unravel, the threads hopelessly bound up with the fate of those who left the village long ago.

Rinni discovers that those beliefs are based on a deception that will rock the foundation of her entire people. To save them, she must learn to open her heart and sacrifice... everything.

For more information about *The First*, as well as other books by Lisa M. Green, visit *lisamgreen.com/books*.

THE FIRST

A tale of myth, mystery...

...and a past long forgotten

LISA M. GREEN

CPSIA information can be obtained
at www.ICGtesting.com
Printed in the USA
LVHW090353210121
676997LV00023B/719/J

9 781952 300066